FURTHER
FRIDAYS

Other Books by John Barth

The Floating Opera

The End of the Road

The Sot-Weed Factor

Giles Goat-Boy

Lost in the Funhouse

Chimera

LETTERS

Sabbatical
A Romance

The Friday Book
Essays and Other Nonfiction

The Tidewater Tales
A Novel

The Last Voyage of Somebody the Sailor

Once Upon a Time
A Floating Opera

FURTHER FRIDAYS

Essays, Lectures, and Other Nonfiction
1984–94

John Barth

LITTLE, BROWN AND COMPANY
BOSTON   NEW YORK   TORONTO   LONDON

First Edition

Lines from "Lapis Lazuli" by Willian Butler Yeats from *The Poems of W. B. Yeats: A New
Edition*, edited by Richard J. Finneran. Copyright 1940 by Georgie Yeats, renewed 1968
by Bertha Georgie Yeats, Michael Butler Yeats, and Anne Yeats. Used by permission of
Simon & Schuster.

Excerpt from *Chaos Bound: Orderly Disorder in Contemporary Literature and Science* by
N. Katherine Hayles. Copyright © 1990 by Cornell University Press. Used by permission
of the publisher.

Excerpt from "Romantic Arabesque, Contemporary Theory, and Postmodernism" by
G. R. Thompson. Copyright © by G. R. Thompson and *ESQ: A Journal of the American
Renaissance*. Used by permission of the author and publisher.

Illustrations page 316 from *The Fractal Geometry of Nature* by B. B. Mandelbrot. New
York: W. H. Freeman, 1982.

Several pieces in this book have been published previously, and the author gratefully acknowledges the following sources: *Harper's* for "It's a Long Story: Maximalism Reconsid-
ered" and "Teacher"; *Washington College Magazine* for "Browsing"; *New York Times Book
Review* for "Can It Be Taught?," "A Few Words About Minimalism," and "Kenosis: 'I
Think It's Trying to Tell Us Something'"; *Review of Contemporary Fiction* for "The Spanish Connection"; Duke University Press for "The Limits of Imagination" from *Facing
Texts: Encounters Between Contemporary Writers and Critics*, edited by Heide Ziegler; *Mississippi Review* for "It's a Short Story"; *Antaeus* for "'Still Farther South': Some Notes on
Poe's *Pym*" and "Borges and I: a mini-memoir"; *Johns Hopkins Magazine* for "Once Upon
a Time: Storytelling Explained"; *Washington Post Magazine* for "Goose Art, or, The Aesthetic Ecology of Chesapeake Bay"; *Paris Review* for "'Jack and Jill': An Exegetical Aria";
Boulevard for "Ad Lib Libraries and the Coastline Measurement Problem: A Reminis-
cence"; Anchor Press for the forewords to *The Floating Opera*, *The End of the Road*, *The
Sot-Weed Factor*, *Giles Goat-Boy*, and *Lost in the Funhouse*.

Library of Congress Cataloging-in-Publication Data

Barth, John.
    Further Fridays : essays, lectures, and other nonfiction,
1984–94
    John Barth. — 1st ed.
        p.   cm.
    Includes bibliographical references.
    ISBN 0-316-08324-0
    I. Title.
PS3552.A75F87 1995
814'.54 — dc20   94-40723

10 9 8 7 6 5 4 3 2 1

MV-NY

*Published simultaneously in Canada
by Little, Brown & Company (Canada) Limited*

Printed in the United States of America

for Shelly

Contents

Foreword:
TGIF

⟋⟍ FOR THE PAST FIFTEEN YEARS, my household's habit through the academic season has been to live and teach in the city of Baltimore for the first four days of each week and then, after our last Thursday classes, to shift across Chesapeake Bay to our country retreat on Langford Creek, off the tranquil Chester River, one of the Bay's forty-odd major tributaries.

On workday mornings, I write fiction — novels, typically, and typically of some heft. It used to be that every four years or so, when a new one was launched and commissioned, I would refresh myself by writing an essay-lecture or two, in order to discover what I thought about some subject or other, before reconfronting the vacated ways and laying the keel for the next substantial fiction project. As our Bay-straddling city/country rhythm established itself, however, I came to find it more agreeable and convenient to leave the novel-in-the-works back in Baltimore on those Thursday shiftings, with its accumulating worknotes, research materials, and draft pages, and to spend the Friday mornings (in "bad" weather, the Saturday and Sunday mornings, too) with what presently became my country muse, the muse of nonfiction. So congenial did this rhythm grow — a reciprocal respite for all parties, like the city/country alternation itself — that in the summer months, when my wife and I leave off straddling the Bay and settle in at Langford Creek, I enjoy maintaining the Friday habit of switching muses.

Ten years ago I published a collection of nonfiction pieces called, for the reasons above, *The Friday Book*. Five hundred further Fridays have gone by since then, by no means every one of which was spent writing anything. More of them than not, however, were, and of those, most were addressed to my creekside muse. Herewith, some fruits of those further Fridays: lectures and essays mostly on literary-aesthetical subjects, but occasionally on such broader topics as memory and imagination; author's forewords to new editions of my earlier novels, the reissue of which afforded me the ambivalent experience of surveying my backtrail; and a group of previously unpublished addresses to the higher-tech subject of "Postmodernism, Chaos Theory, and the Romantic Arabesque," which I have here prefaced with a separate introduction.

The greater part of my nonphysical life is spent writing, reading, thinking, and teaching. This is not to say that those agreeable pursuits aren't also partly physical, or on the other hand that eating, sleeping, lovemaking, errand-running, house- and yard work, traveling, sailing, biking, hiking, and tennis don't have their mental aspects — but we know what I mean, I trust. These Friday-pieces address those four cardinal pursuits, and so my first thought was to organize them under those headings. But the four are multiply intertwined: What teaching I do these emeritus days is the coaching of talented apprentice writers, which coaching involves a fair amount of thinking about writing and reading and the corpus of literature, my own productions included. A considerable fraction of what I read is my past and present coachees' writing and my own — forty years of teaching generates a lot of former students, a gratifying number of whom are now working writers themselves. And my fiction, not to mention my nonfiction, comes out of my reading and thinking as well as from other categories of experience. Inasmuch as lecture- and essay-writing are a kind of thinking out loud, even a kind of teaching — if only teaching oneself what one thinks of some subject at some point in one's life — it turns out that every one of these pieces is more or less about writing/reading/thinking/teaching. Their final arrangement here, therefore, is the approximate order of their concoction, except as otherwise specified in their headnotes.

— *Langford Creek, Maryland: Fridays 1984–94*

FURTHER FRIDAYS

Teacher
(for Shelly, on her birthday)

This Friday-piece was written in 1986 for a little anthology called An Apple for My Teacher *(Chapel Hill: Algonquin Books, 1987), subtitled* Twelve Authors Tell About Teachers Who Made the Difference. *The anthologist, Louis D. Rubin, Jr. — himself a notable author, literary historian, professor at the University of North Carolina, and founder of Algonquin Books — had once upon a time been* my *teacher at Johns Hopkins, where he had indeed "made a difference." The essay, however, concerns another teacher, formerly my student, presently my wife and this volume's dedicatee. As the essay's own dedication parenthetically declares, it was written as a little birthday tribute to her, to be published appropriately in my old friend and coach's tastefully low-profile small-press anthology.*

But the thing sort of got away from me, and what was meant as a quiet testimonial to an extraordinary teacher turned into a minor embarrassment for her. Having posted the manuscript to Chapel Hill and been paid my token payment (the essay, like the whole anthology, was a labor of love), I decided impulsively, without consulting the tributee, to send a copy off to Harper's; *the extra money would be nice. They accepted it just as my wife and I were setting out for a lecture visit to Alaska, and when I told her the news en route, she pointed out immediately that a panegyric from one's husband would be out of place in a national magazine. No problem, I assured her: Such periodicals have a lead time of months; once back from Anchorage and environs, I would call* Harper's *and withdraw the essay. Alas, we found on our return that the magazine had already set it in type for their upcoming issue. There it appeared, much edited, in November 1986, a year before the anthology for which it was written, with a surprise subtitle that further embarrassed us*

("Teacher: The Making of a Great One" — edited down at our insistence to "a Good One") — and then Reader's Digest *picked it up ("Talk About Teachers!" March 1987) and then* Best American Essays 1987 *(NY: Ticknor & Fields/Houghton Mifflin, 1987) and several subsequent anthologies. I have even retold the tale myself in the novel/memoir* Once Upon a Time: A Floating Opera *(Boston: Little, Brown, 1994).*

Ah well, Shell. I meant it then, I mean it now: Happy birthday, student, teacher, lover, friend, and wife. And I still prefer the original version, photographs and all, here reprinted for the first time since the modest occasion for which it was intended.

IN THE FEATURELESS, low-rise, glass-and-aluminum box in which, back in the early 1960s, I taught Humanities 1 (Truth, Goodness, and Beauty) at the Pennsylvania State University, her hand was always up: usually first among those of the thirty undergraduates enrolled in my section. Many were seniors from the colleges of Education, Home Economics, Psychology, Engineering, even Forestry and Agriculture, fulfilling their "non-tech elec"; Hum 1 was not a course particularly designed for liberal-arts majors, who would presumably pick up enough TG & B in their regular curriculum. But Miss Rosenberg of the bright brown eyes and high-voltage smile and upraised hand, very much a major in the liberal arts, was there (1) because it was her policy to study with as many as possible of that university's huge faculty — almost regardless of their subject — who she had reason to believe were of particular interest or effectiveness; (2) because other of her English professors had given me okay notices; and (3) because the rest of my teaching load in those days was freshman composition (a requirement that she had easily absolved) and the writing of fiction (an art for which she felt no vocation).

Hum 1, then:

What is Aristotle's distinction between involuntary and nonvoluntary acts, and what are the moral implications of that distinction? Miss Rosenberg?

Miss Shelly Rosenberg, spring 1965

What does David Hume mean by the remark that the rules of art come not from reason but from experience. Anybody? Miss Rosenberg.

What are all those *bridges* for in *Crime and Punishment*? Let's hear from somebody besides Miss Rosenberg this time. (No hands.) Think of it this way: What are the three main things that a novelist can do with a character on a bridge? (No hands. Sigh.) Miss Rosenberg?

Her responses were sound, thoughtful, based unfailingly upon thorough preparation of the assigned material, and always ready. If she was not the most brilliant student I had ever taught — I was already by then a dozen years into the profession, with more than a thousand students behind me — she was the best. Brilliance is often erratic, capricious, cranky, sometimes indolent, sometimes

John Barth, teaching, spring 1965 (Joe Graedon)

troublemaking. Which is not to say that Miss R. (the Sixties weren't yet in high gear; in central Pennsylvania, at least, most of us still lectured in jackets, white shirts, and neckties and called our students Miss and Mister, as they called us Professor) was docile: If she didn't understand a passage of Lucretius or Machiavelli or Turgenev, she interrogated it and me until either she understood it or I understood that I didn't understand it either. Her combination of academic and moral seriousness, her industry, energy, and animation — solid A, back when A meant A.

The young woman was physically attractive, too: her skirt-and-sweatered body trim and fit (from basketball, softball, soccer, tennis, fencing), her brown hair neatly brushed, her aforecited eyes and smile. Ten years out of my all-male alma pater, I still found it mildly exciting — diverting, anyhow — to have girls, as we yet thought of them, in my classroom. But never mind that: As a student, for better or worse, I was never personally close to my teachers; as a teacher I've never been personally close to my students. And on the matter of *physical* intimacies between teacher and taught, I've always agreed with Bernard Shaw's Henry Higgins: "What! That thing! Sacred, I assure you. . . . Teaching would be impossible unless pupils were sacred."

Now: What is the first rung on Plato's "ladder of love"? Nobody remembers? Miss Rosenberg.

All the same, it interested me to hear, from a friend and senior colleague who knew her better, that my (and his) star student was not immune to "crushes" on her favorite teachers, who were to her as were the Beatles to many of her classmates: crushes more or less innocent, I presumed, depending upon their object. This same distinguished colleague I understood to be currently one such object. She frequented his office between classes; would bicycle across the town to drop in at his suburban house. I idly wondered . . . but did not ask him, much less her. Sacred, and none of my business.

I did however learn a few things further: That our Miss R. was from Philadelphia, strictly brought up, an overachiever (silly pejorative; let's say superachiever) who might well graduate first in her four-thousand-member class. That she was by temperament and/or upbringing thirsty for attention and praise, easily bruised, traumatically strung out by the term papers and examinations on which she scored so triumphantly. That her emotional budget was high on both sides of the ledger: She expended her feelings munificently; she demanded — at least expected, anyhow hoped for — reciprocal munificence from her friends and, presumably, from her crushees.

Mm hm. And the second rung, anybody? (No hands, except of course . . .) Miss Rosenberg.

En route to her A in Hum 1 we had a couple of office conferences, but when she completed her baccalaureate (not only first in her class but with, in fact, the highest academic average in Penn State's hundred-year history, for which superachievement she was officially designated the university's 100,000th graduate at its centennial commencement exercises), I was still Mister Barth; she was still Miss Rosenberg. She would have prospered at the best colleges in our republic; circumstances, I was told, had constrained her to her state university, to its and our benefit. What circumstances? I didn't ask. Now (so my by-this-time-ex-crushee colleague reported) she had seven several graduate fellowships to choose from among; he believed she was inclining to the high-powered University of Chicago.

I, too, as it happened, was in the process of changing universities. I neither saw, nor heard from or about, nor to my recollection thought of excellent Miss Rosenberg for the next four years.

There is chalk dust on the sleeve of my soul. In the half-century since my kindergarten days, I have never been away from classrooms for longer than a few months. I am as at home among blackboards, half-desks, lecterns, and seminar tables as among the furniture of my writing room; both are the furniture of my head. I believe I know my strengths and limitations as a teacher the way I know them as a writer: Doubtful of my accomplishments in both métiers, I am not doubtful at all that they *are* my métiers, for good or ill.

But, autodidact, I resist being taught by others. Years of childhood piano lessons failed to "take"; later I taught myself to play jazz drums and baroque recorder, as I taught myself tennis, skiing, sailing, novel-writing, even teaching. In literature as well as in general, my school-education was harum-scarum. For the years between kindergarten and college, I can pass some of the blame for that deficiency on to a procession of well-meaning but uninspired teachers in an economically depressed, semi-rural public-school system, teachers who neither messed up my head nor much educated it. Miss Ridah Collins, however, who ran a little private kindergarten in Cambridge, Maryland, back in the 1930s, was as accomplished in her corner of the profession as were my formidable, in some instances famous, Johns Hopkins professors in theirs: the aesthetician and historian of ideas George Boas, the Spanish poet Pedro Salinas and the American poet Elliott Coleman, the romance philologist Leo Spitzer, the historians C. Vann Woodward and Sidney Painter, the literary scholars Charles Singleton, Kemp Malone, Earl Wasserman, my writing coaches Robert Jacobs and Louis Rubin. If most of what I know I learned from my own teaching rather than from my teachers, the fault does not lie in such stars as those, but in myself.

Having learned by undergraduate trial and error that I was going to devote my adult life to writing fiction, I entered the teaching profession through a side door: by impassioned default, out of heartfelt lack of alternatives. I had had everything to learn; the university had taught me some of it, and I guessed that teaching might teach me more. I needed time to clear my throat, but I was precociously a family man; college teaching (I scarcely cared where or what; I would improvise, invent if necessary) might pay landlord and grocer, if barely, and leave my faculties less abused and exhausted than would manual labor or routine office work, of both of which I had had a taste. Teaching assistantships in graduate school had taught me that while I was not a "natural" teacher, I was not an unnatural one, either. Some of my Johns Hopkins undergraduate students knew more about literature, even about the rules of grammar, syntax, and punctuation, than I did. I pushed to catch up; accepted gratefully a three-thousand-dollar-a-year instructorship in English composition at Penn State, where I taught four sections of freshman comp. Six teaching days a week, twenty-five students per section, one composition per student per week, all papers to be corrected and graded by a rigorous system of symbols, rules, standards. That's three thousand freshman compositions a year, at a dollar per. It drove one of my predecessors, the poet Theodore Roethke, to drink. But there were occasional half-days free, some evenings, and the long academic holidays and summers. I stayed on there a dozen years, moving duly through the ranks and up the modest salary scale; got novels written and children raised; learned a great deal about English usage and abusage. And I had a number of quite good students among all those hundreds in my roll-book . . . even a few superb ones.

My academic job-changes happen to have coincided with and corresponded to major changes in recent U.S. cultural history. As America moved into the High Sixties, I moved from Penn State's bucolic sprawl — still very 1950ish in 1965, with its big-time football, its pom-pommed cheerleaders, its more than half a hundred social fraternities, its fewer than that number of pot-smoking counterculturalists among the fifteen thousand–plus undergraduates, its vast experimental farms and tidy livestock barns, through which I used to stroll with my three small children when not writing sentences or professing Truth, Goodness, and Beauty — moved to the State University of New York's edgy-urban new operation in Buffalo. The Berkeley of the East, its disruptivist students proudly called the place. The Ellis Island of Academe, we new-immigrant faculty called it, also with some pride, so many of us were intellectual heretics, refugees from constrained professional or domestic circumstances, academic fortune hunters in Governor Nelson Rockefeller's promising land.

Those next four years were eventful, in U.S. history and mine. Jetting once a month to guest-lecture at other universities, I literally saw the smoke rise from America's burning urban ghettos. More than once I returned from some teargassed campus to find my own "trashed," on strike, or cordoned off by gas-masked National Guardsmen. It was a jim-dandy place, SUNY/Buffalo, to work out the decade. My marriage came unglued; I finished *Giles Goat-Boy,* experimented with hashish and adultery, wrote *Lost in the Funhouse* and "The Literature of Exhaustion," began *Chimera.* Education, said Alfred North Whitehead, is the process of catching up to one's generation. Even for autodidacts, the tuition can be considerable.

One afternoon in the Sixties' final winter I took off from Buffalo in a snowstorm for my monthly off-campus lecture, this one at Boston College. The flight was late. My Jesuit host, who was to have taken me to a pre-lecture dinner, had his hands full just getting us across the snowed-in city to the B.C. campus, where most of my audience kindly waited. Promising dinner later, he hustled me onstage to do my number and then off to the obligatory reception (invited guests only, in this case) in a room above the auditorium. Since we were running late, we skipped the usual post-lecture question period. Even so, as happens, people came forward to say hello, get their books signed, ask things.

Such as (her head cocked slightly, bright eyes, bright smile, nifty orange wool miniskirted dress, beige boots — but my host was virtually tugging at my sleeve; we had agreed to cut short this ritual and get upstairs to that reception as quickly as courtesy allowed): "Remember me?"

*   *   *

For a superachiever in the USA, public-school teaching is a curious choice of professions. Salaries are low. The criteria for employment in most districts are not notably high; neither is the schoolteacher's prestige in the community, especially in urban neighborhoods and among members of the other professions. The workload, on the other hand, is heavy, in particular for conscientious English teachers who demand a fair amount of writing from the hundred or more students they meet five days a week. In most other professions, superior ability and dedication are rewarded with the five P's: promotion, power, prestige, perks, and pay. Assistant professors become associate professors, full professors, endowed-chair professors, emeritus professors. Junior law partners become senior law partners; middle managers become chief executive officers; doctors get rich and are held in exalted regard by our society. Even able and ambitious priests may become monsignors, bishops, cardinals. But the best schoolteacher in the land, if she has no administrative ambitions (that is, no ambition to get out of the classroom), enters the profession with the rank of teacher and retires from it decades later with the rank of teacher, not remarkably better paid and perked than when she met her maiden class. Fine orchestral players and repertory actors may be union-scaled and virtually anonymous, but at least they get, as a group, public applause. Painters, sculptors, poets may labor in poverty and obscurity, but, as Milton acknowledged, "Fame is the spur." The condition of the true artisan, perhaps, is most nearly akin to the gifted schoolteacher's: an all but anonymous calling that allows for mastery, even for a sort of genius, but rarely for fame, applause, or wealth; whose chief reward must be the mere superlative doing of the thing. The maker of stained glass or fine jewelry, however, works only with platinum, gemstones, gold, not with young minds and spirits.

Sure, I remembered her, that snowy night: Penn State, Hum 1, hand raised. After a moment I even recalled her name, a feat I'm poor at in company. My sleeve was being tugged: the reception. So what was she doing there? She'd seen notice of my reading in the newspaper and hauled through the snow from Brookline to catch her old teacher's act. No, I meant in Boston: Ph.D. work, I supposed, somewhere along the River Chuck, that cerebral cortex of

America. Or maybe she's finished her doctorate — I couldn't remember her specialty — and was already assistant-professoring in
the neighborhood? No: It was a long story, Ms. R. allowed, and
there were others standing about, and my sleeve was being tugged.
Well, then: Obliging of you to trek through the drifts to say hello
to your old teach. Too bad we can't chat a bit more, catch up; but
there's this reception I have to go to now, upstairs. You're looking
fine indeed.

She was: not a coed now, but a city-looking smart young
woman. Where was it she'd been going to go after Penn State?
What interesting things had her ex-crushees among my ex-col-
leagues told me about her? Couldn't remember: only the hand invariably raised (sometimes before I'd reached my question mark)
in Truth, Goodness, and Beauty, the lit-up smile, and maybe one
serious office conference in her senior year. Was there a wedding
ring on that hand now? Before I could think to look, I was Jesuited
off to an elevator already filled with the invited.

As its doors closed, she caught them, caused them to reopen,
and lightly asked, "May I come along?" Surprised, delighted, I answered for my host: former star student, haven't seen her in years,
we did her out of her Q & A, of course she may come along.

No wedding ring. But at the reception, too, I was rightly pre-
empted by the Boston Collegians whose guest I was. Ms. Rosenberg and I (but it was Shelly now, and please call me Jack) had
time only to register a few former mutual acquaintances and the
circumstances of my being in Buffalo these days (she'd read that)
and of her having left Chicago (a long story, Jack) to teach in
Boston. Aha. At Boston U.? Tufts? Northeastern?

The incandescent smile. Nope: in the public schools. First at
Quincy Junior High, then at Weston Junior High, currently at
Wayland High. She was a public-school teacher, of English. A
schoolteacher is what she'd wanted to be from the beginning.

We supposed I ought to mingle with the invited. But as she had
already taken two initiatives — the first merely cordial, the second
a touch audacious — I took the next four. The kindly priest, my
host, meant to dine me informally after this reception, at some
restaurant convenient to my motel, into which I'd not yet been
checked. I urged her to join us, so that we could finish our catch-

ing up off company time. She agreed, the priest likewise. As she had her car with her and the weather was deep, they conferred upon likeliest roads and restaurants (one with oysters and champagne, the guest of honor suggested) and decided upon Tollino's on Route 9, not far from the Charterhouse Motel, where I was billeted. She would meet us there.

My duty to the invited done, she did. Tollino's came through with half-shell Blue Points and bubbly; the priest had eaten, but he encouraged us to take our time (although the hour was late now) and to help ourselves. He even shared a glass with us. We tried politely to keep the conversation three-way; it was clear to all hands, however, that our patient host was ready to end his evening. Initiative Two: The Charterhouse was just a few doors down the road; Miss Rosenberg had her car. If she was agreeable . . .

Quite. The good father was excused; he would fetch me to the airport in the morning. Another round of oysters, then, another glass of champagne to toast our reacquaintance. Here's to Penn State, to old mutual friends and ex-crushees, to Truth, to Goodness, to Beauty. Here's to lively Boston, bumptious Buffalo, and — where was it? Chicago, right. A long story, you said. On with it: Long stories are my long suit.

A schoolteacher is what she'd wanted to be from the beginning. Although she'd used to weep at her difficulties with higher math and was unnerved even back then by the prospect of examinations and term papers, she'd loved her Philadelphia public-school days. At the Pennypacker Elementary School and especially at the fast-track Philadelphia High School for Girls, where straight-800 SAT scores were not rare among her classmates, Penn State's future academic superstar had regarded herself as no more than a well-above-average performer. But she had relished each new schoolday; had spent the long summer breaks enthusiastically camp-counseling, the next-best thing to school. Unlike me, she'd had any number of inspired, inspiring teachers well before college; her freshman year at Penn State had been unexciting by comparison with her senior year at Girls' High. Even later, when she'd sought out the local luminaries and seen to it that she'd got herself a sound undergraduate education, her resolution to "teach school" had never wavered. At the urging of her professors she'd gone on to graduate study in literature and art history with the University of Chicago's Committee on the Humanities; she'd done excellent work there with Norman Maclean, Elder Olson, Edward Rosenheim, Joshua Taylor. She had even charmed her way into one of Saul Bellow's courses, to check that famous fellow out. But she had no ambition for a doctorate: Her objective was *school teaching!* (she said it always with exclamation mark and megawatt smile), and she wanted to get on with it as soon as possible. On the other hand, she'd had no truck with "education" courses: Mickey Mouse stuff, in her opinion, except for the history and philosophy of education, which she'd found engrossing. Her baccalaureate was in English; her M.A. was to have been in the humanities. Neither had she been a teaching assistant; hers was a no-strings fellowship.

I pricked up my ears: *Was to have been?*

Yes: She had left Chicago abruptly after a year and a half, for non-academic reasons, without completing the degree for which she had already more than enough credits. This irregularity, together with the absence of education courses on her transcripts, had made it necessary for her first employer, in Quincy, to diddle benignly her credentials for certification to teach in the Commonwealth's public schools, especially as she had come to Boston in mid–academic year. She was hired, and was being paid, as "M.A. equivalent," which she certainly was.

Abruptly, you said? For non-academic reasons?

Yup. A love-trauma, only recently recovered from. Long story, Jack.

Tollino's was closing. Initiative Three: I supposed there was a bar of some sort in or near my motel, where we could have a nightcap and go on with our stories (I, too, had one to tell). Should we go check me into the Charterhouse and have a look?

Sure. We made the short change of mise-en-scènes down the snowplowed highway in her silver-blue Impala convertible, behind the wheel whereof my grown-up and, it would seem, now seasoned former student looked quite terrific in those beige boots and that orange miniskirted dress under that winter coat. And in the motel's all-but-empty lounge I was told at last the long story and some shorter ones, and I told mine and some shorter ones, and presently I took Initiative Four.

Plato has Socrates teach in *The Symposium* that the apprehension of Very Beauty, as distinct from any beautiful thing or class of things, is arrived at by commencing with the love of, even the lust for, some particular beautiful object or person. Thence one may proceed to loving beautiful objects and persons in general, the shared quality that transcends their individual differences; may learn even to admire that shared quality without lusting after it: "Platonic love." Thereby one may learn to love the beauty of nonmaterial things as well: beautiful actions, beautiful ideas (a philosopher-colleague back at Penn State, remarking to me that he could not read without tears the beautiful scene near the end of Turgenev's *Fathers and Children* where Bazarov's old parents visit their nihilist son's grave, added, "But I weep at the Pythagorean theorem, too"). Whence the initiate, the elect, the Platonically invited, may take the ultimate elevator to Beauty Bare: the quality abstracted even from beautiful abstractions. This is the celebrated Ladder of Love, as I understood and taught it in Humanities 1 at Penn State, Miss Rosenberg's hand raised at every rung. Our relationship began at the top of that ladder, with those lofty abstractions: Truth, Goodness, Beauty. Now my (former) student taught her (former, and not *always* autodidact) teacher that that process is reversible, anyhow coaxial; that ladder a two-way street; that ultimate elevator — May I come along? — a not-bad place to begin.

She was and is the natural teacher that I've never been. Distraught by the termination of her first adult love affair (emotionally extravagant, as such affairs should be), she had abruptly left Chicago and her almost completed graduate degree and found asylum in Boston with a Girls' High classmate, now a Harvard doctoral candidate. In the midst of this turmoil — and in midyear — she entered the profession she'd known since first grade to be her calling, and with no prior training or direct experience, from Day One on

the chair side of the teacher's desk she was as entirely in her element as she'd known she would be. M.A. or no M.A., she was a
master of the art; personal crisis or no personal crisis, she impro-
vised for the Quincy Junior High fast-trackers, later for the whiz
kids at Weston and Wayland, a course in literature and art history
as high-powered and high-spirited as its teacher. She flourished under the staggering workload of a brand-new full-time supercon-
scientious public-school English teacher. She throve in the life of
her new city: new friends, apartment-mates, parties, sports, explorations, liaisons non-dangereuses — all worked in between the
long hours of preparing lesson-plans and study questions, assem-
bling films and projector-slides, critiquing papers, grading quizzes
and exams, and teaching, teaching, teaching her enthusiastic students, who knew a winner when they learned from one. Those first
years of her professional life, which turned out also to be the heal-
ing interim between her two most serious engagements of the
heart, were the freest and in some respects the happiest of her
story thus far.

On subsequent Boston visits (No need to fetch me to the airport
this morning, Father; I have a ride, thanks) I would meet various
of her colleagues — most of them likewise energetic, dedicated,
and attractive young men and women — and a few of her students, bound for advanced placement in the Ivy League. I would
come to see just how good good public schooling can be, how
mediocre mine was, how barely better had been my children's.
Alas, I was unable to witness my former student's teacherly perfor-
mances (my new lover's, my fiancée's, my bride's), as she had witnessed a semestersworth of mine. Public schools are not open to
the public; anyhow, my presence would have been obtrusive. By all
accounts they were superlative, virtuoso. From what I knew of her
as a student, from what I had learned of and from her since, I
could not imagine otherwise.

Yet she came truly into her professional own when, after our
marriage, we moved to Buffalo — returned to Buffalo in my case,
from a honeymoon year as visiting professor at Boston University — and, beginning to feel the burden of full-time public-
school teaching, she took with misgivings a half-time job in a pri-

vate girls' high school, the fine old Buffalo Seminary. Its non-coed aspect gave her no trouble, much as she had enjoyed her male students in Boston, she'd enjoyed even more the atmosphere of the Philadelphia High School for Girls. But the notion of private schools — "independent schools," they call themselves — ran counter to her liberal-democratic principles. Buff Sem's exclusiveness was not academic, as had been that of Girls' High and the Wayland fast track; she feared it would be social, perhaps racist: a finishing school for the daughters of well-to-do Buffalonians who didn't want their kids in the racially and economically integrated city system.

Her apprehensions were not foundationless, but they evaporated within a week in the sunny company of her new charges. The girls as a group were no brighter than those at Quincy, Weston, Wayland; *less* bright, as a group, than her fast-trackers in those public schools or her own high-school classmates back in Philadelphia. But they were entirely likable, not at all snobbish, and wondrously educable. There are next to no disciplinary problems in a good private girls' school, at least not in the classroom. And with only twelve or so students per class, and with only two classes, and without the powerfully distracting sexual voltage of coeducation at the high-school level — what teaching could get done!

We stayed for only one academic year. My bride was not yet thirty. But more than a dozen years later she is still remembered with respect and affection by her Seminary headmaster and by her students from that *Wunderjahr*, older now than she was then. She had become Mrs. Barth in two respects: It pleased her to append her husband's last name to her own (to be called "Mrs. *John* Barth," however, rightly rankles her; she is herself, not Mrs. Me), and she had become the pedagogical phenomenon that her students refer to among themselves as "Barth." One does not speak of taking "Mrs. Barth's course" in myth and fantasy, or in the short story, or in the nineteenth-century Russian novel, or in the literature of alienation; one speaks of "taking Barth." For along with large infusions of the curricular subject matter, what one gets from "taking Barth" is a massive (but always high-spirited, high-energy) education in moral-intellectual responsibility:

responsibility to the text, to the author, to the language, to the muses of Truth, Goodness, and Beauty . . . and, along the way, responsibility to the school, to one's teachers and classmates, to oneself.

Very little of this came via her husband. I don't doubt that "Barth" learned a few things from her undergraduate professor about the texts in Hum 1 — texts on which, however, I was no authority. No doubt too her newlywed daily life with a working novelist and writing coach sharpened her understanding of how fiction is put together, how it manages its effects. But she is a closer reader than I, both of literary texts and of student essays, and a vastly more painstaking critic of the latter, upon which she frequently spends more time than their authors. The Barth who writes this sentence involves himself not at all with the extracurricular lives and extraliterary values of the apprentice writers in his charge. My concern is with their dramaturgy, not with the drama of their personal lives, and seriously as I take my academic commitments, they unquestionably rank second to my commitments to the muse. The Barth "taken" by the girls at the Buffalo Seminary, and thereafter (since 1973, when we moved from Buffalo to Baltimore) at Saint Timothy's School, gives them 100 percent of her professional attention: an attention that drives her to work time and a half at her "half-time" job, and that is directed at her charges' characters and values as well as their thought processes, their written articulateness, and their literary perceptivity. I'm at my best with the best of my students, the ones en route to joining our next literary generation, and am at my weakest with the weakest. She works her wonders broadcast; the testimonial letters — I should get such reviews! — pile in from her C and D students as well as from the high achievers, and from their parents. Often those letters come from college (wimpy, the girls complain, compared to taking Barth; we thought college would be *serious!*); sometimes they come years later, from the strong young professionals that many of those students have become. You opened my eyes. You changed my life.

*   *   *

This she has done for more than a dozen years now at St. Tim's, an Episcopal-flavored boarding school in the horse-and-mansion country north of Baltimore. It has proved a virtually ideal place for the exercise of her gifts. She has her complaints about it (as do I about my dear, once-deadly-serious Johns Hopkins). She worries about grade inflation, about the risk of softening performance standards, about the unquestioning conservatism of many of her students. She freely admires, however, the general fineness of the girls themselves, who wear their privileges lightly and who strive so, once their eyes are opened, to measure up to her elevated standards, to deserve her praise. (I have met numbers of the best of these girls and am every time reminded of Anton Chekhov's remark to his brother: "What the aristocrats take for granted, we paid for with our youth." Encircled by a garland of them at a party at our house, Donald Barthelme once asked my wife, "Can't I take a few of them home in my briefcase?")

She hopes to go on with this wonder working ... oh, for a while yet. She doubts she has the metabolism for a full-length career, sometimes wonders whether she has it for a full-length life. As her habits of relentless self-criticism and superpreparation have required a half-time situation on which to expend more than full-time energy, so — like some poets and fictionists — she will accomplish, perhaps must accomplish, a full professional life in fewer than the usual number of years. We feel similarly, with the same mix of emotions, about our late-started marriage, consoling ourselves with the reflection that, as two teachers who do most of our work at home, we are together more in one year than most working couples are in two. At the front end of her forties, unlike some other high-energy schoolteachers, she has no interest in "moving up" or moving on to some other aspect of education. For her there is only the crucible of the classroom — those astonishing fifty-minute bursts for which, like a human satellite transmitter, she spends hours and hours preparing — and the long, patient, hugely therapeutic individual conferences with her girls, and the hours and hours more of annotating their essays: word by word, sentence by sentence, idea by idea, value by value, with a professional attention that puts to shame any doctor's or lawyer's I've known. How I wish that my children had had such a high-school teacher. How I wish *I* had!

So: for a while yet. A few years from now, if all goes well, I myself mean to retire from teaching, which I'll have been at for four decades, and — not without some trepidation — we'll see. An unfortunate side effect of the single-mindedness behind my best former student's teaching is that, like many another inspired workaholic, she's short on extraprofessional interests and satisfactions. And both of us are socially impaired persons, so enwrapped in our work and each other that our life is a kind of solipsism *à deux*. We'll see.

My university's loss will easily be made up. Talented apprentice writers doubtless learn things from a sympathetic and knowledgeable coach in a well-run writing program; I surely did. But they acquire their art mainly as writers always have done: from reading, from practice, from aesthetic argument with their impassioned peers and predecessors, from experience of the world and of themselves. Where the talent in the room is abundant, it scarcely matters who sits at the head of the seminar table, though it matters some. The Johns Hopkins Writing Seminarians will readily find another coach.

But if when I go she goes too — from schooling her girls in art and life, nudging them through the stage of romance, as Whitehead calls it, toward the stage of precision, which she can't do if we put the strictures of the academic calendar behind us — *there's* a loss that can nowise be made good. Writers publish; scholars, critics publish. In a few cases, what they publish outlives them, by much or little. But a first-rate teacher's immortality is neither more nor less than the words (spoken even decades later by her former students to their own students, spouses, children, friends): "Mrs. Barth used to tell us . . ."

I like to imagine one of hers meeting one of mine, some romantically sufficient distance down the road. *He* has become (as I'd long since predicted) one of the established writers of his generation; *she* is a hotshot young whatever, who's nevertheless still much interested in literature, so exciting did her old high-school English teacher make that subject. They're in an elevator somewhere, upward bound to a reception for the invited, and they're

St. Timothy's Barth, left, and Johns Hopkins's Barth, right, spring 1985

quickly discovering, indeed busily seeking, additional common ground. Somehow, the city of Baltimore gets mentioned: Hey, they both went to school there! Later, over oysters and champagne, they circle back to that subject. She'd been in high school, he in graduate school: St. Timothy's, Johns Hopkins. Hopkins, did he say, in the mid-Eighties? She supposes then (knowledgeably indeed for a young international banker) that he must have worked with her old English teacher's husband, the novelist. . . .

Sure, we all had Barth.

What a smile she smiles! You think *you* had Barth, she declares (it's late; the place is closing; they bet there's a nightcappery somewhere near his motel). Never mind *that* one: Out at St. Timothy's we had *Barth!* Talk about teachers!

Let's.

Can It Be Taught?

"Talented apprentice writers doubtless learn things from a sympathetic and knowledgeable coach in a well-run writing program," declares the preceding Friday-piece. *"But . . ."*

   The essay following (first published in the New York Times Book Review, *June 16, 1985) addresses both that confident proposition and that* but. *It is my response to the most frequent, banal, and reasonable question asked of the many American writers who, in the second half of this century, have chosen for better or worse to help pay their rent by teaching "creative writing" in our colleges and universities.*

Can It Be Learned?

Sure. Not by everybody, but by more writers per annum than anyone has time to read. Whatever the demand for their product, the supply of able American poets, novelists, and short-story writers has not declined in the second half of this century. An annual national poetry competition, for the Walt Whitman Award, a few years back received 1,475 manuscript *volumes* of verse from which to select and publish the winner; a poetry magazine with 520 subscribers may receive 10,500 poems from 1,875 contributors in a single year.* The fiction and poetry editors of the few American large-circulation periodicals that still publish fiction and poetry are comparably deluged, as are the directors of the nation's better-known graduate programs in creative writing. Lots of literature out there.

*Figures borrowed from Stephen Minot's 1977 essay "Hey, Is Anyone Listening?" in the *North American Review*.

Is the stuff any good? My experience of winnowing fiction applications to the Johns Hopkins University Writing Seminars is that if not many of them knock our socks off (and we don't want to be de-socked by more than ten or a dozen yearly), only a few are downright incompetent. Somehow, somewhere, these multitudes of aspiring authors have somehow learned their trade, even before they apply to us or others for fine-tuning.

It has been argued that while the supply of reasonably competent American literary artists may exceed their interested readership (the number of over-the-counter sales of that aforementioned Walt Whitman Award poetry collection was smaller than the number of entries from which it was selected), we have presently no writer of great international stature; that our Saul Bellow and John Updike, our James Merrill and John Ashbery, are not in the transcendent league of William Faulkner, Ernest Hemingway, T. S. Eliot, Robert Frost; that since the death of Vladimir Nabokov (a non-native at that), the most commanding figures in contemporary Western literature happen not to be Americans: Samuel Beckett, Jorge Luis Borges, Gabriel García Márquez. In short, that production is up, but quality is down.

My own feeling is that a chapter of our literary history that includes the compatriots mentioned above, plus Donald Barthelme, Robert Coover, Stanley Elkin, William H. Gass, John Hawkes, Bernard Malamud, Grace Paley, Thomas Pynchon, and Kurt Vonnegut, Jr. — to mention middle-aged fictionists only, and only a few of those — is a bright and busy chapter. If it turns out to be, after all, an entr'acte, then the entr'acte, like some of Molière's, may prove livelier than the play. But no matter; the question is beside our point. Genius, like matter in the universe, is thinly distributed; first-magnitude stars are nowhere common. According to the *New York Times* Winter Survey of Education in 1984, there are presently more than three hundred degree-granting creative-writing programs in American colleges and universities; but not even in America can one major in Towering Literary Artistry.

The writing that people have in mind when they put the question "Can it be taught?" is not usually "The Waste Land" or *One Hundred Years of Solitude*; nor is it on the other hand greeting-card doggerel and bodice-rippers. It is your average pretty-damn-good literary artifact as published by *The New Yorker* or *Esquire* or *The Atlantic*, say, or the *Paris Review* or *Antaeus*, or one of the better New York trade-book publishing houses, to be read with more pleasure than not by those who still actually read literature for pleasure.

Most such artifacts are the work of men and women who consider themselves writers by trade (rather, by calling; as the critic Earl Rovit has observed, the novelist in America practices a vocation that is seldom quite a profession, economically speaking, and for the poet or short-story writer it is even less so). The rest are the work of able now-and-thenners. All have more or less mastered the art of imaginative writing, as did their predecessors one way or another over the 4,500-year history of written literature. Doubtless there are people whom no amount of patient observation, instruction, or practice can teach to serve a shuttlecock or tie a bowline on a bight; such folk find other métiers than badminton and marlinespike seamanship. But "the artful rendition of human experience into written words" (my version of Cleanth Brooks and Robert Penn Warren's definition of literature) gets mastered by the quite talented and approached by the rather talented, generation after generation. Given the inclination and the opportunity, those with any aptitude for it at all surely hone what skills they have, in the art of writing as in any other art, craft, skill.

It gets learned.

Can It Be Studied?

Boyoboy, can it ever. Since long before the invention of universities, not to mention university programs in creative writing, authors have acquired their authorship in four main ways — first, by paying a certain sort of attention to the experience of life, as well as merely undergoing it; second, by paying a certain sort of attention to the works of their great and less great predecessors in the medium of written language, as well as merely reading them; third, by practicing that medium themselves, usually a *lot* (the writer and critic Charles Newman declares that the first prerequisite for aspiring writers is sufficient motor control to keep their pens moving left to right, line after line, hour after hour, day after day; I would add year after year, decade after decade); and fourth, by offering their apprentice work for discussion and criticism by one or several of their impassioned peers, or by some more experienced hand, or by both.

None of this, obviously, implies an organized practicum course in creative writing, much less a degree-granting program in it. Many and many an eminent writer has spoken out against such courses and programs, but none that I know of against the Fourfold Path that such programs at best may conveniently embody. In his excellent book *The Art of Fiction*, the late John Gardner cites Ernest Hemingway's remark that the best way for a writer to learn the craft is simply to go away and write. Gardner then properly adds, "Hemingway, it may help to remember, went away for free 'tutorials' to two of the finest teachers then living, Sherwood Anderson and Gertrude Stein." The most reclusive of apprentices usually flashes his or her scribblings at *somebody* and tremulously or truculently hangs upon response, for unlike a diary, a poem or story seen by no eyes except its author's can scarcely be said to exist.

Those four obvious, all but universal ways of learning how to write correspond roughly to what I take to be the proper objects of study for all serious writers — their material ("human life," says Aristotle, "its happiness and its misery"), their medium (the language in general, the written language in particular), their craft (the rudiments of, say, fiction, together with conventional and unconventional techniques of their deployment), and their art (the inspired and masterful application of their craft and medium to their material). Not only does the first of these — the material — not imply a creative-writing course; it is beyond the proper province of one, although the study of great literature is one excellent handle on "human life, its happiness and its misery." And real mastery of the fourth — the art, as distinct from the craft — is more the hope than the curricular goal of a sound writing program; it comes from mastery of the other three plus a dash of genius. But these four objects of authorial study, and those four ways to authority, were as surely the Egyptian scribe Khakheperresenb's in circa 2000 B.C. as they are the freshman poet's in this year's class at Iowa or Stanford, Columbia or Johns Hopkins.*

Well, but what about those three hundred–plus creative-writing operations I mentioned earlier, a phenomenon scarcely to be found outside our republic and scarcely to be found inside it before V-J Day, since when it has proliferated like herpes simplex or the gypsy moth? The sheer numbers involved in that quixotic enterprise are certainly dismaying, as is the immense and touching irony that as fewer and fewer of us incline to read fiction and verse, more and more of us aspire to write it. Not economic recession, not declining literacy, failing bookstores, the usurpation of the kingdom of narrative by movies and television — nothing quenches the American thirst for courses in creative writing. In day school, night school, high school, college, graduate school, correspondence school, summer school, prison school, in writers' colonies and conferences and camps and cruises it is scribble, scribble, scribble, scribble, scribble, scribble, scribble. A very few of these student scribblers will become part of the next crop of American writers; the rest of that next crop are presently scribbling away too, more or less on their own, without benefit of departments and professors and classmates and diplomas in creative writing.

Either way, the thing gets learned, all right; and it gets learned, where it does, because it got studied, practiced, and reacted to, in or out of school.

*Khakheperresenb was a postmodernist of the Middle Kingdom in Egypt, anticipator of Donald Barthelme and William H. Gass and author of one of the earliest extant literary documents, a papyrus I call "Khakheperresenb's Complaint": "Would I had phrases that are not known, utterances that are strange, in new language that has not been used, free from repetition, not an utterance which men of old have spoken." Compare Mr. Barthelme's *Snow White* — "Oh I wish there were some words in the world that were not the words I always hear" — and Mr. Gass's *Willie Masters' Lonesome Wife* — "Why aren't there any decent words?" Written literature appears virtually to have begun with the eloquent fret that it is perhaps already played out: writing about writing. Moreover, as one might have guessed, the complaint is not original with Khakheperresenb; he's working an established Egyptian literary genre with a considerable history already by 2000 B.C. See the discussion "Complaint Literature" in Miriam Lichtheim's anthology *Ancient Literature, Vol. 1: The Old and Middle Kingdoms*, which includes Khakheperresenb's specimen, among others.

Then Should It Be Taught?

Absolutely not, if it can't be; else 'twere fraud. But why on earth not, if it can be, when so astonishingly many want to learn it?

Whether it should be offered as a university major leading to the baccalaureate or merely as an elective adjunct to a rigorous general education; whether in either case there should be autonomous departments of creative writing; whether a master's degree, not to mention a doctorate, is the proper accolade for a typescript volume of poetry or fiction neither more nor less likely to see eventual print than any other graduate thesis; whether, if I aspire like Joyce's Stephen Dedalus "to forge in the smithy of my soul the uncreated conscience of my race," I should do my apprentice racial-conscience forging in Dublin's Trinity College or the Trieste Berlitz school (where the aspiring writer Italo Svevo found a pretty good teacher, James Joyce, to look over his stuff) or Palo Alto or Baltimore or none of the above — these are questions about which the reasonable and knowledgeable, not to mention the unreasonable and ignorant, may disagree. Kay Boyle, late of San Francisco State U., opined not long ago that all creative-writing programs ought to be abolished by law. John Gardner, on the other hand, in his preface to the work aforementioned, declares, "I assume from the outset that the would-be writer using this book [which Gardner worked up out of his writing courses] can become a successful writer if he wants to, since most of the people I've known who wanted to become writers, knowing what it meant, *did* become writers."

I am less sanguine in this matter than Mr. Gardner ("knowing what it meant" is a participial escape hatch, to be sure), but far less absolute than Miss Boyle. A majority of the advanced apprentice writers that I've coached at Johns Hopkins over the past dozen years — not one of them untalented, or he/she wouldn't have been invited — have not in fact become "successful writers," at least not yet, if success means rather often publishing what one writes. On the other hand, a very fair minority of them have. Of the two thieves crucified along with Jesus, St. Augustine writes "Do not despair; one thief was saved. Do not presume; one thief was damned." Although many more of our diplomates than not will publish the occasional poem or story here and there along their subsequent way, the odds that one of them will turn into Mary Robison or Frederick Barthelme or Louise Erdrich are less favorable than Augustine's fifty–fifty.

I think it just as well that this is so. As a Chesapeake waterman said about the fact that only one in a million blue crab eggs gets to be an adult crab, "It's a damn good thing; otherwise we'd be arse-deep in crabs." How many important new writers must emerge from an annual seminar of ten or a dozen to justify that seminar? One every several years would be an impressive score, in my opinion — so long as (1) the odds are understood, so that there's no false advertising (and what apprentice in any art doesn't understand them?); (2) it is understood further that extraordinary talent tends to cut through those odds, especially when that developing talent receives sustained and intelligent critical attention; and (3) all hands are learning something useful about the ancient medium and craft of literature by working in that seminar room.

Among undergraduate writing majors, as might be expected, the success rate is considerably lower, if success is measured by subsequent careers as publishing poets and fictionists. But that is the wrong measure, I think. How many undergraduate majors in history, economics, philosophy, or literature expect or even wish to become professional historians, economists, philosophers, literary scholars? Their undergraduate major is the focus of their liberal education. A few will proceed to preprofessional graduate training in those fields — or come to it from other fields, as is the case with graduate-student writers. Most will become businesspeople, lawyers, civil servants, teachers, journalists, or administrators of this and that. Typical students in Johns Hopkins's Peabody Conservatory of Music, it is true, may hope to become celebrated musicians, but what they reasonably *expect* is a professional career involving music. What most of them in fact become is full- or part-time orchestra players, vocal and instrumental teachers, band and choir directors, piano tuners, music-store operators. A certain number will remain gifted amateurs.

Imaginative writing as a major field of study for college undergraduates is somewhere between the traditional liberal arts and the visual and performing arts. Among my own undergraduate classmates and near-classmates in the Hopkins seminars back in the Truman era, only two or three turned out to be professional writers in the usual sense (of those, the best known is Russell Baker of the *New York Times*); most have become the other things that our current undergraduates will become. Rather a lot of them have published the odd item, maybe even a novel or a book of verse, somewhere along the line. Nearly all of them write, in some significant capacity or other, in connection with their work — speeches, reports. My guess is that they all write at least a little better for their season in the seminars, immersed in the study and practice of literary craftsmanship.

I'll bet that they all *read* more knowledgeably and appreciatively, too, from having attempted literature themselves, just as those who have taken ballet lessons understand things about Baryshnikov and *Firebird* that we more innocent onlookers don't. If the chief product of all those hundreds of American creative-writing courses is successful readers rather than successful writers, what a service they render.

Which is not at all to argue that it should be taught even if it can't be.

But . . .

Of course it can, though not to everybody, and not by just anybody, and not necessarily in an official course on any sort of campus (though quite possibly and conveniently and effectively there). Not necessarily by a hotshot writer, either, though not impossibly by one.

So how come we do it in the university only in America? Because we're Americans; we do *everything* in our universities. A Pennsylvania State University colleague of mine in bygone years was a senior professor in the department of dairy science whose professional specialty was chocolate almond ice cream (I'm not exaggerating half so much as you wish I were). That chap was the emperor of ice cream; his lab was the cutting edge of chocolate almond research. One ate high-tech ice cream in those parts. Oxford and Cambridge, Tübingen and Heidelberg — they'll catch on by and by.

Yes, yes, yes: The thing can be taught, here and there. Can you be taught it? Who knows? We can't squeeze blood from a turnip, but chances are we can get the turnip juices flowing, or help to, if they're in there.

If You Go,

as they say in the *Times*'s Travel section, to one of our college-level American author factories, or have it in mind to apply to one, here's a handful of tips, the fruit of thirty years of writing, teaching, teaching writing, and looking in on maybe a hundred of those three hundred–plus enterprises:

1. Remember that good writers are not necessarily good coaches of writing, and conversely. There is no correlation either way between these separate gifts. An inspiring literary role model in the flesh, a living master of the language and of human experience, is no paltry thing to have at the head end of your seminar table. More important, however, are sustained, patient, sympathetic, intelligent critical attention to your manuscripts, both line for line and overall; a reasonable degree of aesthetic pluralism together with high standards of excellence and, farther along, some savvy about the facts of literary life, perhaps even some assistance in getting your work into print when it's ready for print. These virtues may be found among the less celebrated, sometimes even among the scarcely published.

Indeed, one risk of going to school with a very successful writer is that he or she may seriously (in a few cases scandalously) shortchange the students in favor of the Muses, or the Sirens, but be too famous and tenured to be cashiered. As in other departments, of the university and of life, the liveliest action is sometimes among the junior faculty. Another risk (it strikes me as small) is that a writer noted for a particular kind of writing — blue-collar realism, say, or Postmodernist fabulation, or high-tech formalism — will be unsympathetic to quite different though equally serious kinds. Would Vladimir Nabokov have been a good coach for Raymond Carver? Maybe; good writer-teachers almost always recognize and are delighted by gifted apprentice work in any mode that takes its readers seriously. Indeed, so far from turning out clones of themselves, most celebrated writers of my acquaintance shy away from would-be protégés whose work uncomfortably resembles their own. Perhaps a more serious risk of apprenticeship to the eminent is that their presence will intimidate more than it inspires, even when they don't at all want it to. "Nothing grows well in the shade of a great tree," young Constantin Brancusi is said to have said, declining Auguste Rodin's invitation to be his mentor. If I'd had Nabokov for my teacher, I fear I'd have been speechless. But I have met most of our current well-known American writer-teachers, some famous indeed, and have in many instances talked with their students as well. I report that wholesale intimidation in their workshops seems to be rare, while the opposite is abundant.

Going to school with a writer whose career misfired, on the other hand, or never really got started, has its own peril. One sees a fair amount of embittered truculence, downright paranoia, and jealous mini-empire-building here and there in the foothills of Parnassus, though probably no more so than in other academic departments. Word of mouth is reasonably reliable in this matter, unless the mouths are all too inexperienced to recognize the sour taste of frustrated ambition.

Scout the territory a bit; make sure that the chefs you want are scheduled to cook when you're scheduled to dine (writers move around). If you're an undergraduate, make sure that the *famosos* you're after don't teach graduate seminars only. And it's a good idea to train with more than one coach — but consecutively, not concurrently.

2. Go to the most celebrated writing program that you can win admission to. Its director is likelier to know which good writers are also effective mentors and coaches, and likelier to have the wherewithal to attract a staff of them. At least as important, the competition for admission to the good programs — especially at Columbia, Hopkins, Iowa, Stanford,* Brown, Virginia, et cetera — is considerable; your fellow apprentices in such programs will be sharp. As much of what happens in successful workshops happens outside them, among the apprentices, at all hours, as in their official meetings and conferences with the boss writer.

*Stanford University terminated its distinguished graduate writing program in 1990 but still offers its much-sought-after Stegner Fellowships, named after the program's longtime chief coach and regnant novelist, the late Wallace Stegner.

The best thing they can offer you is the finest audience any writer can have until his/her work is famous enough to attract wide critical attention. The busy interaction of the writers-in-the-room *out side* the room is the real smithy in which their working aesthetic principles — as well as particular images, characters, and story ideas — are forged, tested, and sharpened. Typically, by the time we go at a manuscript in class, it has been gone over assiduously with the author by a half-dozen talented classmates already. The conversation is likely to continue, in coffee shop or bar, well after the class is dismissed and the boss has gone home; it may continue by letter for years after commencement day. That interaction can be intense. "It took pounds off me," Mary Robison told a *Times* interviewer of her year in the Hopkins seminars. But she gained weight.

The success of the better-known programs tends to be self-sustaining. Since good writers compete to get in, good writers come out, usually better for having spent busy time in one another's company. You will likely learn more from the more talented than from the less; where everybody in the room is pretty sharp, competition in the counterproductive sense goes down, reciprocal respect goes up, and your craft improves. Moreover, those programs are in good universities, with superior faculty outside their writing workshops. It will do your apprenticeship no harm to study great literature with great professors of it as you practice its manufacture. Finally, while neither the muses nor professional editors take notice of advanced degrees from distinguished universities, academic hiring committees do, other things being equal. To have taught undergraduates in Charlottesville or Providence while taking your M.F.A. there may help you get a teaching job elsewhere, if you want one, to tide you over until your royalties pour in.

3. But be advised that some of the very best writing programs around are not yet so celebrated as they ought to be. At Washington University in St. Louis not so long ago, you might have studied with Stanley Elkin, William H. Gass, Charles Newman, Howard Nemerov, Donald Finkel, and Mona Van Duyn; at the University of Houston, your menu would have included Donald Barthelme, Cynthia Macdonald, and Stanley Plumley; at Syracuse, Raymond

Carver, Tess Gallagher, and Tobias Wolff. There are lively pods of metafictionists, among other species, in Buffalo and Boulder. No doubt, like restaurants once given good notices, such places will be overcrowded by the time you apply. But the action then may well have shifted to Gainesville, Tucson, Hattiesburg, who knows where — maybe back to Kenyon College in Gambier, Ohio, where for a truly extraordinary while it used to be.

4. For that matter, some quite interesting programs are scarcely known at all outside their immediate region, or they don't become so until they've entered literary history. The Black Mountain school under Charles Olson's rectorship in the 1950s is a case in point. Washington College in Chestertown, Maryland, not far from where I write these lines, is a tiny liberal-arts school with an unusually able writer-teacher (Robert Day), an international parade of distinguished visiting writer-lecturers that is our envy across the Chesapeake at Johns Hopkins, and — get this — an annual undergraduate literary award that once ranked second in monetary value only to the Nobel Prize (the Sophie Kerr Award: It remains at the $35,000 level, but several other "real" literary prizes now surpass it). The University of Kentucky, not everywhere regarded as a seedbed of American writing, once turned out a surprising clutch of notable literary alumni, including the poet Wendell Berry and the fictionist Bobbie Ann Mason, all coached by the poet and novelist Robert Hazel, who dwelt some seasons there. You might just luck into tomorrow's action at East Apathy Vo-Tech; the probability, though, is that your fellow apprentices there won't be of the caliber of those at the five-fork operations.

5. Finally, if fortune does land you at Southwest Sauerbraten Community College, do not despair of subsequent admission even to Iowa or Stanford or Hopkins, to say nothing of the Academy of the Immortals. It is not only the muses and their New York representatives who are more interested in your writing sample than in your undergraduate career. Surely it can be no handicap for a writer to have taken a baccalaureate summa cum laude from Harvard or Princeton and then to apply to us with through-the-roof scores on the Graduate Record Examination and salivary recommendations from distinguished scholars and writers-in-residence. Other things being equal, such goodies are useful tie-breakers. But

other things seldom are, and although I believe that a writer who elects to spend apprentice time in a good university ought to function creditably in graduate-level courses other than the writing seminars (*must* do so, to take the degree), the fact is that most of the former writing students of whom I am most proud did not cut their undergraduate teeth in the Ivy League. A couple of them never quite managed even to complete the B.A. for one reason or another, and were thus admitted into our graduate program under discreetly bent rules. Their talent simply wowed us, as it now wows the wider world.

Do not despair; do not presume. It can be learned, by the able; it can be studied, by everybody and his/her brother; it can even (you know what I mean) be taught, even in school.

The Spanish Connection

This lecture was delivered in Málaga in December 1984 to an annual convention of Spanish professors and students of British and North American literature. One writer from each of those literary venues was invited to address the convention. I was the North American; my "British" teammate was, delightfully, Salman Rushdie, in those happy days before the Ayatollah Khomeini's outrageous fatwa *against that distinguished writer. My novel-then-in-progress, referred to in what follows, was* The Tidewater Tales, *published in 1987. A version of the lecture itself first appeared in* Review of Contemporary Fiction *10, no. 2, Summer 1990; it was subsequently collected in* Studies in American Literature: Essays in Honor of Enrique García Díez *(Valencia: Colleció Oberta, 1991).*

That Festschrift volume is a memorial to our host at that Málaga conference and the moderator of Rushdie's and my presentations: the energetic and charming Enrique García, whom I had met briefly once before in America and who subsequently became a much loved family friend as well as an astute translator of and commentator upon my writing. I am most moved that before his early death from cancer, Enrique chose as his epitaph a line from my story "Night-Sea Journey": " . . . it is we spent old swimmers, disabused of every illusion, who are most vulnerable to dreams."

I write this headnote with Enrique's treasured Montblanc Meisterstück pen, in honor of my most prized "Spanish Connection."

I BEGIN WITH two confessions, of which the first is that against all common sense and against the explicit prohibition of Miguel de Cervantes Saavedra, I am in the process of writing a novel in which Don Quixote makes a minor but significant appearance. Kindly enter this first confession in your memory bank; I intend to circle back to it after a long detour.

The second confession is that in my most recently published novel (*Sabbatical: A Romance*, published in 1982) one of the main characters tells a story about Spain — specifically, about losing his *boina* in the Tajo de Ronda back in 1962 and subsequently refinding it. It is a story in which neither Spain nor the narrator comes off very well. My confession is that there is a tiny bit of autobiography in that story, to which also I shall circle back. Before I do, however, I want to recount yet a third story, neither by me nor by any character of my invention nor by Miguel Cervantes, but by my American contemporary Mr. Thomas Pynchon.

Early in Pynchon's novel *Gravity's Rainbow*, the principal character, a Harvard undergraduate named Tyrone Slothrop, gets drunk in 1938 at a certain famous American dance hall with some of his fellow students (including young Jack Kennedy). He becomes ill and goes to the men's room to vomit (the shoeshine boy in that men's room is young Malcolm X, the future leader of the Black Muslims). In the process of vomiting, Slothrop loses one of his favorite possessions, a harmonica: It slips out of his shirt pocket into the toilet and is flushed away. This happens on page 63 of the first American edition of the novel. Nearly six hundred pages and several years later, wandering through the wreckage of Germany at the end of World War II, Tyrone Slothrop catches sight of something glinting on the ground, in a forest. It is a harmonica. He washes it off in a pristine mountain stream and puts it into his pocket. Although he doesn't know it, it is the very same harmonica that he lost down the toilet of the Roseland Ballroom in 1938; it has surfaced in Germany as mysteriously as Edgar Poe's hero Arthur Gordon Pym surfaces in New York City after disappearing into the abyss at the South Pole.

In my judgment, this is one of the bright moments of contemporary North American storytelling — indeed, of the literature we call Postmodernist. Together with a certain little domestic coincidence, it inspired the Spanish story in my novel *Sabbatical*. Here is the little domestic coincidence:

About once a month, I visit some American university campus or other to read from my fiction or to lecture on some literary topic. A few years ago, in the course of one such visit, I happened to lose my favorite hat: a Basque *boina* that I regarded as immortal. It was the last of several boinas that I had bought in Spain nearly twenty years before, and although I had worn it almost daily for a decade, in every kind of weather, it never seemed to wear out. But it fell from my coat pocket somewhere on that college campus and was lost. In the course of a seminar that afternoon with some young writers and literature students, I asked them please to keep an eye out for that hat of mine and to return it to me at The Johns Hopkins University in Baltimore if they happened to find it. Then I told them the true story of how in 1962 I had visited the ancient town of Ronda in Andalusia and had walked out on the Puente Nuevo, wearing that hat or one like it, in order to have a look at the famous gorge that bisects the city. How a wind had come down the mountainside and blown my hat off my head into the Tajo de Ronda, out of sight. How my young family and I had then hiked down to the bottom of the gorge to inspect the ruins of the Roman baths down there, and how as we climbed down we made a joke out of looking for my boina, as if there were really any chance of finding it. And how, against all odds, we actually *did* find it, not very far down the path below the bridge.

The anecdote reminded me of that harmonica business in the Pynchon novel. I told the students *that* story, too, and declared my confidence that my lost boina would come back to me again, one way or another, in one country or another, as Tyrone Slothrop's harmonica had come back to him. Eternal return, etc. A few months later, on yet another American college campus, my host handed me my boina. A student at the first campus, who had heard my story, had found that hat and given it to his professor, who had also heard my story. Rather than mailing it to me directly, she had thought it more appropriate to mail it to a colleague on that second campus, which she happened to know I was scheduled to visit.

*   *   *

The story that I have just told you is true, to the best of my memory, and the chain of associations inspired by it became the armature of my *Sabbatical* novel. Its hero, Fenwick Turner, is an honorable, middle-aged former CIA officer who has published an exposé of some of the agency's less admirable activities and who currently aspires to become a novelist. (Many retired government people in America become novelists, especially those who retire in disgrace; it is almost a national habit.) Fenwick Turner and his wife, a young professor of American literature on sabbatical leave, are just completing a nine-month sailing cruise from Chesapeake Bay in Maryland down to the Caribbean and back. They are beset by a number of large problems and small adventures. Re-entering their home waters at the beginning of the novel, Fenwick accidentally loses his boina over the side, into the tidewater, and tries unsuccessfully to retrieve it. Never mind, he says finally: It will float back to him sooner or later. How does he know that? Because at certain other major crossroads of his life he has lost that hat and found it again. It is, he declares, a charmed hat.

That night, the couple happen to anchor near a secret CIA facility in Chesapeake Bay. (There are no fewer than eighty Pentagon facilities along the shore of the fragile Chesapeake, and only God knows how many CIA safe houses and such, including of course the headquarters of the Central Intelligence Agency itself. Dead spies are among the contaminants of my historic and otherwise fairly tranquil home waters.) Before they go to sleep, Fenwick tells his wife *his* Ronda story: how and why he abandoned his early ambition to be a writer and became a CIA operative instead. His story is more interesting than mine, though more depressing.

He came to Spain as a young man with his first wife, he says, and settled in for the winter near Málaga to try to write a novel. He had a brother in Madrid at the time who worked for the U.S. Central Intelligence Agency and whose career was going well; but Fenwick Turner's career as a writer was not going well at all, nor was his marriage. Spain did not help: It was a particularly cold and depressing winter here on the Costa del Sol; the couple's living quarters were chilly by American standards, damp, uncomfortable. Mrs. Turner was bored and unhappy. Although the year was 1962, the couple kept running into grim reminders of the

Spanish Civil War. Moreover, Fenwick's novel was not progressing satisfactorily. Instead of being a lively work of the imagination, it threatened to turn into a tedious roman à clef about unhappy Americans in Spain.

At one critical point, Fenwick says, the Turners made an excursion to Ronda, taking the manuscript with them as fearful novelists sometimes do. It is a cold, wet, miserable day. Husband and wife enjoy a marital quarrel en route; when they reach the old city, Mrs. Turner will not even get out of the car. Fenwick and his young son walk out on the Puente Nuevo to look at the Tajo, and the wind carries Fenwick's boina into the gorge. At this point, exasperated, Mrs. Turner threatens to drive back to Málaga with the boy and leave her husband there in Ronda if he does not terminate the wretched sight-seeing expedition at once. Angry, he challenges her to go ahead, and stalks off down into the Tajo to view the Roman ruins. At the very bottom of the gorge, he miraculously finds his missing hat. What the miracle signifies, he cannot imagine. He climbs back up to the bridge and finds that his son has bravely defied his mother and is waiting for him there. Moreover, the boy has rescued his father's manuscript from the car, lest his mother destroy it in her anger. Fenwick kisses the boy, but throws the failed novel into the Tajo de Ronda, and with it his ambition to be a writer. He returns with his wife to the United States, but the marriage ends soon after. By that time, our hero has joined his brother in the Central Intelligence Agency.

At the end of this story-within-the novel, Fenwick's present wife astutely observes: "Not only did the Tajo return your hat; it keeps returning the story you threw into it."

Now: Except for the circumstances of the lost and found boina and the chilly Andalusian winter, there is not much autobiography in the story just recounted. If I were rewriting it today, there would be even less, for I would not let Fenwick Turner get his hat back out of the Tajo so easily. In the *Sabbatical* novel, the hat he loses in Chapter 1 doesn't come back to him until the climax of the book, at the far end of Chesapeake Bay from where he lost it, after he and his wife have run the obstacle course of the plot. In the same way, I think that he should not have been able simply to go down into the Tajo (as I did), retrieve his boina, and come back up. I believe that he who goes down into the Tajo de Ronda in search of something lost ought to be obliged, like Dante in the Dark Wood, to take the long way home: not back uphill to the Puente Nuevo, but down the Guadiaro River to the Mediterranean and out through the Pillars of Hercules to the Gulf of Cádiz; then, like Columbus, westward across the Atlantic to the Caribbean; then, like Fenwick and his wife Susan, up from the Caribbean to North America, to the Chesapeake, to Maryland — and then, like my wife and me last year, back to Iberia, where I had not been for twenty years. But not even then would Fenwick Turner come quite back to Málaga and Ronda, no; he would return to the USA after observing the great changes in Portugal and Spain since he and I both lost our hats here in 1962. Then, having pondered these changes and begun to write yet another Spanish story, we would come back again to Spain, this time to revisit Málaga at the kind invitation of this conference; and only tomorrow would we go at last again to Ronda, where our boinas patiently await our return.

What was I doing in Andalusia in the winter of 1962? I was not working for the CIA, let me quickly assure you. I was working for the muses, upon a long novel called *Giles Goat-Boy*, and my domestic situation was quite all right, thank you. It is true that my literary output that season was reduced somewhat by the profound distraction of being abroad for the first time, in a language I cannot speak well at all, with not one but three small children. Nevertheless, unlike Fenwick Turner, I managed to get a satisfactory amount of work done as well as a little sight-seeing.

I must acknowledge that I did not have "fun." Like Fenwick, I was an American innocent abroad; some of his reactions to Spain were my reactions. In 1962 the scars of the Guerra Civil were still much more in evidence than they are today; even a tourist with no great facility in the language did not have to look far to find them. As an American and a Marylander, I know something about civil wars. Maryland was a border state back in our American Civil War, and thus deeply divided against itself — especially that part of Maryland where I was born and raised. Since the capital cities of both the Union and the Confederacy are not far from that neighborhood, Maryland in the 1860s was also a battleground, crossed and recrossed by the armies of both sides. When I was a boy, people still spoke of that bloody war as if they had lived through it. In Málaga in 1962, people still spoke of your civil war — when they spoke of it at all — because they *had* lived through it. On a certain headland, I was told, overlooking a certain beach not very far from this hall where we are here gathered . . .*

But never mind: Let us all pray for the continued health and prosperity of Iberian democracy.

Okay: Why was I writing that novel in Spain rather than in Baltimore or Barbados, since the story itself has nothing to do with this country? I am tempted to answer: Because I needed to lose my hat and find it again. But in fact my hat was already off to this country and its language; before I ever got to Ronda, Spain had already given me more than I can ever give back. Here is the story of my Spanish connection.

I am a writer partly because of the example of one of my undergraduate professors at Johns Hopkins, the first flesh-and-blood writer I ever knew. The United States has famously been the cultural beneficiary of the political misery of other nations. Two or three of my professors in Baltimore were refugees from Nazi Germany and Austria: Leo Spitzer, with whom I read Flaubert and the *Chanson de Roland*; Arno Schirokauer, with whom I read Thomas Mann. Pedro Salinas was a refugee from Franco's Spain, and it was my immense privilege to read under his guidance Menendez y Pelayo's *Las cien mejores poesías liricas de la lengua castellana*; also *Lazarillo de Tormes* and some Lope de Vega and some Caldéron, even some Unamuno — and above all, of course, *Don Quijote*.

I should explain that my prior education was unimpressive; indeed, almost nonexistent. I was the first of my family ever to attend a university, and I had everything to learn. I had no idea what I intended to do with my life after graduation. I understood that Professor Salinas was a famous Spanish poet — second only

---

*As many as 4,000 Malagueño Republicans were massacred when Franco's Loyalists captured the city in February 1937, according to Hugh Thomas's *The Spanish Civil War* (NY: Harper, 1961).

to Lorca in his generation, somebody said — but I didn't know yet who Lorca was, and I didn't have enough Spanish to make sense of Salinas's poetry even if I'd had enough sense to buy his *Poemas escogidas* in the Espasa Calpé edition (I bought that book years later, here in Málaga, and still had trouble with it). Alas, I cannot report to you anything that Pedro Salinas told us young North Americans about classical Spanish literature, for I have forgotten it all. What I can report to you is that that gentle, patient, dignified fellow, with his patchy English and his bald head and his gold teeth and his great cigars — and his brown pinstripe suits, much worn and badly pressed, as I recall, and the long green woolen underwear that he wore in our damp Baltimore winters, and which I noticed the cuffs of when he crossed his legs and puffed his cigars and spoke to us quietly of Don Quixote — I report to you that that quite uncharismatic fellow became for me the embodiment of an idea: namely, that to dedicate one's life to the passionate manufacture of literature — to be a writer, whatever the consequences — can be a noble destiny indeed.

That adjective — a *noble* destiny — sounds to me like the Spanish connection. Thanks to Pedro Salinas, I still hear the word *literature* with a Spanish accent.

And now that I think about it, I do recall two things that Salinas told us American sophomores about *Don Quijote*, and one thing that he told me about myself. Salinas warned us not to be surprised if Cervantes's great novel disappointed us a little the first time through. There are a few literary images, he said, so profound and so powerful that no mere procession of sentences can quite measure up to them. The image of Quixote and Sancho Panza wandering across Spain is one such. Years later I heard an American critic (Leslie Fiedler) say a similar thing, in more technical language: that one index to the mythopoeic quality of a work of literature is what stays with you when you have forgotten all the words, and what therefore translates readily into other media, even into gift-shop souvenirs. Such images, said Salinas, are larger than their books.

I quite agree. In my personal pantheon there are four such cardinal images, along with a host of lesser ones. Don Quixote is one of those four.

Salinas also advised us to reread the novel every ten years, in order to measure our own kilometrage down the road. I have done that, and have been properly impressed by the Borgesian way that the book keeps changing.

Adios now to Pedro Salinas: May he rest in peace down in the exiles' graveyard in San Juan, Puerto Rico. One day he asked us to identify the first truly *quixotic* moment in Cervantes's novel. Most of my classmates agreed that it was the first night of Quixote's first sortie, when he mistakes the prostitutes for noble ladies and the innkeeper for the governor of a fortress. A few said it was earlier than that, when he sees Rocinante as a splendid charger and re-names Aldonza Lorenzo as Dulcinea del Toboso. Well, I saw how the game was going and declared in effect that true *quijotismo* was not the mere glamorous misperceiving of things, but a way of act-ing on those misperceptions, and that therefore the first truly quixotic moment occurs even earlier in Chapter 1, when, having fashioned a helmet-visor out of pasteboard and tested it with his sword and seen it slice easily into pieces, Quixote fashions another from exactly the same material, reinforcing it just a little bit, but prudently tests it no further, declaring it instead to be a perfectly satisfactory helmet-visor. (The episode reminds me now of a mem-orable moment during America's war in Vietnam, when a wise senator recommended that we should simply declare victory and get out before we lose our shirts.)

Pedro Salinas was delighted with my answer. Beaming at me with his gold teeth around his great Havana cigar, he declared that only three people in the world recognized that crucial moment for what it was: a certain Spanish critic (whose name I have forgot-ten), himself, and now Señor Barth. Surely it was then that I de-cided to become an *escritor*.

The next stages of my Spanish connection came not directly from Spain but — following the route of Columbus and then of the con-quistadors — from Iberia by way of Latin America. Gabriel Gar-cía Márquez has spoken with wry delight of what he calls "the his-panification of North America": the great waves of immigration in recent decades from Puerto Rico, from Mexico and the West Indies, from Cuba, from Argentina and Chile, and most recently from Guatemala, Nicaragua, and El Salvador. I shall now speak briefly, also with delight, of the further hispanification of this particular North American.

Having resolved somewhat quixotically to become a fiction writer, it remained for me to learn how to write fiction; that art requires more than knowing what the first quixotic moment is in *Don Quijote*. Like most of my U.S. contemporaries in the 1940s and fifties, I cut my apprentice teeth on the great Modernists, especially James Joyce and William Faulkner, though I was also deeply impressed by certain older storytellers, in particular Scheherazade. For several years I wrote bad imitations of those writers, attempting to do with tidewater Maryland what Joyce had done with Dublin and Faulkner with Mississippi. Fortunately, none of that apprentice-work was published.

Then somehow I came upon the fiction of the late-nineteenth-century Brazilian writer Joaquim Machado de Assis* — his novels *Braz Cubas*, *Quinças Borba*, and *Dom Casmurro* had just been translated, belatedly, into English — and something clicked. In their American translation, at least, those novels read as if they had just been written. We did not have the term "Postmodernism" in our critical vocabulary back in the 1950s, but Machado's combination of formal playfulness, narrative self-consciousness and self-reflexiveness, political skepticism, and emotional seriousness tempered with dry comedy — they add up to a kind of proto-postmodernism which appealed to me very strongly indeed. My first novel, *The Floating Opera*, was written under the benign influence of Joaquim Machado de Assis. Later in my education I learned that behind Machado stands the first English postmodernist novel: I mean *Tristram Shandy*, no doubt a more brilliant performance than any of Machado's. But much as I honor Laurence Sterne, I have never been able quite to finish *Tristram Shandy*. There is a larger humanity in Machado de Assis than there is in Laurence Sterne; I prefer the kind of technical fire-

---

*More on Machado, Borges, and García Márquez later in this volume, in the essay "Borges and I: a mini-memoir," and the forewords to *The Floating Opera* and *Lost in the Funhouse*.

works that speak to my heart as well as to my mind and my funny-bone — formalism with a Latino accent: *formalismo*.

A while ago I used the adjective "Borgesian": my next important Hispanic connection. I have paid ample public homage to Jorge Luis Borges elsewhere and shall not dwell upon his importance to me here, except to remark that I was in my teens and twenties when Joyce and Faulkner and Kafka and Scheherazade and Machado de Assis swept me off my feet, and it is rather easy to be swept off one's feet at that age. Indeed, it is the responsibility of a twenty-year-old apprentice to be swept off his feet repeatedly by his great predecessors. At age thirty-five and forty it is another matter: You discover new writers with more or less excitement, but by that time you are pretty much who you are, and you go on with your work. However, upon first encountering Borges's *Ficciones* at that age, I had the disorienting though familiar feeling that everything must stop until I had assimilated this extraordinary writer. A little series of short fictions called *Lost in the Funhouse* and an essay called "The Literature of Exhaustion" are my attempts to make that assimilation.

Whether or not those attempts were successful, by the age of forty I was tired of being influenced by Iberia, whether directly by Cervantes and Salinas or indirectly by way of Machado de Assis and Borges. From the distance of Baltimore I applauded the restoration of democracy to Portugal and Spain; I applauded "*el boom*": the explosion of Latin American literary talent (mostly expatriate talent, alas) in the 1960s and Seventies — a boom that still reverberates through my country. But those lively writers left me alone, and I left them alone.

Then in 1973 I had the interesting experience of reading two quite extraordinary novels back to back: the aforecited *Gravity's Rainbow*, by Thomas Pynchon, and *Cien años de soledad*, by Gabriel García Márquez. The difference in their effect on me was analogous to that of Laurence Sterne versus Machado de Assis. I admired *Gravity's Rainbow* as an astonishing performance, but the novel did not touch my heart, and (except for the business of that lost and found harmonica) it did not touch my writing, either.

Reading Pynchon was for me like visiting a remarkable, memorable country with which however one makes no emotional connection. On the other hand, like many another reader, I fell in love with *Cien años de soledad*. I had almost forgotten that new literature can be not only important, not only impressive, but wise and wonderful, life-affecting, as Dickens and Dostoevsky, Homer and *Huckleberry Finn* are life-affecting. García Márquez showed me not what Postmodernism is, necessarily, but what it ought to be if it is to be anything worth taking seriously. Its author gave *magic* back to modern storytelling: not literary magic, but literal magic: the literally marvelous. With all due respect to my countryman Thomas Pynchon, I know for certain that the hero of the novel *Sabbatical* could not have dropped his boina overboard at the mouth of Chesapeake Bay and fished it out again two hundred kilometers and three hundred pages later at the head of Chesapeake Bay without the assistance of Gabriel García Márquez. I even suspect that the sea-monster who surfaces briefly and swims away at that novel's climax might be Sr. García Márquez himself, headed home to Macondo.

Now it is time for me to come back to Spain, by this roundabout route, and to re-retrieve my own boina. The "hispanification of North America" that so pleases Gabriel García Márquez (perhaps especially after our benighted Passport Agency denied the great man a visa) is after all not truly a hispanification, but a Latin-Americanization. I welcome it anyhow as one more enrichment of our culture, just as I welcome the more recent influx of Southeast Asians, while lamenting the political-historical causes of their immigration. Nowadays every provincial American town half the size of Ronda has its taco stand and its all-purpose Asian restaurant, along with its pizzeria and its McDonald's hamburgeria; our small-town supermarkets have ever-growing shelves of Chinese, Japanese, Mexican, Jewish, and other ethnic foodstuffs. We are better off for that: a bit less parochial than we were before.

But *my* Spanish connection begins in Spain, not in Latin America, and I would be happy to have it return here. It begins with the real inventor of postmodern fiction: the author of Part Two of *Don Quijote*. The little Don Quixote story I am presently writing

(1984) is a small part of a large novel-in-progress called *The Tidewater Tales*. I won't take up your time with this story-within-the-story except to say that it begins in the Cave of Montesinos (*Don Quijote* II:22, the most mysterious episode in Cervantes's novel) and that it carries Alonso Quijano not directly back up again out of that cave to Sancho Panza on his two-hundred-meter length of rope, but rather down the Rio Guadiana to Portugal and the sea; on across the Atlantic at the 37th parallel of north latitude, which runs just a little above Málaga and Ronda, exactly from Sagres, Portugal (one of my favorite places on this planet), to the entrance of Chesapeake Bay, another of my favorite places on this planet. The voyage carries him from the sixteenth/seventeenth century briefly into the twentieth; he strays into my home waters in a battered old sailboat named *Rocinante IV* (I saw such a boat sail by one day over there); he is still looking for the end of that length of rope, with which to pull himself back out of the Cave of Montesinos so that he can go on with Cervantes's story — whose ending he has read and approves.

Cap'n Donald Quicksoat, as he is called in my novel, may very well be inventing his whole history. Americans do that; maybe we learned the trick from Odysseus. In any case, if he wants to find that rope, Cap'n Don will have to make his way back home, taking the long way around to La Mancha. When Mrs. Barth and I revisited Portugal and Spain last year, we were excited by the likelihood, in your present climate of freedom, of an Iberian artistic renaissance: an art that draws upon, integrates, and departs from cultural-historical resources that both South and North Americans might envy.* I mean especially the tremendous Moorish input, which Cervantes made good use of, and the tremendous Jewish input, which I believe he unfortunately ignored altogether, as well as the Christian-European input. (When we got home, we were informed by the *New York Times* that such a *renacimiento* is indeed stirring.) The new Spanish connection that I quixotically look forward to being influenced by in my fifties and sixties will reach back not only before the Guerra Civil, but before the Reconquista

---

*Or might not, since we have the enviable inputs of both black African and indigenous, "Native American" cultures as well as Asian and European at our artistic disposal.

and the expulsion of the Jews, and there will burst upon our astonished American eyes a new Spanish Postmodernist literature that will make the great Latino boom sound like a mere overture to the real opera.

Who knows? Perhaps we shall even find in it some Yankee input along with all those other inputs. The best connections, after all, are coaxial: The signal goes both ways.

The Limits of Imagination

First delivered as a lecture in the 1985 series "Limits and Constraints" at the College of Wooster, Ohio, as described in its opening paragraphs, this Friday-piece was subsequently published in the anthology Facing Texts: Encounters Between Contemporary Writers and Critics *(ed. Heide Ziegler; Durham, NC: Duke University Press, 1988), with commentary by the German critic Manfred Pütz, of Augsburg University.*

MY PRINCIPAL LINE of work is making up and setting down stories, not holding forth upon subjects of a philosophical character. Some while ago, however, the brochure of a lecture series sponsored by a small college in Ohio so caught my imagination's eye that I set aside a few Friday mornings to write a bona fide lecture on the subject of the limits of imagination.

Three things about that lecture-series brochure particularly interested me. First, the general subject of the series was fascinating: *Limits and Constraints.* Mr. McGeorge Bundy, the late President Kennedy's Special Assistant for National Security Affairs, was to speak on the limits of unlimited power, and the scholarly syndicated columnist Garry Wills on the limits of national autonomy; other authorities were to address the limits of culture, the limits of personhood, the limits of law. As it happens, I am a writer who has spent his professional life exploring some the limits of the ancient art of storytelling, setting the bar ever higher on my personal high jump at the risk of ending up with a mouthful of turf (and I have learned the taste of turf, though I shall never learn to enjoy it). I wished I could hear every one of those lectures: The Limits of Dissent, The Limits of the Unknown. . . . It was easy to imagine extending the series: The Limits of Love; The Limits of Any Human Being's Capacity to Understand Another Human Being. The subject of limits struck me as limitless.

The second thing that interested me about that lecture-series brochure was that *my name* was on the list of speakers. Indeed, it came back to me that in a long-ago telephone conversation I had agreed to lead off the series with a lecture upon the limits of imagination, if I could imagine anything on that topic worth saying in public. Having thus tentatively committed myself, I had gone back to my novel then in progress — my latest expedition to the limits of my own imagination — and I more or less forgot about the subject of limits and constraints until that brochure arrived in the mail.

Whereupon — this was the third thing that arrested my attention — I found that for some reason *my* subject was advertised not as The Limits of Imagination, but as The *Limitations* of Imagination.

Think about it: the limitations of imagination! I did think about it, and was hooked. Not how far can imagination go; not whether that human faculty has its bounds, and, if so, what those bounds might be and what might imaginably lie beyond them; but as it were the shortcomings, even the hazards, of the faculty itself. The Limitations of Imagination: irresistible.

Why was Imagination the only topic on the list thus singled out? I couldn't imagine — and so off we go: first into the preliminary definitions and distinctions that every lecturer likes to test the public-address system with (though not every storyteller; storytellers prefer to begin with action and then interstitch the exposition as they go along); thence into a little cadenza on the inherent paradoxes of the subject; finally into a chorus or two of what I take to have been meant to be my real theme: the *limits* of imagination. Specifically — since I am a writer of fiction and not even an amateur philosopher — the limits of artistic, especially of literary, imagination.

To conclude this overture: When I arrived at that little college in Ohio, I learned that the "limitations" business in their brochure was a mere clerical inadvertence. Happy fault: It had prompted me to reflect as follows upon some home truths about the art I practice.

*   *   *

Let's tune the calliope with those preliminary definitions: the *limits* of imagination, as distinct from the *limitations* of imagination, as distinct from *limited* imagination, which we might as well throw in too.

In fact, I'll begin with that last one:

A "limited imagination," as I understand it, gets things wrong. From its mere incapacity, like limited intelligence or limited physical strength, it fails to anticipate accurately and to come up with the really new or more effective idea. Never mind that even the most powerful imagination may not be literally unlimited; "limited imaginations," as we commonly use the term, have low aptitude scores, so to speak, in that area — like those political imaginations that in 1985 advised President Ronald Reagan to celebrate the fortieth anniversary of VE-Day by visiting the German military graveyard in Bitburg, where a number of SS troops are buried, and there declaring the murderers and their victims equal in death. That I would call limited imagination, among other things.

In the literary sphere, limited imagination is likely to be limited to the most conventional and obvious: a mere lack of originality in the material, the form, the treatment. In the case of otherwise capable apprentice writers such as those I coach in the Johns Hopkins Writing Seminars, this defect may come from too much irrelevant information about, or insufficient distance from, their material: Why does the young woman on page five of the story drive up to her lover's Cape Cod beach house in a milk-colored Chevy Camaro rather than a mustard Mercedes or a gamboge Cadillac? Because she *did*, replies the limited literary imagination. You can bet that when the hero of Flannery O'Connor's 1952 novel, *Wise Blood*, steers through that story in a "high, rat-colored car," it is not because — at least not *simply* because — some factual fellow did.*

I am reminded of Henry James's habit of interrupting the teller of a potentially usable anecdote, lest he hear too much about the matter and thereby limit his imagination. I am reminded of several

---

*The contemporary American literary fetish of automotive specificity, I am convinced, can be traced back to that wonderful "high, rat-colored car" of Flannery O'Connor's. The milk-colored Camaro and the gamboge Cadillac come from apprentice stories by two distinguished ex-coachees of mine: Mary Robison and Frederick Barthelme, respectively, who knew very well what they were doing.

of Thomas Mann's early artist-protagonists, who at a certain point turn their backs upon capital-K Knowledge in order to liberate, to unlimit, their artistic imaginations. Typically, though, limited imagination is a defect of the individual, or the committee, not of the human imaginative faculty as such. When William Makepeace Thackeray begins or ends a novel-chapter with such words as "Words cannot describe the scene that followed," etc., we may legitimately imagine that perhaps Dickens's or Tolstoy's words *could* have described that scene, perhaps unforgettably. A sly genius may even do so after declaring that it cannot be done: Dostoevsky, for example, says of Raskolnikov's terrible dream in Chapter 5 of *Crime and Punishment* that such dreams "are so plausible, the details so subtle, so unexpected, so artistically in harmony with the whole picture, that the dreamer could not invent them for himself in his waking state, even if he were an artist like Pushkin or Turgenev." Dostoevsky then proceeds to give us Raskolnikov's dream in its unforgettable entirety. Your problem, Mr. Thackeray, we may say to ourselves, may be not in the language but in your limited imagination of its possibilities.

The *limitations* of imagination, on the other hand — assuming a high score on one's imaginary aptitude test in that area — strike me as likely to proceed from a contrary deficiency: from an insufficient ballast of information or experience. As an undergraduate apprentice writer myself in the late 1940s, too young to have served in World War II, I had the chutzpah to try to write a military combat story in a workshop that included several combat veterans among my fellow apprentices. Indeed, the class was presided over by a gentle former Marine Corps combat officer (then an Edgar Allan Poe scholar) who had survived a number of amphibious landings in the Pacific Theater of Operations.* In my story, I blush to remember, a young soldier, en route to hit the beach of

---

*Robert Durene Jacobs, then a doctoral candidate and teaching assistant at Johns Hopkins, subsequently a professor of English at Georgia State University until his retirement. His real specialty was Faulkner and other contemporary Southern writers, but the then-conservative Hopkins English department did not permit dissertations on living writers. Jacobs is the "Bob" affectionately remembered in my Friday-pieces "Some Reasons Why I Tell the Stories I Tell the Way I Tell Them Rather Than Some Other Sort of Stories Some Other Way," in *The Friday Book*, and "It's a Short Story," to follow.

Iwo Jima in an LCI or whatever, is duly dismayed by the sound of heavy caliber machine-gun bullets ricocheting off the bow ramp of his landing craft; that ramp will soon be lowered so that he and his comrades can storm ashore. The veterans in the classroom were patient with my naive poaching on their preserve; they granted that I had a pretty good imagination. But the former combat officer gently pointed out to me that heavy-caliber machine-gun bullets did not, as a rule, ricochet off the bow ramps of infantry landing craft; they came right through and hit people. Forty years later, I still stand humbly corrected upon that datum. I hadn't imagined.

In writing workshops at every level, as well as in the larger, more important workshop of the world, we see this variety of limitation all the time, with respect both to particular details and to the author's — or our neighbor's — general inability to "project" with sympathetic authority his or her sensibility across gender, class, age, race, culture, whatever. And we understandably admire the opposite, for that ability, or its lack, affects our relations with one another as well as our relations with literature. A Russian writer once praised Leo Tolstoy's story "Kohlstomer," which happens to be written from the point of view of a horse, by saying, "But Count Tolstoy, surely you must have *been* a horse, in some earlier incarnation." That is high praise — particularly coming as it did from no less an authority than Ivan Turgenev. On the other hand, an American critic some seasons ago took John Updike to task for having one of his female characters reflect (in the novel *The Witches of Eastwick*) that it takes a woman longer than it takes a man to begin to urinate, once she sets about it, her plumbing being more considerable. I forget now whether the criticism was of that datum itself or of Mr. Updike's having the female character reflect upon that datum. In any case, the critic found the passage unconvincing; she compared it unfavorably with a passage in a novel by a woman of her literary acquaintance describing a *male* character's pleasure in urinating over the leeward rail of a sailboat under way, instead of having to go below to the "head." *There,* she believed, was genuine transsexual literary imagination.

Let us leave this fascinating aspect of our subject: what I call in my fiction-writing seminars "the lower criticism," although we take it seriously indeed. Even writers of fantasy need to get their facts straight, and not put carburetors on fuel-injection engines. We ought not to move on, however, before remembering that the phrase "limitations of imagination" covers also, or shades off into, the more interesting subject of imagination's being a liability, at least a potential liability, as well as an obvious asset.

The phenomenon is too general and familiar to warrant more than a mention. When a dog bites another dog, the bitten dog hurts but presumably does not worry — about rabies, for example. When my wife, on the other hand, was bitten one spring not on the other hand but on the right leg, by a Maryland farm dog whose rabies inoculation turned out to have expired, the bite itself caused less pain in our household than our imaginations did. All of us have felt this edge of imagination's two-edged sword, which so often enhances our fear of both the known and the unknown. The fish in our family fish tank in Baltimore are presumably unaware that they are alive and therefore that they are going to die. The tank's owners know not only that they themselves must die but also that they don't know when or how their passing will come to pass. I can't decide which of us is better off. I think of Jorge Luis Borges's Czechoslovakian playwright (in the story "The Secret Miracle"), arrested by the Gestapo and condemned to death for the crime of being Jewish; in his death cell, he reflects that reality very rarely conforms to our anticipation of it, and therefore — "armed with this weak magic," Borges says — he deliberately imagines in vivid detail the most gruesome and excruciating deaths, precisely so that they will not happen to him. The consequence, of course, is that he suffers scores of deaths before he undergoes his actual one.

On the less dramatic scale, we have all known persons whose comfortably successful, even quite enviable lives are rendered wretched — at least less than satisfying — by their implacable imagination of how things might have gone even better for them; *much* better for them, had they only made *that* move rather than this, chosen *that* partner, taken *that* road.

Good old imagination.

The last item in this parade of distinctions that probably go without saying is a touch slipperier and maybe a touch more technical, but it brings us closer to our real subject: It is the distinction between the limits of artistic imagination and the limitations of particular media — a not-uninteresting subset of the larger topic.

It cannot be doubted that every medium of art has its inherent limitations. The narrator of Samuel Beckett's novel *Molloy* says at one point, "It was raining. It was not raining." I cannot imagine that disorienting assertion effectively translated into film, any more than I can imagine filming the lyrics of "Oh! Susannah" ("Sun so hot I froze to death, Susannah don't you cry," etc.). On the other hand, we cannot literally verbalize primary physical sensation; the medium of writing, alas, is strictly anesthetic. Written literature may render indirectly any and all of the physical senses,* but it is the only medium of art I can think of that deals directly with none of them — not even the visual, although its symbols are apprehended through the eyes (or through the fingertips, if you're reading in Braille). Characteristically there are no literal sights, sounds, smells, tastes, or feels in written literature: only their names.† The best verbal description of a chase is not likely to approach the impact of the literally kinetic depiction of one in a movie, or the well-directed enactment of one on the stage. On the other hand, neither film nor television nor theater nor opera nor ballet nor pantomime, for example, can render directly the universe inside our heads and under our skins: the nonphysical universe of sensibility; the *registering* of sensation. That interior universe is at least as important in our human lives as the exterior physical universe is, and the written word, alone among artistic media, has direct access to it. Literature cannot give us the sights, sounds, smells, tastes, and feels themselves, but it can dwell at any length upon what things look, sound, smell, taste, and feel *like*, to the characters. And it can reflect, deliberate, decide, generalize, and interpret, without anyone's necessarily moving or speaking aloud.

*See, e.g., Diane Ackerman's lovely *Natural History of the Senses* (NY: Vintage, 1991).
†These generalizations exclude certain Modernist literary experiments with visual effects, and the anticipations of those experiments in earlier literature. They exclude also many children's books, with their wonderful three-dimensional pop-ups, their scratch-and-sniff effects, and, of course, their pictures. "What good is a book without pictures?" asks Lewis Carroll's avant-garde Alice.

"Happy families are all alike," declares Tolstoy. "The great shroud of the sea rolled on," declares Melville. "Once upon a time," proposes every storyteller since human narrative time began. We can't film or stage *those* propositions, either.

No need, I suppose, to dwell further upon the strengths and limitations of the several media, although it is a subject I am perennially fascinated by: the sea itself, say, versus the English word s-e-a, or Homer's "wine-dark sea" or James Joyce's "snotgreen, scrotum-tightening sea," or a briny passage from Hart Crane, or the above-quoted ending of Melville's *Moby-Dick*, or any of those versus Debussy's tone-poem *La Mer*, or Hokusai's famous drawing called *The Wave*, or Géricault's painting *The Raft of the "Medusa"* and Winslow Homer's *Breezing Up*; or all of those versus a still-photograph seascape or some marine footage for a TV nature series. Each has qualities that the others cannot duplicate or in some instances even approach, whatever the artist's skill.

That, to be sure, is why some artists become poets or novelists and others become photographers, composers, painters. It is also why most people enjoy the experience not only of love, for example, but of love stories, love songs, love poems, love sculpture, and the rest. We humbly (perhaps gratefully) recognize not only that each medium of art has its assets and its limitations, but that our own experience does, too — as does for that matter our experience in experiencing experience, so to speak, and our experience in experiencing art, which is part of our experience of living. The unforgettable story of Dido and Aeneas in Virgil's *Aeneid* is not likely to move a reader inexperienced in the ups and downs of love as deeply as it moves one who has him or herself painfully abandoned a lover, or who has been by one abandoned. It will move even more a reader experienced in poetry as well as in love. Needless to say, the connection is coaxial: Our ability to experience life may be more or less limited by *in*experience of art, as well as vice versa, since each tends to increase the wattage of the great illuminator of both — namely, the imagination.

To move from the consumer of art to its producer, and directly to our subject: Let us suppose a strong, mature artistic imagination,

soundly ballasted (but not swamped) by information and experience both of life and of the artist's particular medium; powered by
high intelligence and energy; controlled and focused by artistic discipline and training to the point of mastery. Is anything beyond the
reach of such an imagination? Are there, in the history of the
medium, effects that it cannot hope to surpass? Are there subjects
that it cannot compass, or should not even attempt?

Some knowledgeable people have certainly thought so. In our
time, the grim test case has been the Nazi genocide of European
Jewry, an evil so appalling in its scale and nature that some critics
have argued not only that art fails in the face of it, but that the
unassimilable fact of it may call into question the very values that
make art meaningful, that give our art its cultural validation. The
argument, much simplified here, is that in a civilization whose
members can admire Rilke and Goethe and Beethoven while perpetrating Dachau and Belsen and Auschwitz, art may be effectively rendered spurious: not just Holocaust novels and Holocaust
television miniseries, mind, but *all* art. Most attenders to my remarks here will be familiar with this troubling argument* and
with its counterarguments, such as William Styron's defense of his
Holocaust novel, *Sophie's Choice*.† The well-warranted fuss over
Ronald Reagan's ceremonial visits to the Bitburg military cemetery
and the Bergen-Belsen death camp, along with the more recent tri-
als of Klaus Barbie in France and Ivan Demjanjuk in Israel and the
unpleasant revelations about Kurt Waldheim's military service, re-
freshed many folks' memories in this area and perhaps introduced
some younger people to the darker corners of the subject. I hope
so — and I'll come back to the matter presently.

Turning to the positive side of the essentially negative topic of
imagination's limits, we find that well before the Holocaust — in

---

*Notably advanced by George Steiner in *Language and Silence: Essays on Lan-
guage, Literature, and the Inhuman* (NY: Atheneum, 1967). Steiner's eloquent
and forceful argument is *not* as simple as my bald reduction of it above; it merits
reviewing in its entirety.
†More a reply than a defense, the opening pages of the novel's ninth chapter directly acknowledge the force of Steiner's proposition that "in the face of certain
realities, art is trivial or impertinent" and then proceed — successfully, in my
opinion — to justify the author-narrator's project of at least attempting to address the perhaps uncompassable.

fact, through the whole history of western literary criticism —
knowledgeable people have been moved to say, of some particular
passage or of some entire literary artifact, "Beyond this, art cannot
go." The late dilettante Huntington Cairns (I use the term in its
best sense: a person who delights in the exercise of a large and various personal culture in addition to his or her professional specialty, which in Cairns's case was the office of treasurer of the National Gallery of Art in Washington) was even moved to publish in
1948 an anthology as fat as it is ingenious, called *The Limits of
Art:** 1,400 pages of such selections in their original languages,
followed by English versions when necessary, followed by some
critic's declaration that this is it: a perfect 10 on the scale of literary possibility. The texts themselves in this remarkable anthology
run from Homer and the Bible up to Marcel Proust and James
Joyce; the critical superlatives come from as far back as Aristotle
(praising Homer's metaphors) to as recent as the French critic
Denis Saurat's praising Paul Valéry in 1946 — the anthology, remember, was put together in 1948. Cairns's book is an ideal place
to explore our subject.

Most of the superlatives in it, as one might expect, are hedged,
and not to our purpose. To say, for example, that no verbal picture
of girlish bashfulness, together with the daring of first love, sur-
passes the poet Walther von der Vogelweide's "*Unter den Linden*"
(as the German critic Kuno Franke declared in 1901) is not to propose a bound on the possibilities of either language itself or the
imagination itself: It is at best a historical assertion, like the proposition that no building on Earth in 1939 was taller than the Empire
State Building — only less subject to empirical verification. Amus-
ingly, a declaration by the Greek rhetorician Longinus — that
Homer's version of blinded Ajax's prayer for light in Book 17 of
the *Iliad* is superhumanly majestic — is followed by a declaration
by the French critic Charles de Saint-Evremond that Longinus's
praise of that passage in Homer is itself as fine a passage as anything in *that* literary category.

Et cetera. But here and there in *The Limits of Art* we find what
we're looking for: the knowledgeable critic who declares of a cer-

---

*Washington DC: Bollingen Series XII.

tain text not only that no one so far has ever done *better* than this,
but that this *cannot be surpassed* — and that that is the case not
because of the circumstance that we cannot nowadays write authentic late-Latin elegics, for example, or medieval French rondelo,
but because the author cited has achieved the very limits of linguistic imagination; because beyond this, art cannot go.

Would any critic really stick his neck out so far? Yes indeed.
Sometimes, of course, the assertion is mere hyperbole: When Francis Thompson says of three lines in Edmund Spenser's *The Faerie
Queene* that "the mournful sweetness of those lines is insurpass-
able," all he's really saying is "Wow, those are three really dynamite mournful sweet lines, those three." But when the eminent
George Saintsbury says of certain passages in Shakespeare's *Tam-
burlaine* that they are "examples of the NE PLUS ULTRA of the
poetic powers, not of the language but of language," or when T. S.
Eliot says famously of the closing canto of Dante's *Paradiso* that it
is "the highest point that poetry has reached or ever can reach," I
believe them to have meant just what they said: not "This really
knocks my socks off"; not "This is the best example of this sort of
thing that I myself happen to know of in all of literature"; but
rather "Here is the absolute limit of artistic *possibility*, at least in
the category specified. Beyond this, art cannot go."

What can we say of such assertions, other than "Well, you have
our attention"? One thing we can say is that they involve us in the
essential paradox I mentioned earlier. When we declare that we
cannot imagine poetry or language or even the creative imagination itself going farther than this, or dealing commensurately with
that, are we describing real limits of the medium and/or of the
imaginative faculty? Or are we merely demonstrating the limitations of our own imaginations, which the experience of a new
masterpiece might disprove tomorrow, if such things were really
measurable?*

I suppose it's foolish to imagine that the imagination is literally
unlimited. Whatever it is, like other qualities and aspects of mind

---

*The title of one of Samuel Beckett's later and bleaker works, *Imagination Dead
Imagine*, embodies this paradox.

it is a function of the physical human brain; and while human brains, no less than other parts and systems of the human body, admit of a considerable range of capacity, that range is not infinite. Granted, for example, that athletic records are always being broken: What physical and disciplinary evolution was required in the sport of foot-racing to achieve in 1954 the first officially recorded less-than-four-minute mile! But within a mere thirty years thereafter, the record had been shaved down from Roger Bannister's 3:59:4 to Nourredine Morceli's 3:44:39.* Who would presume to say now that a three-and-a-half-minute mile is beyond human capacity, especially with steroidal assistance? But who on the other hand would therefore presume the possibility of a *two*-minute mile? A two-*second* mile (I mean on this planet, run by somebody indisputably of our species, steroids or no steroids)? No: A prodigy, a genius, may astonish us like Kafka's Hunger Artist with a performance so different in degree as to seem almost different in kind; but that difference will not be infinite. The average lobster caught commercially off the New England coast weighs about a pound and a quarter; the largest ever known to have been caught, there or anywhere, was a forty-four-pounder taken near Nova Scotia on February 11, 1977. It is not difficult to imagine that there is yet a larger lobster down there somewhere; perhaps even one twice as large: an eighty-eight-pounder! But is there one the size of Nova Scotia itself? The fact is, we can *imagine* such a beast, as in a Japanese monster movie or Edward Albee's play *Seascape*; but with fair confidence we may assert that there are intrinsic physical design constraints upon the upper magnitude of lobsters.

With the creative imagination the case is more problematical, by reason of the now-familiar inherent paradox: The human imagination would appear to be limited only by the limitations of our human imaginations. And the parameters are softer in the area of art than in the areas of foot-racing and lobsterology. We have no electronic stopwatch or objective calipers with which to verify that such-and-such a play or novel refutes that earlier-mentioned argument concerning art and the Holocaust. Indeed, the same Holo-

---

*Set in 1993 and still the record as of this writing.

caust novel that proves to one reader that the argument is unten-
able may demonstrate to another that it is valid.

And yet, even if I myself happened to agree with that second
reader in some particular (hypothetical) case, I could nevertheless
imagine the imagination's doing what some "post-Holocaust"
critics, for example, declare that it cannot do. I shall conclude
these remarks with a little thought-experiment, the specific terms
of which I invite you to exchange for others more to your liking:

There are certain literary-artistic images, most of us would
agree, of such extraordinary imaginative power — one might say,
of such mythic resonance — as to be larger than the works that
contain them, or rather fail to contain them. They live on force-
fully in our imaginations long after we've forgotten the details of
the texts (or whatever) in which we first encountered them. Indeed, because it is characteristic of such transcendent images that
they translate readily from one medium to another, we may be
quite familiar with the image even though we're unfamiliar with
its source.

The short-short list, in my shop, comprises just four such images: In literary-historical order, they are Odysseus, striving homeward from Troy across the wine-dark sea; Scheherazade, yarning
through the night to save her neck; Don Quixote and Sancho
Panza, chatting their way across the plains of La Mancha; and
Huckleberry Finn, rafting down the heart-waters of America. After these four cardinal images — the very compass-points of my
own narrative imagination — come a host of powerful but, to my
mind, somewhat lesser ones: Dante touring the underworld, Ahab
chasing after his great white whale, Rip Van Winkle sleeping while
the world turns upside down, Gregor Samsa waking to find himself metamorphosed into a big bug, Alice tumbling down the
rabbit-hole or through the looking-glass on a Victorian summer
afternoon. But in my personal pantheon, those first four are the
regnant deities; for me there is no fifth, yet. And after calling
your attention to the fact that what I said a minute ago applies to
them (many, many more people know who Scheherazade and Don
Quixote are than have actually read *The 1001 Nights* or Cervantes's novel, just as millions know the iconography of the passion of Jesus who have forgotten or never actually read the gospel

narratives, and millions know who Mickey Mouse is who have never seen the original Walt Disney cartoons and comic books), I shall close by rubbing these four touchstones of mine against our subject: the limits of imagination.

First, without attempting to rank the four, I cannot myself imagine more profound, multifaceted, transcendently appealing narrative icons than these: Odysseus, Scheherazade, Don Quixote, Huckleberry Finn. For me, as I have declared, there is no fifth. Yet (this is my second point) although the creation of such transcendent icons is by no means the only literary virtue, and although numerous of my very favorite novels, for example, do not happen to contain such sublimely uncontainable images (*Tom Jones* doesn't, nor do *Bleak House* or *Ulysses* or *One Hundred Years of Solitude*), nevertheless I cannot imagine a happier destiny for a storyteller than to add an item to that short list, or even to the somewhat longer one. I myself, after thirty-five years of professional storytelling, have not managed to do so; nor at my age am I now likely to. (Though it is not altogether unimaginable that I yet might. That consideration is among the things that keep me going, along with the cheering truth that most of the writers I most admire have not done so either. It is simply not given to the human imagination to come up with an Odysseus or a Scheherazade or a Don Quixote or a Huck Finn very often; 4,500 years of writing have produced — by my standards — only those four: about one every eleven centuries.)

But look here, I then tell myself: If I had been a well-read citizen of thirteenth-century Persia — the Huntington Cairns of Baghdad or Basra — I guess I would have thought that there was only one such image, Homer's Odysseus, when in fact the second — Anonymous's Scheherazade — was being imagined right under my nose. And if I had lived in seventeenth-century Spain, I might well have said that there are only two — Homer's Odysseus and Anonymous's Scheherazade — never imagining that my countryman Cervantes was about to prove me wrong. And had I been an American book reviewer in 1885, I might even have added my voice to the chorus of those who found Mr. Mark Twain's new novel mainly vulgar, not realizing that what I was hearing was the very voice of America.

And so here we are, at the close of the twentieth century, some of us imagining it to be unimaginable at this hour of the world that the human literary/mythopoeic imagination can dream up yet another image with the profundity and staying power of those great predecessors — when for all we know, the thing might be being done next door, right now, by someone too busy doing it to attend these remarks of mine. Or it might already have been done, but not yet recognized for what it is, like Odysseus in his beggar's rags, mocked by the bona fide beggars in his own house. Or it might imaginably be about to be done, by some hitherto not especially remarkable writer who, like late-middle-aged Cervantes, finds himself possessed by an image that he himself, till it possessed him, imaginably thought to be beyond the limits of imagination.

A Few Words
About Minimalism

*The three following Friday-pieces have to do with questions of length
and scale in fiction: minimalism versus maximalism and the short
story versus the novel. This first of them was delivered originally at a
1986 symposium on minimalism at the University of Southern Mississippi — where Frederick Barthelme's excellent* Mississippi Review
*was preparing a special issue (MR 40/41) on the then-fashionable
subject of "the new American fiction." It was published in the* New
York Times Book Review *on December 28 of that year.*

"LESS IS MORE," said Walter Gropius, or Alberto
Giacometti, or László Moholy-Nagy, or Henri Gaudier-
Brzeska, or Constantin Brancusi, or Le Corbusier, or Ludwig Mies
van der Rohe; the remark* has been severally attributed to all of
those more or less celebrated more-or-less-minimalists. Like the
Bauhaus motto "Form follows function," it is itself a memorable
specimen of the minimalist aesthetic, of which a cardinal principle
is that artistic effect may be enhanced by a radical economy of
artistic means, even where such parsimony compromises other
values: completeness, for example, or richness, or precision of
statement.

The power of that aesthetic principle is easy to demonstrate:
Contrast my eminently forgettable formulation of it above — "ar-

---

*First made in fact, it appears, by Robert Browning's Andrea del Sarto, in lines
76–78 of Browning's verse monologue of that title: "Yet do much less, so much
less, Someone says/(I know his name, no matter) — so much less!/Well, *less is
more*, Lucrezia: I am judged." Italics mine. I am indebted to Mr. Robert Schreuer
for this reference. In our century, the proposition became Mies van der Rohe's
working slogan, and is his epitaph.

tistic effect may be enhanced," etc. — with the unforgettable assertion "Less is more." Or consider the following proposition, first
with and then without its parenthetical elements:

Minimalism (of one sort or another) *is the principle* (one of the
principles, anyhow) *underlying* (what I and many another interested observer consider to be perhaps) *the most impressive phenomenon on the current* (i.e., 1980ish) *literary scene* (in North
America, especially in the United States: our gringo equivalent to
"el boom" in the Latin American novel): *I mean the new flowering
of the* (North) *American short story* (in particular the kind of
terse, oblique, realistic or hyperrealistic, slightly-plotted, extro-
spective, cool-surfaced fiction associated in the last five or ten
years with such excellent writers as Frederick Barthelme, Ann
Beattie, Raymond Carver, Bobbie Ann Mason, James Robison,
Mary Robison, and Tobias Wolff, and both praised and damned
under such labels as "K-Mart realism," "hick chic," "Diet-Pepsi
minimalism," and "post-Vietnam, post-literary, post-Postmodernist blue-collar neo-early-Hemingwayism").

Like any clutch of artists collectively labeled, the writers just
mentioned are at least as different from one another as they are
similar. Minimalism, moreover, is not the only and may not be the
most important attribute that their fiction more or less shares;
those labels themselves suggest some other aspects and concerns of
The New American Short Story and its proportionate counterpart,
the $\frac{3}{8}$" novel. But it is their minimalism I shall speak of (briefly)
here, and its antecedence: the idea that, in art at least, less is more.

It is an idea surely as old, as enduringly attractive, and as ubiquitous as its opposite. In the beginning was the Word; only later
came the Bible, not to mention the three-decker Victorian novel.
The oracle at Delphi did not say "Exhaustive analysis and comprehension of one's own psyche may be prerequisite to an understanding of one's behavior and of the world at large"; what it said
was "Know thyself." Such inherently minimalist literary and par-
aliterary genres as oracles (from the Delphic shrine of Apollo
to the modern fortune cookie), proverbs, maxims, aphorisms,
epigrams, pensées, mottoes, slogans, and quips are popular in
every human century and culture — especially in oral cultures and

sub-cultures, where mnemonic staying-power has high priority —
and many specimens of them are self-reflexive or self-demonstra-
tive: minimalism about minimalism. "Brevity is the soul of wit."
"Silence is golden." "*Ars longa, Vita brevis es,*" Seneca warns;
"Eschew surplusage," recommends Mark Twain.

Against the large-scale classical prose pleasures of Herodotus,
Thucydides, and Petronius, there are the miniature delights of Ae-
sop's fables and Theophrastus's *Characters*.* Against such verse
epics as the *Iliad*, the *Odyssey*, and the *Aeneid* — and the much
longer Sanskrit *Ramayana*, *Mahabharata*, and *Ocean of Story* —
are such venerable supercompressive poetic forms as the palin-
drome (there are long examples, but the ones we remember are the
short ones: *Madam, I'm Adam*; *Sex at noon taxes*; perhaps even
the ancient Greek *NIΨONANOMHMATAMHMONANOΨIN*,
which translates: "Wash my transgressions, not only my face"), or
the single couplet (a modern instance is Ogden Nash's "Candy is
dandy/But liquor is quicker"), or the feudal Japanese haiku and
its western echoes in the early-twentieth-century Imagists (Ezra
Pound's "The apparition of these faces in the crowd:/Petals on a
wet black bough") — up to the contemporary "skinny poems" of,
say, Robert Creeley. There are even single-word poems, or single
words that ought to be poems; the best one I know of is the Tierra
del Fuegan word "mamilapatinapei," which in the language of the
Land of Fire is said to mean "looking into each other's eyes, each
hoping that the other will initiate what both want to do but neither chooses to commence."

The genre of the short story, as Edgar Poe distinguished it from
the traditional tale in his 1842 review of Nathaniel Hawthorne's
first collection of stories, is an early manifesto of modern narrative
minimalism: "In the whole composition there should be no word
written, of which the tendency . . . is not to the pre-established
design. . . . Undue length is . . . to be avoided." Poe's codification
informs such later nineteenth-century masters of terseness, selec-

---

*From Greek *kharax*, a pointed tool for making sharp impressions. The literary
genre — familiar social types "characterized" in a few pungent, usually satirical
sentences — was revived in the English seventeenth century by Sir Thomas Over-
bury and John Earle: "A Fop," "A Courtier," "A Whoore," "A *Verie* Whoore,"
etc.

tivity, and implicitness (as opposed to leisurely once-upon-a-timelessness, luxuriant abundance, explicit and extended analysis) as Guy de Maupassant and Anton Chekhov. Show, don't tell, said Henry James in effect and at length in his prefaces to the 1908 New York Edition of his novels. And don't tell a word more than you absolutely need to, added young Ernest Hemingway, who thus describes his "new theory" in the early 1920s: ". . . you could omit anything if you knew that you omitted, and the omitted part would strengthen the story and make people feel something more than they understood."

The Bauhaus Functionalists were by then already busy unornamenting and abstracting Modernist architecture, painting, and design; and while functionalism and minimalism are not the same thing, to say nothing of abstractionism and minimalism (there is nothing abstract about those early Hemingway stories), they spring from the same impulse: to strip away the superfluous in order to reveal the necessary, the essential. Never mind that Voltaire had pointed out, a century and a half before, how indispensable the superfluous can be (*"Le superflu, chose si nécessaire"*); just as, in Modernist painting, the process of stripping away leads from Post-Impressionism through Cubism to the radical minimalism of Kasimir Malevich's *White on White* of 1918, Ad Reinhardt's all-but-imageless "black paintings" of the 1950s, and the materially nonexistent projects of the Conceptualists, so in twentieth-century literature the minimalist succession leads out of Poe and Maupassant and Chekhov through Hemingway's "new theory" to the shorter *ficciones* of Jorge Luis Borges and the ever-terser texts of Samuel Beckett, perhaps culminating in his play *Breath* (1969): The curtain opens upon a dimly lit stage, empty but for scattered rubbish; there is heard a single recorded human cry, then a single amplified inspiration and expiration of breath accompanied by a brightening and redimming of the lights, then again the cry. Thirty-five seconds after it opened, the curtain closes upon this minimalist life history.

But it closes only upon the play, not upon the modern tradition of literary minimalism, which honorably continues in such next-generation writers as, in America, Donald Barthelme ("The fragment is the only form I trust," declares a character in his story

"See the Moon?") and, in the literary generation overlapping and following his, the plentiful authors of The New American Short Story.

Old or new, fiction can be minimalist in any or all of several ways. There are minimalisms of unit, form, and scale: short words, short sentences and paragraphs, super-short stories,* those $\frac{3}{8}$"-thin novels aforementioned, and even minimal bibliographies: Borges's fiction adds up to a few modest though powerfully influential short-story collections; of the late Mexican writer Juan Rulfo, who published nothing in the last thirty years of his life and not much in the preceding thirty-seven, one eulogist said: "No one could carry on Rulfo's work; not even its author." There are minimalisms of style: a stripped-down vocabulary; a stripped-down syntax that avoids periodic sentences, serial predications, and complex subordinating constructions like these; a stripped-down rhetoric that may eschew figurative language altogether; a stripped-down, non-emotive tone. And there are minimalisms of material: minimal characters, minimal exposition ("all that David Copperfield kind of crap," says J. D. Salinger's catcher in the rye), minimal mise-en-scènes, minimal action, minimal plot.

Found together in their purest forms, these several minimalisms add up to an art that — in the words of its arch-priest, Samuel Beckett, speaking of the painter Bram Van Velde — expresses "that there is nothing to express, nothing with which to express, nothing from which to express, no power to express, no desire to express — together with the obligation to express." But they are not always found together: There are very short works of great rhetorical, emotional, and thematic richness, such as Borges's essential page, "Borges and I"; and there are instances of what may fairly be called long-winded minimalism, such as Beckett's stark-monumental trilogy from the early 1950s: Molloy, Malone Dies, and The Unnameable. Parallels abound in the other arts: The miniature, in painting, is characteristically brimful (miniaturism is not minimalism); Joseph Cornell's little boxes contain universes.

---

*One excellent selection of these is "Minute Stories," the Winter 1976 issue of Tri-Quarterly.

The large paintings of Mark Rothko, Franz Kline, and Barnett Newman, on the other hand, are as undetailed as the Washington Monument.

The medieval Roman Catholic Church recognized two opposite roads to grace: the *via negativa* of the monk's cell and the hermit's cave, and the *via affirmativa* of immersion in human affairs, of being *in* the world whether or not one is *of* it. Literary critics have aptly borrowed those terms to characterize the difference between Mr. Beckett, for example, and his erstwhile master James Joyce, himself a maximalist except in his early works. Other than bone-deep disposition, which is no doubt the great determinant, what inclines a writer — sometimes almost a cultural generation of writers — to the Negational Path?

For individuals, it may be by their own acknowledgment largely a matter of past or present personal circumstances. Raymond Carver writes of a literary apprenticeship in which his short poems and stories were carved in precious quarter-hours stolen from a harrowing domestic and economic situation; although he now has professional time a-plenty,* the notion besets him that should he presume to attempt even a short novel, he'll wake to find himself back in those wretched circumstances. An opposite case is Borges's: His near-total blindness in his latter decades obliged him to the short forms that he had elected for other, nonphysical reasons when he was sighted.

To account for a trend, literary sociologists and culture-watchers point to more general historical and philosophical factors — not excluding the factor of powerful models like Borges and Beckett. The influence of Chekhov and early Hemingway upon Raymond Carver, say, is as apparent as is the influence of Carver in turn upon a host of other New American Short-Story writers, and upon a much more numerous host of apprentices in American college fiction-writing programs. But why this model rather than that, other than its mere and sheer artistic prowess, on which after all it has no monopoly? Doubtless because this one is felt, by the

---

*So it appeared to him and to the writer of this essay in 1986. He had, alas, only three more years.

writers thus more or less influenced, to speak more strongly to
their condition and that of their readers.

And what is that condition, in the case of the cool-surface
realist-minimalist storytellers of the American 1970s and Eighties?
In my conversation with them, my reading of their critics both
positive and negative, and my dealings with recent and current apprentice writers, I have heard cited, among other factors, these
half-dozen, ranked here in no particular order:

• Our national hangover from the Vietnam war, felt by many
to be a trauma literally and figuratively unspeakable. "I don't
want to talk about it" is the characteristic attitude of "Nam" veterans in the fiction of Ann Beattie, Jayne Ann Phillips, and Bobbie
Ann Mason — as it is among many of their real-life counterparts
(and as it was among their numberless twentieth-century forerunners, especially after the First World War). This is, of course, one
of the two classic attitudes to trauma, the other being its opposite,
and it can certainly conduce to hedged, non-introspective, even
minimalist discourse: One remembers Hemingway's early story
"Soldier's Home."

• The more or less coincident energy crisis of 1973–76, and the
associated reaction against American excess and wastefulness in
general. The popularity of the subcompact car parallels that (in literary circles, at least) of the subcompact novel and the mini-
fiction — though not, one observes, of the miniskirt, which had
nothing to do with conserving material.

• The national decline in reading and writing skills, not only
among the young (including even young apprentice writers, as a
group), but among their teachers, many of whom are themselves
the product of an ever-less-demanding educational system and a
society whose narrative-dramatic entertainment and tastes come
far more from movies and television than from literature. This is
not to disparage the literacy and general education of those writers
mentioned above, or to suggest that the great writers of the past
were uniformly flawless spellers, punctuators, and grammarians of
wide personal literary culture. Some were, some weren't; some of
today's are, some aren't. But at least among those of our aspiring
writers promising enough to be admitted into good graduate writ-

ing programs — and surely they are not the *inferior* specimens of their breed — the general decline in basic language skills over the past two decades is inarguable enough to make me worry in some instances about their teaching undergraduates. Rarely in their own writing, whatever its considerable other merits, will one find a sentence of any syntactical complexity, for example, and inasmuch as a language's repertoire of other-than-basic syntactical devices permits its users to articulate other-than-basic thoughts and feelings, Dick-and-Jane prose tends to be emotionally and intellectually poorer than Henry James prose. Among the great minimalist writers, this impoverishment is elected and strategic: "simplification" in the interest of strength, or of some other value: richness under wraps, power under restraint, grace under pressure. Among the less great, it may be faute de mieux. Among today's "common readers," it is pandemic.

• Along with this decline, an ever-dwindling readerly attention span. The long popular novel still has its devotees, especially aboard large airplanes and on beaches; but it can scarcely be doubted that many of the hours we bourgeois now spend with our TVs and VCRs, and in our cars and at the movies, we used to spend reading novels and novellas and not-so-short stories, partly because those glitzy other distractions weren't there and partly because we were more generally conditioned for sustained concentration, in our pleasures as well as in our work.* My grandson snaps together a plastic model spacecraft in a few seconds; his father used to assemble flying model aircraft in a day from pre-cut balsa parts; his grandfather spent days carefully cutting those parts from pre-stamped balsa sheets before beginning the long, painstaking labor of assembly; and the how-to books for turn-of-the-century children advised the lad who wished to build a model steamboat to go first to his neighborhood blacksmith for scraps of tin, then to the druggist's for naphtha or paraffin, then to the hardware store for tin snips and solder. . . . The Austrian novelist Robert Musil was already complaining by 1930 (in his maxi-novel

*More on this subject in the essay "Inconclusion: The Novel in the Next Century," later in this volume.

The Man Without Qualities) that we live in "the age of the magazine," too impatient already in the twitchy Twenties to read books. Half a century later, in America at least, even the large-circulation magazine market for fiction had dwindled to a handful of outlets; the readers weren't there. It is a touching paradox of the New American Short Story — so admirably straightforward and democratic of access, so steeped in brand names and the popular culture — that it perforce appears mainly in very small-circulation literary quarterlies instead of in the likes of *Collier's*, *Liberty*, and the *Saturday Evening Post*. But *The New Yorker* and *Esquire* can't publish everybody.

• Together with all the above, a reaction on these authors' part against the ironic, Black-Humoristic "fabulism" and/or the (sometimes academic) intellectuality and/or the density, here byzantine, there baroque, of some of their immediate American literary antecedents: the likes of Donald Barthelme, Robert Coover, Stanley Elkin, William Gaddis and William Gass, John Hawkes, Joseph Heller, Thomas Pynchon, Kurt Vonnegut (and, I shall presume, myself as well). This reaction, where it exists, would seem to pertain as much to our successors' relentless realism as to their minimalism: Among the distinguished brothers Barthelme, Donald's productions are no less lean than Frederick's or the up-and-coming Steven's; but their characteristic material, angle of attack, and resultant flavor are different indeed. The formal intricacy of Elder Brother's story "Sentence," for example (a single nine-page non-sentence), or the direct though satirical intellectuality of his story "Kierkegaard Unfair to Schlegel," are as foreign to the K-Mart Realists as are the manic flights of *Gravity's Rainbow*. So it goes: The dialogue between fantast and realist, between fabulator and quotidianist, like the dialogue between maximalist and minimalist, is as old as storytelling, and by no means always adversary. There are innumerable combinations, coalitions, line-crossings, and workings of both sides of the street.

• The reaction against the all but inescapable hyperbole of American advertising, both commercial and political, with its high-tech manipulativeness and glamorous lies, as ubiquitous as and more polluted than the air we breathe. How understandable that such an ambiance, together with whatever other items in this catalogue, might inspire a fiction dedicated to homely, understated, programmatically unglamorous, even minimalistic Telling It Like It Is.

That has ever been the ground inspiration, moral-philosophical in character, of minimalism and its kissing-cousin realism in their many avatars over the centuries, in the fine arts and elsewhere: the feeling that the language (or whatever) has for whatever reasons become excessive, cluttered, corrupted, fancy, false. It is the Puritans' reaction against baroque Catholicism; it is Thoreau's putting behind him even the meager comforts of the village of Concord. Count Basie's solid but never flashy drummer Jo Jones, taken some decades ago to hear the young prodigy Buddy Rich, is reported to have said after one of Rich's extravagant solo workouts, "He talking fast, but he ain't saying much." To the Lost Generation of World War I survivors, says one of their famous spokesmen (Frederic Henry in Hemingway's *A Farewell to Arms*), "Abstract words such as glory, honor, courage, or hallow were obscene. . . ." Hemingway's own procedure, as recollected in his memoir *A Moveable Feast*, was this: "If I started to write elaborately, or like someone introducing or presenting something, I found that I could cut that scrollwork or ornament out and throw it away and start with the first true simple declarative sentence I had written." The Bauhaus artist Wassily Kandinsky said that he sought "Not the shell, but the nut." The functionalism of the Bauhaus was inspired in part by admiration for machine technology, in part by revulsion against the fancy clutter of the Gilded Age, in language as well as elsewhere. The sinking of the elegant *Titanic* has come to symbolize the end of that age, as the sight of some workmen crushed by a falling Victorian cornice symbolized for young Frank Lloyd Wright the dead weight of functionless architectural decoration. Flaubert raged against the *blague* of bourgeois speech, bureaucratic speech in particular; his passion for the *mot juste* involved far more subtraction than addition. The baroque inspires its opposite. After the excesses of Scholasticism comes the radical reductionism of Descartes: Let us doubt and discard everything not self-evident and see whether anything indubitable remains upon which to rebuild (in common use, even his famous three-word foundation stone, *Cogito ergo sum*, gets abbreviated to the single word *Cogito*). And three centuries before Descartes, among the Scholastics themselves, William of Ockham honed his celebrated razor: *Entia non sunt multiplicanda*: Entities are not to be multiplied; what can be explained on fewer principles is explained needlessly by many.

In short, less is more.

Beyond their individual and historically local impulses, then, the more or less minimalist authors of The New American Short Story are reenacting a cyclical correction in the history (and the microhistories) of literature and of art in general: a cycle to be found as well, with longer rhythms, in the history of philosophy, the history of the culture. Renaissances beget reformations, which then beget counterreformations; the seven fat years are succeeded by seven lean, after which we, no less than the people of Genesis, may look forward to the recorrection.

For if there is much to admire in artistic austerity, its opposite is not without merits and joys as well.* There are the minimalist pleasures of Emily Dickenson ("Zero at the bone") and the maximalist ones of Walt Whitman ("I contain multitudes"). There are the low-fat rewards of Beckett's *Texts for Nothing* and the high-calorie delights of Gabriel García Márquez's *One Hundred Years of Solitude*. There truly are more ways than one to heaven. As between minimalism and its opposite, I pity the reader — or the writer, or the age — too addicted to either to savor the other.

---

*Celebrated in the Friday-piece following this one: "It's a Long Story."

It's a Long Story:
Maximalism Reconsidered

"Renaissances beget reformations," declares the preceding Friday-piece, "which then beget counterreformations. . . ." Likewise, essays on minimalism may beget counter-essays on maximalism. This one first appeared in Harper's, *July 1990.*

MUCH MAY BE said for minimalism. In the realm of aesthetics, other things equal, less surely *is* more. Except among shaggy dogs, brevity *is* the soul of wit. Art *is* long, in its aggregate anyhow, and life short. Civilized attention spans are measurably not what they used to be: Second intermissions, for example, not to mention third and fourth, have all but disappeared from theater production — given repeated opportunity, audiences these days will likely leave. And Winslow Homer's 1877 watercolor called *The New Novel* — of a teenage girl in the sunny years before that term was coined, recumbent on the summer grass in her summer frock sans Walkman or running shoes and *utterly absorbed* in a printed narrative of some heft — evokes more nostalgia now than recognition.

To be sure, our distracted century did not invent minimality. Spareness has ever been a relief from elaborateness, the puritanical from the baroque. It was no modern, but neo-Gothic Edgar Poe (reviewing neo-Puritan Nathaniel Hawthorne) who articulated the "single effect" economy of the modern short story as opposed to its more diffuse antecedents, and such abbreviated genres as the maxim and the epigram are as old as literature. Undeniably, however, "moderns love brevity," as the arch-maximalist François Rabelais observed in 1532, and twentieth-century Modernism added a special voltage to the venerable aesthetics of parsimony. In short (excuse the expression), other ages took occasional pleasure in the minimal; ours invented Minimalism.

I used to propose to undergraduates, for mnemonic convenience, that if Enlightenment plus industrialism leads to Romanticism, then Romanticism plus cataclysm (including revolutions political and nonpolitical) leads to Modernism, around the margins whereof lurks the apocalyptic suspicion that art, maybe Western Civ itself, is about done with. Kasimir Malevich's White Paintings of 1918 were meant to finish off that medium of art; Pablo Picasso, some decades later, affirms that "there is no more modern art"; Jorge Luis Borges's "footnotes to imaginary texts" (as one critic describes his *ficciones*) are by way of being end-notes to our literary history as well, and such works as Samuel Beckett's *Breath* achieve literal wordlessness, just as John Cage's *4' 33"* achieves (from its performers' instruments, at least) literal soundlessness. The century now closing with fashionable treatises on the end of history and the end of nature opened with whispers (sometimes noisy proclamations) of the end of art. In such an endgame ambiance, it may understandably come to seem not only that "less is more," but that least is most.

At so leanly perceived an hour of the world, is not the big fat novel, the "long read" — that delight of Winslow Homer's *jeune fille en fleur* and of ampler times in general — an anachronism, even an aesthetic embarrassment? Such twentieth-century specimens of it as Jules Romains's twenty-seven-volume *Les Hommes de bonne volonté* (cited by Guinness as "the longest important novel ever published"), Anthony Powell's twelve-novel, four-"movement" *A Dance to the Music of Time*, Proust's seven-volume *A la recherche du temps perdu*, Thomas Mann's four-volume "Joseph" series and Lawrence Durrell's *The Alexandria Quartet*, Robert Musil's three-volume *Der Mann Ohne Eigenschaften*, even Joseph McElroy's recent two-volume *Women and Men** — are they not in the ultrasaurian category of things that attain their maximality just when, sometimes just because, they're obsolete? The *Hindenburg* zeppelin, the Big Bertha field gun, the "Spruce

---

*NY: Knopf, 1986, 1,204 pages — or Vikram Seth's even more recent *A Suitable Boy* (NY: HarperCollins, 1993), published as a single 1,349-page volume.

Goose" flying boat, the *QE2*, the $33\frac{1}{3}$ rpm LP, the multi-decker panoramic or encyclopedic novel.

And yet . . . Although one seldom sees the two-incher, not to mention the two-booker, being read these days except by middle-aged folk on resort beaches and large airliners, before we turn our backs to such gargantuan impositions on modern attention, let's review, and not only nostalgically, some pleasures of literary max-imalism, reminding ourselves that extravagance can be as wel-come a relief from austerity as vice versa and that Mies van der Rohe's celebrated motto, "Less is more," is also his epitaph. I am not James A. Michener's most ardent fan, but his remark to my students some years ago — that he aspires in his novels "to create a world in which [his] readers will pleasurably spend some weeks" — deserves in my estimation to stand as a counterpoise beside Poe's dictum that the short story be readable "at one sit-ting." To create a world: That is it, precisely. One is reminded that the pleasures of the one-night stand, however fashionable, are not the only pleasures. There is also the extended, committed affair; there is even the devoted, faithful, happy marriage. One recalls, among the several non-minimalist Moderns, Vladimir Nabokov seconding James Joyce's wish for "the ideal reader with the ideal insomnia" (we lovers of Nabokov's plump *Ada* are a red-eyed club, but passionate) and Joyce himself insouciantly expecting "nothing of [his] readers except that they spend their lives reading [his] work."

Perhaps maxi-novelists, like canny bargainers, ask for a lifetime in hopes of getting a semester or two? I personally recall, with undying gratitude to Marcel Proust, having survived an under-graduate life crisis by virtually isolating myself with *Remembrance of Things Past*. For two weeks I did little besides eat, sleep, and read Proust; my problems did not go away, but by page 1,124 my sustained and concentrated self-loss had weakened their grip on my spirit.

Getting out of oneself (in order, naturally, to return, bringing something back): If self-forgetfulness is not necessarily a mark of high-quality literary experience, self-transcension doubtless is. Granted, it can happen momentarily in a great short story, and one's most intense experiences are rarely one's longest (William

James goes so far as to include "transiency" among the four hall-marks of true mystical experience). But it's equally true that one's most pleasurable experiences, literary and extraliterary, are not necessarily the most intense. Beside the epiphanic flash of a Chekhov wrap-up line must be set such prolonged, sustained emotional sound-and-light shows as *Don Quixote, Tom Jones, The Brothers Karamazov, War and Peace, One Hundred Years of Solitude*: huge engrossments in midst of which we may find ourselves wishing that they would *never end*. What will we do when this story's over? Why can't it be longer yet?

Well, some are, though their readers may find them not so much gripping as absorbing, conducive more to the marathoner's low-grade, long-run high than to the sprinter's adrenaline rush. One finishes Samuel Richardson's *Clarissa* (2,183 pages in the four-volume Everyman's Library edition) not so much transfigured as relieved. Once the readerly oxygen debt has been achieved, however, and the endorphin/dopamine levels are duly adjusted for the long haul, one is as pleased to have finished *Clarissa* as to be finished with her, or with any other of the less-than-life-altering trilogies and tetralogies so popular in the two centuries of general bourgeois literacy between the invention of movable type and the advent of movies, television, and the VCR.

To change the metaphor: We feed on short stories like diving ducks: take a breath, take the plunge, take our tidbit, and soon surface. "At one sitting," Poe prescribes; I for one am likely in an evening to pop a handful of Chekhovs, or Flannery O'Connors, Donald Barthelmes, Stephen Dixons. Novel readers, however — and novel writers — are like the Weddell seal, which employs one metabolistic mode for "ordinary" dives (your typical 300- to 400-page novel: *The Scarlet Letter, Madame Bovary, A Farewell to Arms*) and quite another for such prolonged submersions as mine with Proust. We batten the hatches, narrow our scope, shut down all ancillary systems, reduce and redirect our essential oxygen, settle down and into enormous reaches and intrications unknown to minimalism: all five books of *Gargantua and Pantagruel* (no skimming allowed; read every item in every one of those interminable Rabelaisian catalogues); all three partitions of Robert Burton's

*Anatomy of Melancholy** — 1,382 pages in the Vintage paperback edition: twice as many as Rabelais, 250 more than Proust,
though still a mere warm-up for Richardson at his most expansive.

With those or equivalent stamina-builders under our belt, we
may aspire to maximalisms beside which even *Clarissa* seems
downright terse: works of sometimes literally Asiatic breadth; worlds
in which to spend pleasurably not "some weeks" but months and
months and months. By now such occasional best-selling U.S. fat-
soes as Ross Lockridge's *Raintree County* (1,066 pages) and Marguerite Young's *Miss Macintosh, My Darling* (1,198 pages) will be
no more than stretching exercises; likewise such Brobdingnagian
classics and demiclassics as Lady Murasaki's *The Tale of Genji*
(1,135 pages in the Modern Library edition), from the folks who
gave us on the one hand bonsai and the seventeen-syllable haiku,
on the other sumo wrestling and perhaps the longest proper novel
ever: Sohachi Yamaoka's *Tokuga-Wa Ieyasu* (serialized in daily
newspapers for some thirty years, which Guinness estimates "will
require nearly forty volumes in book form"), Eugene Sue's *The
Wandering Jew* (1,357 pages), Victor Hugo's *Les Miserables*
(1,781 pages in the Pléiade), William Gaddis's *The Recognitions*
(at 956 pages, a full 150 longer than my own *Sot-Weed Factor*; I
once declined to review Gaddis's formidable novel on the minimalist pretense that anything worth saying in literature can be said
in 806 pages), and Nabokov's maxiest novel, that exhaustively annotated four-volume Englishment of Pushkin's *Eugene Onegin*,
from which *Pale Fire* is a minimalist spin-off. We are ready for *The
1001 Nights*: first the complete but unembellished Mardrus and
Mathers translation (2,341 pages in the four-volume Routledge &
Kegan Paul edition) for the quality of its English prose and incidental verse — 14,000-odd lines of the latter, in appropriate Arab

---

*Not a novel? Sure it is, in this metabolic mode: a novel in which characteristics
take the place of characters. Instead of Musil's *Man Without Qualities*, Burton
gives us the adventures of a Quality without particular embodiment. But the
thing must be read properly, including every one of the Author's Notes — many
per page, all in Latin, an effect the more piquant if, like me, you have but small
Latin — plus the appended glossary and the whole Nabokovian index, from
ABBEYS, *subversion of the*, to YOUTH, *impossible not to love in*. Friedrich von
Schlegel's generous conception of *der Roman* (see the Friday-pieces on Postmodernism, Chaos Theory, and the Romantic Arabesque, farther on in this volume)
would readily accommodate Burton's *Anatomy*.

metrics — then the freewheeling Richard Burton version with its burgeoning apparatus: in the Burton Club Limited Edition, seventeen quarto volumes of narrative prose, poetry, footnotes and appendices on everything under the mothering sun, plus a truly Terminal Essay that, like Tolstoy's essay on history at the close of *War and Peace*, we shall read as part and parcel of this splendid maxi-novel about Scheherazade.

In full deep-dive mode now, shall we not regard the twenty novels of Zola's Rougon-Macquart cycle, like the seven of Proust's *Recherche*, as one grand fiction? Of course we shall, along with the twenty-six of Walter Scott's Waverly series and the ninety-two of Balzac's *La Comédie humaine*, both because the whole product of a single author's imagination has an inescapable organicity, more or less,* whether or not the same characters reappear, Faulkner-style, from book to book (and so we'll throw in the remaining Balzac as well, those most un-"Balzacian" *Droll Stories*), and because we can use the additional exercise before we turn to a *really* long story: one that makes a minimalist of Scheherazade, if not quite of Balzac.

Kathā Sarit Sāgara — ten *folio* volumes in the Tawney/Penzer Englishing most likely to be found in (large) libraries — is Sanskrit for *The Ocean of Story*,† more or less by an eleventh-century Kashmiri court-poet called Somadeva, or "Mister Soma." Granted, it is not, in the original, a work of prose; but we won't be reading the original, not by a long shot, and anyhow the great smorgasbord of literature includes among its offerings a fair number of novels in verse, not to mention in still photographs, comic strips, even videotapes. The title refers to the original author's, or compiler's, mega-maximalist aspiration to tell a story that would encompass *all* stories, as the ocean ultimately receives all the rivers of the world.

Does that project seem superhuman? No less so was the first composer of *Kathā Sarit Sāgara*: the god Shiva himself, lord of creation and destruction, who cooked up the "Great Tale" (*Brihat-*

---

*On this, too, see Schlegel, as cited in Lecture 3 ("The Arabesque") of "4½ Lectures," later in this volume.
†Literally, "the ocean of streams of story."

katha) as a gift to his consort Pārvatī for a particularly divine session of lovemaking. Asked to name her postcoital heart's desire, Pārvatī requested a story that no one had ever heard before and, moreover, that *no one would ever hear again*: an extraordinary request in a literary culture that, like classical Rome's, preferred twice-told tales to original material. Given the goddess's second stipulation, you ask, how did Mr. Soma come by the story? And what is so maximal after all, given our previous examples, about a mere ten folio volumes, including an apparatus of footnotes, appendices, and indices that would do Burton proud? Somadeva's rendering of the *Ocean* comes to no more than 22,000 distichs — twice the length of Homer's *Iliad* and *Odyssey* combined, according to Penzer. No quickie, to be sure, but simple arithmetic tells us that ten folio volumes equal only twenty quartos: comparable to Zola's Rougon-Macquarts (imagine them in couplets!) but far short of Jules Romains's *Men of Goodwill*, not to mention Balzac's *Human Comedy*.

The answer to these questions is a story in itself, and not a short one. It is called *Kathāpītha*, the history of the text, or story of the story; it constitutes half of Volume One of the Penzer edition of *The Ocean of Story*, and, like certain overtures more memorable than their operas, it is in my opinion the best story in *Kathā Sarit Sāgara*. From it we learn that the text in hand, massive as it is, is by no means the whole story of *The Ocean of Story*, and was not even before Mr. Soma's minimalist abridgment. What Somadeva pared down to a radically terse 22K distichs was Shiva's Great Tale as originally versified eight centuries earlier by one Gunādhya, court minister to a certain King Sātavāhana — who represents himself to be the royal author of this Story of the Story. And Gunādhya's version, as received by Sātavāhana, came to no fewer than 100,000 distichs: four and a half times larger than Somadeva's condensation (*Reader's Digest* typically cuts 30 percent from original texts; Somadeva managed 78 percent). That's ninety quarto volumes, if rendered and annotated Penzer-style; right up there with M. Balzac.

Yet even *that* enormous work, the *Kathāpītha* goes on to explain, was but the Bay of Bengal, so to speak, beside the veritable Indian Ocean of Gunādhya's original rendition of Shiva's Great

Tale. Indeed, it was no more than the *final seventh* of King
Sātavāhana's minister's colossal narrative poem, and the reason
for that is the hilarious, heartbreaking (and maximally complicated) story of the Story of the Story: how Pārvatī's private gift-
tale happened to go public and what befell its other six-sevenths.

I have condensed that story elsewhere* — it's one of my favorites — and will recondense it here more radically than Somadeva condensed Gunādhya. Shiva's girlfriend, remember, asks for
a one-off, her-ears-only story; she then sits patiently on her lover's
lap while (after a tactless false-start anecdote involving one of his
previous sexual partners) Shiva spins out the Great Tale: approximately a year and a half of yarn spinning, by my calculation, but
what is time to the immortals? As happens, however — otherwise
there'd be no story — this recitation is overheard by a servant-
god, who repeats it to his wife, who innocently repeats it in turn
(all this would take three years, I reckon) to Pārvatī herself. The
goddess is so incensed at the narrative leak that she sentences the
eavesdropper to serve time on earth in mortal incognito, just as er-
rant Olympians were now and then obliged to do for their transgressions. One of the defendant's buddies receives the same sentence: the future poet Gunādhya, who has loyally if rashly pleaded
on his eavesdropping friend's behalf and is therefore punished as
an accessory after the fact. The particulars of their penance are
exceedingly complex and may be passed over here except for
Pārvatī's stipulation that before Gunādhya can return to heaven he
must hear the Great Tale on earth — not from his pal the eavesdropper, but from a certain hard-to-find hermit (also a demigod,
as it happens, doing time for an unrelated offense) whom the
eavesdropper must track down and relay it to, as he did to his
wife, before *he* can come home to heaven. When Gunādhya finally
hears the thing, moreover, he must *write it down.*

A great many chapters farther on in our maximal prologue, this
consequential transition from oral to written narrative is accomplished as follows: Duly reborn on earth, our man works his way
up the Indian career ladder to a ministry in King Sātavāhana's
court. There, in consequence of a wager as reckless though well-

---

*See "The Ocean of Story," in *The Friday Book.*

meaning as the gaffe that got him earthbound in the first place (it has to do with giving the king lessons in Sanskrit grammar), he is not only banished to the woods with no company besides a couple of his students, but obliged to renounce every language he knows. In this arboreal silence, mirabile dictu, he eventually crosses paths with the Tale-bearing hermit he has been vainly looking for throughout his mortal life, and who is himself more than ready to unload his narrative burden and get back to heaven. But wait: How is Gunādhya to transcribe (and versify) it, when by the terms of his penance-within-a-penance he has no language to write it in nor, as it happens, ink to write it with?

Both problems are solved the hard way, and their solutions make Gunādhya the archetype of many a subsequent author. As to tongue: Like Samuel Beckett, Vladimir Nabokov, Joseph Brodsky, and other writers exiled either by choice or by decree, Gunādhya adopts a new language to replace the ones forsworn; in this case, "goblin language" (Paiśācha), taught him by the hermit-god, who then duly recites the Great Tale in it and takes off for heaven, his own penance done. It remains for Gunādhya to turn oral goblin-prose into written goblin-distichs. This little chore, not surprisingly, requires seven more wooded years; the thing takes a year and a half just to *recite*, after all, and how many rhymes can there be for "goblin"?

As to his medium, what many a maxi-novelist may be said to do figuratively in his/her aspiration to heaven, Gunādhya does literally: Every line of the versified Great Tale is inscribed in the poet's own blood (where the paper comes from, we are not told). His faithful students stand by — growing older, I suspect, in more ways than one — and when the final couplet clots, they dash off to King Satavahana with the enormous finished manuscript, confident of their mentor's vindication.

It would be pleasant to end this Story of the Story just there, with the neglected writer's belated, William Kennedy–like success. The *Kathāpītha*, however, has two more exemplary lessons to teach us — and Gunādhya's students. The first has to do with the capriciousness of literary fortune: The magnum opus delivered, its royal critic takes one look at it and reacts like an unprepared reader first encountering *Finnegans Wake*. "Away with this barbarous Paiśācha tale!" he says in effect (doubtless proud of the Sanskrit grammar he has learned without Guṇāḍhya's help): Get out of here with this goblin-babble! More than one vast work, we reflect, meant to awe and redeem with its monumentality but perhaps overlong in its gestation and ambitious beyond its author's powers, has met with comparable rejection, or at least indifference, when finally it appeared.

Back to the woods the disciples go with the panned masterwork, whose "author" (too modest to have delivered it in person? too proud? or simply bled weak?) is so cast down by its rejection that he ends up reading the thing aloud to the only audience left him: himself, presumably his students, and . . . all the animals of the forest. Unfettered by linguistic prejudice, these last stand transfixed day after day and month after month after month, weeping not only at the beauty of Guṇāḍhya's goblin-verse epic but at the spectacle of the poet's burning each page of his manuscript after he reads it, like Puccini's Rodolfo in *La Bohème*.

The situation, we note, has come symbolically almost full circle. Pārvatī had asked for a novel story that would never be repeated, and inasmuch as only the gods can commit such megaworks to memory, it looks as though Shiva's Great Tale is fated never to be retold on earth. But *The Ocean of Story*'s Story of the Story has a splendid final twist, and moral. As I can testify from more than one perpetration, maxi-novels take maxi-time in every stage of their production: planning, composition, revision, copyediting, printing, even lead time for reviewers. Likewise, obviously, for their consumption, by the reader and/or by fire (did the Muslim book-burners who lately incinerated Salman Rushdie's *Satanic Verses* use a few mini-novels for tinder?). As the months go by and liter after liter of Guṇāḍhya's bloodscript goes up in smoke, the critic-king Sātavāhana falls mysteriously ill. His physicians determine that the wild game provided by his royal huntsmen has lost its nutritive value, and that this circumstance in turn is owing to the animals' being so enthralled by a certain strange bard-in-the-bush that, rapt in another sort of rumination, they have forgotten to eat. It is not explained why the rest of the royal household has been spared the king's malnutrition: poetic justice, perhaps, which at least in this instance means also justice for a poet. Sātavāhana himself leads a search-and-retrieve party into the woods, recognizes his ex-minister, and takes into his own famished hands the remaining manuscript pages. He restores Gunādhya to full favor (but the poet, vindicated, elects to return to heaven rather than to civil service), rewards the faithful students, and, to complete his own penance for literary-critical rashness, not only publishes what little is left of the versified Great Tale but prefaces it with the story here retold: the story of the story from which *The Ocean of Story* is condensed.

And just how long a story was Gunādhya's version of Shiva's tale, whereof Sātavāhana's 100,000-couplet remnant was but the final seventh, and Somadeva's ten-folio-volume abridgment little more than 3 percent? No fewer than 700,000 distichs, says the *Kathāpītha*: by our previous maximal arithmetic, 630 Penzerized quarto volumes. Instead of "Dr. Eliot's Five-Foot Shelf" (the 51-volume, 418-classic *Harvard Classics*, which I confess to having at least leafed through *in numerical order*, Indexicon and all, like the serial installments of a maxi-novel, one undergraduate summer while working as a night-shift timekeeper in a Baltimore Chevrolet factory*), imagine Dr. Gunādhya's 62-Foot Shelf. Or, by Penzer's own, more conservative equivalence, imagine an *Odyssey* 127 times the length of Homer's: a readerly odyssey indeed, which, if perused at the leisurely rate of one Homersworth per month, would take as long to reach the end of as it took Odysseus to get home from Troy. Although Somadeva's *Kathā Sarit Sāgara*, when we finally get past its remarkable prologue, turns out to be in fact not one great tale after all, but rather a compendium of earlier Sanskrit story-collections, in Gunādhya's third-century macroversion it must have been the longest literary work ever written.

Did it actually exist? I prefer to think not. I like to imagine that Mr. Soma made the whole thing up to entertain his patron, the queen of Kashmir; that he invented Shiva's love-gift to Pārvatī (the queen would have appreciated so magnificent a gesture), dreamed up the eavesdropping, the poet-minister Gunādhya, the elaborate penance, the masterwork written in poet's-blood, and — to disarm his own potential royal critic — the consequences of King

*See "Ad Lib Libraries and the Coastline Measurement Problem," farther on in this volume.

Sātavāhana's ungenerous response. Thus regarded, Somadeva is working a more or less Platonic literary theme known to Hebrew tradition as "the mother of the book": the tradition that our present Pentateuch, for example, with its occasional obscurities and apparent discrepancies, is the fallen remnant of a once-perfect Septateuch, one of whose books has disappeared altogether and another shrunk to but a pair of verses (10:35, 36) in the book of Numbers. This is among other things the Cabalists' way of accounting for, the artist's of excusing, possible imperfections in the text in hand. And its spirit is the very antithesis of Mme de Staël's wonderful apology for logorrhea (which must never be invoked by maxi-novelists): "Forgive me this too long letter; I had not time to write a short."

Considered from yet another angle, however, even Gunādhya's original transcription of Shiva's complete Great Tale may not be the longest "novel" in the world. In Nabokov's posthumously published *Lectures on Literature*, after speaking of major versus minor writers, the author distinguishes between major and minor readers ("All great reading," he remarks by the way, "is rereading" — a chastening proposition for the reader who has successfully swum the whole *Ocean of Story*). It is perhaps such major readers, at any rate those with a major appetite for fiction, who may incline to regard any one storyteller's complete works, however disparate — even the South African Kathleen Lindsay's Guinness-record-holding 904 published novels, composed under several noms de plume — as a single superfiction: a supernovel, I imagine, given that genre's notorious elasticity, multiformity, and powers of accommodation. Nabokov's minimalist contemporary Borges speculates that all the literal steps a person takes in his/her lifetime may trace out a figure as readily apprehensible to the mind of God as is a triangle to our human minds; in that spirit, may we not imagine all the written sentences that any of us reads in a lifetime, from "See Dick run" to "Rest in peace," as adding up to one maxi-novel? A work short on unity and architecture, it may be, but, if we're lucky, long on incident and invention, playfulness and passion, levity and gravity, ups and downs and energy and variety and beauty: quite like (may it be maximal) the story of our life?

I believe we may. In any case, I invite this speculation (and invoke the Mother of *The Ocean of Story*) in order to put in more favorable perspective that grand old animal, lately an endangered species, the Big Read: the kind of novel to which we bring, or in which we learn, a different way of reading, a different sense of attention and mode of economy. *Don't skip*, I earlier enjoined; but there are meganovels that may be approached, and especially revisited by major readers, like a large foreign country: from any of many entry-points; for a preliminary reconnaissance or a follow-up review, a walking or flying tour; for a week's vacation or a semester's study or an extended-visa sojourn or a permanent residency. "I expect nothing of my readers, except . . ." etc. No Joyce, I myself have been gratified enough to hear from readers of my own larger novels, "I read it in traction," ". . . in Viet Nam," ". . . snowbound in Fairbanks," ". . . in jail."

But at this advanced hour of the printed word, this heyday of the TV newspaper and the sound bite, is not *quixotic* the gentlest adjective for the novelist who attempts so maximal a project as the Big Read?

Just so. Commonly called the first modern novel, *Don Quixote* is in several respects the first postmodern one as well: in its incremental awareness of itself as fiction, in its impassioned and transcendent parody of the genre it ends up glorifying, and not least in its half-ironic amplitude ("My master can go on like this to the end of the chapter," Sancho Panza remarks of Quixote's effusions). As we end our century and our millenium, we may well have come to wish an end to endgames as well; to the modern, and particularly the Modernist, apocalypticism intimately bound up with minimalist aesthetics. To the postmodern spirit, less and less does less seem more. Those who used to worry about "the death of the novel" are more likely nowadays to be worrying about the death of the reader, the death of the planet; and although the nuclear arsenal is still much with us, thermonuclear holocaust appears a less likely nemesis now than resource depletion and pollution of the biosphere: good arguments for another sort of minimalism than the aesthetic kind.

*   *   *

Wait long enough, in short, for the end of art or of the world, and you may be inspired to build a half-ironic monument to mark if not redeem your prolonged attendance. In that monumental labor, moreover, you may well find your irony fired after all with a profound though post-innocent passion; so much so that should Godot in fact arrive, anticlimactically, you would shrug your shoulders and go on with what you're now much more committed to than waiting. Among the opportunities of Postmodernism, for the novelist, is the quixotic revivification — with the right irony to leaven its pathos and the right passion to vitalize the irony — of that noble category of literature: the exhaustive but inexhaustible, exhilarating novel; the long long story that, like life at its best, we wish might never end, yet treasure the more because we know it must.

But not in a hurry.

It's a Short Story

The First International Conference on the Short Story was held in Paris in 1990. The Second, in sharp but not inappropriate contrast, convened two years later in Iowa, home of America's oldest and best-known creative-writing program. The following confession is adapted from my address at the University of Iowa to that second gathering. It was subsequently published in the Spring 1993 number of Mississippi Review, *an issue dedicated to the subject of the short story in general and the contemporary American short story in particular — the efflorescence whereof in recent decades can be attributed to the proliferation in our republic of writing programs modeled on the Iowa example.* *

MY HIGH REGARD for the short story — the literary genre codified by Edgar Poe and purified by the likes of Maupassant and Chekhov — is long-standing and ongoing, but our actual love affair was brief. An early-middlescent fling is all it was, really, in the tumultuous 1960s, when the form was a-hundred-and-thirtysomething and pretty well domesticated, but I was thirty-plus and restless. An unprecedented (and unsuccedented) infidelity, it was, to my true love and helpmeet, the novel — whereto my steadfast commitment had produced four robust offspring already by the time I tell of, and has produced another four since, and bids to produce at least one more yet.† For a

---

*See, e.g., my remarks on this subject in the preceding Friday-pieces "Can It Be Taught?" and "A Few Words About Minimalism."
†This it has duly done, in the interval since delivery of this address. Furthermore, muse willing, *Once Upon a Time* (1994) may not be its author's last novelistic words.

season, however (a maxi-novelist's season: about six years), I strayed. It was a sweet and productive *liaison dangereuse*, the fruits of which were one volume of short stories in 1968 and a trio of novellas in 1972: resonant dates (the first especially) in our nation's political-cultural history, with a special poignancy in my personal scriptorial history.

One notes in what terms I recollect that interlude, no doubt pumping up the recollection a bit in its retelling. That is because I am by temperament monogamous; it was a relief to put that memorable aberration behind me and come back to husbanding the genre of the novel. And I have gone straight ever since — twenty years clean now! Though I still remember . . .

Well: It *is* a short story, even though it commences with a digression. I shall retell it discreetly, as such stories should be told. I'll even drop the sexual metaphor: *Auf Wiedersehen*, sexual metaphor.

The story goes, no doubt apocryphally, that in 1872, just after *War and Peace* had been published, Count Leo Tolstoy woke from a nightmare crying "A yacht race! A yacht race!" (in Russian, it goes something like *"Párusnaya regátta!"*), dismayed that he had neglected to include that item in his vast novel: his only omission from the whole panorama of nineteenth-century human activity.*

Whatever the truth of the story, it certainly sounds to me like the bad dream of a novelist, not a short-story writer. That the genre of the novel tends toward inclusion, that of the short story toward exclusion, goes without saying, once one has allowed for plenty of exceptional instances on both sides — minimalist novels, maximalist not-so-short stories. Those exceptions granted, we may safely generalize that short-story writers as a class, from Poe to Paley, incline to see how much they can leave out, and novelists as a class, from Petronius to Pynchon, how much they can leave in. Many a fictionist of the last century and this has moved with apparent ease between the modes, not only at some point in her or

---

*For that reason, I made certain to incorporate in one of my own novels both a yacht race and this Tolstoy anecdote, so that when unfriendly critics charge me with insufficient social realism, I can reply that I have touched bases overlooked even by Tolstoy.

his career, but right through it: Joyce Carol Oates, John Updike, who have you. Plenty more work the short form abundantly in the earlier part of their careers and then, for one reason or another, practice it seldom or never thereafter: James Joyce, Ernest Hemingway, William Faulkner, Kurt Vonnegut — the list is long. Do we know of any writers, I wonder, who abandoned the novel form in mid or late career and devoted their literary energies exclusively thereafter to the short story?

In any case, more populous than any of those three categories are the categories (*a*) of congenital short-story writers who seldom, perhaps never, publish a novel (Chekhov, Borges, Alice Munro, Raymond Carver) and (*b*) of congenital novelists who never or seldom publish a short story (Ralph Ellison, William Styron, most of the big Victorians, not to mention Richardson, Fielding, Smollett, Jane Austen, and the other pre-Poe novelists — this category is the most populous of all). It seems reasonable to infer that despite numerous exceptions, by and large there is a temperamental, even a metabolical, difference between devout practitioners of the two modes, as between sprinters and marathoners. To such dispositions as Poe's, Maupassant's, Chekhov's, or Donald Barthelme's, the prospect of addressing a single, discrete narrative project for three, four, five years (perhaps seventeen or twenty-two), would be appalling — *atrocious*, I imagine, would have been Borges's adjective — not to mention aesthetically unseemly, perhaps presumptuous, at this advanced hour of the print medium. Such novels as such writers perpetrate, if any — I think of Barthelme's four, of Maupassant's four also, I believe — are slender, economical: They are the hors d'oeuvres or side dishes, paradoxically, to the chef d'oeuvre of their short stories. Knowing that Donald's novels did not come to him as naturally as his short stories, I once very tentatively asked him, in the period of his wrestling with *The Dead Father*, how that project was coming along. "Oh, it's finished," he replied. "Now all I have to do is *write* the damn thing."

Conversely, to many of us the prospect of inventing every few weeks a whole new ground-conceit, situation, cast of characters, plot, perhaps even voice, is as dismaying as would be the prospect of improvising at that same interval a whole new identity. Indeed, for some of us that analogy is so rigorous as to be more an identity itself than an analogy. Like hermit crabs (up to a point), we comfortably *live* in the shell of our project-in-progress, and do not shed it until we must, and feel naked and uncomfortable until we've found another to inhabit. Once every few years is quite often enough for that.

I say "we," because except for the six-year lapse aforecited I am willy-nilly of the camp of the congenital novelists. This circumstance is nowise an aesthetic principle (congenitality doesn't operate by aesthetic principle; it cobbles up a suitable aesthetics ex post facto); it's a metabolical donnée. I didn't plan or presuppose it; congenitality doesn't make such plans and presuppositions. Like everybody else in post–World War II America, I started out writing short stories in an entry-level creative-writing workshop. More particularly, I happened to stumble into virtual charter membership in the second oldest creative-writing program in our republic, although not the second oldest creative-writing *course*. This was 1947; the Johns Hopkins program had been established just the year before, and the only other such operation in existence then (so we at Hopkins believe, anyhow) was Paul Engle's out in Iowa, already by that time of some dozen years' standing. Up at Harvard, Albert Guerard was coaching the likes of John Hawkes and Robert Creeley, but his was an isolated workshop, not a degree-granting program — of which we now have, god help us, above four hundred in the USA.

The poetry workshops at Johns Hopkins in those maiden years were respectably professional, presided over by Elliott Coleman and Karl Shapiro (who had just won a Pulitzer Prize for *V-Letter and Other Poems*), with the distinguished Spanish poet Pedro Salinas standing by in a neighboring department. But the fiction operation was unavoidably makeshift; one would have had to look far to find a career fiction-writer of any stature employed by an American university in the 1940s.*

I myself had signed up as a journalism major, an even more makeshift curriculum — although it doesn't seem to have dam-

---

*Robert Penn Warren is about the only name that comes to mind — and Warren was one-third poet and one-third critic.

aged Russell Baker, who was one year ahead of me. Our journalis-
tic requirements, interestingly, included the entry-level fiction
writing course, and so it came to pass that my first creative-writing
coach was a veteran Marine Corps combat officer and fledgling literary scholar pressed into service by our shorthanded department
while he finished his dissertation on Edgar Poe. The departmental
reasoning must have been that inasmuch as Poe first defined the
modern short story, a Poe scholar could run the workshop.

I have written of this chap elsewhere:* a gentle Southerner who
encouraged us raw recruits to call him Bob; whose deep-Dixie accent charmed *writing* into *rotting*; who urged upon our attention
such exemplary rotters as William Faulkner, Eudora Welty, and
R. P. Warren (one discerns Bob's principle of selection); who, because he had no creative-rotting aspirations himself, was oddly respectful, even a touch deferential, to those of us who callowly so
presumed. Bob's seminar — we seem not to call them *workshops*
at Johns Hopkins — was a whole academic year long and could be
repeated for credit, as the department had not many course offerings in those days. His gentle requirement of apprentice aspirants
to the craft of rotting fiction was a story every two weeks — and
these, mind you, were the bygone days of honest fifteen-week semesters, before the campus riots of the 1960s frightened administrators into shortening the U.S. college semester to thirteen weeks,
a whole storysworth of time (*two* storiesworth per academic year;
four storiesworth over two years). So: Fifteen weeks times two
times two divided by two gives thirty stories minimum that I must
have written for Bob in my first two years' apprenticeship. Nowadays the number would be a piddling twenty-six, if any workshop in the land still requires a story every fortnight, no excuses or
late papers accepted. Bob was gentle; Bob was respectful and soft-
spoken; but Bob was a veteran Marine combat officer, whose
deadlines one tended not to diddle with.

It is well for me that all this was the case, for I had been ill-
educated in general, had next to no familiarity with the vast corpus of literature and no prior experience of or interest in the art of

*In "The Limits of Imagination" in this collection; also in "Some Reasons Why I
Tell the Stories I Tell . . ." in *The Friday Book*, and in the novel/memoir *Once
Upon a Time: A Floating Opera*.

writing fiction. I was a disappointed musician, a Juilliard dropout scrabbling around for some other vocation, and I had squandered my high-school reading budget mainly on the likes of Ellery Queen and Agatha Christie in mass-market paperbacks, which had just been invented.* What I turned out for Bob and my fellow novices in those two years was unrelievedly abysmal in every particular except grammar, spelling, and punctuation, at all of which I was reasonably competent. Those manuscripts were letter-graded: Mine scored C's, mainly; the odd D, the occasional B, for two full years, and this from the most considerate of coaches — who, however, had his standards. It was rotten rotting, altogether talentless twaddle, for although I was in that same period taking unto myself a freight of literature — not just the canonical classics plus Bob's Southerners plus the monumental European and expatriate American High Modernists, Pound/Eliot/Joyce/Proust/Mann/Kafka (whom the literature departments back then wouldn't touch, but our maverick writing department did), but also, and extracurricularly, the likes of Rabelais and Boccaccio and Scheherazade and Somadeva — although, as I say, I was onloading the literary corpus in straight shifts, it was going unsystematically into an all-but-empty cargo hold, and so it took some stevedoring indeed before the vessel ballasted into even rudimentary stability.

But that is not what this present story means to be about. I don't want, either, to give the impression that *literature* is the main thing one needs to learn about if one aspires to write it, although I certainly do believe it to be *one* of the main things. I can't help wondering, though, how it would have gone with my apprenticeship if semesters in those days had been of their present abbreviation, for it was not until story number thirty — more particularly, it was not until the *closing passage* of that final item of my two-year stretch of random Bobbing on the ocean of story — that I had what amounted, by my then standards, to a "breakthrough." Number Thirty itself was little better than its twenty-nine predecessors: a presumptuous bit of bogus realism about the postwar adjustment problems of . . . *a Marine combat veteran*, of all

---

*See "Ad Lib Libraries and the Coastline Measurement Problem," elsewhere in this volume.

imaginable human categories — the whole thing largely derivative from Hemingway's "Soldier's Home" without Hemingway's authentic knowledge of his material, not to mention Hemingway's literary skills. But the story's denouement contrived to soar from wretchedness up to mediocrity with a most un-Hemingwayish purple stream-of-consciousness passage that, while also bogus, derivative, and overwritten to boot, was nonetheless not without a certain rhetorical force. It was duly praised therefor by Bob and my fellow seminarians, and published in an ephemeral undergraduate lit mag — tautological adjectives, I suppose.

It took no more than that to persuade me of my vocation, although by no means yet of my talent for that vocation. Still a junior undergraduate, two years shy of voting age, I immediately married the woman I was living with and commenced churning out children and fiction with equal facility and no thought for the morrow. "The Fifties," John Updike somewhere says with a sigh, "when everybody was pregnant." The babies survived and thrived; the short stories (for that is what I was writing: stories, stories, stories) suffered a 100 percent infant mortality rate. Their constituent prose sentences, it may be, slowly improved in grace and efficiency; the case could scarcely be otherwise, given the number of them that I was generating and the stacks of good literature — literal library stacks of it — that I was unsystematically running through. But my plots were gimmicky and my characterizations inauthentic; my psychological penetration was barely subcutaneous and my texture of rendered sensory detail unimpressive. Moreover, like many another American undergraduate writing apprentice, I had not anything to say nor, had I had, any Weltanschauung to afford me a handle on it. (Which of those two is logically prior doesn't matter here; to paraphrase Beckett, having neither chicken nor egg, I had neither egg nor chicken.) What I did have were an all but reality-proof sense of calling, an unstoppable narrativity, and, I believe, a not-bad ear for English. I have coached many an apprentice since who manifested something like that mix of strengths and shortcomings, and relatively few of the opposite sort: young aspiring writers with a strong sense of who they are and what their material and their handle on it is, but little sense of either story or language. I regard that latter case as by far the less promising, although I would be reluctant to tell the patient so. Experience may confer narrative focus and authority, perhaps even a worldview; but essential imaginativeness and articulateness, not to say eloquence, are surely much more of a gift.

My other problem — as I came to understand in retrospect but could not then, nor could any just routinely knowledgeable coach have told me — was the *form* that we all were working, and that nearly every fiction-workshopper cuts his/her teeth on, with good pedagogical reason: I mean the form of the modern, post-Poe short story. Its aesthetics were simply not my cup of tea, but in those days (and in many more fiction workshops than not to *this* day) it was the only aesthetic on the menu. *Compression*, it turns out, was not my strong suit. *Showing instead of telling* was not my strong suit; neither were implicativeness, singleness of effect, epiphanic peripety, psychological realism, or for that matter realism in general. But those suits were regarded almost unquestioningly as the indispensable, indeed the only ones for a properly modern writer, which I certainly aspired to be. It would have taken an extraordinarily large-viewed coach in the American academic 1940s to have seen that a subtle and inhibitory conflation was operating there, of the terms *modern* and *Modernist*. What a few of us really needed to do (I see now but could scarcely have seen then) was to invent or be invented by Postmodernism, as I understand that term in its best literary-aesthetic application — but that's another story, to which I'll presently return.*

Meanwhile, back in the seminar room, there one was, fretting away at that artistically splendid and pedagogically effective but, for some of us, hyperconstrictive, more or less constipative form, the modern short story. Surely it's a truism by now that the admirable efflorescence of the American short story in recent decades is owing to the proliferation of our college creative-writing programs: not simply the raw number of young writers being spawned therein like blue-crab larvae in Chesapeake Bay (and confronting a similar statistical fate), but the prevailing pedagogical assumption, anyhow belief, that the most suitable vehicle for

---

*And about which I have my full say in the Friday-pieces "Postmodernism Revisited" and "$4\frac{1}{2}$ Lectures," to follow.

their training is the "classical" modern short story as afore-described.

Understand, please, that I have no serious quarrel with that prevailing belief; indeed, I rather share it. Novels, to name one alternative vehicle, are more cumbersome and time-intensive to deal with in fiction workshops — more cumbersome to write in timely installments, more cumbersome to revise, to reproduce, to read, to critique, to respond to useful criticism of. The academic year runs out before the dramaturgical bills have been paid; or a whole season of apprenticeship gets invested in what at best is likely to be a single narrative conceit, voice, point of view, cast of characters, and plot, and what at worst may prove to have been a large mistake, without coaching-time left to try something else. A conventional short story, on the other hand, we can hold in the mind's eye of the seminar; in the allotted hour or so we can attend with some critical efficiency both to representative details and to overall matters of pace and plot and narrative viewpoint. What's more, as the season wears on we can come to know the author's *characteristic* strengths and weaknesses and idiosyncrasies of imagination, and can assess a new effort in the light of its predecessors, a sort of mini-*oeuvre*. These are undeniable pedagogical assets. The associated aesthetic values, too — compression, implicativeness, rendition as against mere assertion, precise observation, subtlety of effect — are undeniable literary values (though not the only ones); undeniable especially for apprentices, most of whom will not in fact turn out to be working fiction-writers, but a fair fraction of whom will turn out to be teachers, editors, writers of other sorts of documents, and — the chief and worthy product of those four hundred–plus U.S. creative-writing programs — *readers*, more sensitive and knowledgeable in the art of reading literature than they would likely be if they hadn't practiced writing it.

I assert again, however, that those literary values are not the only ones. In the very best workshops (and by definition there can never be a great many of those), the pedagogical virtues of the conventional modern short story will not be conflated with its aesthetic values, and its aesthetic values will not be assumed to hold for all times, places, temperaments, and talents. There is a narrative metabolism, equally honorable and with at least as long a

pedigree, that valorizes expansiveness, even extravagance, complication, non-linearity, even telling instead of showing (telling, after
all, is one of the things that language can do better than a camera),
and perhaps fabulation or some other admixture of irrealism over
unadulterated realism. Such a narrative metabolism may find the
now-classical short-story form claustrophobic: Rabelais and Laurence Sterne oughtn't to have to walk in Maupassant's moccasins,
or Scheherazade in Chekhov's, and vice versa.

When I first set about, at age twenty, to write a novel, I approached the prospect with all due trepidation. It seemed a presumptuous undertaking, as indeed it was, in a number of ways.
True, Thomas Mann had been only twenty when he wrote *Bud-
denbrooks* — but Mann at twenty was forty already, and what's
more, he was Thomas Mann. I went ahead and perpetrated my
maiden novel, and it was an unpublishable travesty — turgid tidewater ersatz Faulkner, without Faulkner's moral-historical vision
and deep acquaintance with his subject — but I felt immediately at
home in the form, as if my hands and feet had been unshackled.
"The novel, the novel!" I exulted to myself at the time: "Room to
swing a cat in!" "The novel, the novel," I exulted in some novel
many novels later,* "with its great galumphing grace, amazing as
a whale!" I doubted that I would ever go back to the short story.
    And by puristic standards, I never quite did. My very next ap-
prentice project (the last, in fact, of my apprenticeship) involved
short fictions again, but with at least two differences from my earlier Bob-Bob-Bobbing that it pleases me to find significant in retrospect. Having imbibed Boccaccio and Scheherazade and company
along with the big Modernists, what I projected was a cycle of one
hundred tales about my native tidewater county — my salt-marsh
Yoknapatawpha — at all periods of its history, but not in chronological order. In other words, the thing was to be a *book*, a narrative whole like the *Decameron*, larger than the sum of its parts,
not every one of which would need to be free-standing; and those
parts, many of them anyhow, would be in the nature of *tales* or
even anecdotes, not post-Poe short stories. They would *tell*, here

LETTERS, first published by Putnam in 1979.

and there, instead of showing: *He was a jealous and miserly old oysterman; she was a wanton young crab-picker* — whatever. They would ramble and digress; they would deploy narrative effects from the eighteenth and earlier centuries, tongue half in cheek and one foot always in the here and now.

This project, too, was a failure (I aborted it round about tale fifty), but it proved a valuable learning experience, as they say, and in the event I was able to recycle a number of those *Dorchester Tales* into *The Sot-Weed Factor*, three novels later. What I had in place, although I didn't know it yet (this was the front end of the 1950s), were some of the field-identification marks that I now associate with Postmodernist art, at least by my definition: notably, the ironized recycling of premodern forms and devices for modern readers with uppercase Modernism under their belts.

There is, of course, more to the making of fiction than a geographical predilection and the deployment of forms and devices, ironized or otherwise. There is, e.g., the little matter of what one aspires to narrate by means of those predilections and forms and devices. Once the material, the craftsmanly means, and the aesthetic objective have somehow reciprocally clarified one another and jiggered themselves into synergy, with luck a career of "professional" literary production may ensue. In my fortunate case, once I had discovered by trial, error, and serendipity my narrative space and pace, I was not of a mind to do other than vigorously continue exploring it for a couple thousand pagesworth of novels over the next dozen years: short novels, midsize novels, long novels, but novels all. Now that I was not committed to and therefore not straitjacketed by the short story, I was free to admire it uncovetously and its masters unenviously. This I did, and taught their works with respectful pleasure to my literature students and the form with profit to my fiction-writing coachees — until the High 1960s, when three or four factors together led me to give short-storyhood another go.

I happened through the latter Sixties to be living and working in Buffalo, New York, and while many young Americans were crossing the Niagara River from that city into Canada for sanctuary from our war in Vietnam (as Americans had done in numerous of our other wars, long before there was a Peace Bridge to facilitate the crossing), there came back across that bridge, from nearby Toronto, the siren song of Marshall McLuhan advising us "print-oriented bastards" that our Gutenberg Galaxy was not only not the whole universe, but a galaxy perhaps petering out in the electronic global village. Self-bound to the medium of the book like Odysseus to the mast of his vessel, I attended this song with the same constrained fascination that I lately bring to Robert Coover's and George P. Landow's serenades to the medium of hypertext:* About Hypertexties in the Nineties, as about Death-of-the-Bookies in the Sixties, I think and thought, "Maybe they're right, maybe they're wrong, maybe some of each; but most important, maybe there's something here that a writer can make good use of."

I had, as it happened, just published my fourth novel, and the latter pair of those four were baggy monsters indeed: *The Sot-Weed Factor* and *Giles Goat-Boy*. The notion of re-attempting brevity, perhaps even terseness, was understandably seductive. Moreover, I had discovered and been duly wowed by the *ficciones* of Jorge Luis Borges, who certainly made maximalist novels seem *demasiado* at that hour of the world. Finally and less creditably (as I have acknowledged in the foreword to the current American edition of *Lost in the Funhouse*†), I had by the 1960s been teaching long enough to notice that we congenital novelists do not normally find ourselves included, for obvious reasons, in the standard short-story anthologies on which I had cut my own apprentice teeth and which I regularly assigned to the teething apprentices in my charge. (William Styron, for example, wasn't in those anthologies, either; he doesn't teach school, however, and so perhaps was less aware of his exclusion.) But there were Donald Barthelme and Flannery O'Connor and Grace Paley and John Updike and Eudora Welty, not to mention their illustrious predecessors back to Poe and Hawthorne. Along with the more creditable attractions of the

---

*See for example Landow's *Hypertext: The Convergence of Contemporary Critical Theory and Technology* (Baltimore and London: Johns Hopkins U. Press, 1992) and Coover's pioneering reports, "The End of Books" and "Hyperfiction: Novels for the Computer," in the *New York Times Book Review* of June 21, 1992, and August 29, 1993, respectively.
†Reprinted in "Four Forewords," later in this collection.

short form was admission to that distinguished club, which I unabashedly hankered after. Even today, I confess, when a new anthology comes across my desk, I look first to see how my stock is
doing. If I'm included, I check out my new, younger shipmates
with benign interest (aha, Graham Swift; aha, Jane Smiley; ahoy
there, Julian Barnes); but if the turkeys leave me out, I toss
the thing — unless, as has increasingly become the case, former
coachees of mine are represented there, supplanting their erstwhile
mentor. Pleasant pain.

Anyhow, for all these reasons I embraced at last the sharp-eyed,
relaxless muse of the short story, who, unlike good longwinded
Homer, *never* dozes off, even for a second. Just as wary Odysseus,
when romancing formidable Circe, covered his butt (let's say) with
a sprig of moly, so I put an anchor out to windward by writing a
short-story *series* — a book, a book, "for print, tape, and live
voice" — in order not to get lost in my own funhouse, excuse
the hybrid metaphor. I decided to pay my initiation fee by writing the shortest story in the whole corpus of literature, which
however would at the same time be literally endless and a paradigm for the book to boot: a ten-word Möbius-strip narrative
called "Frame-Tale" (*ONCE UPON A TIME THERE WAS A
STORY THAT BEGAN*, etc. ad inf.). Short on characters, short
on plot, short on social realism — but short is the name of the
game, no?

That done, I spent an invigorating couple of years fabricating
tales to be framed by that frame-tale, enjoying most the longest
and most intricate of them, for that is who I am, but attempting
here and there as bona fide an old-fashioned modern short story as
I could contrive for future anthologists, and where possible looking to see what other marks I might set in my private Guinness
Book of World Literary Records. Some years of casual homework
on frame-tale literature, for example, had revealed to me that
the maximum degree of narrative imbeddedness in the corpus of
such literature was about the fifth degree — a tale within a tale
within a tale within a tale within a tale — and that the relations
among such nested tales was generally at best thematic, seldom

functionally dramaturgical.* Purely *pour le sport*, therefore, I went for seven degrees (in a story called "Menelaiad"), and saw to it moreover that their concentric plots were rigged for sequential climax-triggering from the inmost out. I hasten to add, however, that Menelaus's story is about love, not about plot-mechanics, for I was in love (love, love, love, love, love, love) with the short story.

And after the short story, with the novella — that sweet, that delicious narrative space, so much neglected in our century. I do hope that there'll be an international conference someday on the novella and that I won't be too superannuated to attend, for there's another love story altogether. Meanwhile, two cheers minimum for the exhausting muse of the short story — exhausting anyhow to us congenital novelists, who are likely to leave her embraces in the condition of Peleus after Thetis's, or Anchises after Venus's.† I romanced the novella form for three or four years in the same sidelong and tracks-covering but truly heartfelt way as I had romanced the short-story form, pretending that my trinity of more or less linked novellas was really a unity — a book, a book, a book — and even allowing my publisher to market that book (*Chimera*) without any indication whatever on jacket or title page that it's not a novel. This was, after all, exactly twenty years ago, just before the wholesale resurgence of the American short story, when the conventional wisdom among New York trade publishers was that volumes of short fiction don't earn their keep. And the original Chimera, we remember, was neither a menagerie nor a congeries nor a colonial organism, but a tripartite, fire-breathing, single-spirited entity, however genetically self-disparate and, well, chimerical.

Then on Yom Kippur 1973, as you may have noticed, the American Sixties ended. Overnight, women's skirts got longer and men's sideburns shorter; the national economy simultaneously recessed and inflated, and in the general reaction against the 1960s, Ameri-

---

*For more on frame-tales, see "Tales Within Tales Within Tales" in *The Friday Book*.
†One notices, however, that those old studs aren't complaining in their wheelchairs — and that the issue of their life-altering one-nighters was Achilles, was Aeneas.

can fiction swung back to its prevailing aesthetic conservatism and
for better or worse has pretty much dwelt there to this hour; nor
does it show much sign that I can see of venturing therefrom. At
this state of affairs, I shrug my shoulders: Traditionalist excellence
is no doubt preferable to innovative mediocrity (but there's not
much to be said for conservative mediocrity, and there's a great
deal to be said for inspired innovation). This particular congenital
novelist went contentedly — nay, happily — back to congenital
novelizing; I even made a working rapprochement with social/psy-
chological realism, though not enough of one, evidently, to mollify
certain critics.

Ah well, *mes amis, je ne regrette rien*, certainly not my invigorating liaisons with those slender, demanding forms, the short
story and the novella. Single-shot dalliances, in their way, but each
a novelist's single shot, of several years' concentrated, undivided
commitment: quality time. I remain profoundly, satisfyingly wedded to the space of the novel, most particularly the longish-haul
novel. Every four years or so, however, when a new one slides
down the ways to whatever post-launch fate awaits it, I confess to
resolving that I will have one more go, this many decades later and
this late in the afternoon, at the perennially beautiful possibilities
of the short story. At this hour of our cultural history, I ask myself,
who needs another large novel — not to say, more particularly, another hefty *Barthbuch*? In no time at all I accumulate project-notes
toward that end — notes not for a story, never for a story, but for
a *book* of stories, a book, a book. Next thing I know, the frame
has subsumed the picture, the book its constituent stories, and
what I'm writing is no longer a book of stories but another book-
length story. That mode remains as fitted to my spirit as Homer
says Penelope was to Odysseus's, and vice versa. To that question
aforeproposed — Who needs another et cetera? — I sigh and reply, "*I* do."

Or rather (as bridegroom says to bride), "I *do*."

It Goes Without Saying

Logically prior to questions of length and scale in fiction are the fun-
damental ones asked in the opening paragraph below. I put them
to myself privately every time I begin a new novel, and to my
advanced-apprentice coachees every time a new clutch of them first
assembles. For a season I asked them to myself publicly on the lec-
ture/reading circuit, and responded as follows: *

1.

What is fiction? What's a *story*? What accounts for the circumstance that people in every time and place appear to enjoy,
whether as individuals or as cultures, making up nonfactual stories and telling or writing or acting them out and hearing or reading or spectating them?

Such questions are so elementary that their answers would
seem to go without saying. But (1) when I was a young apprentice
fiction writer, newly certified as a Master of Arts but still a long
way from mastering my art, I decided by passionate default or
heartfelt lack of alternatives that I would pay the rent by university teaching, at least until my literary royalties showered down
upon me; and I resolved further to devote the academic side of my
life to saying over and over again, like mantras, all the things
about the art of fiction that go without saying, until the obvious
sheds its obviousness and becomes strange and new, the way your
signature does after you've inscribed it 1001 times in a row: an
interesting exercise in ontological defamiliarization. And (2) —

*First published together with the preceding Friday-piece, "It's a Short Story," in
Mississippi Review, Spring 1993.

perhaps in consequence of (1) — forty years and five thousand published pages later, after a career of full time writing and full-time teaching, I remain happily perplexed by a number of basic things about the nature of stories and storytelling — the more perplexed the more directly I confront them.

It goes without saying that it isn't *necessary* for a working artist to question continually the first principles of his or her art. Unremitting interrogation can lead to a disabling self-consciousness, like thinking too much about the nature of bow-knots while you're trying to get your shoelaces tied. Many skills are best exercised when they've been mastered to the point of subroutinization — what we call "second nature" — so that our best attention can be directed to strategy and tactics and priorities rather than to rudimentary operations on the one hand or cosmic overviews on the other. "Microscopes and telescopes," Goethe somewhere remarks, "distort the natural focus of our eyes." A fine tennis player in action has no time to think consciously of such intricate, "microscopic" subroutines as maintaining physical balance and keeping an eye on the ball; and the center court at Wimbledon is probably not the best place to raise such "telescopic" questions as What is the game of tennis really *about*? What does it *mean* for two highly developed bipeds to whack a little yellow ball back and forth over a net until one or the other of them fails to do so?

But sports and crafts and other such human skills are not the same as the fine arts, although they share such attributes as virtuosity. And in the Western tradition of the fine arts, at least since the Romantic period, the most notable accomplishments have often been those of artists who have *not* taken for granted the processes and history of their medium. All of that goes without saying, as does the corollary that an interrogative or skeptical spirit (not to mention an iconoclastic spirit) does not in itself produce notable artistic results. There has to be inspiration behind the interrogation — including, most importantly, a knack for not throwing out the baby with the bath water.

So: What is this stuff we call fiction? Cleanth Brooks and Robert Penn Warren's definition from the 1940s sounds inarguably commonsensical: "The fiction-writer [it goes without saying]

employs prose to tell a story presumed to be made up."* In
fact, every item of that definition, from the implied genus *writing*
through each of the four differentia, is problematical enough to
warrant at least a short lecture: the employment of prose (as opposed to verse, song, mime, dance, or visual images), the nature of
telling (as opposed to showing), the phenomenon of story, the crucial presumption of *fabrication*, which is to say (circularly) of
fictivity — all of these matters become more or less vertiginous, at
least debatable, when you lean on them. And I, for one, lean on
them all the time, both with my muse at the writing table and with
my graduate-student apprentices in the seminar room.

   To consider briefly just one item of that catalogue: the nature of
story. Fiction, it goes without saying, tells a story. As E. M. Forster
said in effect, that's its dirty little secret.† But what's a *story*, as opposed to the mere recounting of more or less related happenings? I
know as well as you do what the difference is, but I really can't explain it in any non-circularly definitive way. In fact, a sure feel for
the distinction between stories and not-quite-stories is typically
the last rudiment of the craft of fiction that gifted apprentice writers master. Such things are learned by osmosis and practice, by
monitored trial and error, more than by the study of cogent definitions. As David Hume said,‡ the principles of art are grounded in
experience, not in reason; the difficulty for apprentices, once they
begin to analyze the question consciously, is compounded by the
circumstance that many stories aren't fictional, and that some
great fiction cannot be said to comprise a story (about a third of
Franz Kafka and of Donald Barthelme, for example). Brooks and
Warren, with Aristotle standing behind them, tell us correctly that
a story is "a meaningful series of events in a time sequence." All
very well, but what do we mean by a *meaningful* series of events,
as that adjective applies to fiction-stories rather than to factual ac-

---

*Brooks, Purser, and Warren, *An Approach to Literature* (NY: Crofts, 1942);
bracketed language mine. More on this definition presently, in "Very Like an Elephant."

†What Forster said, "a little sadly," was "Yes — oh dear, yes — the novel tells a
story" (*Aspects of the Novel*, NY: Harcourt, Brace, 1927) — and it is the novel
that Forster has particularly in mind, but its dirty little secret is shared by the
novella and the short story, if not by such anomalous prose-fictive genres as the
prose poem.

‡In the essay "Of the Standard of Taste," in Hume's *Four Dissertations* (1757).

counts and anecdotes? It turns out that what we mean by mean-ingful is "dramatically meaningful" (more accurately, *dramaturgically* meaningful) — which is to say, meaningful in the way that a made-up story is meaningful, and around we go. Really, it's easier for a talented writer to *write* a story than to explain what a story is — which is exactly why I enjoy raising the question.

I won't even go into such more particular mysteries as what a *novel*, for example, is, except to point out that the poet Randall Jarrell's charming definition of the novel — "a prose fiction of a certain length that has something wrong with it" — has several things wrong with it. There are verse-novels and photonovels; there was once said to be such an animal as the nonfiction novel; and, mirabile dictu, some critics even go so far as to maintain of certain novels that they have nothing wrong with them (Flaubert's *Madame Bovary* is sometimes cited in this regard).

Let's shift the subject. I happen to be not optimistic about the future of literature in the electronic global village,* but the usurpation of the kingdom of narrative by the visual media, while I myself regard it as unfortunate, obviously hasn't diminished the human appetite for made-up stories; it has only changed the medium of their popularity, from the oral through the written to the visual. Why aren't people satisfied with the facts? (By which I mean factual reality, by which — it goes without saying — I *don't* mean either "truth" or aesthetic realism, neither of which is to be confused with factual reality.†

To tell the truth, I don't know *why* we crave anything beyond the facts, but over the decades I've entertained a number of speculations in that line. Before I mention a couple of them, it ought to be acknowledged that at least a few apparently healthy people *do* seem to be imaginatively satisfied by factual reality, to the point of having a positive distaste for most kinds of fiction. If they read, they would rather read nonfiction than novels and short stories; they don't enjoy movies and stage plays; when they watch television, they prefer documentaries and sports broadcasts and talk

---

*See this volume's concluding Friday-piece, "Inconclusion: The Novel in the Next Century."
†More on this distinction in "Very Like an Elephant."

shows to sitcoms and soap operas and other sorts of made-up drama. "Just give me the facts, ma'am," as *Dragnet*'s detective Joe Friday used to say in midst of that particular fiction. I confess to having gotten increasingly this way myself over the years — an occupational side effect, I believe, in the case of those of us for whom the experience of fiction can never be innocent entertainment. We're forever sizing it up, measuring ourselves against its author, watching to see how the effects are managed and whether all the dramaturgical pistols that were hung on the wall in act one get duly fired in act three. We're like those musicians who can't abide background music: They can't listen except professionally, and if they're not in the mood to do that, they prefer conversation, street noise, silence — anything but music.

Most normal people, however, have a healthy appetite for made-up stories, whether "realistic" or more or less fantastical, and whether on the printed page or the "satanic glass screen," as Mark Helprin calls television.* Why *is* that? Granting for the sake of argument Aristotle's observation in the *Poetics* that "history" deals with what was and "poetry" with what might have been, why are we fascinated with "what might have been" — by which let's understand, with Aristotle, "what might be plausibly imagined even though perhaps factually impossible"? It goes without saying that there are abundant explanations, more or less cogent and/or interesting, applicable in various combinations to various people experiencing various sorts of fiction. For my own bemusement I have a list of such explanations — Fiction's Functions, you might say — pinned to a corkboard over my worktable. That list keeps getting longer; it started out as one face of a three-by-five card, then spilled over onto the card's backside, and has now been recopied in such small printing that I can't read it from where I sit writing fiction. I suspect that that's just as well, since enumerating fiction's functions is like enumerating human copulatory positions: The catalogue is no doubt virtually endless, and anyhow quality is more important than taxonomy, passion than position. From both the manufacturer's and the consumer's point of view, there is fiction as *escape* (probably two dozen different kinds of escape; as

*In "The Canon Under Siege," his introduction to *Best American Short Stories of 1988* (NY: Ticknor & Fields, 1988).

many kinds of escape as there are kinds of things to be escaped from), fiction as *anti*-escape, fiction as propaganda (moral or political or what have you), fiction as scenario or thought-experiment or virtual-world modeling, fiction as exorcism ("our revenge upon our childhood," John Hawkes has said), fiction as reality-testing or reality-mapping, fiction as linguistic/aesthetic R&D, fiction as aphrodisiac, anaphrodisiac, analgesic, prophylaxis, soporific, fiction as prayer, confession, therapy, curse, or hymn of praise, fiction as ontological validation, as vicarious autodestruction, et cetera, et cetera, et cetera.

Needless to say, these categories of fiction's functions are not at all mutually exclusive. More than half of them might be subsumed under the attempt or desire to make sense out of our experience of life, and for at least some of the others I once upon a time cooked up a formulation that I still enjoy repeating, if only for the sound of it: *Of of what one can't make sense, one may make art.* I like the quasi-stammering hendecasyllable;* I like the mimetic syntax, the element of self-demonstrativity. Such formulations caress the ears of unreconstructed romantic formalists like yours truly.

If there were any space left on that overcrowded three-by-five card, I would add one jim-dandy high-tech fiction-function that I learned of only recently and quite accept. Daniel C. Dennett, a philosopher at Tufts University who knows both neuroscience and computer science, argues that consciousness itself has an essentially narrative aspect, grounded in the biological evolution of the brain. I am not competent to summarize Dennett's argument,† but I am immediately persuaded by his conclusions — at least as an explanatory fiction. He conceives of consciousness as essentially a "multi-draft scenario-spinner"; of the self as an *as if*, a "posited Center of Narrative Gravity" — in short, a magnificent on-spinning fiction. "We *are* the stories we tell ourselves and others about who we are," declares Professor Dennett — stories that we edit continually, and that continually edit us.

*That phrase, I note — "quasi-stammering hendecasyllable" — is itself a quasi-stammering hendecasyllable.
†See his *Consciousness Explained* (Boston: Little, Brown, 1991). Some distinguished neuroscientists, however — Jerome Edelman, for example — remain unconvinced. More on Dennett's theory of consciousness in the Friday-piece "Once Upon a Time: Storytelling Explained."

Now, I ask you: Did the pondering of questions like this ever make anybody a better writer? Wouldn't any fictionist be better advised to ponder the casuistries of love, the details of a sunset, even the vicissitudes of the starship *U.S.S. Enterprise*? Maybe so, maybe not. But in putting such questions, as in spinning out scenarios, we're doing what comes naturally — perhaps more naturally to some people than to others.

2.

Having acknowledged my uncertainty about what fiction is and what it's for, I turn now briefly to the burning questions of why I myself write it and, given that I do, why I incline, more often than not, to perpetrate relatively long and sometimes complex novels rather than short, straightforward, more user-friendly ones, quicker and less taxing to read and no doubt more profitable to write. If I don't know the answer to *these* questions, either, with any certainty, it is not for want of putting them to myself.

As to the first of them, I can say this much with some confidence: I write fiction because in the summer of 1947 I learned at the Juilliard School of Music in New York City that I hadn't enough talent to be the professional jazz player and orchestrator that I had aspired all through high school to become, and I subsequently learned at the Johns Hopkins University in Baltimore that I had a genuine vocation for writing fiction, whatever my degree of talent in that line. I had everything to learn; I worked hard and indiscourageably at learning it; I got to be pretty good at the *craft* after half a dozen years of heavy reading and constant practice; I found my real handle on the *art* at age twenty-three or -four; and I still enjoy practicing it every weekday morning forty years later — the way most people enjoy doing things that they do reasonably well with at least moderate success. In my case, the product is mainly novels instead of short stories for metabolical reasons, not for any lack of admiration for the short form.* And I write *my* novels instead of Stephen King's or James Michener's or Tom Clancy's novels because despite my considerable respect for the novel as commercial popular entertainment (even in the age of

*See "It's a Short Story."

television), my own ambitions have been unabashedly in the direction of capital-L Literature, the very best that I can coax my language and imagination to do. From the outset I have aspired un-
apologetically and no doubt quixotically to add to the corpus of
twentieth-century American fiction — to the corpus of *world*
fiction, if possible. If I could have it both ways, as Charles Dickens
and Mark Twain managed to, I would be delighted. But evidently
I'm not able to have it both ways, and given that inability, I would
rather be the author of my novels than of Mr. King's, Mr. Michener's, or Mr. Clancy's, much as I envy them their wide nonprofessional readership and their enormous royalty incomes.

On the other hand, I freely acknowledge that I would rather
have given the world the novels of Gabriel García Márquez, for
example, than my own. But I truly find this sort of thought-
experiment all but impossible as well as profitless. I'm stuck with
being me — a latter-twentieth-century straight male American
WASP romantic formalist with neither more nor less talent than I
have — and I not only accept that characterization but rather enjoy it, without for a minute turning it into a manifesto.

No manifesto, no agenda: That's as close as I come to having a
literary manifesto or a literary agenda. I have heard Kurt Vonnegut acknowledge that he's an old-fashioned utopian socialist
whose fiction is written from that perspective and toward that
end. I have heard Joyce Carol Oates acknowledge that she writes
in private hope of changing the world. I have heard the South
African novelist J. M. Coetzee declare that in his country there can
be no nonpolitical fiction, that for him to write a novel that makes
no political statement would be to make a loud and egregious political statement. I respect such positions as these (and I particularly sympathize with the last-mentioned of them), but for better
or worse I don't share them. Even the "romantic formalism" that I
mentioned earlier* is neither a manifesto nor an agenda; it's simply a description of something I notice about my fiction. As an

---

*By which I mean simply a preoccupation with fiction's architecture — espe-
cially, where possible, the investing of that architecture with emblematic
significance — but not an inclination to "classical" forms except as they may be
postmodernly renovated. See the Friday-pieces "Postmodernism Revisited" and
"$4\frac{1}{2}$ Lectures."

ethnic-majority American man of exactly the right age to have been spared all the wars thus far of this catastrophic century, I have enjoyed the tremendous privilege of being pretty much left alone by politics and history, and I have pretty much returned them that courtesy.

All of which is not to say that my novels aren't "about" anything beyond their own language and processes and architecture. They certainly *are* to some extent about themselves and about the phenomenon of storytelling, but various of them have also managed to be "about" such matters as the problematics of history, of love, and of personal identity; about the myth of the wandering hero as it applies to our lowercase lives; also the locale of tidewater Maryland, the several differences between art and life, and (on the other hand) the equatability of narration — of the transmission and reception of stories — with being humanly alive.

But that, if you happen to have read them, goes without saying.

Postmodernism Revisited

Follow-up to a follow-up, this essay is a reconsideration and qualified reaffirmation of a 1979 Friday-piece called "The Literature of Replenishment," itself a reassessment of my 1968 essay "The Literature of Exhaustion."* The subject of all three is what in the 1970s came to be called by the awkward but evidently indispensable name "Postmodernism" — a term by now in such common and various use as to have become all but meaningless, for a concept by now so exhaustively analyzed by critics so numerous and sophisticated that it takes some chutzpah for a mere working artist to have a go at its definition. On the other hand, if one finds oneself pigeonholed, one may understandably feel the urge to comment on pigeonholes in general and one's particular PH especially. For the cross-my-heart last follow-up to this follow-up follow-up, see the Friday-piece "Postmodernism Visited" in "4½ Lectures," farther on in this volume.

1. The Tragic View of Categories

Perhaps because I'm a novelist by trade, I am by temperament much more Aristotelian than Platonist in my attitude toward reality: more nominalist than realist, especially as regards human beings and the things they do and make. Fred and Shirley and Mike and Irma seem intuitively realer to me than does the category *human beings*; the cathedrals at Seville and Barcelona and Santiago de Compostela strike me as more substantial than the term *Spanish Gothic*; and the writings of Gabriel García Márquez and Italo Calvino and Salman Rushdie and Thomas Pynchon — even the

*Both may be found in *The Friday Book*; their arguments are summarized in what follows.

writings of John Barth — have ontological primacy, to my way of thinking, over the category *Postmodernist fiction*. To me it seems self-evident (although I know very well that it is not) that *this* rose and *that* rose and *that* rose — Fred, Irma, and Shirley Rose — are real items in the world, whereas the term *rose* names an idea in our minds, a generality that we achieve only by ignoring enough particularity; and further, that such generalities, while not necessarily illusions, are of an order of reality secondary to that of individual roses. In my innocent universe, in short, classes of objects are not *un*real, but they're less real than their members.

On the other hand, categories and similar abstractions, such as common nouns themselves, although they are (to my way of thinking) more or less fictions, are nevertheless indispensable fictions: indispensable to thought and discourse, to cognition and comprehension, even to sanity. How blithely I have divided reality already, in just a couple of paragraphs, into Aristotelians and Platonists, classes and members, novelists and cathedrals and roses and paragraphs and human beings, like a fisherman culling his catch. How glibly I deploy even such a fishy fiction as the pronoun *I*, as if — although more than half of the cells of my physical body replace themselves in the time it takes me to write one book (and I've written ten*), and I've forgotten much more than I remember about my childhood, and the fellow who did things under my name forty years ago seems as alien to me now in many ways as an extraterrestrial — as if despite those considerations there really is an apprehensible antecedent to the first person singular pronoun. It is a far-fetched fiction indeed, as David Hume pointed out 250 years ago;† but if I did not presume and act upon it, not only would I go insane; I'd be insane.

This is the Tragic View of Categories. Terms like Romanticism, Modernism, and Postmodernism are more or less useful and necessary fictions: roughly approximate maps, more likely to lead us to something like a destination if we don't confuse them with what they're meant to be maps of.

---

*As of the date of this essay's first publication in *Review of Contemporary Fiction*, Fall 1988 ("The Novelist as Critic"). Thirteen, for better or worse, as of this volume's completion.
†In his *Treatise of Human Nature*, 1738.

Why do people bother their heads with such categories, and even write essays about them? For a number of reasons, no doubt, some implied above:

- We do it as a kind of shorthand. It's more convenient to say "Postmodernist architecture"* than it is to recite a list of buildings here and there around the world that seem to us to share certain significant characteristics.

- We do it out of the human urge to articulate widely felt changes in perceived reality. Certain decades, for example, acquire names — the Gay Nineties, the Mauve Decade, the Roaring Twenties, the Swinging Sixties — although the fine-tuning of those terms (sometimes even their gross-tuning) may be problematical indeed. I may feel that "the Sixties" began on November 22, 1963, with the assassination of John F. Kennedy by Lee Harvey Oswald,† and ended on Yom Kippur 1973 with Egypt's attack on Israel and the consequent Arab oil embargo; you may have quite other benchmarks. One of my undergraduate professors, the Romance philologist Leo Spitzer, used to say that it's very useful for students to imagine that something called the Renaissance began at half past two on a Thursday afternoon in 1274, let's say, with the death of St. Thomas Aquinas, and ended with the announcement on the eleven o'clock news of October 31, 1517, that Martin Luther had nailed ninety-five theses to a church door in Wittenberg. Later on, said Spitzer, we may want to adjust those benchmarks by a decade or maybe half a century. Some revisionists may even dispute the whole concept: How many people truly swung in the Sixties, roared in the Twenties, felt a spirit of cultural rebirth in the three hundred years we're calling the Renaissance? The only answer is: a small but (for users of the category) epoch-making minority.

- Finally, it must be acknowledged that in the twentieth-century art world in particular, one may "declare a kingdom in

---

*On the weighty matter of distinguishing "postmodern" from "postmodernist" and "postmodernist" from "Postmodernist," not to mention the hyphenated from the unhyphenated spellings of each, see the Friday-piece "Postmodernism Visited" in "$4\frac{1}{2}$ Lectures," to follow.

†The art critic David Hickey has declared that for him, American Postmodernism begins with this event, the subsequent assassination of the assassin, and the endless television replays of both: the death of a certain diehard U.S. optimism.

order to proclaim himself king." My former Johns Hopkins colleague Hugh Kenner has made this observation vis-à-vis literary Postmodernism, for which he has little use. As a general observation I would not only second it, but extend it to literary critics as well: They may declare an entire era — "the Pound era," for example — in order etc.

Confining ourselves to the more creditable of those motives just mentioned, most of us would agree, I'll bet, that our culture lives in time and that there really do seem to be significant differences of spirit between the American 1950s and Sixties, say; or between the works of the nineteenth-century painters who came to be called Impressionists and the works of the twentieth-century painters who called themselves Abstract Expressionists; or between novels that begin with sentences like "Happy families are all alike; every unhappy family is unhappy in its own way" and novels that begin with sentences like "riverrun, past Eve and Adam's, from swerve of shore to bend of bay, brings us by a commodius vicus of recirculation back to Howth Castle and Environs." We may even agree that there are significant differences of spirit between Ludwig Mies van der Rohe's Seagram building in Manhattan and Philip Johnson's AT&T building in that same neighborhood, whatever we happen to think of the buildings themselves; and that there are aesthetic differences, perhaps even comparable ones, between the opening words of James Joyce's *Finnegans Wake* and those of Gabriel García Márquez's *One Hundred Years of Solitude*, as well as between the novels that follow those opening sentences.

"Many years later, as he faced the firing squad, Colonel Aureliano Buendía was to remember that distant afternoon when his father took him to discover ice."

We have arrived at Postmodernism, which is where I came in a couple of decades ago. More exactly, my first visits to that mildly vexed subject were two little essays written between novels: "The Literature of Exhaustion" (1968) and "The Literature of Replenishment" (1979). If my approach here to a revisit has been particularly tentative and crabwise, that is because my experience with the term and with the various phenomena that it has been used to name has been similarly so. I shall review now that experience: my personal and particular interest in Postmodernism beyond my general interest, as a sentient citizen, in understanding what's going on around me: what my artistic predecessors, contemporaries, and successors have been and are up to.

2. Postmodernism Arrived At

The writer of these words is a fifty-eight-year-old* storyteller, mainly a novelist, who — as a student in the 1940s and Fifties — cut his apprentice literary teeth on the likes of Franz Kafka, Thomas Mann, James Joyce, T. S. Eliot, and Ezra Pound: the old masters of what we now call literary High Modernism, as that last term is understood in many parts of the world.†

When my first novel (*The Floating Opera*) was published in the mid-1950s, it was approved by the critic Leslie Fiedler as an example of "provincial American existentialism." The description intrigued me; like a good provincial, I went and read Sartre and Camus to learn what Existentialism was, and I concurred with Mr. Fiedler (who later became a colleague and friend), if not altogether with Sartre and Camus. If people had done such things in those days, I'd have had a T-shirt printed up for myself: PROVINCIAL AMERICAN EXISTENTIALIST.

My second novel — *The End of the Road*, published two years later — was generally assigned to a new category called Black Humor. I buckled down and read such alleged fellow Black Humorists as John Hawkes, Kurt Vonnegut, Bruce Jay Friedman, and (when he arrived on the scene) Joseph Heller, and I decided that this was not a bad team to be on: the Existential Black Humorists.

But my third, fourth, and fifth books, published through the 1960s,‡ came to be described no longer as Existentialist or Black Humorist, but as Fabulist, and the term was made retroactive to

---

*As of back when he was a ten-book author.

†But not in all: *el modernismo*, in Spain and Latin America, has a quite different reference, and when the Spanish writer Federico de Onís apparently coined the term "postmodernism" in 1934, he was describing a Hispanic reaction within Hispanic *modernismo*, no more relevant to our subject here than Arnold Toynbee's use of the term "postmodern" a few years later in *A Study of History*. This Hispanic distinction seems still to apply: Professor Enrique García Díez reports from the University of Valencia that the adjective "postmoderno" is applied derisively by his students to the latest clothing styles from Madrid.

‡*The Sot-Weed Factor*, 1960; *Giles Goat-Boy*, 1966; *Lost in the Funhouse*, 1968.

those earlier productions too, as well as to the fiction of John Hawkes again and now of Donald Barthelme, Robert Coover, Stanley Elkin, William Gass, and Thomas Pynchon, to name only some of my new (and old) teammates. As before, I dutifully did my homework: read up on those of my fellow Fabulists with whom I wasn't already familiar, and decided that I liked that term — and that team — even better than I had liked its predecessors. But of course I went right on doing what it seemed to me I'd always done: not particularly thinking in terms of Existentialism, Black Humor, or Fabulism, but putting this sentence after that one, and the next one after this one.

Sure enough, just when I had got a pretty good idea what Fabulism was, in the 1970s the stuff began to be called Postmodernist. With increasing frequency I found myself categorized under that label, not only with my old U.S. teammates but with some first-rate foreign ones: Samuel Beckett, Jorge Luis Borges, Italo Calvino, Gabriel García Márquez. I had hoped that some women would sign on next time the ship changed names — would *be signed on*, I should say, since the artists themselves are not normally consulted in these matters.* In any case, the crew was certainly strengthened by those world-class additions. But what exactly were the critics referring to?

You will understand that by this time I found that familiar question less than urgent. All the same, it interested me that those who used the term "Postmodern," at least with respect to literature, seemed far less in agreement about its reference than had the users of labels like Fabulist and Black Humorist. If Joyce was a Modernist, was Beckett then a Postmodernist? Indeed, if the Joyce of *Ulysses* was a Modernist, had the Joyce of *Finnegans Wake* already moved on to Postmodernism? Was Laurence Sterne's *Tristram Shandy* proto-Modern or proto-Postmodern? More important, was the whole phenomenon, whatever it was, no more than a pallid ghost of the powerful cultural force that international Modernism had been in the first half of this century, or was it a positive new direction in the old art of storytelling, and in other arts as

---

*Grace Paley in the U.S. and Angela Carter in the U.K. are sometimes assigned (or consigned) to the Postmodernist pigeonhole, but we are, alas, a predominantly male pigeonry.

well? Was it a repudiation of the great Modernists at whose figurative feet I had sat, or was it something evolved out of them, some next stage of the ongoing dialectic between artistic generations that has characterized Western Civ at least since the advent of Romanticism in (I'm going to say) the latter eighteenth century?

My opportunity to find out came at the close of the decade. The *Deutsche Gesellschaft für Amerikastudien*, an association of German professors of American subjects, convenes annually at Whitsuntide in one or another of that nation's universities, as our Modern Language Association does between Christmas and New Year's in one or another of our Hilton hotels.* In 1979 the Gesellschaft took as the general subject of its conference "America in the 1970s," and the Literature section chose as its particular topic "Postmodern American Fiction." Three U.S. writers — William Gass, John Hawkes, and myself — were invited to Tübingen as guests of the conference, a kind of live exhibit. By that time the term really had gained wide currency in literature as well as in architecture and painting; I even had a rough idea how it might be applied to what was going on in my own shop. But when I looked over some of the standard critical texts (faithfully doing my homework again), I was surprised to find that although the century was 79 percent expired, there was still considerable disagreement about what "Modernism" means, or meant, not to mention Postmodernism, about which no two authorities seemed to agree.

Therefore I leaped into the breach — rather, I sidled crabwise into it — and drafted a little talk for the Gesellschaft on what I thought the term *ought* to mean, if it was going to describe anything very good very well. Armed with my tentative definition/prescription, I went off to Tübingen with my fellow former Fabulists Et Cetera, and found to my mild dismay that our German hosts, the object of whose meticulous curiosity we were, spoke of literary Postmodernism as if it were as indisputable a cultural-historical phenomenon as the Counter-Reformation or the Great Depression of the 1930s. Their discussion, and there was plenty, had to do with refining the boundaries and establishing the canon; there was

*And as AEDEAN, the *Associacion Español de Estudios Anglo-Norteamericanos*, convenes annually at the latter season in one or another southern-Spanish city. See headnote to "The Spanish Connection."

so much confident bandying of adjectives and prefixes — High Postmodernism, Late Postmodernism, Proto-Postmodernism, Post-Postmodernism — that at the end of one session an American student remarked to me, "They forgot Post Toasties."*

Moreover — perhaps on the principle that birds have no business holding forth on ornithology — our hospitable hosts weren't interested in hearing my lecture on their subject. My fellow exhibits and I read from our fiction instead, no doubt a sounder idea.

All the same, I had thought what I'd thought and I'd seen what I'd said (to myself) on the subject of Postmodernist fiction. When I got home I published my reflections in *The Atlantic* (the monthly magazine, not the nearby ocean), where a dozen years before I had published some reflections on what I called "the literature of exhaustion." Here is the summarized conclusion of that Tübingen essay, "The Literature of Replenishment":

> If the Modernists, carrying the torch of Romanticism, taught us that linearity, rationality, consciousness, cause and effect, naive illusionism, transparent language, innocent anecdote, and middle-class moral conventions are not the whole story, then from the perspective of these closing decades of our century we may appreciate that the contraries of these things are not the whole story either. Disjunction, simultaneity, irrationalism, self-reflexiveness, medium-as-message, political olympianism† . . . these are not the whole story either. . . .
>
> My ideal Postmodernist author neither merely repudiates nor merely imitates either his twentieth-century Modernist parents or his nineteenth-century premodernist grandparents. He has the first half of our century under his belt, but not on his back. Without lapsing into moral or artistic simplism, shoddy craftsmanship, Madison Avenue venality, or either false or real naiveté, he nevertheless aspires to a fiction more democratic in its appeal than such late-Modernist marvels as Beckett's *Texts for Nothing*. . . . The

---

*Indeed, it was in Germany again — Stuttgart, in 1991 — that the seminar topic "The End of Postmodernism: New Directions" prompted my "$4\frac{1}{2}$ Lectures," to follow.

†And, I wish I had added, the *topos* of artist-as-hero, from Goethe through Byron down to Joyce.

ideal Postmodernist novel will somehow rise above the quarrel between realism and irrealism, formalism and "contentism," pure
and committed literature, coterie fiction and junk fiction. . . .

What my [earlier] essay "The Literature of Exhaustion" was really about, so it seems to me now, was the effective "exhaustion"
not of language or of literature but of the aesthetic of High Modernism: that admirable, not-to-be-repudiated, but essentially completed "program" of what Hugh Kenner has dubbed "the Pound
era." In 1966/67 we scarcely had the term *Postmodernism* in its
current literary-critical usage . . . but a number of us, in quite different ways and with varying combinations of intuitive response
and conscious deliberation, were already well into the working out,
not of the next-best thing after Modernism, but of the *best next*
thing: what is gropingly now called Postmodernist fiction. . . .

Et cetera: There is more to the definition and more to the argument, but that's the general idea.

3. Postmodernism Revisited

Now, then: The difference between professional intellectuals and
professional artists who are perhaps amateur intellectuals is that
the former publish articles and essays in order to share their learning, whereas we latter may publish the odd essay-between-novels
in order to share our ignorance, so that those more learned can
come to our rescue. My little essay on Postmodernism has been
translated and reprinted a number of times over the years since its
first publication, and my rescuers have been many. Although I still
hold to my basic notion of what Postmodernist fiction is — or
ought to be if it's to deserve our attention — I have happily with-
drawn from the ongoing disputes over its definition and its canon:
over who should be admitted into the club or (depending on the
critic's point of view) clubbed into admission. Postmodern, I tell
myself serenely, is what I am; ergo, Postmodernism is whatever I
do, together with my crewmates-this-time-around, until the critics
rename the boat again. Moreover, *it is what I do whether I do it
well or badly*: a much more important critical consideration, to
which I shall return.

But as I go on doing it, I note with respect and mild interest observations on the subject made by my peers and betters. Octavio Paz, in the Mexican literary organ *La Jornada Semanal*, declared huffily that since I've got *el modernismo* all wrong (that special Hispanic distinction again), I can scarcely be trusted with *el postmodernismo*, which anyhow he was already writing about decades ago, under a different term, as I would have known were I not just one more gringo ethnocentric. There's a rescuer for you.* The writers whom I call Postmodernist, Susan Sontag and William Gass call Late Modernist; for them, the American Postmoderns are the minimalist-realists of the 1970s and Eighties: Raymond Carver, Ann Beattie, and company. The Australian-American art critic Robert Hughes dates Postmodernism, at least in its Pop Art manifestation, from that moment in Walt Disney's 1940 movie *Fantasia* when Mickey Mouse mounts the conductor's podium and shakes hands with Leopold Stokowski. I like that. But yet another art critic (and novelist), Tom McEvilly, speaks of an Egyptian postmodernism from the Middle Kingdom and a Roman postmodernism from the Silver Age; for McEvilly, lowercase postmodernism is the periodic swing of the pendulum of Western Civ from the spiritual-romantic (of which twentieth-century Modernism is an instance) toward the rational-skeptical.†

The Italian semiotician/novelist Umberto Eco, in his 1983 book *Postmodernism, Irony, the Enjoyable*, is a good deal kinder to my essay than Señor Paz was, and very illuminating on the ironic "double coding," as he calls it, characteristic of much postmodern art and life. I quote Signor Eco:

> . . . the postmodern attitude [is] that of a man who loves a very sophisticated woman and knows he cannot say to her, 'I love you madly,' because he knows that she knows (and that she knows that he knows) that these words have already been written by Barbara Cartland. Still, there is a solution. He can say, 'As Barbara Cartland

---

*More on "Pazmodernism" in "Postmodernism Visited" ("4½ Lectures").
†I too, in "The Literature of Replenishment," referred to the Middle Kingdom scribe Khakheperresenb as a postmodernist. As for twentieth-century literary Postmodernism, I date it from when many of us stopped worrying about the death of the novel (a Modernist worry) and began worrying about the death of the reader — and of the planet — instead.

would put it, I love you madly.' At this point, having avoided false
innocence, having said clearly that it is no longer possible to speak
innocently, he will nevertheless have said what he wanted to say to
the woman: that he loves her, but he loves her in an age of lost innocence. If the woman goes along with this, she will have received a
declaration of love all the same. Neither of the speakers will feel innocent, both will have accepted the challenge of the past, of the already said, which cannot be eliminated, both will consciously and
with pleasure play the game of irony. . . . But both will have succeeded, once again, in speaking of love.

I like that, too (but would add that in a properly postmod heterosexual romance, it will as likely be the woman as the man who
makes that uninnocent declaration): If for "Barbara Cartland" we
substitute "the history of literature up to the day before yesterday," it is the very point of my essay "The Literature of Exhaustion." Eco's illustration makes clear also, incidentally, the difference between the premodern English novelist William Makepeace
Thackeray, for example, and the Postmodern Chilean novelist José
Donoso. When Thackeray, at the end of *Vanity Fair*, says of his
novel and its characters, "Come, children, let us shut up the box
and the puppets, for our play is played out," he is making in 1848
an author-intrusive rhetorical flourish of a sort familiar at least
since the early seventeenth century (e.g., in *Don Quixote*), and he
is making it in the same spirit as Cervantes; it is not really anti-
illusionary at all. When such early-twentieth-century writers as
the André Gide of *The Counterfeiters* and the Miguel de Unamuno
of *Mist* and the Luigi Pirandello of *Six Characters in Search of an
Author* begin to challenge the reality of their characters (or to have
their own reality challenged by their characters) and otherwise
foreground the inescapable artifice of their art, we recognize that
we are in the land of Modernism. But when Donoso declares to us
elegantly and elaborately from time to time in *A House in the
Country* (1984) that he has no wish to trick us into believing that
his characters are real or that their joys and sufferings are any
more than ink marks on paper — and then immediately beguiles
us back into the gorgeous, monstrous reality of his fable — he is
"double coding" like Umberto Eco's lovers; he is having it both

ways with illusionism and anti-illusionism. That strikes me as legitimately Postmod, and in the hands of a good storyteller it
works.

I'm interested too in the observation by the British architect
Charles Jencks that whereas for Modernist artists the subject is often the *processes* of their medium, for Postmodernist artists it is
more typically the *history* of their medium. On the basis of this
distinction, Jencks classifies the Pompidou Center in Paris, for example, with its abstract patterns of boldly exposed and brightly
painted pipes and trusses, as Late Modernist, and Robert Graham's
Olympic Arch in Los Angeles — with its truncated classical nude
bronze torsos balancing on inverted metal cones on a black granite
dolmen like a streamlined ruin — as Postmodernist. But I'm not
sure how far this interesting distinction carries over into literature.
It is true that many of the writers called Postmodernist have
looked to various sorts of myth for their material — whether classical myths or such pop mythologies as old Hollywood movies —
as well as to premodern narrative forms, like the tale, the fable,
and the gothic or the epistolary novel; also to premodern narrative
devices, such as Donoso's intrusive, commenting author. *I've* certainly made use of things like that. But then so did Joyce, in
Ulysses,* and if that benchmark of novelistic Modernism must be
reclassified as Postmodernist, I for one begin to experience vertigo.
I think I'll stick with Umberto Eco's "double coding"; in fact, I
think I'll stick with my own rough-and-ready definition of Postmodernism, quoted earlier. All the same, I recommend Charles
Jencks's little treatise *What Is Post-Modernism?* (London/New
York: Academy Editions/St. Martin's Press, 1986), an especially
sound review of Postmodernist architecture, painting, and sculpture, with side glances at literature.

So how is literary Postmodernism doing these days, and what
Post-Postmodernism, if any, lies around the next corner? In architecture, there seems to be no question that Postmodernism is
where the action is, for better or worse. Almost nobody builds

---

*E.g., in the "Oxen of the Sun" chapter, which lovingly parodies the evolution of
English literature in echo of Mrs. Purefoy's pregnancy and difficult labor.

plain old International Style curtain-wall boxes anymore; even shopping malls have their ironic steel-and-glass gable ends, false fronts, cupolas, quotations from the Victorian, whatever. The style has triumphed,* with the usual distribution of excellent, mediocre, and horrendous specimens that one finds in any established style. But although most of the leading practitioners of what is called Postmodernist fiction are by no means finished yet with their careers, and may feel themselves to be still in the process of defining the style (just as their critics are still defining and debating the term), it cannot be doubted that in (North) American fiction, at least, the pendulum has swung from the overtly self-conscious, process-*and*-history-conscious, and often fabulistic work of Barthelme, Coover, Elkin, Gass, Hawkes, Pynchon, & Co. toward that early-Hemingwayish minimalist neo-realism aforementioned, epitomized by the short stories of Carver, Beattie, Frederick Barthelme (the Houston Postmodernist Donald's next-younger brother), and others. Indeed, I suppose that just now these are the two main streams of contemporary U.S. fiction of the literary sort — fiction that, in Joseph Conrad's words, "aspires to the condition of art" — although there are many who would say that the best American work in the medium is being done by more "traditional" pigeons not usually associated with either of these holes: writers such as Saul Bellow, Norman Mailer, Joyce Carol Oates, William Styron, Anne Tyler, John Updike.† That may be.

In any case (back to my starting point), be it remembered that the question whether a particular novel or painting or building is Late Modernist, Postmodernist, Post-Postmodernist, or none of the above, while it's not an unworthy question, is of less importance — at least it ought to be so — than the question *Is it terrific?*

In this connection, it's worth remarking that in literature, at least, an artist may be historically notable without being especially good (for this reader, Theodore Dreiser is one such, Gertrude Stein

---

*With particularly happy results, to my eye, in the area of residential architecture, where with few exceptions the Modernist style was especially inhospitable.
†And we are speaking of identifiable mainstreams, not of significant alternatives like Toni Morrison's "operatic realism," as William Gass aptly calls it, or the nonlinear computer-fiction of the Hypertexties (see the essay "Browsing," farther on in this collection).

another; others will have other examples). Conversely, a writer may be quite good without being otherwise especially "important" (I think of the late Joyce Carey, of the late Henry Green, of others, not yet late, whom I shall not name). Alas, it is the misfortune of many, many published writers, perhaps of most, to be neither especially good nor particularly important; and it is the fortune of a very few to be both artistically excellent and historically significant. Since art is long and life short, *those* are the writers (if we can name them) to whom we ought to give our prime-time attention. Among our contemporaries, I quite believe, a few of these few are what has come to be called Postmodernist.

A Body of Words

"Historically," I noted in The Friday Book, *"the Johns Hopkins University has been the distinguished tail upon a very large dog: the Johns Hopkins Medical Institutions, across town." There is, however, connection between the beast proper and its appendage, involving not only the university's science departments and engineering college but, to a lesser extent, the humanistic disciplines as well. In 1987, the JHMI's new Mind/Brain Institute (now called the Krieger Mind/Brain Institute, after its generous endower) sponsored a symposium of assorted scientists and humanists on the general matter of the ancient dualism of mind and body. Herewith my contribution thereto, a till-now-unpublished Friday-piece.*

WITH RESPECT TO the famous distinction between our bodies and our minds, it occurs to me that the practice of fiction writers, even without their thinking about it in abstract terms, may illuminate the practice of other, less professional liars — including us fiction writers when we're not writing fiction.

What I mean by that is this: Like most folks, I go about assuming (in my off-duty hours, at least) that there is some rough-and-ready reality to the antecedent of the first-person-singular pronoun. From long-standing habit, I take that antecedent to comprise a gross or more pounds of live meat, bone, blood, and gristle, embodying this other thing that I think I have, mainly inside the first thing's head end. This other thing I think of as to some extent monitoring and controlling the first thing — setting an agenda for the meat/bone/blood/gristle and endeavoring to coordinate its lurches and perpetrations — and to some extent being reciprocally agenda'd and controlled by it: a less than masterful jockey upon a not invariably docile horse.

And I don't stop there: It is my comfortable habit to imagine further that what I am is pretty much the complex of these components — the proprioceptive carnal robot and its synapsing wet microprocessors and software — plus my imperfect memory* of the history of a half-century of its lurches and perpetrations, plus whatever notions I entertain of its trajectory, plus my consciousness of its consciousness et cetera. Usually I quit thinking about the matter somewhere around there, if not sooner, because my body has other things on its mind.

So far, we're all alike: our minds thinking of themselves as embodied in a body that cohabits with something centered somewhere above its shoulders, which perhaps it shrugs. We habitually distinguish between these aspects of ourselves, even if we're not always perfectly easy about the distinction when our minds have occasion to take a closer look at it — as normally they seldom do. Even the odd philosopher among us who might for one reason or another quarrel with the distinction would most likely agree that there's more to what he's quarreling with than the mere language of his quarrel: On the level of our lives as lived, at least, it certainly appears that *something* lurches and perpetrates, registers and reasons, broods and bruises.

In the feature section of my morning newspaper I read the first-person account of a forcible rape. The victim (a woman, in this instance, assaulted by a man) reports that throughout the assault she experienced a numb dissociation of mind and body, as if what was happening was somehow happening "not to me but to somebody else, or only to my body, while I looked on like a helpless spectator." I believe that I understand the victim's psychological state of affairs, but whatever my ontological persuasion (or almost whatever), if I trust the sadly familiar account I believe not only that some real body was victimized, but that *somebody* really was.

Then I go to my writing table, where I am in midst of composing *Clarissa*, by Samuel Richardson, or *Justine*, by the Marquis de Sade, or even *The Tidewater Tales*, by Yours Truly. Having filled

*For more on the subject of memory, see "Once Upon a Time: Storytelling Explained," to follow — another JHMI symposium presentation.

my pen and sharpened my word processor, I set to my work in progress, which happens this particular morning to be the creation (literally from scratch, since I draft in longhand first) of a woman, both her body and her mind: a little chapterlet called, in fact, "Do the Woman":*

... Here's the woman of us, in her man's opinion: Katherine Shorter Sherritt at thirty-nine is a rangy, long-limbed looker looking thirty-three tops and topped with beach-colored hair (both the dry beach and the wet), streaked straight past fine strong shoulders when she lets it down. She has [her father's] Episcopalian bright gray eyes, [her mother's] twenty-four-carat skin and cultured-pearl dentition. She'll dress to the nines when occasion calls and sophisticate in three languages, Kate, but she's easy in the preppie drag she wears to work: tweed skirts, cable-knit crewnecks over oxford-cloth buttondowns; easier yet in soft jeans and hiking boots and flannels, swapping stories ... across an Ozark campfire; easiest of all in the all-but-altogether with [her husband,] Peter Sagamore, spanking along in [their little sailboat] *Story* through a summer afternoon or splashing naked by moonlight with the noctilucae. When Katherine takes her clothes off later in this prologue and stands in [her parents'] First Guest Cottage wearing only earrings, wedding band, and fine gold chain necklace, you'll see those aforesung breasts engorged by pregnancy beyond their normal trim, their russet aureoles stretched cookie-size; athletical buttocks fairly firm even this far gone; smoothmuscled, fineskinned calves and thighs, flawless; and what was till the turn of the year a hard flat belly with God's thumbprint for a navel. All this, mind, in her husband's opinion. ... She's an Outward Bound type, Kath: back-packer, white-water canoeist, distance swimmer. She's a green-belt karatiste as well as raconteuse, don't mess with K.S.S., though that belly's thrown her balance off. Under all that skin she is intuitive but clearheaded, even hardheaded when necessary. She is memorious, practical, capable, Kathy, but more dependent than she wishes upon Peter's stability and good humor to level out her swings from up to down to up. Life having been generous to her, she is in his

The Tidewater Tales: A Novel (NY: Putnam, 1987), pp. 29–31.

opinion generous with hers: Much of that [public library] work is hard-core inner-city, and she is forever volunteering for good-citizenly chores over and above. . . . She has enjoyed vigorously, Katherine, every stage of her privileged life — her childhood, girl-hood, adolescence, young womanhood, mature adulthood — except the period of her [first] marriage. . . . Strong-charactered and principled, she learned from that experience to prize good character above all else in others. She dislikes pettiness, foolishness, weakness, coquetry, moral laziness, snobbishness, cowardice, dissembling, bad faith; also drunkenness, narcosis, philandering, and sexual sadism. She is not, is Katherine Sherritt, modish, intellectual, high-style, cute, very worldly, "sexy," very political, submissive, very dependent, carping, devious, vain, contentious, affected, very fastidious, "passionate," fearful, reckless, jealous. She is neither genius nor virtuoso, though she's a whiz at collecting stories and getting better all the time at telling them. What she is, in her husband's view, is knowledgeable, sensible, well-organized, ardent, reasonable, energetic, sexual, loyal, dependable, moodier than she approves of being, quick-minded and intelligent, well-educated, physically and morally courageous, articulate, resourceful, prevailingly cheerful, self-reliant but not entirely, damned good-looking, we said that already, and, she adds, much drawn to genuine talent and virtuosity.

Kathy Sherritt knows who she is. She does? She does. With the strength of a certain WASP cultural tradition behind her, of which she largely but not uncritically approves, she relates easily to others who know who *they* are, however foreign: an asset in her ethnic-oral-history work. She would hit it off with a Masai chieftain or the Baal Shem Tov. Homosexual men are not uncomfortable in Kathy's company; straight women like her; lesbians are powerfully drawn herward . . . , as are heterosexual men of various classes, races, ages.

Katherine, Kathy, Katie-Kath-Kate! *He's* drawn to you, too, who just now helped draw you! Lucky the man whose woman is Katherine Sherritt.

You get the picture. Having in this preliminary fashion "done the woman" (the novel's female lead), like Yahweh working backwards I next create her mate, in a chapterlet called "Now Do the Man." Him too I supply with the particulars of a body and a mind, character and characteristics. I assign him a name whose noise satisfies my ear (Peter Sagamore, QED) and the enviable role of being Katherine Sherritt's husband for 656 pages. As he is the second man to hold that happy office, however, he arrives in her story too late to prevent her being (or having been) brutally raped, seventeen years earlier but 260 pages later, at my instigation, by her then-estranged first husband — whom also I invented, partly for that vile purpose. Dear Katherine's mind, unlike the woman's in the newspaper account, does *not* dissociate from her body on that sore occasion. I shall pass over the scene, although I am not displeased with it.*

Now: What on earth am I doing? Sometimes I wonder. I don't mean, in this instance, what is it that impels me to imagine and to depict in English words the sexual violation of this splendid though imaginary woman, Katherine Sherritt Sagamore,† who is as real to me in her way as I am in mine. That may be a legitimate question — for what clinical interest the datum may have, I note that rapes (usually though not invariably of women by men) are to be met with in no fewer than seven of my nine book-length works of fiction‡ — but it is not the question I want to ask (or face) just now. I mean what on earth am I doing in that "Do the Woman" chapter, for example: the thing that I do four or five mornings a week, and that Richardson and de Sade and Jane Austen and Anne Tyler and every other novelist did or does too, each in his/her way: dreaming people up and choreographing marriages and murders among them, rapes and ratiocinations, epiphanies and peripeties, lurches and perpetrations?

---

*Op. cit., pp. 303 ff.

†In the noise of *her* name, I here confess uncomfortably, is to be heard a deliberate echo of the vast Sanskrit tale-cycle *Kathā Sarit Sāgara*, The Ocean of Story, for more whereon see "It's a Long Story." Declares hugely pregnant Kath, with Walt Whitman, "I contain multitudes."

‡As of this footnote (1994), eight of my eleven: an improvement from 78 percent to 73 percent. Happily, if not significantly, in my novel-cum-memoir *Once Upon a Time: A Floating Opera*, nobody gets raped.

I'm damned if I know, for sure, but here are a couple of things that occur to me when my mind thinks about the question:

Imagining that Clarissa Harlowe or Justine or Katherine Sherritt Sagamore has a body, to which such and such happens, together with more or less of a mind, which registers this and that thus and so, is similar to, but not quite the same as, imagining that *I* have a body et cet or that you have one. Wherever our minds may suppose that our bodies stop and our minds start, when we talk about them we're talking about something beyond the images conjured by our words; something that we imagine those images to be images of. Although I do not know the victim of that newspaper rape account, when I imagine her mind's dissociating from her body during that traumatic episode, I am attempting to reconstruct an actuality in my imagination. But what is the body, and for that matter the mind, of Clarissa Harlowe? Of the misfortunate Justine? Of my Katherine Sherritt Sagamore? Words on the page. Finally, says the distinguished philosopher/novelist William H. Gass, *no more than* words on the page:

"On the other side of a novel," Gass writes,* "lies the void. Think, for instance," he invites us, "of a striding statue; imagine the purposeful inclination of the torso, the alert and penetrating gaze of the head and its eyes, the outstretched arm and pointing finger; everything would appear to direct us toward some goal in front of it. Yet our eye travels only to the finger's end, and not beyond. Though pointing, the finger bids us stay instead, and we journey slowly back along the tension of the arm. In our hearts we know what actually surrounds the statue. The same surrounds every other work of art: empty space and silence."

Clarissa, Justine, Katherine — words on the page; language, not quite for its own sake, but not for the sake of pointing at the world, either.

But what about that newspaper rape victim, whom I don't know at all and who is nothing to me, personally, compared to Katherine Sherritt Sagamore? Isn't *she* just words on the page as far as I'm concerned, and her rapist likewise, and the investigating officer and prosecuting attorney and the rest? Sure they are — but

*In his essay "The Concept of Character in Fiction," in *Fiction and the Figures of Life* (NY: Knopf, 1970).

not at all in the same sense, for the humble but crucial reason (which fiction writers themselves frequently lose sight of) that while literature in general may be defined as "the artful rendition of human experience into words" (and could thus imaginably include the newspaper rape account if it had been artfully, transcendently done), *fiction* is specifically a variety of literature that employs prose to tell a story *presumably made up.**

I direct your attention to that crucial presumption, which rigorously applies (or ought to apply) even where we happen to know that in fact the author is drawing from life. It applies even to the works of a novelist such as J. P. Donleavy, for example, who once defined novel-writing as "the fine art of turning one's worst experiences into money." You tell me that Marcel Proust's tantalizing Albertine was in fact based upon the family chauffeur, a chap named Albert; I say *zut alors*, or maybe fact shmact: Get out of here with your factual Albert, about whom I care nothing; he has been Prousted into the tantalizing Albertine, about whom I care intensely. The legal presumption of innocence ends upon reasonable proof of guilt, but the aesthetic presumption of fictionality prevails over all evidence to the contrary — or at least it ought so to prevail. At the risk of talking under all hands' heads, I'll conclude by applying this presumption to the matter at hand:

Although our minds are strictly embodied, our bodies may be thought of as being all in our minds. Mind and Body, and any distinctions between them, are concepts, like the concept Distinction itself. We apprehend them in what we call our minds, and we deploy and manipulate them by *calling* them: that is, by means of (what we call) language — another concept, another product of our minds, bodied forth by our bodies. Those bodies, yours and mine, no less than our minds, come down to words: my left thumb, your medulla oblongata, our apprehensions and misapprehensions, lurches and perpetrations. The same is true, a touch more obviously, of Katherine Sherritt's excellent mind and body, and that's all I meant when I said at the outset that the fiction writer's practice — making things out of words that are finally *just* things made out of words — may perhaps illuminate the way we

---

*Both definitions (echoed earlier in "Can It Be Taught?" and "It Goes Without Saying") are by Cleanth Brooks and Robert Penn Warren.

necessarily make words out of things and then habitually forget the distinction between the two.

There the similarity ends, although we often forget that, too. For I'm not at all suggesting that these noises that we make with our larynxes and the rest to signify the distinctions that we make in our minds correspond to nothing "out there": They do, no doubt, at least approximately enough so that the medical arts and sciences, for example, can proceed and even progress — often by refining or changing their language. The validity of such verbal constructs as that newspaper rape account, like the validity of eloquent case histories written by Sigmund Freud or Oliver Sacks, depends upon our presumption that beyond the words lies an actual, historical person, and it would so depend even if it could be shown that in fact Freud or Sacks stretched a few things here and there. Katherine Sherritt's dear validity, on the other hand — the special quality of her being — depends oddly upon the reader's presumption that my words do *not* describe any actual, historical person, even if it could be shown* that in fact they do. She is first of all, as Gass says, "the noise of [her] name, and all the sounds and rhythms that proceed from [her]." And that's what she is last of all, too, even though her writer no less than her reader may lose sight of that fact.

For it often happens, says Gass, that we novelists mimic the ordinary use of language. "We report upon ourselves," he writes in that same lovely essay:

> . . . we gossip. Normally we are not lying, and our language, built to refer, actually does. When these selfsame words appear in fiction, and when they follow the forms of daily use, they create, quite readily, that dangerous feeling that a real [Nicholas] Nickleby [for example] lives just beyond the page; that through that thin partition we can hear a world at love. But the writer must not let the reader out; the sculptor must not let the eye fall from the end of his statue's finger. . . . Of course, he will; but let the blame be on himself. High tricks are possible: to run the eye rapidly along that out-

---

*It cannot.

stretched arm to the fingertip, only to draw it up before it falls away into space; to carry the reader to the very edge of every word so that it seems he must be compelled to react as though to truth as told in life, and then to return him, like a philosopher liberated from the cave, to the clear and brilliant world of concept, to the realm of order, proportion, and dazzling construction . . . [that is,] to fiction, where [minds and bodies], unlike [our own], freed from existence, can shine like essence, and purely Be.

To that peculiar and luminous mode of being, I say "So be it." Take our words for these minds and bodies, without mistaking those words for minds and bodies.

Very Like an Elephant
Reality versus Realism

*Three times, at least, in my writerly life I have been high among the
targets of published attack by fellow writers (book reviewers are another matter): in the late John Gardner's 1978 treatise* On Moral
Fiction, *cited below; in Gore Vidal's 1974 essay "American Plastic";* and in Tom Wolfe's 1989* Harper's *essay "Stalking the
Billion-Footed Beast."*

*One does well, as a rule, merely to shrug one's shoulders at such
carps and to go on writing what and as one writes. Who are those
turkeys, to set the terms of the debate? And so in face of the Gardner
and the Vidal, I held my peace. Wolfe's anti-Fabulist howl, however,
struck me as so particularly narrow and self-serving that at the*
Harper's *editor's invitation I drafted the following response — with
the stipulation that it be given the same prominence (and payment)
as the piece that provoked it, rather than be run as a mere Letter to
the Editor. No deal. I therefore recalled the piece, satisfied myself by
reading it to the Tokyo chapter of the American Literature Society
(who take a professional interest in U.S. literary-aesthetic catfights),
and here publish it for the first time.*

---

*First published in the *New York Review of Books*; collected in Vidal's *United
States: Essays 1952–1992* (NY: Random House, 1993). Like Gardner's and
Wolfe's polemics from their different perspectives, "American Plastic" is a cate-
gorical derogation of those contemporary American writers sometimes called
Postmodernist: Barth/Barthelme/Coover/Elkin/Gass/Hawkes/Pynchon/etc. — "all
the usual suspects." Acute and entertaining as are Vidal's sociopolitical essays, it
will come as no surprise that I find his literary judgment wanting. Even his praise
(e.g., of the late Italo Calvino's fiction, which both of us admire) strikes me as
wrongheaded.

A DOZEN YEARS ago, the novelist and polemicist John Gardner laid into his fellow fiction writers at kneecap level with the AK-47 of "moral fiction":* Nearly all of us, he charged, were delinquent in the fictive area of moral representation, which Gardner held to be the historical glory, indeed virtually the function, of fiction in general and the novel in particular. If one took him at his word, when the assault-rifle smoke cleared virtually no literary contemporary remained upright except the gunman himself.

Those of us who cordially knew Gardner (and we were his principal targets) mainly sighed: There goes Bad John again, popping off at his peers. Self-serving as his tirade was, however, it was by no means merely so. The man earnestly believed, I think, that the likes of Vladimir Nabokov, Donald Barthelme, William Gass, John Hawkes, Thomas Pynchon, and myself were perpetrating not immoral but amoral fiction — and that in this we were reprehensible.

While not happy to be thus consigned to Hell, I for one was honored to have such splendid company in the Circle of Literary Irresponsibles. On the other hand, I felt that there was enough to be said for Gardner's argument that it deserved a keener arguer: one who would not only choose his targets more judiciously (I see much exemplary morality in the writers named above, and much clunky art in more programmatically "moral" novelists) but would also distinguish more consistently between the moral *aspect* of most great literature, which I readily affirm, and the notion of a writer's moral *duty*, which I resist as I would resist the wholesale conscription of art into any other propaganda service, however worthy. I believe it to be the reader's privilege to take no interest in novels that fail to address his/her pet cause: feminism, animal rights, political revolution, general social justice, whatever. Let it be the writer's privilege to enlist his art in such causes if they happen to energize his imagination, as not infrequently they do: witness Dickens, Dostoevsky, Hugo, García Márquez. But let him be

On Moral Fiction (NY: Basic Books, 1978).

free as well to pursue nothing more edifying than "aesthetic bliss" (Nabokov's declared objective — but don't be fooled) or even "nothing" (what Flaubert remarked that he would "really like to write a novel about"). If the author is a genius, excellent art will follow in either case; if a mediocrity, then, as computer programmers say, it's "garbage in, garbage out," however high-minded the writer's moral principles.

May John G's driven spirit rest in peace.* Now — just when you thought it was safe to re-enter the waters, or jungle, of contemporary fiction — along comes the old New Journalist and new old-fashioned-realistic novelist Tom Wolfe, packing the elephant gun of Social Realism. In a recent, much-ballyhooed essay called "Stalking the Billion-Footed Beast,"† Wolfe declares the recent literary landscape a neo-fabulist wasteland and proceeds to bang away, Gardner-style, not at the "billion-footed beast" of Reality after all, but at his fellow fictionists — until, when the smoke clears, voilà (and déjà vu): He stands almost alone, beside an uncomfortable-looking John Updike (in whose stated opinion Wolfe's essay was "not deeply felt"), under the inspiring portraits of . . . Sinclair Lewis and William Makepeace Thackeray.

But the smoke hasn't cleared. Let us ventilate:

"A child of seven," G. K. Chesterton observed,‡ "is excited by being told that Tommy opened the door and saw a dragon. But a child of three is excited by being told that Tommy opened a door. In fact," Chesterton adds, "a baby is about the only person, I should think, to whom a modern realistic novel could be read without boring him."

That is the "strong" objection to literary realism, which I'll define as the endeavor to focus quotidian "reality" in a high-resolution verbal lens. Chesterton's implication is that the more the endeavor succeeds, the less interesting it becomes: Why pay admission to see the Firth of Forth reflected in the great camera

---

*His second posthumously published treatise, *On Becoming a Novelist* (NY: Harper & Row, 1983), goes far toward a more judicious, less pugnacious restatement of his argument in *On Moral Fiction*.
†*Harper's*, November 1989.
‡In "The Logic of Elfland," 1908.

obscura of Edinburgh, when one can stand outside and view that noble waterway for real and for free?

My own position in the matter is a good deal more temperate — indeed, it's not an objection to the literary-realistic enterprise at all, of which I approve and in which I have often joined, but merely some observations on reality versus aesthetic realism. The difference between the aforecited Firth as apprehended by the unmediated eye and as recomposed in light reflected, refracted, and refocused is half the difference between life and art. The other half — for realists and irrealists alike — is artistry, by which (to echo Coleridge) the familiar may be rendered marvelous and the fantastic commonplace.

"Out there" — and also, importantly, in our heads — is what we're accustomed to thinking of as Reality. It was not invented by "realistic" novelists and painters, although our perception of it can doubtless be influenced by art as surely as changes in a culture's perceptions influence what passes for artistic realism (compare the "realistic" dialogue of the 1942 film *Casablanca*, as impossibly stagey to our present ears as is some Hemingway talk, with that of the 1989 film *sex, lies, and videotape*, say, which persuades us now but half a century hence will likely sound every bit as stagey). Our experience of this protean reality — of "human life, its happiness and its misery," Aristotle says — is the subject of literature; not *ought to be*, but *is*, as shall be shown. It is an experience that significantly includes our experience of language and even, for audiences as well as for artists, our experience of art. Without this latter experience, no given artwork is likely to be intelligible, much less meaningful; Chesterton's exemplary baby cannot enjoy a story until he has learned that it *is* a story.

Human life, its happiness and its misery; the manifold human perception and experience of reality, which will not ignore our at least occasional feelings of irreality ("Un*real!*" American teenagers exclaim about many sorts of things): Whatever uppercase Reality may be, our human experience of it in sickness and in health, in prosperity and in adversity, as children and as adults of sundry cultures in sundry mise-en-scènes, is a subject too enormously large and multifaceted to be encompassed by any of the various species of aesthetic realism, and equally of irrealism. Mr.

Wolfe's "billion-footed beast" is very like the elephant of the parable, of whom the most comprehending among us can lay hold of
no more than a part and declare, like the blind sages holding
trunk or leg or ear: "Very like a snake!" "Very like a tree!" "Very
like a fan!" Leo Tolstoy reports his multitudinous impressions
of the creature, Franz Kafka his more narrow but no less profound. Jane Austen, François Rabelais, Nikolai Gogol, Lewis
Carroll, Theodore Dreiser, Scheherazade, Edgar Poe, Yukio
Mishima, Gertrude Stein — even Stephen King and Dr. Seuss —
each has a handle on our common subject; each has a piece of the
elephant. Programmatic social realists like Émile Zola, I sometimes think, have it by the tail ("very like a tiger"), and it them by
the eyes, blinding them to much else. But not even miraculous
Chekhov has it by the balls.

There is more to it: more to reality than realism, and more to
my argument. "Literature," say Cleanth Brooks and Robert Penn
Warren (after Aristotle), "is the artful rendition of human experience into words." Every term of that definition merits an essay;*
sufficient to note here that the writer's ineluctable *subject*, human
experience, is only one (or two) of those terms. One notable way
to get at that subject is represented by the daily newspaper, and
one of the uses of the novel in particular, both historically and ety-
mologically, has been to bring us "the news." Fiction as a kind of
secular news report or camera obscura is an honorable tradition
still very much with us, and it can be practiced with great art or
with apparent or real artlessness. But another way of getting at the
subject, equally famous and even more venerable, is the defamiliarization of the familiar so that we see it afresh, as when ordinary
Alice goes through the looking glass to its extraordinary other
side, or when (conversely) Gregor Samsa wakes up in his familiar
surroundings to find himself metamorphosed into a big bug.
Fantastic tales, says Chesterton, "make rivers run with wine only
to make us remember, for one wild moment, that they run with
water."

No use praising one of these approaches and damning the
other; they're simply different handles on the subject, different

*E.g., the essay "It Goes Without Saying," earlier in this volume.

lenses, and either can effectuate great art, mediocre art, or non-art, for the elementary reason that there is more to literature than its subject. If the realist happens to be Anton Chekhov, deal me in; if the irrealist happens to be Italo Calvino, deal me in. Aesthetic orthodoxy, no matter which orthodoxy, will never make a silk purse out of a sow's ear, whereas great artists of every sort perform that miracle routinely. On the other hand, a mediocre writer can make a sow's ear out of a silk purse whether the mode is realism, irrealism, or any of the innumerable alloys of the two. So it is not after all quite so simple as "garbage in, garbage out." The rendering is crucial.

The *artful* rendition of human experience, our definition stipulates, *into words*. It has been the defensible ambition of certain literary realists (by no means all of them) so to foreground their "material" that their medium — language, artfully deployed — appears to disappear; it is the naive error of some of them to imagine that it can be truly effaced. Speaking to my students at Johns Hopkins, James A. Michener once declared that he wants his readers to forget that they're reading; using a metaphor as old as window glass, he declared his ideal language to be as invisible as a spotless pane, through which his readers would see not a novel about Hawaii, but Hawaii. Balzac and many another great novelist might well have agreed with Michener as to the merits of this "Windex" approach, as I call it, to the medium (Charles Dickens and Mark Twain would not have). But it is to be noted that where the result is formidable art, that will be owing not to artlessness, but to the masterful deployment of the artifice of "invisible language." Verity may be the goal of such writers, but cunning verisimilitude is their means: not reality, but realism; not "truth," but trompe-l'oeil.

The opposite approach is "stained-glass" language: the medium so foregrounded that exterior reality may appear to serve mainly to backlight it: Consider Rabelais's "Whether a chimera, bombinating in the void, can be nourished by second intentions," and Carroll's "'Twas Brillig, and the slithy toves did gyre and gimble in the wabe," and Joyce's "riverrun, past Eve and Adam's," and Stein's "A rose is a rose is a rose." At its most radical, this approach may lead to a misconception corresponding to the naive realist's: that literature is "nothing but" language, an assertion as wrongheaded as that a Canaletto (or a Kasimir Malevich or a Jasper Johns) is "nothing but" pigment on canvas, or the cathedral at Chartres (or the Pompidou Center) "nothing but" stone and mortar, glass and steel. The fact, aforenoted, is that our experience of life centrally includes our experience of language, and thus the most abstruse, even perverse literary experiments — the generation of literary texts by algorithm, such as Georges Perec's novel without the letter *e* in it — will interest us, if they do, by reason of the light they cast, however odd, upon that experience, as well as upon human ingenuity, which is also part of our experience of life. How much odder, after all, is a novel without an *e* than a "man without qualities" (the antihero and title of Robert Musil's social-realist epic of prewar Austria)?

There is yet more to it — or perhaps there is not. I had been going to point out that all of the foregoing takes for granted, one way or another, the Platonic premise that art "holds a mirror up to life," and that alternative premises may be valid. Is there no room at the inn of literature for the writer who sets about to create — whether in Windexed or stained-glass language — either alternatives to reality or alternative realities? The millions of enjoyers of fantastic fiction — of Odysseus's and Sindbad's voyages, Dante's *Divine Comedy*, Rabelais's *Gargantua and Pantagruel*, Tolkien's hobbits (and "realist" Charles Dickens's ghosts and spontaneously combusting villains) — would vociferously protest. And so would I, except that no protest is necessary. It may sound like sophistry to say that even the artist who tries to hold a mirror *away* from life — toward another mirror, perhaps — is still mirroring "life," in the sense that our experience of life includes experience of mirrors literal and figurative; but it is not mere sophistry, for what applies to literature's language applies to its material as well. If we enjoy a novel about little green extraterrestrials, say, that will likely be for three main reasons, none of them finally divorced from "life":

  • First, as aforesuggested, the extraterrestials may revealingly defamiliarize our own terrestriality: "The disease of the agglutinated dust, lifting alternate feet or lying drugged with slumber;

killing, feeding, growing, bringing forth small copies of himself; grown upon with hair like grass, fitted with eyes that move and glitter in his face; a thing to set children screaming. . . ." That's *us*, described by Robert Louis Stevenson in "Pulvis et Umbra."

• Second, likewise aforenoted, we are not enjoying *a* novel about extraterrestrials;* we are enjoying *this particular* novel about them, by an author whose imagination and/or language we find appealing. Our pleasure is the very human, terrestrial pleasure in human inventiveness and virtuosity.

• But, third, we are not, after all, *mere* narcissists and anthropocentrists. Our curiosity extends beyond ourselves and our society, beyond the here and now and even the real (not to mention the merely social), to the possible, even to the irreal and the impossible — if only, once again, for what they tell us about the possible, the real, the here, the now. How vast and rich human reality is! How blinkered and myopic is some realists' view of it! To assert that it can be compassed or even best approached by Realism — whether social, Socialist, bourgeois-domestic, psychological, or magical — is to rob the bank of human experience, in which every one of us has a more or less substantial deposit.

"Very like a newscast"; "Very like a dream (or nightmare)"; "Very like a funhouse"; "Very like a madhouse" — we all are partly in the right, and all are in the wrong. If some writers' reports on the shape-shifting beast of Reality are more persuasive, memorable, beguiling, beautiful than others — for this is *fiction* we are making here, not journalism old or New — that circumstance will be owing much less to their aesthetic program, their handle on the elephant, than to their literary genius, on which neither "realists" nor "irrealists" have a monopoly.

---

*Readerly tastes, however, can be very category-specific. A librarian of audio-taped books for the blind reports being asked not "What else do you have written by Virginia Woolf?" but "What else do you have narrated by Alexander Scourby?"

"Still Farther South"
Some Notes on Poe's Pym *

⊙——IN 1838, AT the age of twenty-nine, Edgar Allan Poe
published his first and only novel: *The Narrative of
Arthur Gordon Pym of Nantucket*. Its teenage hero, with a little
help from a friend, stows away on a ship outbound from that island and undergoes the adventures summarized in Poe's subtitle:

COMPRISING THE DETAILS OF A MUTINY AND ATROCIOUS BUTCHERY
ON BOARD THE AMERICAN BRIG GRAMPUS, ON HER WAY TO
THE SOUTH SEAS, IN THE MONTH OF JUNE, 1827.

WITH AN ACCOUNT OF THE RECAPTURE OF THE VESSEL BY THE
SURVIVERS [sic]; THEIR SHIPWRECK AND SUBSEQUENT HORRIBLE
SUFFERINGS FROM FAMINE; THEIR DELIVERANCE BY
MEANS OF THE BRITISH SCHOONER JANE GUY; THE
BRIEF CRUISE OF THIS LATTER VESSEL IN THE
ANTARCTIC OCEAN; HER CAPTURE, AND THE
MASSACRE OF HER CREW AMONG A
GROUP OF ISLANDS IN THE

EIGHTY-FOURTH PARALLEL OF SOUTHERN LATITUDE;

TOGETHER WITH THE INCREDIBLE ADVENTURES AND
DISCOVERIES

*No headnote needed, as this essay begins with one, describing the subject in
terms that would go without saying to a conference of Poe scholars. Written as a
keynote address to the Nantucket Island *Pym*fest therein cited, this Friday-piece
was subsequently published in the quarterly *Antaeus*, Autumn 1989, and collected with other, more scholarly papers from that conference in *Poe's Pym: Critical Explorations*, ed. Richard Kopley (Durham NC: Duke U. Press, 1993).

STILL FARTHER SOUTH

TO WHICH THAT DISTRESSING CALAMITY GAVE RISE.

Like many a tall tale before and since, *Pym* presents itself as a sober, factual account of an increasingly fantastic voyage, in this instance culminating in the hero's imminent disappearance (in the final sentence of his first-person narrative) into a watery abyss at the South Pole. In a straight-faced preface dated some ten years later ("New York, July, 1838"), "Pym" informs us that "Mr. Poe" has lately published, with his consent, two early installments of his adventures *as fiction*, and that he wishes now to set the record straight; he does not, however, explain how he got from the polar abyss to Richmond (where he claims to have met Poe) and New York. In a similarly straight-faced appendix to the narrative, an anonymous "editor" mentions, also without explanation, "the late sudden and distressing death of Mr. Pym" — immediately after his composing the preface, evidently — and regrets that "the few remaining chapters which were to have completed his narration . . . have been irrecoverably lost through the accident by which he perished himself." He informs us further that "the gentleman whose name is mentioned in the preface" — that is, Mr. Poe — has expressed "his disbelief in the entire truth of the latter portions of [Pym's] narration."

In short, the fiction that the fiction is factual includes its dismissal, by its factual author, as fiction.

Such ontological mirror tricks, a stock-in-trade of contemporary "metafiction," did not sit well with *Pym*'s nineteenth- and early-twentieth-century readers. "Imaginative bankruptcy," Robert Louis Stevenson said of the novel's ending — acknowledging however that at least Poe "cheats us with gusto." Henry James, no fan of Poe's in any case, declared that *Pym*'s "climax fails . . . because it stops short, and stops short for want of connexions. There *are* no connexions." Others dismissed the novel as a hoax, meant to fool unsuspecting readers into thinking it a factual account of South-Polar misadventure. Poe himself, having written and published the novel quickly between editorial jobs in Richmond and Philadelphia, apparently had second thoughts about its merits.

In our time, however, *The Narrative of Arthur Gordon Pym of Nantucket* has enjoyed considerable and sophisticated critical attention: enough so that in honor of the sesquicentennial of its publication, Poe scholars from around the country convened on foggy Nantucket Island in May 1988 for a three-day conference on that novel, sponsored by the Pennsylvania State University. What follows is adapted from my remarks to that conference, which I was invited to address not as a high-tech Pymster but simply as one novelist sizing up another.

My late acquaintance Italo Calvino was once commissioned by the publishing house of Ricci in Milan to write a short novel involving the Tarot cards, to accompany a facsimile edition of a medieval Tarot deck fully annotated by a scholarly tarotologist. Calvino told me that his first artistic decision in this instance was to purge his imagination altogether of the cards' traditional significances; to look at those famous icons as if he knew nothing whatever about them, like an intelligent visitor from an alien culture. The happy result was his novel *The Castle of Crossed Destinies*, on the facing pages of Ricci's beautiful volume *I Tarocchi.**

That is the spirit in which (on this conference's commission) I have lately taken another look at *The Narrative of Arthur Gordon Pym of Nantucket*. The task of purging my imagination of 150 years of critical commentary on that novel — beginning, I suppose, with Poe's own remark that it is "a silly book" — was made immeasurably easier for me by the circumstance that I have read virtually none of that commentary. Indeed, though the author died where I live, and though I feel certain other connections with him as well, I happen not even to have read his first and last voyage upon the bounding main of the novel until maybe ten years ago, when I had conceived and was in the early gestation of my own half-dozenth novel: one called *Sabbatical: A Romance*.

The story of Poe's Pym drifts in and out of that novel like a bit of saltwater flotsam on the brackish tides of Chesapeake Bay. The time of its present action is the last weeks of spring, 1980. Su-

---

*Parma: F. M. Ricci, 1969; subsequently Englished by William Weaver as *Tarots* (Ricci, 1975).

san Rachel Allan Seckler, a young professor of classical American literature on sabbatical leave (to finish a study of Poe's *Pym*), and her husband, Fenwick Scott Key Turner — an ex–CIA agent turned exposeur and aspiring novelist — have just returned to the Chesapeake from a nine-month sailing cruise to the Caribbean in their $33\frac{1}{3}$-foot cutter. In the course of this sabbatical adventure they have confronted but not yet successfully dealt with various big-ticket problems and questions in their recent past and their present — including the question whether to beget children at this possibly late hour of the world. Their sailboat's name, *Pokey*, is among other things an amalgam of the surnames of one each of the couple's real or putative ancestors: in Fenwick's case, Francis Scott Key, of whom Fenn is a lineal descendant; in Susan's case, Edgar Allan Etc., an obviously more problematical genealogy.

Susan Seckler is alleged to be descended from Edgar Poe, but she can't account for the allegation since Poe had no known children, as neither will she. Similarly, the narrative that she shares the lead in can be said to be a maverick, recycled descendant of *The Narrative of Arthur Gordon Pym*, at least in a few respects — and I can't really account for that, either, except to say that like many another American writer, no doubt, I think of Poe as among my literary forebears, for better and worse: not my great-grandfather, but a brilliant though erratic great-uncle, maybe. There have been in my literal genealogy a couple of sharptongued maiden aunts, more or less dotty, in whom (as in all the fish in one's gene pool) I have seen alternative, in this case cautionary, versions of myself. When I contemplate the famous face of my fellow Baltimorean, my great-uncle Edgar, I never fail to be struck by the certain familiar looniness in it: that flakey-Romantic strain most uneasy-making to me not in his overtly gothic fictive preoccupations — live burial, putrefaction, sibling crypto-incest, and the rest — but rather in his more apparently calm and reasoned productions. Hugh Kenner has remarked that nothing looks more Victorian than a Victorian pagoda, for example; just so, I think I hear my great-uncle's half-hysteria most clearly when he's trying to keep it out of his voice: in his reasoned refutation of Maelzel's chess-playing automaton, for example, or his prescient explanation (in *Eureka*) of why the night sky happens to be dark instead of ablaze with the aggregate luminosity of stars, whose number is infinite and one of which must therefore occupy absolutely every line of sight from Earth.* If (like Fenwick Scott Key Turner in the novel *Sabbatical*) I myself feel more affinity for Henry Fielding's and Laurence Sterne's eighteenth century than for Susan's and Poe's "self-tormented, half-hysterical" nineteenth, there is in that feeling an element of prophylaxis, or exorcism. Susan no less than Fenn c'est moi, in this regard; I feel honored that the venerable house of Putnam's, which published *Eureka* (though not *Pym*), was also the publisher of *Sabbatical: A Romance*.

As for *Pym Pym Pym Pym Pym Pym Pym*:† Lord knows it is, if not "a silly book," a very odd duck of a novel, as impossible in its way as Melville's *The Confidence Man* (though mercifully shorter) and as likely to be overvalued, I fear, by ingenious readers for its real or projected ingenuities in the teeth of its patent tiresomeness, its gothic preposterosities, and its dramaturgical shortcomings. And yet . . . and yet, by gosh and by golly, the thing works, sort of — especially the opening paragraphs of Chapter 1 and the closing paragraphs of the magical last chapter (25, in which the hero goes down the drain), if the non-specialist reader has, with young Pym, survived the twenty-three chapters between. Captain Edgar manages after all to skipper his maiden (and final) novel out of some fairly shaky heavy-weather realism, down through gothic Doldrums into latitudes of rather more plausible irrealism, and finally "**STILL FARTHER SOUTH**" (as Poe's subtitle advertises in boldface caps) into a realm where I too have done some narrative navigation: a realm whose resistless current I recognize and, reading *Pym*, give myself over to at last, whether or not I have ever attained it in my own novelistic expeditions.

---

*A contemporary astronomer, Edward Harrison, in his recent book *Darkness at Night: A Riddle of the Universe* (Cambridge MA: Harvard U. Press, 1988), reviews Poe's explanation of why the night sky is in fact dark and judges it essentially correct. Harrison accounts for *Eureka*'s being all but ignored by scientists and literary scholars alike by saying, "Its science was too metaphysical and its metaphysics too scientific for contemporary tastes."
†Poe-folk will recognize the echo of Daniel Hoffman's memorably titled study *Poe Poe Poe Poe Poe Poe Poe* (Garden City NY: Doubleday, 1972).

Speaking not as an expert critic or scholar but as a fairly sea-soned fellow novelist and, by the way, a not-inexperienced ama-teur sailor, I report that I find *The Narrative of Arthur Gordon Pym* sometimes less credible in its more realistic stretches and more so in its less. I won't comment here on its metafictive narra-tive frame, which Susan Seckler and many another contemporary critic have spoken much to. What most impresses me about the opening paragraphs of the story proper [in which sixteen-year-old Pym and a school chum go night-sailing and are run down by a homeward-bound Nantucket whaler] is the tone of the cama-raderie of the two boys' escapade in Pym's little sloop *Ariel* that October night in 1825. Young Augustus Barnard's drunken post-party oath — "that he would not go to sleep for any Arthur Pym in Christendom, when there was such a glorious breeze from the southwest" — and young Pym's counterboast that he too is "tired of lying in bed like a dog, and quite as ready for any fun or frolic as any Augustus Barnard in Nantucket" — these and the other details of their setting out I find as refreshing as a breeze out of the English eighteenth century: out of a scapegrace-*roman* by Fielding or Smollett, say. I don't recall anything elsewhere in Poe, certainly not in *Pym*, quite as appealing and convincing in this line. God forgive me, I myself have undertaken such reckless, not-quite-sober late-night sails in years gone by (it's always a southwesterly that promotes them), and Poe has got it right: the little sloop chafing against the dock-piles, the boys' underestimation of the wind and overestimation of their abilities after Substance Abuse, the fast-sobering scariness, for Pym anyhow, of the night-sea out there, from which one is lucky to return intact. The author even supplies, somewhat belatedly, the bright moon normally required, along with a glorious southerly, to inspire such lunacies. Yo, Poe!

Already by the fifth paragraph, however, I'm having trouble, as are the young night-sailors. In keeping with his temporarily realist mode, Poe describes *Ariel* in some detail as a *sloop*, under whose unreefed mainsail and jib the boys have set out. But when an acci-dental downwind gybe in Paragraph 5 "carrie[s] away the mast short off by the board" (that is to say, the apparently unstayed mast breaks off just above deck level and is lost over the side along

with the boom, the gaff, and the mainsail), Arthur and his passed-
out buddy roar along downwind "under the jib only," without
Poe's troubling to tell us from what — on a single-masted boat
which is now a no-masted boat — that jib is flying.

Okay: Sometimes even good Homer nods, and in a novel whose
principal characters zonk out as often and completely as do those
in *Pym*, it would be a miracle if the author didn't blink from time
to time — particularly in the realistic passages of his voyage,
which have about them the clenched-jawed metonymity of a
driver determined to stay awake on a featureless stretch of inter-
state. I certainly find this lapse more acceptable as a simple lapse
than as a deliberate challenge to the "merely proairetic reader," as
one recent critic has called the likes of us low-tech Pymophiles.

In the same spirit, I don't fret overmuch at my question marks
in the margins of *Pym*'s jury-rigged chronology, such as the narrator's declaration in his preface of July 1838 that he returned to the
United States "a few months ago" from "the South Seas and elsewhere" and met Poe in Richmond, etc., when his return would
seem to have to have been closer to two *years* ago to jibe with the
publication of the story's first installments in the *Southern Literary
Messenger* in January and February 1837 — dates that "Pym"
verifies. Never mind, while one is at it, that the most meticulous
reconstruction of the schooner *Jane Guy*'s movements in Chapters
14 and 15, in the neighborhood of Christmas Harbor, won't quite
add up.* Let it go: Who among us novelists has not had such
gaffes pointed out by sharp-eyed readers? The important thing
about *Jane Guy*'s log is that it picks Pym up from the drifting hulk
of the brig *Grampus* on August 7 somewhere off Brazil's Cabo de
San Rocas — about 7°S. Latitude by my calculations, of which
more presently — and delivers him on the winter solstice (summer
solstice down there) to the 60th parallel of latitude and Capt.
Guy's decision on that portentous date to push on Still Farther
South.

---

*Try it; you'll hate it: The schooner first arrives there on October 18, 1827, and
her crew explore the neighborhood in the schooner's boats "for about three
weeks." Then on November 12 she sets out in search of the Aurora Islands and
"in fifteen days" (i.e., on November 27) passes Tristan da Cunha en route, but
manages nevertheless to reach the reported area of the Auroras a whole week *before* that, on November 20.

I wouldn't even have mentioned *Ariel*'s mastless jib (which has also been noted by Professors Burton Pollin and Herbert F. Smith) if not that it foreshadows my first more serious crisis of belief, just as the dismasting itself foreshadows the sloop's being run down in the dark by the whaleship *Penguin*. Three paragraphs later, after Pym revives from the first of his many, many losses of consciousness, we learn that the crewmen of the *Penguin*, having risked their lives valiantly to look for survivors, had turned back in the ship's jolly boat. The whaler rolls in the heavy seas, and along with First Mate Henderson we see our hapless and unconscious young hero . . . *bolted through the neck?* Yup: bolted through the neck (and through the collar of his jacket) to the vessel's coppered bottom, alternately buried at sea and resurrected, like a funhouse corpse, as the ship rolls.

I know: The shot symbolizes A, B, and C and foreshadows D, E, and F later on in the movie. But I groan all the same at its sensational implausibility: the first of many such groans to come from this "proairetic reader." *Bolted through the neck*, and so securely that all that slow-rolling and dunking in a gale of wind don't dislodge him! Yet he neither drowns nor requires so much as a suture for his wound! The *end* of Chapter 1 charmingly wears its portentousness up its sleeve rather than on it — I mean the boys' coming down to breakfast next morning at Mr. Barnard's as if their night-sea adventure had not happened, and getting away with it — but I am not deceived by Poe's winning observation that "School-boys . . . can accomplish wonders of deception." I know now that it's to be the Rocky Horror Picture Show after all; I sigh and settle in with my popcorn, and take not a word of the story straight thereafter, not even the mesmerizing last chapter. So you scared those hard-case *Grampus* mutineers out of their wits by making like a zombie? Sure you did. And later on you saw a boatload of deadies under full sail with seagulls chewing on the crew, and later yet you cannibalized your shipmate Parker, and after that your dead pal Augustus's leg came apart in your hands like . . . oh, like that putrefied leg of mutton from Chapter 2, let's say, and you could hear the sharks chomping him up from a *whole mile away*, and on the island of Tsalal (where both the natives and the sea-birds cry "*Tekeli-li!*") you were reburied alive and re-resurrected for the fifth time out of six in twenty-five chapters? Right, right.

The documents of the days of sail are rich in actual such horrors, which in our time the Vietnamese boat people could doubtless match. In Poe's hands, alas, they almost invariably turn not into "challenges to the proairetic code," but into genre effects. And for all Pym's elaborate subsequent logging of his psychological weather, as a credible, palpable novelistic character he goes down with the *Ariel* in Chapter 1 and never resurfaces. Even in proto-metafiction, that's a casualty to be regretted.

Yet through even the barfiest of ghoul-flicks the deep myths sometimes speak, more or less, and through the tellings of a canny and intuitive though erratic genius like Poe they may speak strongly, however much or little their "medium" (in the spiritualist sense) might be conscious of them. Autodidact Edgar was unpredictably knowledgeable as well as plenty smart; the paradigmatic image of him in Dominick Argento's opera *The Voyage of Edgar Allan Poe* is surely not the whole story, though it seems a fair piece of it: I mean the tenor zapped flat onstage by his *daimon* after every second aria, the vessel of his rational consciousness overwhelmed. As I tour Great-Uncle Edgar's floating gothic funhouse, my own authorial consciousness respectfully notes that the shipwright managed some admirable and not so obvious formal touches along with the more conspicuous gee-whizzers; and something "still farther south" in my sensibility rides on the undercurrent of myth, stronger and stronger as we descend the parallels of south latitude. Umberto Eco reports that the last words of his friend Italo Calvino were *"I paralleli! I paralleli!"*: It's a better exit line for a writer than Poe's "Reynolds! Reynolds!" and regarding certain of *Pym*'s *paralleli* I shall speak next as the author not of *Sabbatical: A Romance* but of certain earlier fictions inspired by the Wandering Hero myth: the Ur-myth, which my imagination once upon a time became possessed by after critics pointed out to me that my imagination was possessed by it.*

---

*See "Foreword to *The Sot-Weed Factor*," farther on in this volume; also "Mystery and Tragedy: The Twin Motions of Ritual Heroism," in *The Friday Book*.

Inasmuch as every literary person nowadays knows at least the outlines of that myth, I don't doubt that Poe's commentators in our time have long since noted its parallels in *Pym*. The *Ariel* episode prefigures it in miniature, even down to the time-zapping and the returned hero's appearing as if nothing remarkable had happened, as if he'd never been away — in short, as if he were not who he is, the man who has come through. The voyage proper (serial voyages, rather, in serial vessels) incorporates literally or figuratively most of the cyclical myth's classic features: in its first quadrant, the reputable ancestry, with a particular role for the maternal grandfather and a mother so royal-virginal in this case that she's not even mentioned; the undetailed childhood in "another country" (New Bedford, where Pym is sent to school — by his maternal grandfather); the nocturnal summons to adventure; the sidekicks and helpers, tokens and talismans; in its second quadrant, the threshold-crossings, the initiatory ordeals, disguises, contests, riddles, trips-out-of-time, incremental divestitures and subterranean (or submarine) weekends, all culminating in mysterious, even mystical passage from the Twilight Zone to a *coincidentia oppositorum* at the Axis Mundi: the transcension of categories; the "oxymoronic fusion" of dark illumination, winter and summer, et and cetera. And from there, from the edge of the South Polar Abyss itself (a place as spookily, equivocally white as the icy center of Dante's Inferno leading to the white-rose peak of Paradiso, or the Whiteness of the Whale and for that matter the white white room on the far side of time in Arthur Clarke's *2001*), our hero is cycled *still farther south* into the quadrants of Return and Death. . . .

To which *I* shall return after nodding Yes to my fellow skipper's large-scale calendrics and making a point about his structural navigation, so to speak. I mean in the former instance that rhythm of equinox and solstice, for example, a common feature of such myths. I confess to having done that sort of calendar-diddling myself in more novels than one, even before I understood why. Ditto Poe's scheduling the death of Pym's "first-stage" helper, Augustus, not only on the first day of his eponymous month but at the formal center of the novel: Chapter 13 of the twenty-seven narrative divisions, with thirteen units before it (the prologue plus twelve chapters) and thirteen after (twelve chapters plus the epilogue). Indeed, it's very nearly at the center of the center: Augustus dies at twelve noon on Day Nine (August 1) of the fifteen journalized days that comprise that central chapter, adrift in the hulk of the *Grampus*. The *very* center of the center would be Day Eight of the fifteen (July 31), and if nothing special is noted in Pym's log of that pivotal day, it's because the desperate survivors are in no position to know at the time what Pym could have calculated in retrospect but didn't, quite, although I daresay that his author did: that it will have been on that day that our hero drifted across the Equator into the Southern Hemisphere of the novel.

The necessary numbers are all given in Chapter 14: The survivors were rescued by the *Jane Guy* on August 7 "off Cape St. Roque" in longitude 31°W.: that is to say, comfortably off the nose of Brazil, which extends from Cabo de San Rocas (at latitude 5°south) nearly 200 miles down to Recife (at latitude 8° south), its eastmost tip being at about the 7th parallel. Given the intruments of the time, the schooner's positions are approximate indeed, the longitude more so than the latitude, since sextants back then were more reliable than chronometers. Even so, young Pym reckons after the fact that *Grampus* must have drifted south *"not less than twenty-five degrees!"* (italics and exclamation mark his; distance 1,500 nautical miles; probability nil, since in fact the prevailing ocean currents in those latitudes set inexorably west instead of south — but never mind). Conveniently for us armchair navigators, that drifting began on July 14: twenty-five days in all, which comes neatly to one degree (sixty nautical miles) per day. That's a 2.5-knot current, almost a Gulf Stream in reverse, and though it does not exist in fact (until you get well *below* the nose of Brazil), we know where it's going. As for where it's coming from, if we dead-reckon from a rescue at latitude 7°S. and plot backward (which is how both novelists and navigators often do their plotting), we'll find *Grampus* to have been at latitude 20°N. back there on Bastille Day (i.e., just under the Tropic of Cancer) and smack on the Equator of the globe smack at the equator of the story. Another symbolic threshold crossed: one with its own initiatory traditions, as sailors and cruise-ship passengers know.

Way to go, Poe. Back to the myth now, and then to the novel: The first half of the generic wandering hero's night-sea journey (or whatever) ritually fetches him to the heart of mystery. The second half, as I read it, fetches him from mystery to tragedy and then re-cycles him. What there is of this latter half-cycle in Poe's novel is in "Pym's" preface and, glancingly, "the editor's" afterword (both written of course by Poe himself). The wanderer returns "home" from the bright heart of darkness in the netherworld unrecognized or unrecognizable, bringing something precious with him. He manifests himself, routs the usurpers, and delivers his message or whatever, which, being ineffable, must always be more or less garbled in transmission. He reigns peacefully for a time (about eight years, says Lord Raglan in *The Hero*) and then leaves his city to meet his mysterious end. No one knows for sure where his grave is; several cities claim him as theirs; one day he may return.

On the vernal equinox of 1828, when he goes down the hole, Arthur Gordon Pym is still a very young man: nineteen years old, though he seems to have been initiated out of boyishness back there between the Tropic of Cancer and the Equator (his senior shipmates Parker and Peters never refer to him as "the kid"). By my calculations, the median age for these things is $33\frac{1}{3}$; like his author, Pym's precocious. Eight blank years later he pops up in Richmond, and in the ninth and tenth years he endeavors to truthify his message, which has been cordially usurped and betrayed as fiction by "Mr. Poe"; when he dies in July '38 immediately after writing his preface, in circumstances even more equivocal than those of his author's death eleven years later, he's still only in his thirtieth year to heaven, a threshold more poetical than mythical. In the epi-logue, at second or third hand, his creator disclaims the factuality of the bottom line of his creature's account, and the vertiginous paradox of that passing disclaimer at once betrays and affirms the ontological status of Arthur Gordon Pym and of the narrative: They are factual in the fiction but in fact fictional; what truth is in them is the truth of myth.

Yet despite "*i paralleli*," every professional intuition tells me that Poe's novel is *not* a systematic and pointed reorchestration of the myth of the wandering hero. There are about as many and

significant disanalogies as analogies (including the compass directions, which are all wrong), and lots of missing pieces. Some of
those are supplied by Pym's sidekicks (it's Dirk Peters who makes
the Odysseus-like inland trek — to Illinois — at the voyage's end),
and several more can be supplied from the author's biography —
Poe's late-adolescent setting out for his "true" home, the shrines to
his memory in several cities, etc. — but surely that's cheating.
More important, the *sense* of the great myth is absent from *The
Narrative of Arthur Gordon Pym*, as it is not from the stories of
Odysseus, Aeneas, Oedipus, Perseus, Jesus, and even Paul Morel
of D. H. Lawrence's *Sons and Lovers*. Poe's novel rides on the
myth the way the *Grampus* and then the canoe ride on that current, but it is not a rendition of the myth, nor is it sensibly about
the myth. Beyond the metafictive paradoxes of its framing text,
which I find to be of real though not unlimited interest, and beyond, in the story proper, the sundry contaminations of reality by
irreality (as Borges puts it) and vice versa, I think I don't after all
know quite *what* the presenting sense of Poe's novel is: I mean its
situational premise, its thematic center, and its moral-dramatical
bottom line, apart from its symbolical razzle-dazzle and any en-
crypted messages about its author.

The problem is that Pym, and therefore his narrative, has no
mainspring. As we say in fiction-writing workshops, his story is all
"vehicle" and no "ground situation"; his actions, consequently
(on the several occasions when he *takes* action rather than passively enduring what befalls him), seem to this reader meaningless,
dramaturgically speaking, however resonant they may be from
our experience of myth and of initiation novels. Moreover, as I
have said, after that fine opening of the *Ariel* episode he is scarcely
apprehensible as a character. To compare Pym and company with
Billy Budd and company or Roderick Random and company or
even Odysseus or Sindbad and company is to be reminded how
little gift Poe had for the "realistic" aspects of characterization,
even as we find them in fantastical mythographers like Dante and
Scheherazade. And this defect is more conspicuous in a pseudore-
alistic narrative like *Pym* than in the flat-out gothics of "A Cask of
Amontillado" or "The Fall of the House of Usher." Indeed, I think
I know Fortunato and Roderick Usher better than I know Dirk

Peters and Arthur Gordon Pym. Poe's gifts, like Borges's, simply lie elsewhere.*

In short, I confess to sharing the reservations of Henry James and Robert Louis Stevenson concerning our subject. The way I'd put it is that the young hero of *Pym* is altogether without the moral-dramatic voltage required of protagonists in particular, and desirable even in metafiction if it is not to become mere metaphysics. Pym is not a dramatic character but rather the simulacrum of a dramatic character, and Poe's novel ought to be regarded as some sort of simulacrum of a novel: not a counterfeit but an isomorph; not a hoax but a mimicry. *Pym* echoes the bildungsroman and the Ur-myth and mimes the contours of dramatic action the way a praying mantis mimes a green twig but is not a green twig. I am less than confident that Poe understood the difference (and his own motives) as clearly as the mantis may be said to understand them; novels were truly not his métier. I believe, however, that the reader who approaches *Pym* as if it were a bona fide novel, like the fly who approaches the mantis thinking that *lean* plus *green* plus *stationary* equals *twig*, is in for difficulties — less consequential ones, I trust.

I trust too that the scholars gathered here in conference on the island where Pym's voyage began, on the sesquicentennial of Poe's curious novel about it, are of all readers the least likely to make so innocent an approach. I have to hope, on the other hand, that in distinguishing the mantis from the twig, they don't mistake it for an eagle or a bird of paradise. Who ever heard one of those cry "*Tekeli-li!*"?

*See "Borges and I: a mini-memoir," to follow.

Kenosis
"I Think It's Trying to Tell Us Something"

My two most often reprinted essays are "The Literature of Exhaustion" (1968) and "The Literature of Replenishment" (1979), both originally published in the Atlantic Monthly *and collected in* The Friday Book, *and both fumbling toward an understanding, if not a definition, of Postmodernism. The little Friday-piece that follows has to do with the interval — familiar to novelists and to serial parents, among others — between exhaustion and replenishment. It first appeared in the* New York Times Book Review *(January 20, 1991).*

THE DECADES HAVE taught me patience with my muse: Before she'll sit in my lap and sing, she visits me less like one of Zeus's daughters by Mnemosyne than like one of those vintage Hollywood monsters, almost human, whose inchoate grunts and rumbles move the heroine to declare, "I think it's trying to *tell* us something." Always, in the past, in her own good time, she has cleared her throat, refound her voice — which is to say, mine. But she won't be hurried.

It happened that in 1990 a number of things in my life and work came more or less to an end in rather quick succession. Through that year I wound up the final editing of a new novel — my eleventh book, tenth volume of fiction, eighth novel — with the terminal-sounding title *The Last Voyage of Somebody the Sailor*. It is a comedy whose dark muse is, in fact, that figure called by Scheherazade "the Destroyer of Delights, Severer of Societies, and Desolator of Dwelling-Places": lethal Time. Near midyear I turned sixty and, per personal program, retired on that birthday from my full-time professorship at the Johns Hopkins University:

"early-early phased retirement" by the university's standards and in the language of its benefits administration office; but I had been teaching for nearly forty years, the last seventeen of them at my alma mater. I swapped my endowed chair for emeritus rank and reduced my academic responsibilities to one graduate-level fiction-writing seminar — this out of my attachment to university life, the pleasures of coaching a small group of selected advanced apprentices, and the practical benefits of a campus office and secretarial privileges.

That same year, making random notes toward whatever next major fiction project might follow *The Last Voyage* (two had been conceived already since January and had spontaneously aborted), I happened to turn and fill the final page of a spiral-bound stenographic notepad reserved for that purpose. I had begun that notepad twenty-three years, or seven books, earlier, in 1967 — a world ago. It is only the third such that I've filled in my professional lifetime; the other two, although the same size, span a mere seven years each. I have delayed finding a new steno-pad to cover 1991–____, whether because there are still in Pad Three notes toward enough possible projects to fill out my remaining creative lifetime or because, as I enter my seventh decade, that space after *1991–* looks disagreeably gravelike.

In another sort of notebook (I keep all kinds: travel logs, ship's logs, house logs, even fish-tank maintenance logs) — this a small black one for the registration of what are, occasionally, small black thoughts — I noted that just as I had filled Page Last of Steno-Pad Three, *1967–1990*, I had turned the last blank leaf of my old academic roll-book, also numbered Three: *Johns Hopkins, 1973–____*. I ought now to fill that blank, too, with eventful *1990*, but I find that as of this writing, although the semester's finished and the calendar year all but, I've not yet done so. Nor have I bought a fresh roll-book for autumns to come, although I intend to maintain for a while my attenuated connection with the university.

Roll-Books One and Two must have been mislaid in our last house-move, and I miss them. The three together would name every student I've taught since 1951, from my maiden graduate-teaching-assistant class at Johns Hopkins, through my through-the-ranks years at Penn State, Buffalo, and Boston, to my current handful of Hopkins hotshots. Those students must total several thousand, for although in recent years I've taught only small seminars, for decades before that I carried a full load of lecture-courses as well. The record-keeper in me craves the precise numbers on which his pleased fatigue is based; the academic burnout wants the stats of the fire.

Among that missing myriad would be found the maiden name of my wife, whom I met and taught at Penn State in the mid-sixties and serendipitously re-met in Boston some years later. In the final days of 1990, having wound up my circa–five-thousandth published page, my sixth decade of life, my full-time academic career, and my third musely steno-pad and student roll-book, I'll be celebrating with her our twentieth wedding anniversary: not the end of anything except the second decade of a graced connection, but we'll toast the milestone with feelings beyond reciprocal gratitude. Ours will be, as of that date, the longest-standing intimacy in either of our lives: Duly time-tested, it is a bond we're confident now is breakable only by death — and we know that break to be exactly twenty years nearer than it was in December 1970.

L'Chaim.

Outside our house, meanwhile, the cold war ended, Germany reunited, the French and British Chunnel-diggers shook hands under the Channel, the new Persian Gulf crisis bade equally (as of this writing) to midwife a new world order or to abort it, and, depending on one's way of counting, either the 1980s ended or the Nineties began.

There it is. Absent fatal accident, by when this page is published my marriage will have begun its third blessed decade. With so few students now to keep track of, I may not bother with a new roll-book for my emeritus seasons; won't the registrar's computerized rosters and grade-sheets serve as well? But no doubt I'll get around to picking up Steno-Pad Four: *1991–____*, and no doubt I'll find seeds to sow in it for possible future cultivation. Although the muse's pause this time has been somewhat longer than usual, experience leads me to expect that by the time *The Last Voyage* officially hits the stands, I'll be scribbling away on the Next, whether it's CPR on one of those two casualties shelved while I was seeing *Voyage* through the press or something "new," suggested by the umpteenth reinspection of those aging bits in Pad Three: *1967–1990.*

For poets and short-story writers, the case must be different, and I've known novelists who work on several projects at once. But my sort of congenital, one-thing-at-a-time novelist confronts this empty interval between imagination's exhaustion and replenishment, between delivery and reimpregnation, only once every several years (the stats: a mean 3.3 years, in my case, with a minimum of two and a max of seven; but the interpause is typically no longer than a temperate-zone season). I've learned to use the well-filling intermission to write an essay or two, often of a stock-taking or position-fixing character, while monitoring my new and old jottings like those radio astronomers listening for extra-terrestrial signals against the low-level buzz of the expanding universe — except that these are *my* signals, my mutterings; it's *me* I'm awaiting word from, whose garbled transmissions I'm trying to decipher. King Kong and Fay Wray both; my muse, *c'est moi.*

Dum dee dum.

Well, it *has* gone past the norm, this particular repollinative pause, given that its prompt first pair of tentative new blooms look nipped now in the bud. What pause doesn't lengthen for gents my age? Not one season this time, but a virtual cycle; not an essay or two, but three or four and here's another, amid *Voyage's* copyedits and galleyproofs, lecture and vacation travel, seminars and business matters and houseguests and housework and play — the background noise of one's personal universe, whether expanding or contracting, against which one listens, listens for the Signal; life's busywork, which lets the muse sidle up as if idly, like your secret lover at a public party, to murmur (with the gestures and expression of one commenting on the canapés) exactly what you've been waiting to hear.

Scratch that adulterous trope. *Your* muse may wear designer duds and carry on like that, but mine's some combination of E.T.'s avatars aforenoted and Sindbad the Sailor's magic isle of Serendib, with its peculiar navigational aspect of being unreachable by direct intention. To get to Serendib, one must plot one's course in good faith elsewhere and then lose one's bearings — serendipitously. No problem for old Sindbad up through Voyage Six, when he first attained that fortunate isle: He was in good faith headed elsewhere; hadn't known the place existed. But how to hack Voyage Seven, the caliph's explicit commission to sail straight for Serendib? My muse is Serendib-like, a low-magnitude star that disappears when gandered frontally. She's like that slippery Christian grace unattainable by ardent direct pursuit, which taints her pursuer with the sin of pride.

Deedly dee dee.

Kenosis, the Greeks called this emptying of the spirit's vessel in preparation for a refill. Early Christian theology picked up the term to describe Christ's relinquishment of godhood to take human form and die. See Philippians 2:5–8.

Dee diddly die.

And you know, don't you, scribbler of these lines, that beyond a writer's untimely demise (Italo Calvino's, Raymond Carver's, Donald Barthelme's) lies the prospect of his or her *not*-so-untimely demise (old Sophocles's, old Thomas Mann's, old Jorge Luis Borges's) — if not in this decade, then in the next, at latest the one after — and that these musely recovery times are as likely to lengthen as one's other recovery times, until comes the intermission that no next act follows. You're in robust health (*for your age*, the put-down parentheses add), but you're not age-proof. Your knack for slaloming on one water ski upped and vanished some summers back and hasn't been heard from since. You can't jog the four flights from your university office up to the seminar room as erst you did and still speak sentences when you get there. They gave you a twenty-one-geared beaut of a mountain bike at last spring's retirement party, and you've used all twenty-one on Maryland's near-flat Eastern Shore. Where'd you put Roll-Books One and Two, by the way?

John Keats sonnetized his youthful fears that he might cease to be before his pen had "glean'd [his] teeming brain," and not long thereafter joined the ranks of the illustrious Untimelies. 'Twould be no picnic (you permit yourself in passing to counterfear) to go on being and being and being *after* your pen hath glean'd etc. Or say you're Scheherazade — Who isn't? — and you took your maiden deep narrative breath all those nights ago, and now it's this many plots and characters and themes and situations later, foreshadowings and reprises and twists and pace-changes and even Weltanschauung-evolvements, for pity's sake, and here's yet another longish yarn, neatly denouemented if you do say so yourself, and maybe the king's wowed and maybe not (What does *he* know about storytelling?), but anyhow he's not offing your head, and so now it's time to launch your thousand-and-whatevereth before the muezzin cries from the minaret that prayer is better than sleep, and let's just see now, maybe the one about — nope, you used that on Night 602 or thereabouts, so maybe work up instead the bit you tucked away in midst of the Sindbad series, wasn't it, that bit about what *was* it now, had a sort of spin to it, charm to it, color, tippy-tip of your tongue, dum dee dum dum, and there *he* goes now, restless already for his next, you know well enough that little sniff and twitch of his. . . .

Scheherazade, *c'est moi*. King, too. That muezzin, even, whom ever at my back I hear while with some third ear listening, listening —

What was that?*

---

*It was, in fact, the first fetal stirrings of the earlier-mentioned novel/memoir *Once Upon a Time: A Floating Opera*, in which may be found an extended and reorchestrated version of this ode to pregnant emptiness. On with the stories!

Borges and I
a mini-memoir

WE LEARN FROM our students, perhaps in order to teach our teachers. It was two students of mine, their names now lost to me, on two different university campuses, who serendipitously introduced me to the work of Latino writers profoundly consequential to the way I myself think about the art of fiction and the way or ways that I have attempted to practice that art. The second of those writers happens to have been the late great Argentine Jorge Luis Borges; I was pleased recently to drive up from Johns Hopkins to the Pennsylvania State University to join in honoring him once again,* as I have numerous times gratefully paid homage to him elsewhere.

My story begins with a leisurely digression:

In 1953, when I *first* came up from Johns Hopkins to Penn State — to begin my professional academic career in the English Composition Department of what was then still the Pennsylvania State College — I had not yet found my voice as a writer of fiction. The shortest way to put it is that the muses would not sing for me until I found some way to book Scheherazade, James Joyce, and William Faulkner on the same tidewater Maryland showboat, with myself at both the helm and the steam calliope. To put it another way, I needed to discover, or to be discovered by, Postmodernism — but I had not yet grasped that truth (much less that aesthetic concept, not to mention its label) when I arrived in State College PA with my young and ever-increasing family and con-

---

*At the conference "Borges Revisited," held in University Park, Pennsylvania, April 12 and 13, 1991. This mini-memoir is adapted from my address to that conference. It was published in Korean (in the international journal *Contemporary World Literature* 29, 1991) before its first appearance in English (*Antaeus* 70, Spring 1993).

fronted the gloomy prospect of perishing academically for want of publishing, and the gloomier yet of putting aside what I had come to feel deeply was my true calling, however inadequately I was responding to the call.

But then, mirabile dictu, it came to pass that one of my Penn State students — I wish I could recall which one, for I owe him or her much thanks for a great unintended service — indirectly showed me the way, by introducing me to a turn-of-the-century Brazilian writer named Joaquim Machado de Assis, several of whose novels were just then appearing in English translation from the Noonday Press. I checked Machado out of the Pattee Library — first his *Braz Cubas* (retitled *Epitaph of a Small Winner* in its English translation) and then *Dom Casmurro* and *Quinças Borba* (the latter retitled *Philosopher or Dog?* in its English version) — and those novels supplied me with model resolutions of a problem whose terms I could not have articulated before it was well behind me. Never mind the particulars: I have retailed them elsewhere,* and I really do intend to arrive at Jorge Luis Borges by this circuitous route. Never mind as well that various happenings in my lived life, as well as happenstances in my reading, turned me around corners necessary for writing my first published novel and all the books since; this is not about those, although it may seem for a while yet to be.

Paul Cézanne is said to have said, vis-à-vis painting, that "the road to nature leads through the Louvre, and the road to the Louvre leads through nature." Similarly, for a writer of fiction the road to "life" may well lead through the library, and the road to the library — to the shelf with one's own books on it — will no doubt lead through life. Life teaches the storyteller his themes and subject matter; literature teaches him how to get a handle on them: what has been done already, what might be redone differently, what's a *story* anyway, and what is to be found in the existing inventory of situations, attitudes, characters, tonalities, forms, and effects accumulated over four thousand years of written literature. If that writer happens also to be a teacher, his students and

---

*E.g., in "The Spanish Connection" and "Foreword to *The Floating Opera*," both in this volume.

colleagues may occasionally point him toward something important that he was ignorant of in the vast corpus of the already said,
just when he was ripe for the revelation. My thanks to the forgotten Penn Stater who, nearly forty years ago and unwittingly
to both of us, did me this favor. Joaquim Machado de Assis
(1839–1908) happens *not* to be a writer of ongoing importance to
me; in a recent conversation about him on the BBC, I realized (in
midst of praising him as a proto-Postmodernist) that I haven't
reread him since the Penn State 1950s and scarcely remember now
what his novels are "about." But once upon a time he showed me
how to become the novelist I was trying to be, and for better or
worse I up and became that novelist.

Twenty years subsequently, in conversation in East Lansing,
Michigan, with Señor Jorge Luis Borges — who by that time had
become as important to my thinking about the art of fiction as
Machado de Assis had briefly been — I asked the eminent Argentine what he thought of his eminent Brazilian predecessor. I am
sorry to have to report that although I remember quite a number
of things from my three personal path-crossings with Borges, I
cannot remember his response to that question. I happened at the
time to have recently sat in on the Ph.D. dissertation defense at
Johns Hopkins of an Argentinean young woman whose thesis
topic was the fiction of Borges's Buenos Aires crony and some-
time collaborator Adolfo Bioy-Casares; I had interrogated the
candidate about Machado de Assis as a feasible precursor of "el
Boom" — the explosion of Latino fictive talent in recent decades — and I had discovered that although her background
knowledge of that phenomenon was extensive, she had scarcely
heard of my man Machado. I believe, but cannot swear to it, that
Borges and I shook our heads together in East Lansing over the
prevailing indifference to Portuguese-Latino writers among Span-
ish-Latino writers and their readers.

Borges himself, needless to report, was quite familiar with the
writings of Joaquim Machado de Assis and with the salutary
influence on Machado of Laurence Sterne's *Tristram Shandy*,
which in my earlier Penn State innocence I had not yet encountered either. The consequence for me, I remarked to Borges, had
been Borgesian: When I'd gotten around to reading *Tristram*

Shandy, I'd been delighted by the extent to which the eighteenth-century Englishman had been influenced by the late-nineteenth-century Brazilian. As Borges observes in his essay on Franz Kafka, great writers create their own precursors.

Among those of us less than great but never less than serious about the art of literature, it is a matter not so much either of creating our precursors on the one hand or, once we've found and established our characteristic voice, of being unduly precursed by them on the other, as it is of finding in them some validation of this or that aspect of what we take ourselves to be up to, musewise. That is how it was with Borges and I (regardless of grammatical accuracy, I want always to say "Borges and I": *Borges y yo*, the title of one his loveliest meditations) at another consequential turn in my professional road, when another student, at another university, serendipitously introduced me to the *ficciones* of Jorge Luis Borges, just when, without knowing it, I most needed them.

Borges y yo, Borges and I — him the precursor, me the precursed (in this case, pre-blessed): Herewith the sum and substance of our relation, and selected trivia of our personal encounters. Needless to say, the relation is absolutely a one-way street: Nobody is likely to read Borges differently for having read Barth, the way I read *Tristram Shandy* differently for having read Machado's *Epitaph of a Small Winner*. Furthermore, the Borges street — *Calle Borges* — is only one street among others in my personal city of words. But it turns a meaningful corner, and a quarter-century after first discovering it, I'm still working out its ramifications in my own practice of fiction.

In 1965 I left Penn State after twelve agreeable and productive years: three children nurtured, three novels published and a fourth nearly completed, much innocence lost but an invincible remnant preserved, the warmest academic and personal friendships of my life before or since, and the commonplace tribulations and delights of living through one's twenties into one's mid-thirties — ups and downs echoed and amplified in this case by our culture's moving from what we think of as the American 1950s into the tempestuous, counterculturalist 1960s. I moved to the former University of Buffalo, which had just joined the New York state university

system and was enjoying a virtual carte blanche from Governor
Nelson Rockefeller; the governor wanted a major university center
at each end of the Thomas E. Dewey Thruway as well as one in the
middle, at Albany. Eighty percent of my bustling and distinguished
new department had been recruited within the previous two years,
all as additions to the existing faculty. It was the bloody Fat Sixties; almost anything went. I began my new professorship with a
free semester to finish up the novel *Giles Goat-Boy*, begun at Penn
State and extended in Spain, and after so many bucolic years in
rural Pennsylvania I relished the pleasures of living again in a siz-
able city. It must be acknowledged that Buffalo is not Paris or
Berlin or Madrid or New York; but just then, at least, there was a
remarkable amount of new art going on in town, and the ambitious expansion of the university, coincident with the flowering of
the counterculture, effervesced the whole scene. Even its marginal-
ity, geographical and otherwise, seemed positive: "art on the edge"
at the edge of our troubled republic; Lyndon Johnson's "New
Frontier" on the old Niagara Frontier of the War of 1812; a sometimes volatile mix of avant-garde aesthetics, protest politics, and
hippie culture, with Niagara Falls thundering and crumbling in the
background and great Canada just across the river.

I myself was and remain, politically, just another more or less
passive, off-the-shelf liberal, but I inhaled that radical air deeply
except when the campus was being tear-gassed. I spent time in the
contemporary wing of the Albright-Knox Museum, catching up
on what had been happening since Abstract Expressionism. I was
befriended by iconoclasts like Leslie Fiedler and front-edgers like
the composer-conductor Lukas Foss, who was then directing the
Buffalo Philharmonic and encouraging all sorts of far-out new music both downtown and on the campus. I heard my new colleagues
lecturing on the likes of Marshal McLuhan and Claude Levi-
Strauss, Lacan and Derrida. And — thanks again to some savvy
student in my graduate-level fiction-writing seminar — in 1966, as
Giles was going through the press and I was waiting to see what
my muse would do for an encore, I "discovered" the fiction of
Jorge Luis Borges.

The experience of being stopped cold in one's tracks is not unusual among younger artists. Indeed, I have written somewhere or

other* that I take it to be the responsibility of alert apprentice artists — alert apprentice *anythings* — to be swept off their feet with some frequency in the face of passionate virtuosity: great power under great control, as encountered in their predecessors both distant and immediate. So *I* had been upon first discovering James Joyce and Franz Kafka, for example, back in undergraduate days. It is another matter when one is half through one's thirties and for better or worse has pretty much become who one is. But upon first encountering such astonishing stories as "The Secret Miracle," "The Zahir," "Pierre Menard," "Funes the Memorious," "Tlön, Uqbar, Orbis Tertius," and the rest, I felt again that urgent, disquieting imperative from apprentice days: that everything must halt in my shop until I came to terms with this extraordinary artist.

Whatever their aesthetic merits, the record of my efforts in the way of this assimilation comprises two chief items: an essay called "The Literature of Exhaustion," written in 1967 and first published the following year,† and a short-story series called *Lost in the Funhouse*, written over the same period and also published in 1968. The essay (with its much-misunderstood title) was my attempt to articulate, with Sr. Borges's assistance, what I saw going on round about me and felt in my aesthetic bones in the American High Sixties. With the clarity of hindsight I see it to have been groping toward a definition of the spirit of postmodernism, as I understand that slippery term: an aesthetic for the making of new and valid work that is yet responsible to the exhaustive, even apocalyptic vastness of what has been done before. The *Funhouse* stories, I readily acknowledge, have not the delicacy and depth of their inspirer: The short story has never been my long suit,‡ and my muse's agenda is not coterminous with Borges's. But his example taught me, among other things, not merely what art critics call "significant form," but what I call the principle of metaphoric means: the investiture of every possible aspect of the fiction (let's say) with emblematic significance, until not just the conceit, the

---

*In fact, in "Foreword to *Lost in the Funhouse*," to follow.
†Later collected in *The Friday Book*.
‡See, e.g., the earlier Friday-piece "It's a Short Story."

images, the mise-en-scène, the narrative choreography and point of view and all that, but even the phenomenon of the text itself, the fact of the artifact, becomes a sign of its sense. That is very high-tech tale-telling; the wonderful thing is that Borges can bring it off with such apparent ease and unassuming grace, his consummate virtuosity kept *up* his sleeve rather than worn on it; so much so that only after the initial charm of his best stories has led us to ponder and reread them (their brevity makes light work of rereading) — only then are we likely to appreciate just how profoundly their imagination is wedded to their rendition. (Italo Calvino told me, years later, that his collection of stories called *T-Zero* was a similar response to the impact of Borges on his imagination.)

I was, in a word, wowed — and delighted to learn that my new literary hero was scheduled to be the 1967 Charles Eliot Norton Lecturer at Harvard. Armed with my department's Nelson Rockefeller budget for distinguished visitors, I telephoned Borges in Cambridge the day after his arrival there, introduced myself, and eagerly invited him to come speak at the State University of New York at Buffalo. At that time, I believe, despite the Norton lectureship, he didn't yet appreciate the size of his reputation in the literature departments of North America and the number of such invitations that were about to shower upon him. Before we had even got to the matter of honorarium, Borges said at once that he would be delighted to come: His bride had never seen New York.

Through the literary grapevine, I had heard already that Sr. Borges — then sixty-eight years old and all but sightless, and theretofore customarily escorted on his travels by his mother — had indeed married, for the first time, just a couple of days before leaving Buenos Aires for Harvard, and that among the efficient causes of this late large step was precisely that the quite elder Señora Borges felt herself not up to a New England winter and all the associated junketing. The marriage, alas, turned out to last not much longer than the Norton lectureship, but at the time I called it was brand new, and Borges was touchingly fond of invoking the epithet: *mi esposa* this, *mi esposa* that; *mi esposa* has never seen New York. . . .

I gently explained that we were not exactly New York City; that we were, in point of fact, Buffalo. Quite all right, the great

man came back graciously: "My wife has never seen snow, either."
He then asked me what I would like him to lecture on, and offered
his belief that he could lecture on any great American writer of our
classical period, if I preferred him to lecture on an American
writer. What impressed and depressed me in this was my recognition not only that *I* couldn't do that, even in American on Americans, but that Borges could as easily do it in English on the English
(including Old English: *Beowulf* was a professional passion of
his), in French on the French, German German, god knows how
many more. Anything at all, I assured him, would be just fine.

They arrived in Buffalo — the courtly, amiable, somewhat fragile-
appearing multilingual groom and his vigorous, fiftyish, previously widowed, non-English-speaking bride — and when we had
settled down to chatting, I pressed Borges a bit on that "any great
American writer" business. He acknowledged that while he was
indeed fond of Poe and Whitman and Hawthorne and company,
he had all but ceased to lecture on individual writers of whatever
nationality because of the difficulty of reviewing their works and
checking references since his eyesight had failed; he preferred to
address some more general topic — Metaphor, say, or the Literature of the Fantastic (his Buffalo subject) and then from his remarkable memory summon whatever examples suited his theme.

This he did, that evening, to an overflow audience of Buffalonians. I had asked advice from friends at Harvard and elsewhere
about the choreography of the presentation, as it was my first go
at introducing an all but sightless Latino genius (that "all but" was
important to Borges; he liked to insist on the point himself, remarking that to be totally blind would put him in the company of
Homer and John Milton, for which he felt unready). Excellent instructions came back to me from Cambridge: There should be
both a stand-up microphone and a table mike; I should guide the
guest of honor onstage and then, as we both stood, give him an introduction like a presidential nomination speech, a catalogue of all
the compliments I saw fit to lay on. I was even told that if I glanced
overshoulder while delivering this homage, I might see the great
writer nod a slight acknowledgment of each tribute, as if ticking
off the list. Then I should seat him in his chair at the table mike,
whence he would lecture from memory.

All this came to pass, with but one small glitch. It was no chore at all for me to write the introduction, fulsome but sincere (which I was assured was traditional Latino literary courtesy, though I cannot vouch for that bit of cultural anthropology); I truly believed the man to be a living literary treasure, as I currently believe him to be, alas, a dead one: among the all-time great masters of his art. I said this, and more, and sneaked a peek overshoulder as I did so, and, sure enough, saw him register each superlative with a courteous little nod. I then turned to lead him to his chair, and there came the glitch, for my otherwise detailed instructions had not advised me of the ritual *abrazo* at this juncture, which I ought to have known about but did not. Borges moved his arms. In my own blindness, I supposed he wanted to shake hands; I thrust forth mine, gringo-style, which Borges couldn't see, and there ensued a few marvelous momentsworth of slapstick cross-cultural dumbshow until we got things sorted out. Then he sat, looked up as if at the ceiling of the auditorium or the abode of the muses, and transfixed us for fifty-five minutes.

I say *transfixed* because his notelessness, his sweetly accented English, his dignified but unintimidating mien, and his unwavering sightless gaze above our heads did indeed have some of the effect of a benign Homer or Milton live. But with the *what* he said, apart from the how of its saying, I confess to being disappointed. For the first several minutes, Borges declared in effect that in the literature of the fantastic there may be found a variety of patterns. For example, he then said, there is a story by Henry James called "The Jolly Corner," which goes like this . . . . He summarized it in circumstantial detail, at the end asserting, "There is one pattern." Next he invited us to consider the old Norse saga about So-and-So, who valiantly fared forth to do such-and-such, et cetera, for quite a few minutes: "Another pattern." And on he went for three-quarters of an hour from his prodigious memory of his prodigious reading: this tale from *The 1001 Nights*, this from here, that from there, each summarized in considerable particular and identified as exemplary of yet another pattern, without a clue to what those patterns were or how they related. Through my transfixion I began to fidget, waiting for him to floor us with some brilliant synthesis at the close. But at the hour's end, what he declared in effect was, "And so you see, there are many patterns of fantastic literature" — adding, dutifully, "yet none of them is as fantastic as what we call Reality."

Oh well. In the subsequent Q&A, on the other hand, he was quite wonderful (and indeed, in his later American tours he spent less time on his "prepared" lectures and more on his exchanges with the audience). On science fiction, for example: He did not much care for it, he allowed, and to make his point he brilliantly contrasted H. G. Wells's *The Invisible Man* with Plato's myth of the Ring of Gyges. To imagine a ring that makes its wearer invisible, said Borges, requires one simple impossibility from which all else plausibly follows; but to imagine a *chemical* that makes one invisible requires continual buttressing with plausibilities. The ring is easier to swallow, as it were, than the chemical. *Olé*: a splendid quarter-hour of such graceful obiter dicta.

By the time of our second path-crossing, eight years later, I had returned to Johns Hopkins, the Peronistas had returned to power in Argentina, and Borges, despite his fame, had acknowledged to a *New York Times* interviewer some misgivings about his position under the regime that he had outspokenly opposed. We immediately telephoned Buenos Aires to offer him permanent political asylum in Baltimore, sweetening the pot with Johns Hopkins's excellent geriatric-medical facilities for his now quite ancient but still living mother (the short story of his marriage had long since reached its quiet denouement). Borges politely declined our invitation. His political apprehensions fortunately proved groundless; *un*fortunately, they led him more or less to accept the junta that displaced the Peronistas and to accept as well an award from General Pinochet himself in Chile, and that got him into regrettable hot water with fellow writers of the Latino "boom," quite a number of whom were political expatriates. Anon the ancient mother died. Friends feared for the physical and emotional welfare of her aging son in his bereavement — Borges was in his mid-seventies then. But after registering that bereavement in a delicate elegy or two, in 1975 he accepted Anthony Kerrigan's invitation to a residency at Michigan State, where along with numerous others I went to rewelcome him to the USA and again to pay him public homage.

For me it was a memorable re-encounter, in several ways. Borges himself appeared in excellent fettle, as if drawing new breath from what his friends feared might devastate him. Even his eyesight was said to have very slightly improved. In my essay "The Literature of Exhaustion," I had made the remarkably fatuous assertion that for my "postmodern" literary generation the question was how to succeed "not Joyce and Kafka, but those who *succeeded* Joyce and Kafka and are now in the evenings of their own careers." I was referring, grandly, to Nabokov, Beckett, and Borges. Now in East Lansing, as if by way of exquisite retribution for that presumptuous remark, the several days of public homaging built to the main event, Borges's own presentation — not in the evening of anything, but in the bright Michigan afternoon — whereas the act with the impossible job of succeeding him that evening and wrapping up the proceedings was Yours Truly. After Borges . . . *yo.*

The rationale for this painful piece of programming was the guest of honor's age. I took what comfort I could in the reflection that if he was too old and frail to do his number in the evening, at least he wouldn't be there to audit mine. For an engaging hour that afternoon he chatted easily with his audience about his poetry and fiction and essays and about literature in general, making along the way some surprising responses to predictably routine questions. E.g., to the unexciting query, "What do you regard as the writer's chief responsibility?" he did *not* reply, "The artful contamination of reality with irreality" or "The investiture of every aspect of the fiction with emblematic significance, including even the fact of the artifact." What he said, unhesitatingly, was "The creation of character." Imagine: the creation of character — this from a writer of unforgettable stories whose least memorable aspect is their characters! (Indeed, I can scarcely recall any Borges characters except Funes the Memorious, that poor fellow cursed with the inability to forget, and even he is not so much a character as an extraordinary, pathological characteristic.) I must conclude that it is precisely the relative unimportance of *character* in

Borges's fiction that prompted his reply — although the tone of it was not wistful.

From this entirely satisfying climactic event, the guest of honor and we other invitees withdrew to a testimonial dinner, where — while Anthony Kerrigan read handsomely in Spanish and in English what he called the great writer's "essential page," "*Borges y yo*," and while Borges (I noted) made his polite little nod of registration at each of its graceful periods — I fiddled with my chicken tetrazzini and wondered what in the mothering *world* one does for the evening show after such a matinee. The problem was compounded by the circumstance that I had been invited not to deliver one more critical appreciation, as the scholars at the conference had done, but to read from my own fiction then in progress — a most unBorgesian long novel called *LETTERS*. Ah well, I thought: The old hombre will go to bed; the others will hit the East Lansing hotspots; I'll pay my dues to a chasteningly empty hall, go back to Baltimore, and never again speak metaphorically of afternoons and evenings.

Alas: The entire company moved en bloc from banquet hall to auditorium — a well-filled auditorium, I was for the only time in my career sorry to see, the same auditorium as that afternoon's — where front-row seats had been reserved for the conference participants, and the center front seat, directly before my lectern, for Borges himself, who was escorted thither to general ovation from the house. What ensued I would happily pass over, except that it culminates in two memorable remarks by Sr. Borges. I spoke, of course, of "afternoons," "evenings," and ironies, and then duly read two letters from the novel *LETTERS*: one by my imaginary English gentlewoman, Lady Amherst, the novel's main character, who resents being cast in the belletristic role of Literature personified; the other a manic bit by a literal maniac who may be a very large insect mimicking an avant-garde writer (somewhat the way *I* felt that evening). I was not so transported by my own words that I failed to notice Borges at one point turn to murmur something into the ear of Professor Kerrigan, beside him. At the post-reading party (which Borges also attended, still going strong in the evening of the evening), I took Kerrigan aside and urged him to give it to me straight. He smiled and reported that what Borges had said was, "In John Barth I hear the voice of Macedonio Fernández."

For us nonspecialists, that remark needs a footnote. Macedonio Fernández, Kerrigan explained to me, a near-contemporary of Borges, had evidently been something of a literary eccentric, an "original," perhaps even something of a trickster, of whom nonetheless Borges had been fond. In Borges's wonderful one-pager called in English "The Witness," there occurs this passage (I came upon it en route home from East Lansing; in the quotation that follows I have rearranged the closing members for present effect):

> There was a day in time when the last eyes to have seen Christ were closed forever. The battle of Junín and the love of Helen died with the death of some one man. What will die with me when I die? What pathetic or frail form will the world lose? Perhaps the image of a horse in the vacant lot at Serrano and Charcas, a bar of sulfur in the drawer of a mahogany desk, the voice of Macedonio Fernández?

We ended that evening quite late around a small table in the host's kitchen: my wife, Borges, y yo. I was tired, and no wonder; Borges seemed tireless. He and I spoke briefly of Machado de Assis and of Gershon Scholem and the Kabbalah (I had been in the habit of calling it Kab-*ba*-lah; Borges gently offered the preferred pronunciation). My wife had been teaching a number of Borges stories to her high-school students; she and he spoke at some length of those texts and of the students' responses to them. At the long evening's end, I remember, she thanked him for having given her — and by extension her students and for that matter all of us — so much. Replied Borges with a twinkle (echoing one of the works they'd been discussing): "I have given you Everything and Nothing."

Our final path-crossing was in Baltimore, another eight years later, by when Borges was eighty-four and I in my fifties. Although I still venerated him as a writer, my own muse had long since wound up her visit to the neighborhood of the short story and had lit out for the expansive territory of the novels *LETTERS*, *Sabbatical*, and

The Tidewater Tales, where she felt more at home. Among my living literary idols, Jorge Luis Borges had been edged out by one more Latino, of whose masterpiece I once heard Borges say, "Maybe *ninety* years of solitude would have been sufficient." Gabriel García Márquez is a writer whose genius is no doubt less refined than Borges's, but more wholly human; what's more, he is congenitally a novelist, broadcasting on a wider range of my personal frequencies. Anyhow, I had by 1983 delivered so many encomiums to Borges that they bade to become a sub-genre of my own writing; for that reason I had passed up a couple of opportunities to salute him publicly once again on his several lecture tours between 1975 and 1983 (Borges was by then under the admirable care of his young Japanese-Argentinean factotum, Maria Kodama, whom in the last year of his life he married, and his capacity for being a portable public figure was astonishing in a person his age). I was happy to leave the arrangements for his Johns Hopkins visit in the hands of my department chairman, John Irwin, a high-tech critic at work on a study of Borges and Poe. My contribution was simply to ghost-write an introduction to be delivered by Johns Hopkins's president at Borges's main public presentation — which, by the way, took place not in the afternoon but in the evening; JLB's new companionship really did seem to have replenished his spirit.

In that introduction I spoke — rather, I wrote and President Steven Muller spoke, while Borges nodded acknowledgment — of what it means for a writer to turn into an adjective — Homeric, Rabelaisian, Dickensian, Kafkaesque — and I attempted to itemize some of the field-identification marks of a *Borgesian* situation or phenomenon. E.g. (though I didn't bother President Muller with these particular examples), when I follow my old teacher Pedro Salinas's advice* and reread *Don Quixote* every ten years or so, I find it quite Borgesian the way the text keeps changing from decade to decade. Or consider the more elegant example cited in "The Literature of Exhaustion": the actual history of a text called *The Three Impostors*:

---

*See "The Spanish Connection."

a nonexistent blasphemous treatise against Moses, Christ and Mohammed, which in the seventeenth century was widely held to exist, or to have once existed. Commentators attributed it variously to Boccaccio, Pietro Aretino, Giordano Bruno, and Tommaso Campanella, and though no one . . . had ever seen a copy of it, it was frequently cited, refuted, railed against, and generally discussed as if everyone had read it — until, sure enough, in the *eighteenth* century a spurious work appeared with a forged date of 1598 and the title *De Tribus Impostoribus*.

That's Borgesian, no?

On the evening prior to this public event, Borges y yo had what turned out to be our final hello and good-bye, in the company of colleagues at a dinner hosted by Professor and Mrs. Irwin — a dinner fraught, as I recall, with Borgesian allusions. All these I have alas forgotten, except for rhomboid canapés evocative of the pattern of murders in the story "Death and the Compass" and something quincunxial about the dessert, having to do I believe with Borges's retroactive influence on Sir Thomas Browne's *The Garden of Cyrus*. The whole excellent dinner, I suppose, might have been regarded as a *hrön*: one of those Borgesian phenomena called into literal material existence by their intensely imagined possibility, like that treatise on the Three Impostors.*

Surrounded by deconstructionists, semioticians, and members of the Spanish Department, Borges y yo did not speak much directly to each other. I'm not sure that we would have had a great deal to say if we had had the chance. I would have liked, I guess, to teach my teacher: to make clear to Borges that I've never thought literature to be exhausted or exhaustible (as, evidently, he thought I thought); only that felt ultimacies in an artistic or cultural generation can become a considerable cultural-historical datum in themselves, turnable against themselves by a virtuoso to generate lively new work. That is what I had had in mind in "The Literature of Exhaustion"; indeed, it is what I had said there — but I let it go. I was more interested in observing how graciously the old

---

*This memoir is another. And the *hrön* of *hröns*, of course, is Borges's story "Tlön, Uqbar, Orbis Tertius," in which the phenomenon occurs: The fact of the artifact is a sign of its sense.

monument enjoyed his late monumentality. He was himself as inexhaustible as old Robert Frost had been, with whom I once spent a memorable long evening at Penn State very late in the poet's life.* Maria Kodama kept murmuring, "He's tired, you know; he really should get to bed." But to me it seemed that it was she who was ready to pack it in, and I sympathized; she must have heard all those excellent anecdotes and remarks time after time.

I close with three anecdotes of my own from that final encounter. I managed to ask Borges what might seem a dumbheaded question, but I meant it as one writer to another: What do you think of the language you write in? What is your opinion of Spanish as an instrument of literary composition? Borges replied (and I have learned since that I was not the first to whom he made the remark), "Spanish is my fate." He went on to say that Goethe had felt the same ambivalence about German — indeed, it may be that Borges was paraphrasing some remark of Goethe's to his confidant Johann Eckermann — and then he politely added, "All writers feel that way about their working language, no?"

Well, no. But a) his question was put rhetorically, not (as mine had been) from one writer to another; and b) had it *not* been rhetorical, it would have been hypothetical in my case, for the monolingual cannot speak, so to speak, to that point. If it still appears to me, after forty years of fiction writing and circa five thousand published pages, that the English language is an inexhaustible instrument the range of whose possibilities I have scarcely reconnoitered, that sentiment *macht nichts*, inasmuch as I know no other instrument.

Some other low-tech dinner guest asked him whether in his elder decades he found it harder or easier to write than earlier in his career. That question interested me, as I was not getting younger book by book. Borges's prompt reply had nothing to do with his loss of eyesight, which of course obliged him to compose and revise in memory (like the Czech-Jewish playwright Hladik before the firing squad in "The Secret Miracle") and dictate to Ms.

---

*"Ask me anything," the hard-of-hearing old fellow liked to say: "I can't hear your questions, but I'll answer *something*."

Kodama. What he said was, "It is much easier than it used to be, because I have learned what I cannot do." I suppose I envy him that, inasmuch as my own, rougher muse has yet fully to learn that energy-saving lesson, and I suspect will never.

The final anecdote I report as a mortified auditor from the rear of the auditorium the following evening. At the time of his Hopkins visit (April 1983), Borges had once again been passed over by the Swedish Academy for the Nobel Prize in Literature. For many of us, this dereliction had become an ongoing annual embarrassment. One knows how it is with literary prizes: I once defined a worthwhile literary prize as one that from time to time will be awarded to a writer *despite* the fact that he or she deserves it, and by that rigorous standard the Nobel remains a worthwhile prize. It is true and deplorable that James Joyce, Franz Kafka, D. H. Lawrence, Virginia Woolf, Vladimir Nabokov, and others who would have done honor to the Nobel never received it; on the other hand, aside from the abundant second- and third-raters to whom the prize did honor, we find after all Thomas Mann, W. B. Yeats, Ernest Hemingway, William Faulkner, T. S. Eliot, Samuel Beckett, Gabriel García Márquez. So: It's an okay accolade. But year after year Borges had been passed over (that particular year it had gone to William Golding). And I am obliged to report that our man really *wanted* the thing. I believe it was as embarrassing to him as to us that he hadn't got it; we were all, let's say, embarrassed for the Swedish Academy, for our literary culture. The subject kept popping into Borges's conversation: Even sixteen years earlier, in Buffalo, when I had arranged for the newlyweds to tour Niagara Falls as newlyweds should, he had thanked me afterward by saying, "I would rather have had this afternoon than the Nobel Prize." Et cetera. And now here he was, eighty-four years old, damn it, and passed over sixteen more times since that Buffalo afternoon, and you may be certain that none of us had brought up the subject at dinner with him the night before — but in the public Q&A that last evening in Baltimore, a student went to one of the aisle microphones and said, "Señor Borges: Once again you have been passed over for the Nobel Prize. Would you share with us your feelings about that?" Some of us, at least, were stunned. But Borges, unblushing and unruffled, smiled his twinkliest smile and declared to that space above our heads: "You know, I have been on their short list for so long, I believe they think they already *gave* me the prize years ago."

That is a world-class reply, from a world-class writer and gentleman. Ah, Swedish Academy: Be it on your heads that you passed over Jorge Luis Borges yet three times more after that before his death in Geneva in June 1986.

Well. Borges's great contemporary and fellow Nobel Prize–non-winner Vladimir Nabokov once said mischievously that when he and Vera first discovered Borges's writings, they felt as if they were standing on a wondrous portico — and then they discovered that there was no house. For most of us — certainly for *yo* — that "portico" is a marvelous freestanding specimen of Postmodernist literary architecture, rich in what Umberto Eco calls "responsibility to the already-said," consummately civilized, virtuosically crafted, beautiful even in translation. Its author remains among my principal navigation stars, even though he never attempted a novel and I rarely attempt anything else, and despite my understanding that in my whole literary production he would at best "hear again the voice of Macedonio Fernández." So be it.

In his own product I admire least certain of the stories that some of my higher-tech academic colleagues seem to admire most: such tales as the aforementioned "Death and the Compass," which seem to me to have little or no human interest, only a cerebral ingenuity. Even "Pierre Menard, Author of the *Quixote*" I put in that category, inspired as is its conceit and graceful its rendition. I quite love his short essay-meditations (such as "*Borges y yo*"), as rereadable as good poetry, but I am not floored by the poetry proper, no doubt because my Spanish is inadequate to the originals. Such stories as "Funes the Memorious," however, and "Tlön, Uqbar, Orbis Tertius" are unforgettable (even though "Funes" has in my opinion a serious architectural flaw* that I intend to discuss with the author if there turns out to be a heaven for

---

*In the lingo of dramaturgical analysis, there is no "ground situation" (involving the Borges-like first-person narrator, for example) upon which the extraordinary "vehicle" of Funes's fatal memoriousness does meaningful dramatic work. The story's closing line — "Ireneo Funes died in 1889, of congestion of the lungs" — is dramaturgically meaningless, as the very similar closing line of "The Secret Miracle," for instance — "Jaromir Hladik died on March 29, at 9:02 A.M." — emphatically is not.

Postmodernists, or at least a postmortem Q&A). And his very best stories — such *Meisterstücken* as "The Secret Miracle," "The Zahir" (which I read as an exquisitely oblique love story), "Averroes's Search," and "The Aleph" (another love story) — are in my judgment perfect works of literature, perfect fusions of Borgesian algebra and fire. They can be reread a hundred times with delight. They rise from the printed page directly into the empyrean of transcendent art, and make me grateful that while their author's body was (in Borges's phrase) "living out its life," and mine mine, the separate patterns of our footsteps intersected at three points. Borges speculates (in a footnote to "The Mirror of Enigmas") that all the literal footsteps a person takes in his or her lifetime may trace out a figure as readily apprehensible to the mind of God as is a circle or a triangle to our human minds. To *my* human mind, these three path-crossings of Borges y yo are triangulations, privileged celestial position-fixes, even though I have learned better than to confuse my navigation stars with my destination.

Once Upon a Time
Storytelling Explained

Like "A Body of Words" earlier in this volume, what follows was first presented to a symposium at the Johns Hopkins Medical Institutions — this one called "Perceptions of Memory."* My fellow symposiasts were mainly eminent neuroscientists, such as Oliver Sacks and the Nobel laureates Leon Cooper and Gerald Edelman, but the group appropriately included a literary historian (Paul Fussell), an expert on Proust's Remembrance of Things Past *(Baroness Warnock, of Girton College, Cambridge), and one rather uncomfortable writer of fiction, who spake as followeth:*

BY TRADE I am a storyteller; I'll begin by telling a story.

Once upon a time, in a land close at hand, there lived a storyteller, whose household equipment included two automobiles: a large blue American station wagon with its fuel filler cap on the driver's side, and a small green German station wagon with its fuel filler cap on the passenger side. Our storyteller and his mate owned these two vehicles jointly and used them interchangeably in their separate daily rounds: no particular His and Hers or principle of wagon selection beyond the occasional cargo-carrying requirements of some specific errand.

Now, in those days the teller of this story was a full-time professor as well as a full-time storyteller and the protagonist of this particular story. Being no less absentminded than the next full time professor, when fill-up time came around he would sometimes

---

*April 1992. My remarks were then published in the *Johns Hopkins Magazine* in June of that year.

discover (if he happened to be driving without copilot) that he had docked on the wrong side of the self-service island, having at least momentarily forgotten which car he was driving and/or on which side of that car its gas cap lived. In consequence, he would have either to wrestle the fuel hose over or behind the car (a particular nuisance with station wagons), or adjust the vehicle's position, or even move it around to the correct side of the pump island — all the while chastising himself for reinforcing an egregious stereotype, since his Johns Hopkins professorial parking sticker was in plain view of the full-service attendants. Absentmindedness may or may not be memory-lapse pure and simple, but self-forgetfulness is clearly in the general ballpark of forgetting — out in left field somewhere, I imagine, but even deep left field (let us remember) is still part of the ballpark.

Very well: The household that included these two station wagons — the big blue Pontiac, the small green Opel — had once upon a time included three children as well, now grown, the youngest of whom, at the time I tell of, happened to be just completing his Ph.D. in neuroscience at UCLA. With only a modest effort of memory, I recalled which child that was, and I appealed to him to rescue his failing father from self-service embarrassment by devising for me a mnemonic with which to address the gas-pump problem. The young man replied that his graduate work in brain anatomy and the rest had so freighted him with medical-school mnemonics that he could scarcely remember which mnemonic applied to what, but he promised to see what he and his colleagues could come up with. Meanwhile, I would just have to soldier along.

I did that, and presently there arrived in the mail from Los Angeles a splendid custom-made mock-mnemonic, designed to be all but impossible to remember: *The car that is not the blue Pontiac is not the car whose gas cap is not on the side that is not the driver's side.* The psychological principle involved in this anti-mnemonic (let us charitably suppose) is cousin to that behind the perverse music-lesson trick of deliberately *practicing* a stubborn error until it cannot be committed unconsciously. In this instance, the multiple negative switchings are particularly diabolical (as my son well knew) in their being laid on a fellow whose command of polarities is notoriously shaky; who after twenty-five years of ardent sailing, for example, still occasionally hollers "port" when he means to holler "starboard"; who has been known to have to stop and think about east versus west (east is to port when you're running south on a north wind). I trace this polar shakiness to my being an opposite-sex twin who practices right-handedly (which is to say, left-brainedly) an essentially *left*-handed/*right*-brained calling, the dreaming up of fictions — but what do I know? In any case, I tried deploying my gas-cap mnemonic in the perverse spirit of its devising and found that in fact the thing worked pretty well except when tripped up by that more general deficiency: "Here I am," I would rehearse to myself as I approached the self-service island, "riding south on North Charles Street with a near-empty fuel tank in the car that is not the small green Opel. Ergo, by simple inversion of my handy-dandy mnemonic, it *is* the car whose gas cap is not on the side that is not the driver's side."

So far, so good: Not-Opel = Pontiac; not-driver's side = passenger side; *not*-not-driver's side = driver's side. "It followeth as doth the night the day (east to west) that I am driving the big blue Pontiac, whose gas cap is on the driver's side." Rich in confidence and correct in my reasoning, I would then drive up to the *port* side of the island, so to speak, which is to say the *starboard* side of the car, which in the case of the big blue Pontiac . . .

The lapse, to be sure, was mine, as was the attendant vertigo. To my neuroscientific son, however, I reported that this second-level absentmindedness (let's call it) was owing not to polarity-crash but to my musing, as I approached the gas pump, upon the circumstance that in his letter supplying me with my anti-mnemonic, young Dr. Barth had misspelled the word "mnemonic," reversing the most interesting part of that interesting word: its opening double-nasal consonant, *mn*, or *mu nu*. He acknowledged that he sometimes had trouble remembering how to spell that word, and so in retaliation for his mnemonic gift to me, I devised *him* a mnemonic for correctly spelling the word "mnemonic." It would be too easy, I declared, for him simply to remember that the order of those opening consonants happens to be the same as their order in the Greek alphabet, not to mention the Roman alphabet, not to mention the order of those letters' reappearance later in the word. No: The secret for remembering how to spell "mnemonic," I told him, was to remember that one who forgets how to spell "mnemonic" must be experiencing . . . anmesia.

My son thanked me dutifully, but gave me to understand that my mnemonic for spelling "mnemonic" was awfully East Coast. In California neuroscientific circles, he declared, the mnemonic for spelling "mnemonic" was "Remember to punch up the spell-check program on your processor before transmitting letters to your English-teacher parents."

Now, then: Although he was never a red-hot speller like his dad, the neuroscientist I speak of here is by no means either dyslexic or functionally illiterate. Indeed, he is a publishing doer of neuro-science these days at the University of Colorado, with the best spell-check software that NSF research grants can buy. Whatever *my* memory problems may be, I suspect that his in this instance was owing to a tiny defect in his classical education (by compari-son to his scientific training): a defect by virtue of which, so to speak, he either didn't know or didn't remember Mnemosyne, the Greek goddess of mnemory and, in collaboration with Zeus, the mnother of the mnuses. In my musing upon the word "mne-monic" on final approach to that gas pump in the car that was not the small green Opel, I was in effect courting the mother through the daughter, more or less like the eponymous hero of Thomas Mann's late novel *Confessions of Felix Krull*.

Mnemosyne: If Zeus, in this allegorizing myth, represents fertil-izing power, life force, creative energy, it is Memory — fertilized, energized, and no mean creator herself, who gestates, shapes, and delivers the goods. She is the mom, we note, of *all nine* muses: not merely the patronesses of the six classical categories of poetry and drama plus Clio the muse of history — all pretty obvious verbal jurisdictions — but also Terpsichore (officially the muse of dance, but since her symbols are the lyre and plectrum, we may stretch Terpsichore a bit to represent all the nonverbal arts) and Urania, whose official bailiwick is astronomy, but who can serve as a synecdoche for the inspired-creative aspect of all the sciences. While we're gerrymandering these constituencies, let's extend

Clio's from creative historiography to the inspired-creative aspect of *all* mental activity that is neither science on the one hand nor the fine arts on the other, and Terpsichore's to cover not only the nonverbal arts but the inspired-creative aspect of all mentally directed physical activity, from sports to teppenyaki cookery. Now I think we have the myth just about right: All, all, all are the offspring of Mnemosyne, the fruits of memory.

From among them, I've picked for my topic at this symposium some aspects of memory not as the *subject* of art in general and the art of fiction in particular, although it is a perennially popular literary subject, from Orpheus and Lot's wife's forgetting (let's say) their safe-passage instructions, through Wordsworth's recipe for poetry as "emotion recollected in tranquillity" and Proust's momentous *madeleine* and Nabokov's *Speak, Memory* to Jorge Luis Borges's cautionary "Funes the Memorious" (who fatally can forget no datum once perceived) to Milan Kundera's *Book of Laughter and Forgetting*. I'll speak instead to memory as a factor in artistic invention, an agent on the macro-, meso-, and microscales of imaginative production. (The conventional storyteller's formulation "Once upon a time," for example, invokes both memory and invention, inasmuch as the "time" is both past and presumed to be fictitious.) My illustrations will come from the practice of fiction, but they should apply to other precincts as well, and to *performance* as well as to composition insofar as performance has an element of "inspiration" in it — which I daresay it always does. Second violinists and members of the chorus, no less than stars and soloists, have their good nights — when, like Aeneas clothed in radiance by Mother Venus for his first date with Queen Dido, they become not somebody else but superior versions of themselves — and their not-so-good nights, when the mind's memory — or the body's, or the spirit's — chugs along lacklustrously on autopilot.

Most particularly, I'll have a look at the role of memory in my immediate concerns as a working fictioneer: the fabrication (in both senses of that term) of the project in progress in my own shop. Just now, mirabile dictu, that project happens to be a semi-novel/semi-reminiscence called *Once Upon a Time*. Were that not the fortuitous case, I would not likely be in this distinguished company of neuroscientists and humanistic scholars, feeling a bit like

Kafka's ape making its "Report to an Academy." But as it happens, the subject of this symposium is so right up the alley of my current fictive preoccupations that I had my talk half composed by the morning after the evening of my invitation to give it.

Half composed where? In my memory, to be sure, and here we go — starting at the top, working through the middle to the bottom, and finding at the bottom a trapdoor that opens upon the top, like a Maurits Escher staircase. I refer casually to "my" memory: Whose memory is that? I'm going to maintain that the first and the final question that a storywriter puts to his or her memory, regardless of the subject and kind of story in progress, is not, as we usually take it to be, the question "What happened?" but rather the essential question of identity — the personal, professional, cultural, even species-specific "Who am I?" — and that this primordial and ultimate interrogative resonates through the middle- and microscales of the fictive enterprise, as through other human enterprises as well. I shall even maintain that the question "Who am I?" is what ultimately motivates the reader or hearer of fiction as well as its writer/teller, and further (an assertion not original with me, although until recently I believed that it was) that the creation of fiction and its enjoyment are a model of and a spin-off from the great fictive enterprise of human consciousness itself: the ongoing fabrication of our selves, in which memory is always the coauthor.

Please indulge me another personal anecdote, whoever that person finally turns out to be. Like the muses, I am the offspring of both of my parents: in this instance, a father who compensated for his severely impaired hearing by telling abundant anecdotes, chiefly of a reminiscent, local-historical character; whose education was limited, but whose memory and raconteurial prowess (the one, of course, prerequisite to the other) were formidable — and a mother whose rural childhood must have been quite disagreeable, for she would not speak of it, claimed early to have forgotten it, and indeed, as she passed through her decades, had progressively less memory of *any* of her past, although she was not a particularly absentminded person in other respects. In their terminal years, this couple's memories and consequently their senses of personal identity failed them in appropriately different ways. When my mother, by her latter seventies, could no longer remember for example the year of her marriage or where she and her bridegroom had honeymooned, my father (who remembered in circumstantial detail their modest honeymoon trip to neighboring Virginia, fifty years past) would pretend incredulously, "You don't remember touring Rome and Paris?" "We did no such thing!" Mother would protest — and then ask, usually of one of us grown children, "*Did* we?" For she was accustomed to being teased for her poor memory: *That* she remembered; indeed, to her and to her family it had become a salient aspect of her identity.

In his very last days, uremic poisoning and mismedication made my father intermittently delirious, but although he no longer always knew *where* he was or *when* (and therefore had trouble sorting out who was with him in what *I* took to be his hospital room in Cambridge, Maryland, in 1980), he never for a moment lost sight of *who* he was. He was himself — in 1928, perhaps, impatient to get his little soda-fountain/candy store closed after a long day and join his fellows for a nightcap in Virgil Seward's tavern around the corner before going home. Reliving the proprietary routine in detail, he would gently chide me (whether as "myself" or as some employee of his back then) for sitting there in my visiting-chair instead of doing A, B, and C to get the establishment closed down for the night. Then we were *in* that friendly little tavern; I was metamorphosed into his bartender-buddy Virgil — not, alas, guiding him through the otherworld like Dante's comrade, but attending in pained enthrallment his amusing over-the-counter anecdotes, rich in late-1920s circumstantiality, as his delirium "accessed" in remarkable detail those bygone ordinary days.

The last words I was to hear him speak — as I was exiting the hospital room at the end of visiting hours but in the middle of one of these inexhaustible anecdotes — were the words "And then one day . . ." Perfect "last words" for a born storyteller: in the jargon of my trade, the narrative crux where the generalized or customary past time of the dramaturgical "ground situation" modulates to the specifically focused action of the dramatic "vehicle" — that turn of events in the narrative present (although it's likely to be represented in narrative past tenses, an implicit act of memory) that precipitates a story out of the voltage-potential of the ground-situation.* To put it in terms of our topic, "And then one day" is the foreground-memory zoomed in on from the recollected mise-en-scène. My point is that the antecedent of the first-person narrator of those deliriant anecdotes was unequivocally my-father-the-storyteller — at once the subject, object, and agent of narrative memory — whom *I* remember most clearly and warmly in that aspect.

With my mother it was another story, in which there was no "And then one day" but a gradual dim-down of memory's rheostat, from cheerfully not remembering her childhood and her honeymoon to cheerfully not remembering her marriage, her age, her children, anything of her history, her surroundings, scarcely her name. Significantly, perhaps, from a clinical point of view, while she didn't know where or when she was or really who, she never imagined herself to be any where or when or who she was not — in the way that my father imagined himself back in Whitey's Candyland in 1928. She wasn't *any* where-when-or-who, in the self-reportable way. To us who knew her, however, and presumably "in her own mind" as well, she remained very much herself. The antecedent of her personal pronoun was no longer a remembered name and life story (we are not, after all, our names, and not quite our life stories, but rather — so we like to believe — the *bearers* of our names and *protagonists* of our life stories); it was, instead, a distinctive though vestigial repertoire of attitudes, gestures, and trademark lines — *characteristically* good-humored, self-deprecatory.

"Got to run along now, Mother," we visitors would say; "we'll be seeing you again soon."

"Well, you can be sure of one thing, honey," she would invariably reply: "*I'll be here.*"

Who was that *I*? my wife and I would ask ourselves, en route back to the city. Where was that *here*? No problem, really: The *I* was the uncomplaining twanger of that ritual self-affirming speech-act; the *here* was wherever-it-was that we affectionate familiar strangers called upon that *I* and elicited such all-but-

---

*That apparently mixed metaphor is meant electrochemically.

anonymous, last-ditch-cheerful self-affirmations. In neuroscientific terminology, her "declarative" (explicit) memory was kaput, while her non-declarative (implicit) memory lingered.

Now, then: Where was I, and for that matter who? Ah, yes: So-and-so, digressive American Postmodernist author of *The Last Voyage of . . . Somebody the Sailor** and other fictions, regressive author-in-the-works of a quasi-novel or quasi-memoir inspired by its title, *Once Upon a Time*. I have eaten my breakfast and scanned my morning newspaper; I have done certain stretching-exercises both physical and mental, the latter of a Pavlovian char-acter and the former too, come to that: a combined self-mesmeriz-ing, self-priming warm-up routine and invocation to Mnemosyne and her daughters that began with my waking automatically at 7 A.M. or so, eating breakfast, etc., and continues now with *my* going to *my* writing table, ritually filling *my* venerable fountain pen, opening *my* ancient Johns Hopkins loose-leaf binder that I bought during freshman orientation week in September 1947 and have since first-drafted five thousand–plus pages of published fic-tion in, and regathering in *my* memory and muscles both the threads and the knitting-momentum of a certain complex narra-tive argyle-sock-in-progress: not only the peculiar narrative called *Once Upon a Time*, but the ongoing fabrication of the antecedent of all those *my*s.

Just how is that done? After forty-plus years of doing it (sixty-plus, in the latter case), I find the process still mysterious and fasci-nating. I'm speaking not particularly of the "material," although *its* invention, discovery, or selection is mysterious enough.† You're likely to hear writers say, somewhat Romantically, that their mate-rial chooses them, rather than vice versa; there is an engaging modesty and no doubt some neuropsychological substance in the Hellenic tradition of "inspiration": the poet as agent of or vehicle for the muse; the Homeric singer who sings "Sing, Muse, of the

---

*Suspension points added; novel first published by Little, Brown in 1991.
†One of our undergraduates once asked the playwright Edward Albee, "Where do you get your material?" Albee replied, with a shrug, "Allentown? A little dis-count outlet up there . . ."

man who . . . [etc.]," and who then puts his epical bardic memory at her disposal. The mystery that more engages me, at least this morning, is the singing itself, so to speak: the organization, fabrication, orchestration, articulation of the narrative "song" by a process that, monitoring it in myself, I have come to call *coaxial esemplasy*: the reciprocal shaping of utterance by intention and of intention by utterance, not unlike the "Pandemonium" model of speech adverted to by the philosopher Daniel C. Dennett in his treatise *Consciousness Explained* (I'll circle back to Dennett shortly, if I can remember which side of the gas pump I'm on*). In *Once Upon a Time* — which happens to have a quasi-operatic structure — there appears a quasi-aria on this subject, from which I now quote three and a half paragraphs:

> . . . For first-drafting [my] sentences and rough-polishing them as they unfold, I still prefer, depend upon, even love the smooth muscular cursive of jet black Skrip flowing from this old fountain pen across the blue-ruled lines of three-ring paper in this old binder. True to its advertising, [my British] Parker's nib quickly shaped itself to my autography; its scratch against the paper, minimal to begin with, all but disappeared during the first season's use, and for more than a quarter century I've been no more conscious of effort against resistance in the physical act of penning than in the physical act of breathing. The one comes as naturally as the other.
>
> Each normal workday morning, after breakfast, the agreeable ritual follows of withdrawing to city or country study, thermal coffee mug topped up and in hand. I tuck in the Flents ear stopples (first massaging them to malleability) that I required for concentration in years gone by, when my children were young and at home and my academic course-load constrained my writing to late afternoons and early evenings, and that I cannot now concentrate without, even alone in the house in the quiet countryside. I polish my eyeglasses and blow my nose a number of times — a morning sinus drip inherited from my father, and a salute to his memory. I disassemble and feed this old pen its daily drink, reassemble its barrel,

---

*And for more on the Pandemonium model of utterance, see "Browsing," farther on in this collection.

and fix its cap on the butt as designed for perfect balance. When I take the readied instrument in hand, it roots lightly against the callosities of four decades of authorship. I warm up by reviewing yesterday's production in its first [computer] printout . . . , hand-editing the sentences as I go, until I reach the latest of them and, carried by its momentum, take up its longhand version in this old binder and draw the next with this old pen. I'm scarcely aware of writing English; I'm writing writing. Indeed, unless I happen to be writing *about* writing as I'm doing just now, and that's not often, I am no more than half aware that what I'm doing is *writing*, and I'm altogether unconscious of the complex sub-routines of orthography, punctuation, and penmanship. Even diction, grammar, and syntax are little more than higher sub-routines . . . ; my conscious mind attends mainly to navigation and boat-handling, so to speak: choosing and steering moment by moment the verbal course to the next narrative waypoint (as approximated from the last and course-corrected en route) to my dramaturgical destination (ditto).

Some three hours of this. . . . Then — ideally when the going's good, in mid-passage, even mid-sentence, like Scheherazade — I halt, date the day's drafting in parentheses . . . cap this old pen, pop the earplugs, open for the how-many-thousandth time the rings of this old binder, and take the morning's pages [across the room] from Creation to Production for Macintoshing before lunch.

When we imagine Heaven, Miguel de Unamuno remarks, "the immortality that we crave . . . is the continuation of this present life" — minus its irritations, disappointments, and miseries and plus a few goodies that we've thus far hankered after in vain. I am confident that no heaven of mine would be heavenly without [among other pleasures] the registration of experience into language — not excluding imagined experience (such as the afterlife), the experience of imagining, and the experience of language — into this old binder, with this old pen, amen.

End of quasi-aria, but not quite yet of speech. I have invoked in passing not only the muses but the self-denominated "neuro-philosopher" Daniel C. Dennett, of Tufts University. I have also lately written to Professor Dennett, warmly to affirm a number of the points he makes (or scores) about consciousness, memory, and the self in *Consciousness Explained*.* I'll close now by reviewing those of his points that strike me most strongly as validating my own observations and intuitions about fictive once-upon-a-timery, and then by making a final pass at the great self-service pump of memory:

• I have mentioned already the *Pandemonium model of utterance*, according to which multiple goals or intentions are on the lookout, so to speak, for materials of expression, and those materials (*memes*, as the zoologist Richard Dawkins calls memory units) are reciprocally vigilant for opportunities of incorporation. The model isn't original with Dennett (he aptly remembers E. M. Forster's obiter dictum, "How can I tell what I think till I see what I say?"), but Dennett extends it rigorously to his *Multiple Drafts model of consciousness*, whereby content-discriminations variously distributed in the brain generate *something like* a narrative stream or sequence (the "Joycean machine," Dennett calls it: a very different gadget from the celebrated "Turing machine" of the artificial intelligence folk), subject to continual "editing" by various processes also distributed about the brain and continuing indefinitely into the future. At any point, multiple "drafts" of the narrative fragments constituting consciousness are at various stages of "production" in various brain locations; there is no single, final, "published," canonical draft, for there is no Cartesian "Central Meaner" directing the production, no uppercase Author dwelling somewhere inside the head of the lowercase author sitting at my writing table pushing my faithful British Parker pen. It is only *as if* there were. That sounds like my shop, all right, where

---

*Same publisher and date as my aforementioned *Last Voyage*. Gerald Edelman remarked to me after this symposium presentation that in his opinion Dennett's account does not add up to a genuine "theory of consciousness." Oliver Sacks, praising in the *New York Review of Books* Edelman's own account as set forth in *Bright Air, Brilliant Fire: On the Matter of the Mind* (NY: Basic Books, 1992), inclines to agree. To us lay folk, it appears to be the "wet-brain neuronal Darwinists" ("the *New York Review* crowd," Dennett has called them) versus the mind-as-computer types. But Dennett seems to me to make generous allowance for the *dis*analogies between the workings of computers and brains; I remain an admirer of *Consciousness Explained*, for its careful argument, bright examples, and lucid writing. My neuroscientific son aforementioned, however, on whom I pressed the book, inclines to Edelman's reservations. I suspect that to hands-on doers of science it seems too *easy* to be a philosopher, even a good one.

even the published hardcover edition of my text gets further edited every time I give a reading or have occasion to quote from it — and where the product to some extent keeps on editing me as I edit it. Dennett's description of cognition as involving "feedback-guided, error-corrected, gain-adjusted, purposeful linkages" sounds a lot like what was going on in that quasi-aria aforesung — and among those linkages is the coaxially esemplastic one between recollection and representation.

• *"Something like* a narrative stream," Dennett says; ". . . *as if* there were a Central Meaner": Now we're getting warm, or at least it seems to me *as if* we are — all those quasi-thises and quasi-thats that I've been invoking. Although Dennett acknowledges his debt to David Hume, he doesn't mention Hans Vaihinger's "Fictionalism" (*The Philosophy of As If,* 1924); but the concept of the self as an *as if* — as a heuristic fiction — is central to Dennett's theory of consciousness,* and right up this storyteller's alley. Consciousness as multiply drafted scenario-spinning; language as "not [simply] something we constructed, but something in which we created and recreated ourselves"; storytelling (that is, our concocting and controlling the ongoing story that we tell others and ourselves about who we are) as "our fundamental tactic of self-protection, self-control, and self-definition"; the recognition that "our tales are spun, but for the most part we don't spin them; they spin us"† — all these are waypoints to Dennett's definition of the self as a "posited Center of Narrative Gravity," an *Als Ob* from which our yarns *appear* to spin forth.

The self as a posited Center of Narrative Gravity, *as if* continuous and self-identical from episode to episode of our life stories: Right on, Professor Dennett! "How come *I* can tell you all about what [goes] on in my head?" he asks in his final chapter, and then replies to his rhetorical question, "*Because that is what* I *am* . . . a knower and reporter of such things in such terms is what is me.

---

*He is, to be sure, perfectly aware of Vaihinger's *Philosophie des Als Ob,* but avoided referring to it (as he kindly explained in response to my query) because Vaihinger's "fictionalism" has become associated with a largely discredited philosophy called "instrumentalism," with which Dennett did not want his own argument confused.
†I would say, less helplessly, "We spin them and, coaxially, they spin us."

My existence is explained by the fact that there are these capacities in this body." Which is as much as to say, I take it, that when God says to Job, "I am that I am," He may be said to be saying, "I am that that saith to Job, 'I am that I am.'" Now we see the deepest relevance of the figure of Scheherazade: She is the emblem not only of us professional storytellers, whose continuance is always on the line, but also of the (fictionalistical, *as-if*ish) scenario-spinner that is the continuously auto-creating self of every one of us. Go up an order of generality, and I don't doubt that the same might be said of a subculture, of a culture, perhaps of the species homo sapiens: We *are* the stories that we tell ourselves about who we are.

Let me see now whether "I" can remember in a final paragraph what all this has to do with memory, mnemonics, and self-serve gas pumps. The first and the last are pretty obvious: Memory *is* the Self-serve pump that fuels the consciousness/self-consciousness machine. At least it is *as if* it were: the center of our posited Center of Narrative Gravity, its sine qua non. Musing on my anti-mnemonic, musing on Mnemosyne, I forgot not only which wagon I was (not) driving and/or on which side its fuel-tank cap was (not), but also, for the crucial moment, in effect who the driver was — and that not uncharacteristic auto-forgetfulness or musy absentmindedness, when I remark it to myself and retail it narratively to you, becomes one more thread in the onspinning yarn of my self-knit self — and yours.

Goose Art
or,
The Aesthetic Ecology of Chesapeake Bay

In May 1992, the Chesapeake Research Consortium, an association of sundry institutions studying the Chesapeake estuarine system, together with SEARCH (the Solomons Environmental and Archaeological Research Consortium) sponsored the first-ever Chesapeake Writers Conference, on salty (anyhow brackish) Solomons Island, in the mouth of the Patuxent River — a favorite pit stop for cruising sailors hereabouts, ourselves included. Like Philip Roth on being Jewish, Jorge Luis Borges on being Argentine, and Edward Albee on being gay, I regard myself not as a "Chesapeake writer" but as a writer who happens to be of the Chesapeake persuasion, let's say: who has lived more years of his life than not in the neighborhood of his birthwaters and has drawn upon them, in more of his books than not, for imaginative sustenance. Wary as I am of aesthetic categories* (likewise of writers conferences), I was pleased to address the assembled tidewater scribblers — and folklorists, photographers, naturalists, illustrators, folk singers, environmentalists, etc. — more or less thus:

SPEAKING THIRTY-SOME YEARS ago of his economic hopes for the nation, President John Kennedy borrowed a New England watermen's proverb: "A rising tide floats all the boats." As those familiar with the Chesapeake Bay region know, a real spring tide floats all sorts of other stuff, too,

---

*For the Tragic View of Categories, see "Postmodernism Revisited," earlier in this volume. A version of the present address subsequently appeared in the *Washington Post Magazine*, August 9, 1992.

besides boats: dead wood, assorted synthetics and miscellaneous trash, downright garbage, untreated sewage, and suchlike matters of environmental concern. North America's largest estuarine system has inspired a rich and abundant ecological literature; perhaps it's time to address its *literary ecology*, so to speak — indeed, its aesthetic ecology in general: the rendition of "Chesapeakery" into various artistic media, with tidewater fiction as the focus of our larger view.

During my lifetime, and particularly in the decades since World War Two, the tide of interest in the Chesapeake Bay region — popular interest, "media" interest, literary and general artistic interest — has risen very considerably, for better and for worse. My wife and I lately saw, but did not eat at, a place called something like The Baltimore Oyster House on Pier 39 in San Francisco, where Chesapeake Old Bay Seasoning was also available in San Francisco Bay markets. On the menu in Tokyo's Imperial Hotel we saw, but did not order, Chesapeake soft-shell crabs (we had not gone to Japan for Chesapeake soft-shell crabs). There have been Chesapeake Bay *National Geographic* photo-essays and PBS television documentaries; there are innumerable Chesapeake Bay gift-and-souvenir shops around the watershed purveying Chesapeake Bay calendars and cookbooks and sweatshirts and seasonings and every other merchandisable gizmo that can be caused to bear some item from the now-standard iconographic repertoire: wild ducks and geese, blue crabs, oysters, cattails, oyster-dredging skipjacks, screwpile lighthouses, et cetera ad infinitum, perhaps ad nauseam. Over in Cambridge, Maryland, my native town, a microbrewery brews both a Wild Goose Amber beer, not bad, which I have seen for sale in Seattle, and a Thomas Point Light Lager complete with screwpile lighthouse and red steamed crab on its label (the old Thomas Point Light is just below Annapolis). There are professional Chesapeake folk singers and folktalers and wildfowl-decoy carvers and other tidewater arts-and-craftsers. And there is, if not a flood, at least a vigorous stream of Chesapeake writing, ranging in kind from the texts of Chesapeake Bay coloring books and cruising guides and videocassettes and coffee-table photo albums, through feisty ecological polemics (Tom Horton's *Bay Country*), Pulitzer Prize–winning natural-historical/sociological ruminations (William Warner's *Beautiful Swimmers*), and blockbuster commercial novels (James Michener's *Chesapeake*), to capital-L Literary fiction.

What is one to make of this abundance — besides a few bucks, if that's one's game? The two simplest-minded reactions, I suppose, are these: On the one hand, a kind of blanket anathema, such as some of us feel toward waterfront real-estate developers. When the oyster-dredging skipjack and the blue crab and the screwpile lighthouse attain the status of commercial logos, that circumstance may be taken as a fairly reliable sign that the way of life they vaguely symbolize (in some cases, even the boat or beast or building directly represented) is passing from vigorous, unselfconscious existence into merchandisable nostalgia, or has already so passed. Contrariwise, one might simply welcome and be proud of this "development" of our regional "image," which has put our home waters — native home to some of us, adopted home to ever more millions of others — increasingly on the map of national and even extra-national awareness. In Stuttgart not long ago, I had the interesting experience of presiding over a two-week seminar of young literature professors from such former Communist-bloc countries as Romania, Bulgaria, Hungary, Czechoslovakia, even Albania, as well as a few from what back then was still the Soviet Union; our seminar topic was fairly high-tech* and had nothing whatever to do with tidewater Maryland, but out of curiosity I asked how many of those bright young men and women had some sense of what and where Chesapeake Bay might be, and Maryland's Eastern Shore. Remarkably, more of them than not had at least an approximate idea of the place (How many of us can say the same of the Straits of Otranto or even the Sea of Marmara?). Yet more remarkably, considering the scarcity of Western-bloc literature in the regimes that these young scholars had grown up under, a fair fraction of them knew of the place not only from their general geographical sophistication, but also from having heard of (in a few instances from having actually read) either Michener's *Chesapeake* or — excuse me, but I was surprised and delighted — some novel or other of mine. No doubt they had been politely prepping for their Stuttgart seminar.

---

*See "$4\frac{1}{2}$ Lectures: The Stuttgart Seminars on Postmodernism, Chaos Theory, and the Romantic Arabesque," farther on in this volume.

I have said that these two contrary radical attitudes are the simple-minded ones: "Get that shlock out of here!" on the one hand; "Look, Ma, we're an industry!" on the other hand. In fact, I have a sneaking sympathy for both hands, especially for the former. Every cruising sailor knows the sinking feeling, so to speak, of having a favorite little-known secluded anchorage "discovered," whether by a developer or by the cruising guides and sailing magazines.* There are certain prize spots that some of us won't even tell our fellow sailors about, lest word get around. My wife and I are delighted that handsome Langford Creek (off the Chester River, across the Bay from Baltimore), where we live, is described in one of the standard Chesapeake guidebooks as "unimpressive." We wish they had added *Submerged piles; sharks and shoaling reported; beware of the dog.* Yet, like many another, I have been bonded since childhood to the tidewater scene, and I've spent much of my literary working life trying to wrestle what I feel about the place into prose sentences for other people to read. When, therefore, as sometimes happens, some Japanese or Brazilian or Romanian writes to tell me that she or he hopes to visit one day the locale of my fiction, I am duly gratified — while at the same time recognizing that in my small way I have become part of the problem.

With that recognition comes a loss of innocence that is the end of easy, simpleminded attitudes toward various exploitations of the Bay, including its aesthetic exploitation; and in that loss of innocence is the beginning of real-world complexity, if not inevitably of wisdom. If it were in my power, I would no doubt prohibit all further "development" of tidewatershed real estate for the next generation or two, and take action against lots of other contributors to the ecological and scenic despoliation of the Bay and its surroundings. But I cannot make that high-minded pronouncement from any comparably high moral ground, for not only do the Barths already safely *have* their bit of creekside real estate, but it happens to sit in a more or less failed subdevelopment — thank

---

*E.g., the November 1993 number of *Cruising World* arrives with a feature article entitled "The Hidden Chesapeake," and my heart sinks. What if . . . ? Then I find with relief that once again they've got it all wrong.

heaven for such failure! — a former cornfield (former woods and wetlands, if you go back a couple of centuries) latterly called "Langford Bay Estates." We wince at the pretentious name, for there is not much of a bay there, just dear, "unimpressive" Langford Creek — beware of the dog. The modest houses thereabouts, our own included, are so far from being "estates" that the first time my wife and I sailed up that way, twenty years ago, we noted in the ship's log that the creek was "quite impressive . . . except for a clutch of tacky little houses at its fork." For the past dozen-plus years, one of those . . . unassuming little houses has been us.

The analogy holds, I believe, with the Chesapeake artsy-litsy scene, which is also a growing number of us: I mean the moral complexity, the *complicity*, even, involved in our more or less artistic *use* of the Bay — one more strain on the cultural ecosystem. In a general way, I am turned off by the overload of commercialized, touristical Chesapeake nostalgia; by the ubiquitously merchandised images of what I'm lucky enough to be able to see, live and for real, by looking out of my windows, and have so seen — except for a twenty-year expatriate interval "up north," during which I began to write novels set in tidewater Maryland — literally since the day I was born, in what is now called Dorchester General Hospital, on the south bank of the great Choptank River. For some while after we moved back to the Old Line State,* the Barths had a rule prohibiting any Chesapeake motifs in our house or aboard our boat (where we don't allow any nautical motifs, either): no Chesapeake serving trays, cocktail napkins, placemats, pottery, marquetry, et cetera — on the grounds of image-overkill. It had been another matter up in Pennsylvania, up in New York, up in Massachusetts, where I treasured my Aubrey Bodine Chesapeake photo albums,† my first editions of Gilbert Klingel and

---

*Maryland's two unofficial nicknames, the Old Line State and the Free State, are equally misleading. The former comes not from the Mason-Dixon Line (the state's northern border), but from the creditable performance of troops of the Maryland Line in George Washington's Continental Army. The latter comes not from the antebellum distinction between "free" and slaveholding states (Maryland belonged to the second category), but from Prohibition days, when the state legislature refused to pass a prohibition-enforcement act.

†A photograph from one of which — of the tidewater showboat called *Adams's Original Floating Theater*, inspired my first novel.

Hulbert Footner and Paul Wilstach,* my tidewater maps and charts. But to surround oneself with images of one's beloved when one is in her embrace — that's a touch redundant, no? Not to say kinky.

Well, that admirable house rule of ours lasted for a while, but it was eventually undone by two exemplary subversive factors, which I shall call the Pedagogical and the Aesthetic. Out-of-state houseguests and grandchildren and others sometimes need it explained to them just where they are when they're sitting on our porch or perching on our bowsprit; nothing like a cartographical cocktail table or serving tray or a handsomely framed hydrographical chart to facilitate that bit of instruction, or indoctrination. We have even, on occasion, identified certain ducks out on our unimpressive creek by consulting the hand-painted wildfowl tiles around our fireplace; those somewhat corny but ornithologically correct tiles came with the house, and are a handier reference than Roger Tory Peterson if we happen to be duckwatching from that particular room. And when cruising the Bay, we often plan our day's run over breakfast with the aid of certain cartographical placemats under our bagels and coffee — more convenient for that purpose (despite their clearly posted warning against using them for navigation) than the large-scale nautical charts on which we'll do our actual course-plotting as we go along.

That's the Pedagogical Factor — more of an excuse than a justification for our having the stuff around. The truly operative factor is the aesthetic one. To the question that I posed a while ago — the question "Why should anybody, other than a tourist or an expatriate, clutter up the house with more or less expensive *renditions* of Tidewaterland (graphic and plastic renditions, literary and musical renditions, whatever), when the real article is all around us?" — the answers are (*a*) that even junk renditions have more than mere souvenir value: They are affirmations, however crude, of esteem for the things depicted or symbolized, like Baltimore Oriole and Washington Redskin emblems; and (*b*) that a truly artful rendition has a value, even a reality, transcending the

---

*Authors, respectively, of *The Bay* (NY: Dodd, Mead, 1951), *Rivers of the Eastern Shore* (NY: Rinehart, 1944), and *Tidewater Maryland* (NY: Tudor, 1945), three "classic" treatises on the area.

value and reality of the thing rendered. A living, breathing, honk-
ing Canada goose in flight over the Eastern Shore marshes is one
thing; we may value it as a handsome wildfowl, as an element of
the ecosystem, as meat on the table, even as a symbol of Chesapeake Bay country from September through March. A junk rendition of a Canada goose may still serve that symbolic function,
rather like a bumper sticker exhorting one to HONK IF YOU LOVE
THE CHESAPEAKE. But a *splendid, marvelous* rendition of that
goose-in-flight into photography or paint or poetry or perfect
prose is more than just a reminder of the real thing or a secondary
symbol of what the real thing may symbolize for us: It is a real
thing in itself, a noteworthy addition to the stock of apprehensible
reality, and it may be prized as such even by people who know and
care little about our particular piece of geography; by people who
may never have heard of the place.

I have written about this factor elsewhere* and won't dwell on
it here. Gift shops in Holland, for example, are as full of souvenir
wooden shoes and images of tulips and windmills and canal boats
as our tidewater shops are full of all the stuff I've been speaking of,
at every level of taste — and the second largest customers for that
merchandise, after the tourists, are the Dutch themselves, who as a
people are evidently quite fond of their windmills and canal boats
and tulips and Klompen; they enjoy affirming that fondness in
replicated images even while surrounded by what those representations represent. Their countryman Rembrandt was fond of those
things, too, and he rendered them so well (along with other subjects) that people go all the way to the Amsterdam Rijksmuseum
to see the Rembrandts without necessarily even bothering to check
out the local countryside that inspired him.

That's what I mean by the Aesthetic Factor. Together with the
Pedagogical Factor and the Bumper-Sticker-Affirmation Factor, it
accounts for our house's being just about as full of Chesapeake
Bay stuff as any of our neighbors' houses. Indeed, one room of our
place we have come to call, with some embarrassment, the Goose
Room, by reason of the high wildfowl-image count therein —

---

*E.g., in the essay "Historical Fiction, Fictitious History, and Chesapeake Bay
Blue Crabs, or, About Aboutness," in *The Friday Book*.

more accurately, the high wildfowl-and-other-tidewater-image count. With the same mild embarrassment, but without embellishment, I offer now a far from complete inventory of those images, in order to get to the argument of this sermon:

The fireplace duck-and-goose tiles I've mentioned already: They came with the house, and were painted by a woman down the road who exhibits her work in Chesapeake arts-and-crafts shows. Not bad, not great; we ourselves would never have bought and installed them, but there they were. It would have been too aggressive, too unneighborly (and too expensive) to tear them out and replace them with something more to our taste, something iconographically neutral; and so we pretend that they're sort of useful for duck identification — and there's the entering wedge. The *light-switch plates* in that room have wildfowl decals on them — really kitschy. Those, too, came with the house; in this case, however, we could easily and inexpensively have replaced them. So why didn't we? Well, they happen to resonate in a campy way with those fireplace tiles, so what the heck: We name it the Goose Room, and in it we hang a series of marine-architectural drawings that my brother gave us one Christmas, years ago: structural drawings of Chesapeake bugeyes and skipjacks and log canoes by Howard Chapelle and R. Hammond Gibson. That same brother then picks up on the idea and gives us the following Christmas a stylized, varnished-wood half-model of a goose in flight that looks like a streamlined hybrid of the Lufthansa and the old Ozark Airlines logos; we mount that over one doorway and balance it on the opposite wall with a nifty black-and-white photograph of a stalking heron by Skip Willets, playing off the abstraction of the one against the fine-grained realism of the other. Next thing we know, there's a two-by-five-foot heron marquetry in the next room, and a foot-high heron or crane sculpted out of Hindu sacred-cow horn on the windowsill, and a two-goose Japanese brush-drawing yonder, and a giant full-color photographic blowup of a she-crab over the mantelpiece of the goose-tile fireplace, and on and on and on — including several shelves of literary Chesapeakia ranging from the 1930s WPA Writers Project guide to the Old Line State (re-edited in 1976 by Edward Papenfuse and republished by the Johns Hopkins University Press)* to Warner's *Beautiful Swimmers,* Horton's *Bay Country* — all the usual suspects. Meanwhile, out on the unimpressive creek itself, so many live specimens are rafted up that we suspect we've decoyed them in with all that goose art, and we fantasize some Alfred Hitchcock culmination wherein feathered Reality swarms into the Goose Room from off the flyway and overwhelms Art, leaving our house in the condition of our waterfront lawn in winter, all goose-down and goose-dung. The real thing.

Let me see now whether I can salvage some relevance from the litter of this (partial) inventory; maybe even mold from all these goose-droppings my aesthetic-ecological argument. To begin with, I do *not* propose, at least not on this occasion, any heirarchy of categories. I do not assert that a work of "Chesapeake" literature by Christopher Tilghman, say (of whom more presently), or for that matter by Ebenezer Cooke (colonial author of the original "Sot-Weed Factor" satire) or Captain John Smith or Daniel Defoe† — I do not say, just here, that any of these is inherently "better" than a Chesapeake Bay coloring book or cruising guide or souvenir videocassette. They're in different categories, not to be ranked against one another. Likewise the mallard-and-cattail mailbox in front of our property (it came with the house, I swear) versus the big Audubon blue heron reproduction in the entry hall, for which we're responsible (it echoes the trim paint — Williamsburg Blue). There is no *versus* involved, for the reason that John Audubon and the anonymous mailbox artist were up to different things: ethological accuracy combined with compositional beauty in the Audubon, crude recognizability combined with merchandisability in the mailbox. "Let a thousand flowers blossom," said Chairman Mao Tse-tung once upon a time; let a thousand and one cattails grow, and ospreys wheel, and herons stalk, and wild geese honk along the mainstream and tributaries of our estuarine art.

*From which came my explanation, above, of Maryland's nicknames.
†E.g., the passage in *Moll Flanders* wherein Moll crosses the Bay from the Potomac to the Nanticoke and runs into rougher weather than any she encountered in her transatlantic voyages.

This sweet non-judgmentality need not apply, however, *within* the several categories. Indeed, it *ought not* to apply (this is Proposition Two of my ecological argument), for that way lies the anarchy of indiscrimination. It is one thing — a quite okay thing — to enjoy almost equally a terrific American cheeseburger and a terrific item of French haute cuisine, depending on the occasion. It is quite another thing, and not okay at all for our cultural health, not to recognize the difference between a terrific cheeseburger and a mediocre or abominable cheeseburger; between a terrific and a tasteless *suprême de volaille*; or between those goose-art light-switch plates, which are accurate but tacky, those goose-art fireplace tiles, which are also pretty accurate and maybe just a touch tacky but not uninteresting in their overall composition and in the artist's carrying of the figures across the separate tile-lines in a number of places — and that black-on-white sumi-e brush-drawing of a brace of honkers crossing a full moon, which is arguably the least "accurate" in ornithological detail but of immensely more artistic interest precisely because so much Goose-ness and Full-Moonhood are suggested there with such a radical economy of means and virtuosity of touch.

The sumi-e, in short, is not mere goose-art; it is art that in this instance happens to involve geese as its subject matter. It is "about" geese, for sure, but it is by no means *simply* about geese, in the way that those decaled light-switch plates may be said to be. It is also about the medium of ink and paper, the craft of brush-drawing, and the sumi-e tradition of rich suggestiveness in a few masterful strokes. In a word, it is capital-A Art, and although my interest in it is not altogether pure (the drawing hangs where it hangs because its subject happens to be geese), I could just as readily admire it if I didn't care a honk about geese. Indeed, in another room on the premises is a sumi-e rendition of crabapple blossoms, even more artful than the geese but relatively unconnected with matters Chesapeake. It's there just because it's terrific.

My argument, then, is that while we need not and ought not to make comparative judgments about crabapples and oranges, let's say, we owe it to our cultural-ecological well-being to bring our best discriminatory powers to bear upon the sorting out of good and bad apples; not to mistake a mediocre drawing or sculpture or song or poem or story for a good one simply out of loyal affection for its subject matter — Dutch windmills, Chesapeake Bay water-folk, Parisian boulevards, Polynesian palm trees, whatever.

By way of example, I shall now go out on a loblolly-pine limb and maybe step on a few tidewater toes (good trick when one's out on a limb) by declaring (*a*) that the youngish writer Christopher Tilghman, for example, whom I mentioned before — of Tilgh-mans Neck, Maryland, and Harvard, Massachusetts — is an excellent literary artist whose "Maryland" stories* comprise some of the best fiction we have involving the Chesapeake area; and (*b*) on the other hand, that the late, locally-much-revered Gilbert Byron, formerly of Old House Cove, Maryland (author of *The Lord's Oysters* and other Delmarvania), while a remarkable fellow in many respects, is a (locally) much overrated wordster whose fiction and poetry I cannot imagine any knowledgeable reader taking pleasure in unless that reader's priorities put local-folksy subject matter above every other consideration. There are, to be sure, many such special-taste readers (and art collectors): the kind who say "Give me *anything* involving the Wild West" — or Labrador retrievers, or sado-masochistic bondage, or what have you, even unto crab-and-oyster harvesters. *Chacun à son goût.*

No doubt there is an inescapable element of personal taste involved in any critical pronouncement such as the one just delivered.† But if we go all the way with "each to his own taste," or call *every* comparison apples and oranges, we become critically paralyzed; anything then goes, and we can't communicate with one another even for the purposes of reasoned disagreement. This is not the place to draw point-for-point comparisons between the masterful and the mediocre in the work of the two "Chesapeake" Σwriters I've just mentioned — specific instances of perspicacious versus cornball character-drawing, structural craftsmanship, dramatic technique, descriptive precision, verbal texture, thematic depth, and the rest. I'll simply put in evidence what I've mentioned

*In his collection called *In a Father's Place*, published by Farrar, Straus & Giroux in 1990.

†Which did, indeed, ruffle not a few local feathers, in part because (as I wish I had known before making my criticism) the First Chesapeake Writers Conference was dedicated to the memories of the two Gilberts, Klingel and Byron. It may appease Byronistas to know that his most popular tome, the aforecited *The Lord's Oysters*, remains in print partly because I recommended it to the Johns Hopkins University Press some years ago for their "Maryland" series.

in passing already: that Mr. Tilghman's publishers, reviewers, and readers tend to be people primarily interested in good writing and only secondarily or incidentally (in many cases not at all) interested in Chesapeake Bay writing, whereas with Mr. Byron the case is prevailingly vice versa — as the overall record of his publishers, reviewers, and readership attests.

Enough, however, of that: Gil Byron–bashing is not my concern, except by way of critical illustration. My concern is the aesthetic-ecological argument; that argument may be made with other critical examples than the late laureate of Old House Cove, and from other arts than literature. Let's call Mr. Byron an orange after all, or maybe a ripe Delmarva cantaloupe, and get on with sorting out the apples.

But perhaps the point has been sufficiently made; in any case, I prefer to close on a more ecumenical note. Our Chesapeake has many and diverse tributaries, as has its art: major and minor, fair and foul, local and non-local — from tiny watershed trickles in upstate New York and the high Appalachians down to the great ocean itself, when the recycling tide comes in, the Ocean of Story and Panthalassa of all the arts — and including a fair amount of urban runoff and rural manure. Its brackish waters have about the same average salinity as human tears (what writer can resist that datum?), and one side effect of that circumstance is that you can swim in them with your eyes wide open — as I have tried to do allegorically here. On the other hand, those waters are so rich in suspended matter of every imaginable sort, from turds and topsoil to blue crabs and heavy metal, that while swimming wide-eyed through them, you can scarcely see your hand in front of your face.

Caveat natator.

"Jack and Jill"
An Exegetical Aria*

Jack and Jill
Went up the hill
To fetch a pail of water.

Jack fell down
And broke his crown,
And Jill came tumbling after.

AS IS THE case with most nursery rhymes, the meter of this classic specimen is simple and rigorous, even monotonous, and exactly replicated between the two stanzas.† There are no variations whatever in the elementary alternation of stressed and unstressed syllables, with a slight delay after each stress: a lilting, skipping rhythm suggestive of virtually carefree early childhood, such as my twin sister's and mine in East Cambridge, Maryland, through the dark years of the Great Depression — although the action described is not play but a homely household chore from the days before indoor plumbing.‡

*No headnote needed. A much-edited version of this Friday-piece was first published in *Paris Review* 125, Winter 1992; another appears in the novel/memoir *Once Upon a Time: A Floating Opera*, for which opus this mock-pedantic aria was originally composed. Much ado about almost nothing — but that *almost* is important. The variation here given is my favorite.
†There are other stanzas (see below), but what child remembers them?
‡By 1930, the year of this ariast's birth and likewise his sister's, most East Cantabrigians, our family included, enjoyed this luxury. Our grandparents' house next door, however, although equipped with a manual cold-water pump at the kitchen sink, maintained the classic row of outbuildings: toolshed, woodshed, coalshed, privy.

A simple rhyme-scheme (*aab ccb*) and stanzaic structure (short dimeter couplet followed by a single trimeter), its single, small irregularity would appear to be the off-rhyme of the *b* trimeters, *water/after*.

Close scansion, however, reveals the apparent simplicity of the poem's prosody to be deceptive, especially if one compares the recited and the most familiarly sung versions. Is the foot iambic (da-*da*) or trochaic (*da*-da)? Each stanza opens with an apparent trochee (*Jack* and . . . / *Jack* fell . . .) and closes likewise (*wa*-ter / *af*-ter), but a glance at lines two and three of each stanza persuades us at once that the foot is meant to be the homely English iamb: Went *up* | the *hill* / To *fetch* | a *pail*, et cetera. Once we note that the syllabification of the lines is less simple than their rhyme-scheme and alternating accent — not 4-4-7, 4-4-7, but 3-4-7, 3-4-7 — we can reasonably describe the prosody of the recited poem thus: Two three-line stanzas, *aab ccb*, each consist of an iambic dimeter couplet, its initial unstressed beat not given, followed by an iambic trimeter third line with a supernumerary final soft syllable to compensate for the missing opener.

An alternative, trochaic scanning is possible, with the virtue of eliminating the need for prosodic "epicycles," as it were, to account for the "missing" first syllable and the "supernumerary" closing syllable of each stanza. But such scansion requires an unnatural rearrangement of the lines — *Jack* and | *Jill* went / *Up* the | *hill* to / *Fetch* a | *pail* of | *wa*-ter — and moreover wrenches the happy skipping rhythm of *Jack* . . . and *Jill* . . . went *up* . . . the *hill* . . . into gimpy, unEnglish stresses.

Interestingly (to those who take an interest in such technics, the art of art), the common musical version of *Jack and Jill* accentuates the lilting iambic scansion while measuring the lines trochaically. Scored in 2/4 time, the unstressed syllables become sixteenth-notes before dotted-eighth-note stresses:

Jack and Jill went up   the hill to

Lines three and six become tetrameters instead of trimeters, with full weight given to the stanza's final syllable, unstressed in natural speech but not in song:

fetch   a pail   of   wa - ter.

On the other hand, the musical version is marked by incongruities between melody and meaning: The closing line of the "ascent" stanza, for example (given above), is a *descending* melody, which might be rationalized as foreshadowing the children's fall in stanza two, were it not that the same odd inversion recurs in line four — where, as Jack falls down, the melody springs gaily *up*:

Jack fell down

— and again in line six, where Jill's after-tumble is sung to a sprightly *ascending* melody:

and   Jill came tum-bling af - ter

With the song's harmony, the anonymous tunesmith is more successful in mating sound and sense: The major chords of the cheerful hill-climb give way to minor when mishap befalls the water-fetchers. True, the closing bars shift back to major and reinforce the bizarre melodic suggestion of happy ending; one either accepts the incongruousness as a folk-Mozartian musical irony (nursery rhymes abound in such grim cheeriness) or prefers this less commonly heard but more appropriate variant —

and   Jill came tum-bling af - ter

— which sustains the minor sonority as well as singing Jill's tumble in a melodically descending curve.

These preliminary observations made, we turn to the particulars of the poem's signification, beginning with its Dantesque wedding of form and content in both macro- and microstructural features. Just as the three books of the *Commedia* and their *terza rima* building blocks reflect Christianity's tripartite eschatology and the unity of the Trinity, so this blithe nursery rhyme about the fall of an at least originally innocent couple proceeds by duples: *Two* metrically identical stanzas (*twin* stanzas, one is tempted to say) each commence with a *couplet* in a *dimeter* that, whether scanned iambically or trochaically, employs a *two*-beat foot — more levels of two than Dante has threes. And just as the Florentine's *terza rima* interlinks his stanzas — *aba bcb cdc*, etc. — so the twin stanzas of "J & J" are coupled (slantwise, inexactly) by their *b* off-rhyme, *water/after*.

Would it not have been more in keeping with the theme of dupleness, or doubling (not to say *duplicity*), one might ask, to render the poem entirely in couplets — four of them, perhaps, in two stanzas, to get away from threes altogether? Arguably so, but consider the trade-offs: the hobblingly unrelieved dimeters, the loss of interstanzaic linkage (it's either *aa bb/cc dd* or *aa bb/aa bb*, more a cloning than a coupling; or *aa bb/bb aa*, suggesting an ascent/descent in course of which *nothing consequential happens*, or *aa bb/ab ab* — the metaphorical possibilities of which this exegete declines to consider.

In fact, as shall be seen, that "odd" third line of each stanza serves a number of poetic purposes, not least among them release from the constrictive dimeter couplets: a playing of twos against threes reflected in and reflective of the line's tripedality. "Who is the third," Eliot's "Waste Land" asks, "who walks always beside you?"*

Let's zoom in:

1.

Jack and Jill. On an empty stage, two characters in three monosyllables. In the minimalist way of nursery rhymes, all "background" exposition is dispensed with: no "Once upon a time, in a land far away, there lived . . ."; none of "that David Copperfield kind of crap," as J. D. Salinger's Holden Caulfield calls such introductory résumés. We are afforded scarcely a clue to the pair's age, relationship, or situation. Illustrators of Mother Goose books regularly presume J & J to be young children, no doubt on the grounds that if both *go* to fetch a single pail of water, both must be *needed* to carry the pail; all illustrations show the pair of them lugging even the *empty* pail together in stanza one† — small children indeed, or else they hold the vessel jointly out of simple reciprocal affection, as unself-conscious children might hold hands while walking or skipping along. A reasonable presumption, but only a presumption. All that we can say with confidence is that the characters are two, not one or several; that on the evidence of their given names they are male and female; that those given names are what they are (English, for one thing, like the poem itself, implying an Anglophone venue for the action to follow‡); and that in the order of their introduction, at least, Jack precedes Jill.

*In our house, it was the twins' older brother, peremptorily upstaged and outnumbered by our birth in May 1930, seven months after the Black Friday stock-market crash.

†E.g.:

‡Our own stock was principally German. That tongue, however, was spoken only by our next-door grandparents, who like many turn-of-the-century immigrants chose not to teach it to their children, but reserved it for interparental communication.

A cultural reflex of male primacy? Very likely. Reflective of a customary male initiative in such enterprises as hill-ascending and water-fetching? Likewise likely — though Jill's relegation to the end of the line may be owing to nothing more invidious than the resources of English rhyme. *Jill and Jack / Went out the back? Up the track? Down the crack?* Unpromising openers. It may well be *the hill* that constrains Jill to her secondary position and Jack, a fortiori, to his primary; one might argue that he comes first because she must come second, instead of the other way around — though most likely the supply of apt English rhymes merely happens in this instance to reinforce the cultural case: the steep and slippery hill of male initiative and female response, male thrust and female parry or riposte. Jack leads, Jill follows, and the rhyme — and thus the topography and its consequences — follows Jill's following.*

Went up the hill. The three monosyllables of character are followed by four of action and scene. The attentive reader notes that whatever the age of these presumable children, they are not obliged to *climb* the hill, although that verb would as easily fit the meter; they simply "go up" it. The implication is that their *Wasserhügel* is a gentle grade, not a steep incline† — a circumstance that deepens the mystery of their approaching mishap. Alternatively, they may be not such toddlers as would find a moderately steep slope something of a climb, even empty-bucketed. Perhaps they're vigorous teenagers? Young adults? In any case, up the hill they go, without apparent trepidation or difficulty. As remarked above, the cheery rhythm of both the recited and the sung versions suggests that they fairly *skip* uphill.

---

*The singer of this exegetical aria — who with his opposite-sex twin was consequentially named after the nursery rhyme by our then three-year-old brother — in autobiographical fact *followed* his sister into the world by eighty minutes, invariably played *secondo* to her *primo* in our childhood piano duets, and trailed her in academic performance, as measured on school report cards, even after our curricula diverged with our lives at the onset of puberty and high school. But there is no debating that in other matters (who goes to college, who to secretarial school), through the ballad or tale or opera act of our tidewater childhood, it was Jack and Jill, not vice versa.

†Scarcely even a grade in some illustrations: viz. the woodcut terrain aforefootnoted (reproduced, with the other woodcuts herein, from *The Oxford Nursery Rhyme Book* [Oxford: Oxford U. Press, 1955]), as flat as Maryland's Eastern Shore.

Up what hill? Not "*a* hill"; not "Lake Hill" or "Water-Well Hill" — simply "*the* hill": a proto-Modernist "presumptive exposition" quite in keeping with the minimalistic characterization and not uncommon in nursery rhymes ("*the* mouse ran up *the* clock"), but scarcely to be found in prose fiction before the twentieth century.* Compare the pre-Modernist, folktaling indefinite articles of that lugubrious Protestant hymn "The Old Rugged Cross," which Jill and Jack used dutifully to intone in meetings of East Cambridge's St. Paul's Methodist Protestant Junior Christian Endeavor:

> *On a hill far away,*
> *Stands an old rugged cross:*
> *The emblem of suff'ring and shame. . . .*

A hill, despite every Junior Christian's knowing it to be Calvary, a.k.a. Golgotha: Skull Hill, outside ancient Jerusalem.

A water-well atop or at least aflank a hill? Perhaps a clear mountain spring, in the days before one worried about *Giardia lamblia* and other contaminants. Some pleasant, Cotswoldish "Spring Hill," one imagines, of less ominous connotation than the American locus of Richard Brautigan's poem "The Pill Versus the Spring Hill Mine Disaster." To the wellspring, is where our eager couple skip; *à la source.*

And why? *To fetch a pail of water.* What art is in this seven-syllable line, this three-line stanza, this two-stanza narrative! Syllabically equal to but metrically distinct from the preceding couplet, the trimetric third line's stresses are distributed over its seven syllables in a way that effectively prevents its being mistaken for a second three-four couplet. As to the stanza: First it has given us the actors, then the action and scene (rather than the more conventional vice versa — as though the pair's first priority is *to go* and only secondarily to go some particular where); now, finally, as if in

---

*E.g., the opening line of Ernest Hemingway's early story "Indian Camp." "At the lake shore there was another rowboat drawn up. The two Indians stood waiting." What lake shore? What *first* rowboat? What two Indians? In the interest of immediacy, the Modernist pretends that such things go without saying. Literary *Post*modernists, on the other hand, have been known to revert to "that David Copperfield kind of crap."

afterthought, we get the stated motive. One almost imagines a parent calling, "Jack? Jill? Where are you two going?"

"Oh, just up the hill."*

"Up the hill? Whatever for?"

"Oh . . . [etc.]."

"Mm hm. Well, watch your step."

". . . ."

To fetch *a pail* of water. Every illustration to the contrary notwithstanding, the line itself does not explicitly provide the water-fetchers an empty bucket, any more than "Let's go for coffee" sets us out cup in hand. A pail*ful*, a pail's *worth* is as much as the text gives us undeniably. But we need not imagine Mom querying suspiciously, "So where's your bucket, young man and young lady?" The illustrators are on firm ground, both because hillside springs are not equipped with pail dispensers like those paper-cup holders beside office watercoolers and because our story *needs* that pail from the expedition's outset. As sung already, it is the link between Jack and Jill: their conjunction, the couple's coupling, and a sign to all who might catch sight of them that their errand is innocent, even commendable.

Their ascent may be sans trepidation or difficulty; is it without hesitation as well? The stanza's architecture subtly hints otherwise. Contrast such monotonously deliberate alternatives as the labored but steady *Jack and Jill / Climbed the hill. / Up they went, / Water-bent*; or the unanimously resolute *Vowed Jack and Jill, / "We'll climb this hill. / We will not fail / To fill our pail."* Aside from its pleasing syllabic variety, the 3-4-7 of the stanza as given suggests some initial hesitation (on Jill's part, one imagines, Jack having proposed either the project itself or Jill's accompanying him on his errand), followed by further urging on his part and some yielding on hers (one fancies him leading her by the pail handle, uphillward from the dooryard, she fretting "D'you think it's *okay?*" and he jollying "Sure it's okay! Come *on!*") before she puts by her hesitation altogether and skips merrily with him up the springward path.†

---

*But there were no hills in Cambridge, Maryland, seat of Dorchester County, 80 percent whereof (in the 1930s, at least) comprised Chesapeake estuarine wetlands.

†Jill and I preferred to play on the Choptank rivershore, one block down Aurora Street from our tidewater-gothic clapboard house. Its attractions included a be-

This masterful stanza's final *coup de maître* is its final word —
more particularly (in the recited version) that final word's final syllable. Universal solvent, sine qua non of life, bearer of bottled
messages both fake and bona fide, *water* is also the poem's first
polysyllable. As such, it ominously foreshadows its correlative, the
double disyllables of Jill's downfall in line three of stanza two.
Moreover, whether or not its unaccented final syllable is regarded
as supplying the "missing" first syllable of line one, the word *wa-*
ter breaks the poem's rhythm in two significant ways: It trips the
iambs with a trochee (compare *Jeannine and Joe / Went through*
the snow / To fetch a pail of H_2O, or even *Jack and Jane / Went*
down the lane / To fetch a pail of milk), and the pacing of its unaccented syllable in fact rules out its being regarded as a complement
to the truncated opening foot. Scored rigorously in the accents of
speech, the word would appear not as two quarter-notes —

wa - ter.

— but as a sixteenth and dotted eighth —

wa-ter

— or an even more abrupt pair of sixteenths —

wa-ter

---

creepered "jungle" for hide-and-seek and an unofficial trash dump rich in rats
and empty booze bottles, the latter ideal for the posting of water-messages on
outbound tides.

— followed in either case by the ominous silence of that quarter rest on the measure's closing beat.

Wet flagstones beside the well? Mossy rocks in the freshet below the spring? Some moist boundary-mark overstepped? Whatever the efficient cause, in the word *water* we hear the skip become a trip, the step a misstep, the misstep a stumble, the stumble a teetering silence before . . .

2.

Their fall, of course. Better, their *falls*, for whereas stanza one conjoins the couple in an at least ultimately side-by-side ascent — "mutual assent," one might pun, after small initial misgivings on the part of the party of the second part — stanza two explicitly separates and serializes their come-downance. As the former apportioned its three lines to (1) character, (2) action and scene, and (3) motive, stanza two apportions its to (1) Jack's mishap, (2) Jack's mishap's consequences (for Jack), and (3) Jill's mishap — which last might be read as Jack's mishap's consequences for Jill. Before examining the second stanza — more rapidly than we examined the first, as to fall takes less time than to rise* — we must ask what happened between the two. *What caused Jack's fall*, and subsequently/consequently Jill's?

On this literally central question, the text is as silent as that quarter rest in the amended score. Did the lad slip? Perhaps distracted or unbalanced by his pail-mate, did he misestimate some audacious step? We can only surmise — though the order of events, echoing the order of the characters' introduction, certainly suggests Jack's ongoing primary responsibility. He led, she followed, however willingly; he took her to the heights and then brought the both of them low.† Be it on his crown, then, their downfall — though not entirely so.

But we're getting ahead of ourselves, a fair way to tumble. *Jack fell down* is all we know for sure, though far from all we need or want to know. The poem contents itself with effects, leaving causes to the reader/listener's imagination, and those effects now

---

*In classical Greek tragedy, a single circuit of the sun suffices for peripety; in Mother Goose, three monosyllables.
†My sister and I inclined to blame things on our brother.

concatenate line by line. Whatever the cause, *Jack fell down* — another instance of hubris (that which goeth before a fall) brought low? — *And broke his crown.* The climax of the poem's action is not merely a skull fracture with possible subdural hematoma* on the not-so-gentle slopes of this Anglican Calvary (from Latin *calvāria*, skull [translation of Greek *kranion*, translation of Aramaic *gulgūtha*, whence Golgotha]), but the end of male regnancy, at least of Jack's.

And [read *whereupon*] *Jill came tumbling after*, in an aptly tumbling line of denouement, with its artful double disyllables for closure. One line for Jill to Jack's two, but a strict equality of syllables. Not, however, an equality of consequences; reversing the order of narration in lines five and six (Jack falls, Jill tumbles after, Jack breaks crown . . .) throws the disparity into high relief. Both fetchers fall, but the other shoe to Jack's crown-breaking never drops. The dramaturgical silence concerning non-consequences-to-Jill is as loud as that quarter rest of unspecified action between the stanzas.†

---

*This ariast's crown was near-cracked in mid-childhood by his eldest sibling on a Chesapeake summer afternoon in the side yard of 301 Aurora with a length of two-by-four or equivalent lumber: a non-concussive but stunning blow that I can still summon to mind, so to speak, and in fact an altogether blameless accident (my brother didn't know, when for whatever reason he swung that board, that I was standing close behind him), although I declined to believe it so at the time. No hard feelings, Bill.

†As aforenoted, some Mother Goose compendia add further stanzas in which Jack trots home as fast as he can caper to one Old Dame Dob, who patches his knob with vinegar and brown paper, at sight of which plaster, when Jill comes in, she does grin, whereupon her mother, vexed, does whip her next, at the spectacle whereof Jack does laugh while Jill does cry, but their tears do soon abate, whereafter Jill does say that they should play at seesaw across the gate. No child remembers these addenda, which however make reasonably clear that the pair are siblings — and children, not yet ready for adult responsibilities and adventures, as these alarming woodcuts suggest:

Justice served, we might feel: Jack led her up there by the pail; let Jack's be the crown that breaks. Punishment enough for the party of the second part that she takes her tumble: soiled frock, mussed hair, perhaps skinned knees and elbows; no water to show for their little adventure and all the explaining to do, as poor Jack's out of it. Assuming that she can set things right with the home-folks,* will Jill now wear Jack's erstwhile crown, we may wonder, or choose instead to devote herself to "caregiving" for her injured initiator? If indeed she assumes the crown of instigation and primary responsibility, will she presently lead Jack or some other back up that fateful "hill" (more circumspectly, one bets), or fetch water from some less risky source, or leave water-fetching to those whose fingers, shall we say, have not been burnt in that pursuit?

Such conjectures are beyond our given text, however much it invites them. More appropriate to close readership is the question *What happened to the pail?* Outfielders may dive for a fly ball, roll over several times, and come up holding their catch securely, but nobody ever took a skull-cracking downhill fall or heptasyllabic epitumble without spilling his/her water and very possibly smashing the presumably wooden pail as well. All illustrators of the rhyme agree (with the spill, at least†); and although the singer of this exegetical aria remembers, from his undergraduate fraternity-house-bartending days, drunken Kappa Alphas pitching down the club-basement stairs with their open Schlitz bottles held safely aloft, out of harm's way, he concurs that J & J's fetching-expedition must have been a dead loss, waterwise.‡ Inasmuch as stanza two is altogether silent on the matter of the pail but explicit on the severity of Jack's fall and the posteriority of Jill's, the impli-

---

*In the matter of the two-by-four, Jill joined Jack in blaming Bill.

†E.g.: , which reinforces the causal mystery by showing "the hill" once again to be as level as Aurora Street between the Choptank River and East Cambridge Elementary School, whither and whence we daily tripped — and Jack's right toe beyond the frame, like Jill's left hand.

‡Nor have any of my bottled water-messages, as of this writing, ever been replied to.

cation may be not only that the water was spilled and (as some illustrations have it) the bucket de-coopered into its constituent staves, but — contrary to those illustrations — that *no water was ever fetched*, that the obscure mishap mishappened before the pail was ever filled. In any case, by stanza two the couple has been de-coupled, their symbolic link unlinked. Together they went up; they come down separately.

No use crying over spilt water: In that quarter rest between the paired stanzas, what happened happened, what didn't didn't. But Jack's crown was broke, Jill took a tumble, and it's time to stop playing seesaw across the gate. "Jack and Jill" is a reorchestration of the Fall: Adam and Eve rescored by Mother Goose. The unacknowledged party of the third part is neither "Old Dame Dob" nor anybody's elder brother but the Serpent; on that hilltop is the Garden,* and in that garden the Forbidden Fruit. As my twin sister and I would be taught by our East Cambridge Elementary schoolmates before we knew the facts of life, the insinuating "subtext" of "Jack and Jill" is sibling incest: in our innocent case, a taboo not only unapproached but unimagined. For all our pail-toting general intimacy, we were altogether unself-conscious about (indeed, unconscious *of*) this out-of-hand-predamning aspect of JackandJillery, until the figleaved world pointed its soiled fingers and reddened our innocent ears with prurient variations on the canonical text.†

---

*Hebrew, Christian, and Islamic divine geographies often locate the Earthly Paradise on a hill or mountain: e.g., the top of Dante's Mount Purgatory and the Muslims' Adam's Peak in Sri Lanka. But others place it in or near a tide marsh, such as that at the confluence of the Tigris and Euphrates at the Shatt al-Arab. I hold with those latter.
†E.g.: *Jack and Jill / Went up the hill. / They each had a dollar and a quarter. / Jill came down / With two and a half: / Do you think they went up for water?* Et cetera ad nauseam.

Browsing

In Chestertown, Maryland, not far from where I write these Friday-pieces, is a good small liberal-arts college to which the first president of the United States kindly lent his name upon its establishment in 1782. I have mentioned the place already in passing;* my wife and I often use its library when we're in residence at Langford Creek. For that reason, although I like to keep a low profile hereabouts, in the fall of 1992 I was pleased to contribute to the belowdescribed public celebration the following address, subsequently published in the college's alumni magazine.

MY CONGRATULATIONS TO Washington College and to the staff of its Clifton M. Miller Library on the acquisition of this library's 200,000th volume. My thanks to whoever took it into their heads to invite me to help celebrate that occasion, and equally to you all for troubling yourselves to come hear what I have to say about it.

I confess to have been a little curious on that score myself; that's why I accepted the library's invitation. I am in rigorous accord with E. M. Forster's rhetorical question "How can I tell what I think until I see what I say?" Indeed, I learned recently[†] that that eloquent obiter dictum of Forster's has been updated and elaborated by contemporary neuroscience and language theory into what's known as the Pandemonium Model of Utterance — a

---

*In "Can It Be Taught?"
[†]From Daniel C. Dennett's *Consciousness Explained*, as explained in the earlier Friday-piece "Once Upon a Time: Storytelling Explained."

model that theorizes multiple goals or intentions percolating through our consciousness, on the lookout, so to speak, for materials of expression, while at the same time those materials of expression (what the zoologist Richard Dawkins calls "memes," or memory units), likewise distributed through our brains, are reciprocally vigilant for opportunities of incorporation. What issues from this ongoing, low-level pandemonium inside our heads is what in fact we end up saying or writing — which then we may have to qualify immediately because we see that it's not quite what we meant; perhaps (as T. S. Eliot says) that "that is not it, at all." Contrariwise, we may recognize it to be *exactly* what we think and believe, now that we see how it has gotten itself said.

I don't know how it is with you, but the Pandemonium Model of Utterance certainly reminds me of how things happen in *my* head, and likewise at my writing table. Not to wander irretrievably far from the subject of our celebration, let's imagine individual consciousness as a sort of open library stack (what we call our memory) whose "books" are itching to be borrowed. Our intentions are half-random, half-purposive browsers through that open stack, and our utterances are the more or less serendipitous matchup of books and borrowers: a matchup continuously "feedback-guided, error-corrected, and gain-adjusted" (in the words of the "neurophilosopher" Daniel C. Dennett), but never without an essential, inescapable element of browser-like serendipity, whatever the urgency and momentousness of the occasion. It is a matchup, moreover, in which not only are the "borrowers" more or less modified by the "books" (as is often the case with literal book-borrowers), but conversely, as any librarian can attest to be sometimes the literal case too — the book somewhat modified by its borrower.

The book that I myself most recently borrowed from the Miller Library, for example, is a study of the great sixteenth-century French comic writer François Rabelais by the great contemporary Russian critic Mikhail Bakhtin. It is an utterly humorless (though quite brilliant) examination of the millennia-old tradition of folk humor — the rough, democratic, "Rabelaisian" humor of marketplace and carnival — to which Rabelais gave magnificent literary-expression in *Gargantua and Pantagruel*. Mikhail Bakhtin's book has substantially altered the way I think about François Rabelais — and evidently it impressed some earlier borrower of the volume as well, for he or she altered it by ticking certain passages in the margins and even bracketing a few of them in the text, with the consequence that I found myself interacting not only with Bakhtin's interaction with Rabelais, but also with some prior borrower's interaction with Bakhtin's interaction. Now, I happen to believe that anyone who marks up a library book deserves Islamic justice; all the same, it was a spooky and not uninteresting experience to notice early on that my fore-reader was ticking pretty consistently the very passages that I would have ticked, were I a ticker of passages in library books. Soon enough it became a kind of game between me and him/her: How come you didn't tick *this* passage, which I think memorable indeed? How come you bracketed this other one, which doesn't strike me as all that dazzling an aperçu? Maybe I'd better run it through my head again. . . .

In short, the reader had changed the book, as well as vice versa, and I was reading that reader as well as reading the writer and, by extension, reading the writer that that writer was writing about. This complex transaction took place on the beach at Ocean City in the last week of August, by the way, and despite my best efforts to keep the Atlantic Ocean away from Mikhail Bakhtin and François Rabelais and my anonymous co-reader of *Rabelais and His World*,* a bit of salt water dripped onto the lower front cover. As that happens to be exactly where my left ring finger rests when I read, I too have very slightly changed the book that very slightly changed me: There's a worn spot here that wasn't there when I borrowed the book — but I doubt that that alteration will significantly alter some future borrower of Bakhtin-on-Rabelais.

The Pandemonium Model of Utterance, I was saying: that dating service for Intentions and Materials of Expression. I hope to wander back to this browserish aspect of human consciousness, human verbalization — I would go so far as to say human identity, even — after I've browsed through some other alcoves of my subject, which, right about at this point in the early drafting of these

*Cambridge MA: M.I.T. Press, 1968.

remarks, I realized was going to be *browsing*, and so decided to make browsing my method as well as my subject matter: This is what aestheticians call "significant form" and I call the Principle of Metaphoric Means.* To browse means "to inspect in a leisurely and casual way" (so runs the verb's first definition in my dictionary, which etymologizes it back to Old French *broust*, meaning a twig or shoot). Also and therefore, it means "to feed on leaves and young shoots" (the second definition) — your mode of sustenance if you happen to be a deer, a goat, or a giraffe, for example, or an undecided but decidedly curious undergraduate. Of this, too, more presently: young sprouts browsing through the leaves of books. Libraries have this happy arboreal aspect: Not only do they themselves have branches and even twigs — e.g., the Rock Hall Branch and the Galena Twig of our Kent County Library — but the word "book" itself is an etymological offshoot of "beech," which is how their pages come to be called "leaves" and those who forage therethrough "browsers."

Well. Browsing thus through the *B*s in my desk dictionary to check out the word *browse* reminded me that it was while browsing thirty years ago through the *B*s in the card catalogue and literature stacks of the Pattee Library of the Pennsylvania State University, where I happened to be teaching at the time, that I serendipitously encountered the writings of the great contemporary Argentine Jorge Luis Borges, whose fiction I had begun to hear interesting things about† but hadn't read yet. A writer's muse from time to time whispers, "You'd better check this one out"; I always follow her advice, but not always promptly. I was there among the *B*s, I confess, partly to see whether my own books were included in the library's holdings; there were just three of them back then, and the experience of being a card-catalogued novelist was still rather heady. I don't remember whether I found myself there that day or not (what one hopes to find is one's books in the catalogue but not on the shelf); I do remember discovering Borges, a writer who came strongly to affect the way I thought about contemporary fiction, my own included, and about numerous other

*For a fuller statement whereof, see "Borges and I: a mini-memoir."
†Most particularly from that forgotten student duly credited, if alas not named, in "Borges and I."

things as well. In one of his marvelous stories, for example,* Borges defines "money" as "a collection of possible futures." That's how I feel about libraries: A library is a collection of possible futures. My own future was significantly course-corrected, not for the first or the last time, by that fortuitous encounter in the Penn State stacks.

Señor Borges, I believe, shared my feeling about libraries (for a time he was a librarian himself, at the National Library in Buenos Aires). Another of his *ficciones*, called "The Library of Babel," involves an infinite library, whose innumerable volumes contain every possible combination of alphabetical characters and spaces. Such a library — the verbal equivalent of Lucretius's universe, comprising an infinite quantity of a finite variety of atoms in every possible combination — would therefore include the record not only of "actual" history, but likewise of all imaginable histories; it would contain not only the true prediction of the future, but, alas, the prediction of every possible and impossible future. I say "alas" because in the infinite Library of Babel we would have no way of distinguishing, before the fact, the accurate prediction from all the slightly or grossly inaccurate ones. The truth would be there, somewhere, but only extraordinary chance or special dispensation would lead us to it.

Metaphorically speaking, of course, that is the case with all libraries, despite the best efforts of the most knowledgeable and sophisticated staff and the highest-tech database search programs, for the reason that every general library represents and indeed more or less contains the accumulated mental resources of civilization. In the granary of the past are the seeds of the future, and no doubt the best way to assure a crop is to make the widest possible assortment of cultivars as accessible as possible to as many as possible within the community that the library serves.

The image of Borges's infinite library (along with the phrase "widest possible assortment of cultivars," which I chose because it's not every day that a novelist gets to use the word "cultivars") moves me to browse a bit around the number that occasions our present occasion: 200,000 books. Is that a lot of books?

* "The Zahir"

Quite a few books? "Right many," as we Eastern Shore folk some-times say? Only a few? Too many? Just enough? Unanswerable questions, on the face of them, but some other book numbers might help put ours in perspective. A browse through the *World Almanac* tells us that if we add another nine million volumes to our 200,000, we'll match the stacks of the New York Public Library — the research stacks only. Add another seventy million to that (we're talking 79,200,000 *items* this time, not necessarily volumes), and we approximate the holdings of the Library of Congress. Throughout most of recorded history, on the other hand, 200,000 volumes would have constituted a world-class li-brary: A browse through the wonderful old eleventh edition of the *Encyclopaedia Britannica* reminds or teaches us that the great li-brary of Pergamum, for example, in Asia Minor, second only in its day to the fabled library of Alexandria, at the peak of its flourish-ing boasted some 200,000 "volumes" — scrolls, they would have been, of papyrus and of vellum parchment; scrolls to be *rolled* and un*rolled*, from the Latin verb for which action we get our word "volume" and the Swedes get their word *Volvo*. ("Parchment," by the way, comes from Pergamum both historically and etymologi-cally. I don't mind smarting off to you about these things, because many of them I just learned myself, browsing around for this talk.) Plutarch tells us that when Mark Antony's Roman legions cap-tured the city of Pergamum in Fortysomething B.C., Antony made a gift of those 200,000 scrolls to his friend Cleopatra to add to the holdings of that already-legendary library of hers in Alexandria, part of which had been burned by Caesar's fleet a couple of years earlier.

Well, books *are* nice love-gifts. Two hundred thousand of them might strike some of us as a touch much, a touch over-magnificent, but Aristotle lists "magnificence" among the moral virtues in his *Nicomachean Ethics*; the classical Romans went in for the grand gesture, and in this instance it seems to have had the intended ef-fect. Anyhow, think of trying to select *one book* as a knock-your-socks-off love gift to the owner of the largest library in the world. I like to imagine a whole fleet of triremes ferrying those 200,000 scrolls from Pergamum to Alexandria along with a nicely under-stated cover note: *Thinking of you. Mark. XXXI October, XL-something B.C.*

More numbers: The fiction department of the Barths' personal library on a branch of Langford Creek (we call it our Branch library) has evolved into a steady-state operation of about 1,300 volumes, plus or minus several dozen. Its size is constrained by the fixed amount of shelf space that my wife and I allot to that particular category of literature. Every couple of years we do a triage on the overflow, mostly new novels sent by their publishers in hope of a blurb: *This* one we'll keep, because we hope to get around to reading it someday; *that* one we really must keep whether we get around to reading it or not, since the author inscribed it to us. On the other hand, no way we're likely ever to get to *this* one and *that* one, even though they might turn out to be wonderful or important or both: the books of the decade (if they do, we'll borrow them from some other library in some future decade). For every "new" book we keep, we cull an "old" one from the shelves — old and new in terms of acquisition, not date of composition. The number remains approximately constant; the quality curve, we like to think, gently rises. As for the worthy dispossessed, we donate them to our favorite *Salon des refusés*, the library of the O'Neill Literary House,* for some apprentice writer on the browse to serendip into.

Because who can say what half-random combination of voices from here there and anywhere might happen to inspire a new singer? I know of one instance where a thirteenth-century Persian fabulator (Scheherazade) interbred with, among others, a nineteenth-century Brazilian romantic formalist (Joaquim Machado de Assis) and an early-twentieth-century Irish Modernist (James Joyce) to produce a contemporary American Postmodernist. Most of that wild cross-pollination took place in the classics stacks of the old Gilman Hall Library at Johns Hopkins, where I used to work as a book filer to help defray my undergraduate tuition, and where I managed to read quite a lot of what I was supposed to be returning from cart to shelf: my à la carte education. Library stacks, in their quiet way, can be really swinging places; virtual orgies of cross-cultural insemination go on there, at all hours. If Jesse

---

*Washington College's enviable sanctuary for apprentice writers, most of them in pursuit of the staggering Sophie Kerr Prize (see "Can It Be Taught?").

Helms and Pat Robertson get wind of it, the American Library Association is in for trouble.

Speaking of which (apprentice writers and book numbers, I mean, not virtual orgies), Gustave Flaubert famously remarked that it is enough for a writer to have read five or six books well. He neglected to tell us which five or six, however, and so I caution apprentice writers that only the massively well read, like Flaubert, are entitled to make such dismissive remarks, just as only Nobel Prize–winners are entitled to sniff at the Nobel Prize. (I've heard it said, by the way, that a certain distinguished theoretical physicist, toward the close of his career, once lamented to an interviewer that by his own standards he had never had a really great idea in his professional lifetime. The surprised interviewer asked, "Do you mean a Nobel Prize–winning idea?" "No no no," said the physicist: "I mean a *really* great idea." The disparagement would be more pungent coming from a Nobel laureate — except that the anecdote happens to be not tellable that way.)

How many books are enough? When one of my graduate students asked Donald Barthelme, who was visiting our seminar, what she might do to become a better writer, Barthelme suggested that she might begin by reading all of philosophy, from the pre-Socratics up to last semester. The young woman objected that I had already urged her and her comrades to read all of literature, from the Egyptian Middle Kingdom up to last semester, in order to get some sense of the turf. "That, too," Barthelme said. "You're probably wasting time on things like eating and sleeping. Cease that, and go read everything." Thomas Wolfe, if I remember correctly, attempted to do just that, in his New York years, and was rendered desperate by the fact that the Serious Lit stacks alone of the New York Public grew at a rate enormously faster than even a speed reader could hope to approach.

To wind up this exercise in number-browsing: At the opposite pole we have a reading list even shorter than Flaubert's unspecified "*cinq ou six livres*": that of those Islamic fundamentalists who maintain that only *one* book is necessary, the holy Koran, inasmuch as all the others either agree with it, in which case they're redundancies, or else disagree with it, in which case they're heresies. Christian fundamentalism has sometimes inclined that way, too, substituting "the Book" for the Koran — although "Bible", strictly speaking, comes from the Greek plural *biblia*, meaning books: the books of the Book, to be sure, not just any old plurality of books.* The Arabic *alcoran*, on the other hand, means not the book but "the reading," or recitation, while the Hebrew *Torah* means "the law," or instruction. I don't doubt that subtle and exemplary differences among Christian, Islamic, and Judaic cultures might be extrapolated from these different meanings of their terms for their scriptures, but I'm certainly not going to attempt any such extrapolation — and I'll spare you an aria on the interesting word "extrapolate".†

So: Given these numerical extremes — the single-volume library of fundamentalist Islam on the one hand, Borges's infinite Library of Babel on the other — how big should a library be? Specifically, the general library of a good small liberal arts college like this one? The only acceptable answer is "as big as possible," for while the quality of a collection is no doubt more important than its size, there's much to be said for mere muchness, for raw magnitude. George Boas, the late aesthetician and historian of ideas at Johns Hopkins (and my mentor, although he didn't know it), used to fret about "great books" curricula because they tend to leave out the books that disagree with the Great Books. The reading of non-great books, Boas believed, even of downright bad books — even of inexcusably, unredeemedly wicked books — is important to a truly liberal education: liberal as in "liberating," as in *Veritas vos liberabit*, "The truth shall make you free," which happens to be the motto both of my alma mater and of the United States Central Intelligence Agency, neither of which institutions intends the proposition in quite the same spirit that Jesus intended it in the gospel of St. John, Chapter 8, Verse 32. The *liber* of "liberal" and "liberate," I remark in passing, is an entirely different root from the *liber* of "library," but the two roots indisputably nourish the same tree.

---

*Thus in pre-Gutenberg terms we speak of Book Such-and-Such of the *Iliad* or the *Aeneid*: their several scrolled "chapters." The Pergamum library's 200,000 "volumes," therefore, would not have equaled the 200,000 post-Gutenbergian books of the Clifton M. Miller Library.
†Literally, "to polish out of."

Let's hear it, then, for raw magnitude: I can testify that my undergraduate book-filing days in the orderly labyrinth of Greek and Roman classics and of William Foxwell Albright's Oriental Seminary (which back then comprised Sanskrit, Persian, Arabic, Hebrew, Egyptian, and various other literatures) indelibly impressed me with the sheer size and diversity of the *already said*, and made me a cultural pluralist for life — without, mirabile dictu, intimidating me into respectful silence. If you happen to be a refugee from the Dorchester County tide marshes (another sort of labyrinth), as I was and remain, and particularly if you aspire to keep one foot at least ankle deep back in your native bog while the other foot traipses through the wider world, it is well to have such an off-the-cart smorgasbord under your belt, for ballast.

As big as possible, then, your library, the absolute minimum requirement being that it be big enough for a habitual browser to get lost in.

How big is that? We seem to be back where we started: How many books does it take to lose your average seasoned, half-purposive browser? Sometimes, as has been demonstrated, just one will do the trick. I find a good dictionary or almanac or encyclopedia as difficult to extricate myself from as a good hardware or marine supply store; from any of them I'm likely to emerge with something very different from what I went in for. I even resist interrupting a sentence in progress to check out one of its items in such seductive reference works, lest I mislay the thread that led me into the labyrinth and find myself lost in the funhouse of the *Britannica* or the *Oxford English Dictionary*.

Is this another sort of one-book fundamentalism? Not at all, for the reasons that in this case the "scripture" involved is humanly compiled, not divinely revealed; that it deals in worldish information, not heavenly truths; that it's not a labyrinth, really, but a network, leading always as much back out into the world as on into its own further interconnections. Such secular scriptures, it's worth noting, needn't be reference works. When James Joyce was asked, late in his career, whether he didn't after all demand too much of his readers, the author of *Ulysses* and *Finnegans Wake* is said to have replied, "I demand nothing of my readers, except that they devote the rest of their lives to my books" — and indeed, one could profitably do just that with such a work as *Finnegans Wake*, precisely because in addition to leading always farther into itself it leads always also out of itself: to the rest of literature, to myth, history, languages, the sciences, virtually the whole spectrum of human knowledge and experience. To "master" such an "encyclopedic" text would require a degree of knowledge and understanding approaching the global — but then, if I remember correctly, that is just about what Lord Tennyson says about the prerequisites for understanding a simple flower in a crannied wall: "I hold you here, root and all, in my hand, / Little flower — but *if* I could understand / What you are, root and all, and all in all, / I should know what God and man is." Inasmuch and insofar as the world is regardable as a seamless web of virtually infinite interconnections, anything in it (including any book) may serve as the browser's point of entry — so long as, unlike some scriptural fundamentalists, we keep the connections open to the rest of the web, the rest of the labyrinth, funhouse, library, network, world.

A better answer to the question "How big need a library be for one to get happily and perhaps even profitably lost in it?" would be "Big enough to constitute a network of interconnections sufficiently rich to serve as a model of the mentally apprehensible world." That formulation — in particular the term *network* — leads or at least invites me to the all-but-final twigs of this little browse through the subject of browsing.

I've been speaking of *books*, mainly, as one still tends to do when speaking of libraries. Our occasion, after all, is this library's acquisition of its 200,000th book;* there was probably a similar hurrah at Pergamum in Fortysomething B.C. when the 200,000th scroll joined their collection, just before Mark Antony closed in as Cleopatra's field agent for acquisitions. But every frequenter of libraries knows that the image of the library as a book museum, or even as a storehouse of the printed word, is a severely limited image indeed, not only because audiovisual materials are so important a part of any modern library's resources — cassettes, slides,

---

*The volume officially so designated in this instance was a signed copy of H. L. Mencken's *Treatise on the Gods*, presented to the Miller Library by the businessman/bibliophile John Danz, of Baltimore and Chestertown.

microfilms, laser disks, and the like — but also because more and more of the library's available supply of "written" language is "accessed" these days not directly off the shelf and the page but via modems and video display terminals. For a great many research purposes, the printed book — that handy-dandy object that we cuddle up with on beach or airplane or recliner chair and try not to deface with suntan lotions and marginalia unless it's our personal copy — the printed book is often less useful than the computerized database, the search program, and the electronic network — technologies that are obliging us to rethink our familiar book-oriented notions of "text," "author," "reader," "copyright," and the like. In the scientific community especially, but in the humanities and other areas as well, research findings are exchanged, "papers" are "written" and peer-reviewed and revised and enlarged or subsumed without there necessarily being any officially "published," canonical text at all. There are electronic journals (by which term we do not mean magazines about electronics); there are even on-line literary periodicals, not to mention all sorts of interlinkages among specialized databases. Ever more frequently, our transactions with the "already said" — and with colleagues, business associates, even geographically distant family members or fellow enthusiasts of some particular pursuit — take place not in library stacks of printed books or in any other literal space with literal texts, but in the virtual or hyper-spaces of computer networks, with virtual rather than literal, hard-copy "finished" texts. Even, we are beginning to see, with hypertexts.

What is hyperspace? What are hypertexts? For any of you unfamiliar with these phenomena, it is fortunately too late in this talk — too late in life, I suspect, for some of us print-loving troglodytes perfectly comfortable with the mature but threatened technologies and institutions of books, publishers, authors, readers, and copyright laws — too late for me to do more than browse the very edges of the subject.

Most of us have experienced to some extent the "virtual reality" or "virtual worlds" of computer modelings and simulations, which seem to be used these days in virtually every field of human enterprise from weather forecasting to market research. And whether we employ the term or not, most of us are familiar with the "virtual texts" — unprinted, unfinalized, ever open to emendations small or large — that float about in our word processors or in the hyperspace between our computers and those of our editors, colleagues, accomplices, fellow accessees to some electronic network or other. Now imagine a "text" (the word is already in quotes, the signal or symptom of virtuality) every word of which — at least many a key word of which — is a window or point of entry into a network of associated "texts" (or graphics, music, statistics, spoken language, whatever a computer can reproduce), these several networks themselves interconnected and infinitely modifiable — or *virtually* infinitely so — by "readers" who can enter the text at any point, trace any of a zillion paths through its associated micro- and macro-networks, add or subtract material and modify the linkages as they please, and then exit at any point, in the process having been virtual co-authors or co-editors as well as "readers" of their virtual text. That's hypertext.

The quick brown fox jumps over the lazy dog. Imagine a "loaded" display of that innocent proposition on your VDT, such that "clicking" on any item in it opens a window menu of associations available for exploring, from the relative nimbleness of temperate-zone quadrupeds, through the history of fox hunting and its representation in painting, music, and literature, to soundtracks of hounds in full cry (with or without expert commentary) and disquisitions on animal rights — and every one of those associated "lexias," as the hypertexties call them, similarly loaded, another ring of keys with which one may open yet further doors, and on and on and on — no two routes through the maze ever likely to be the same, and every venturer thereinto not only a Theseus but a Daedalus, remodeling the labyrinth at will en route through it. That's hypertext, more or less, and it alarms and intrigues me at least as much as I hope it alarms and intrigues you, and we're likely to be hearing a lot more about it before our weary century expires, because whether or not it's more hype than text (as some naysayers allege), its impassioned prophets proclaim it to be the third great revolution in language technology, after the invention of writing and the invention of movable type.* So watch out.

*See, e.g., George P. Landow's *Hypertext* and Robert Coover's essays "The End of Books" and "Hyperfiction," cited in the earlier Friday-piece "It's a Short Story."

Hypertext is, I suppose, the ultimate form of browsing. In our virtual way, we library-browsers have been virtually hypertext-ing all along without realizing it, the way Molière's Monsieur Jourdain comes to realize that he's been speaking prose all his life without knowing it. My mental interaction on the beach at Ocean City with that previous borrower's shamelessly marginated inter-action with Mikhail Bakhtin's extended interaction with all previ-ous commentators' critical interactions with the text of François Rabelais's literary interaction with the world of sixteenth-century France can be thought of as a somewhat awkward and limited lin-ear analogue to hypertextual browsing, which is essentially non-linear. And for the past forty-odd minutes, you all have been the patient attendants upon another such limited linear analogue: namely, this demonstrational browse through the subject of brows-ing, which could as easily have followed any number of other ser-ial associations than the ones that it turns out to have followed — except that I happened to have the destination *hypertext* in mind, and so my interlinkages had the aspect more of waypoints than of innocent, freestanding young shoots to be randomly browsed.

But true browsing, QED, is always only partly random. Those "innocent young shoots" that the browser browses upon aren't really freestanding; they're multiply interconnected by a complex network of underground rhizomes, like spartina canes in a marsh or wire grass in your garden or the axons and dendrites of the multibillion neurons of our brains: a network unapparent and scarcely apprehensible until we begin to browse along one of its all-but-infinite possible pathways, sighing, perhaps, at the number of alternative routes that we don't have time to explore. I spoke earlier of the "arboreal" aspect of libraries — their branches and twigs, and the etymology of words like *book* — and now I've mentioned rhizomes. It happens that the terms "arborescent" and "rhizomatic" are fashionable just now in post-structuralist literary theory, employed* to describe two very different kinds of organiz-ing structures. Libraries are "arborescent" not only in their aforenoted woodsy associations, but in their hierarchical classi-fication of verbal subject matter into mainstem categories with

---

*Notably by Gilles Deleuze and Felix Guattari, e.g., in *A Thousand Plateaus: Capitalism and Schizophrenia* (Minneapolis: U. Minnesota Press, 1987).

multiply branching subcategories and sub-subcategories (the Dewey
decimal system of book classification is an elaborate instance of
arborescent structure). But browsing, like hypertext, is essentially
"rhizomatic," as is the human brain and the world apprehended
by it. Whatever its official place in some hierarchical system, every
object of contemplation, every mental datum and sensory image,
like every word in a language, is also a node in a rhizomatic network that may lead to illuminating, beautiful, useful, or at least
unexpected interconnections.

Now that I've seen what I've said on the subject of browsing, I believe I know what I think: that I want to end this talk back in a library with the great Jorge Luis Borges, whose texts may not be hy-
per, but are very often super. One of my favorites among them is
set in what used to be called Czechoslovakia in 1938 and involves
a not especially successful writer named Jaromir Hladík, who is
condemned to death by the Nazis for the crime of being Jewish.
On his last night on earth, Hladík prays for time to complete an
unfinished work in progress, and toward dawn he has a crucial
dream:

> ... he dreamt he had hidden himself in one of the naves of the
> Clementine Library. A librarian wearing dark glasses asked him:
> What are you looking for? Hladík answered: *God.* The Librarian
> told him: *God is in one of the letters on one of the pages of one of
> the 400,000 volumes of the Clementine. My fathers and the fathers
> of my fathers have sought after that letter. I've gone blind looking
> for it.* He removed his glasses,* and Hladík saw that his eyes were
> dead. A reader came in to return an atlas. *This atlas is useless,* he
> said, and handed it to Hladík, who opened it at random. As if
> through a haze, he saw a map of India. With a sudden rush of as-
> surance, he touched one of the tiniest letters. An ubiquitous voice
> said: *The time for your work has been granted.*

The story in which this dream occurs is called, in English, "The
Secret Miracle"; it has a magnificent ending, which I won't give

---

*Borges himself, as has been noted elsewhere in the present collection, was all but
blind.

away. I exhort those of you who don't know it to look it up, here in your splendid 200,000-volume library (already half the size of the fabled Clementine). Do not let the circulation staff look it up or fetch it for you; go into the stacks yourself, with only the most general directions, and do not rush to the correct address. Stroll the neighborhood; handle the merchandise; see what catches your eye. You are not likely to find God while browsing through the stacks of the Clifton M. Miller Library — though who knows? What you might just possibly find, however, is yourself.

Ad Lib Libraries
and the Coastline
Measurement Problem
A Reminiscence

Speaking of and to libraries: Not long after the foregoing address to friends of Washington College's Miller Library, I had occasion to do another chorus on some Friday-riffs sounded here and there already in this volume. The occasion was the 1993 annual meeting, in Baltimore, of the Maryland Library Association. My remarks thereto appeared subsequently in the Spring 1994 number of the literary journal Boulevard.

    I AM NEITHER an impassioned bibliophile nor a systematic collector of books. Moreover, the kind of fiction I write seldom requires extensive library research.* But I am a dedicated browser through any case or cart or stack or alcove of books that I come across.

To my "development" as a writer, few experiences have proved more serendipitous† than my undergraduate book-filing job in the old Gilman Hall Library at Johns Hopkins, where I surreptitiously read a lot of what I was supposed to be reshelving from my book cart. That's where I discovered such wonderful storytellers as Ovid and Petronius and Scheherazade and Somadeva, as well as

---

*The two chief exceptions are *The Sot-Weed Factor*, a historical comedy set in Colonial Maryland, for which I did most of my homework in the Fred Lewis Pattee Library of the Pennsylvania State University, and *LETTERS*, a formalist extravaganza with one foot in the War of 1812, which I homeworked in the Lockwood Library of SUNY/Buffalo.
†Or more often adverted to in these Friday-pieces, I'm afraid.

Boccaccio and Rabelais and company, none of whom was included in my excellent official curriculum. The eventual subject of these remarks is going to be a series of earlier, unofficial libraries of one sort or another — ad lib libraries — that were important to me before I discovered those wonderful official ones like the Gilman (now called the M. S. Eisenhower) and the Pattee — which last, fortuitously for me, happened to include the Archives of the Province of Maryland. But I want to approach that subject sidewise, as storytellers incline to do.

It happens that I've just finished perpetrating my dozenth book, this one called *Once Upon a Time: A Floating Opera*. It is an odd sort of beast, a memoir wrapped in a novel, and to the extent that it *is* something of a memoir, writing it gave me occasion to appreciate a few basic propositions about the stories of our lives — propositions that perhaps go without saying.

The first such is that our lives are not stories. Among the several corollaries to this elementary premise is that the story of our life (*any* story of our life) is not our life; it is our story.* Another is that while most of us who are not of the Buddhist persuasion would probably agree that here on Earth, at least, we have only one life, nevertheless that one life ("that massive datum," John Updike calls it in his memoir *Self-Consciousness*) lends itself to any number of stories — and I'm speaking here not of fabrications but of sincere, straightforward factual accounts. Another way to put it is that any life's story can be told in any number of ways, depending on the teller's "handle," or angle of view, or lens. In fact, of course, the same applies to fictional characters: people made out of words in a novel or words and images on a screen. Any number of stories might be told about a Moll Flanders or a Tom Jones or an Indiana Jones; the ones that Daniel Defoe or Henry Fielding or George Lucas chose to tell were determined by particular dramatic and thematic considerations — which never exhaust the possibilities.

*Variations on this riff may be found in *The Tidewater Tales: A Novel* — specifically, the chapterlet called "The Story of Our Life Is Not Our Life. It Is Our Story."

I'll circle back to this proposition after establishing one other, the storyteller's equivalent to what mathematicians call the coastline measurement problem. James Gleick (in *Chaos: Making a New Science*) reports that the problem itself was first remarked in the 1920s by a scientist named Lewis F. Richardson (Bertrand Russell must have written about it, too, for I cited him on that subject nearly twenty years ago, in an essay on the Chesapeake Bay region*). More recently, the coastline measurement problem has been much invoked by Benoit Mandelbrot and others in such disciplines as fractal geometry and chaos theory. I even saw a painting with the title *Measuring the Coastline* reproduced in a recent issue of the magazine *The Sciences*.

The story goes that for one reason or another, Mr. Richardson wanted to know the length of the Portuguese coast.† Sensibly enough, he went to the library — in fact, to libraries in Portugal, Spain, Belgium, and the Netherlands — where he discovered that the relevant figures in various reputable atlases and encyclopedias differed by as much as 20 percent. When he then fetched out some reliable maps of Iberia in order to measure the thing for himself, it became evident to him that such measurements may have a lower limit, but they have no upper. How long is the shoreline of the Chesapeake tidewater system? Your answer depends, obviously, on your scale of measurement: whether you run a line from the Chesapeake & Delaware Canal, say, straight down to Cape Henry and back, or curve that line somewhat to match the Bay's overall curve along its eastern and western shores, or articulate those two curves to include the major indentations of bights and bays and tidal rivers, or include all of those plus every tidal creek and cove shown on the most detailed of maps, or (if we move from maps to the real thing, which is after all what we're interested in) all of those plus the perimeter of every rock and mud flat and sand spit and for that matter every grain of sand right down to the electron-microscopic level — if we decide arbitrarily to stop there. Measuring "as the crow flies" gives us a rough-and-ready though not very

---

*Foreword to my photographer-friend Robert de Gast's *Western Wind, Eastern Shore* (Baltimore: Johns Hopkins U. Press, 1975).
†In some accounts, the length of the Portuguese/Spanish border.

realistic lower limit; but as soon as that crow (better, that blue heron) begins to deviate from its course to follow the contours of reality, the coast of Portugal or the shoreline of the Chesapeake is as long as you want it to be — approaching infinity, as Mandelbrot points out in his analysis of the problem.* That painting I mentioned (by Mark Tansey) shows huge ocean waves crashing against some rugged headland like the cliffs of Cape St. Vincent, the southwest tip of Portugal, while a team of intrepid cartographers with a very long tape attempts to measure around every crag and crevice.

I like to observe to apprentice fiction writers that the coastline problem applies to every story; in fact, it applies to every narrated action *within* every story. How long does it take Irma to answer the telephone, once she hears it ring? In real life, anywhere from a few seconds up to maybe half a minute, if the caller persists and the answering machine doesn't intervene; in narrated life, however, whether factual or fictional, the answer depends on the author's verbal/narrative waypoints. It may take no longer than the space between the word *dingaling* and the word *"Hello?"* Or it may take eight wordsworth of space and time: *Irma picked up the telephone and said "Hello?"* Or it may be that Irma hesitates and reflects a bit on who might be calling; or she may hesitate and reflect a lot — her narrative, anyhow, may do so. Irma may set down her glass of chablis (What brand of chablis? What sort of glass?); she may tap the ash from her cigarette (What brand of cigarette? Tap the ash into what?), reflecting that she would probably be a non-drinker/non-smoker these days if it weren't that her estranged abstemious party-pooping husband, Fred, always used to nag her so on that subject, and wondering whether that's Fred calling now, or Fred's lawyer, or maybe her own lawyer, Rodriguez, whose interest in her case she's half afraid is becoming more than merely professional. . . . Irma's author may even freeze-frame between ring and response and cut to an extended flashback, perhaps several chaptersworth of retrospective marital case history.

*The *fractal dimension* of the Chesapeake's Eastern Shore (a measure of the degree of its intricacy) has been calculated at 1.46, as compared to 1.8 for the west coast of Britain, 2.9 for the human bronchial system, etc. See, e.g., Lium and Hancock, "Complexity Physics," in *Johns Hopkins Magazine*, April 1993.

Indeed, an entire novel may elapse with Fred (or Rodriguez) on hold, so to speak; Laurence Sterne's account of the biological conception of Tristram Shandy nicely illustrates the coastline measurement problem in its narrative aspect. Likewise these remarks, which are going to concern themselves eventually with unofficial, ad libitum libraries, but are taking their sweet time browsing toward that subject.

Now let's put together the coastline measurement problem and the aforestated propositions (1) that the story of our life is not our life, and (2) that any life lends itself to any number of imaginable stories. As we've established, every story, and each of its constituent actions, gets from its beginning to its ending via a series of narrative waypoints chosen by the teller for their relevance. Relevance to what? To the particular story that the teller has chosen to tell, of course, as against all the other possible stories that might be told about the same characters and/or situation. We cannot tell "the story of Napoleon," or even "the story of Napoleon at the Battle of Waterloo"; all we can do is tell *some* story about Waterloo (like Stendhal's famous battle-chapter in *The Red and the Black*) or *some other* story about Napoleon (like John Vernon's 1991 novel *Peter Doyle*, having to do with the posthumous American adventures of the Emperor's penis after it was stolen from his corpse between St. Helena and his final resting place at Les Invalides — a story with, I gather, some basis in fact). Irma may say "I'm going to tell you just the most important things about myself," but the things most important to her divorce lawyer aren't likely to correspond to the things most important to her doctor (Which doctor? Her gynecologist? Her psychiatrist?), or those to what most interests her potential new lover, although there may be some overlap, or those to what interests a fiction writer making up a story "about" Irma.

Now we add the coastline measurement problem. How long did it take Irma to get from age ten, let's say, to age sixteen? Roughly six years, we bet, in her life as lived. How long is the story of those particular six years of Irma's life? Annie Dillard's memoir of that period of *her* life (*An American Childhood*) runs to 255 lovely pages. A different account of the same time-span might run to a Marcel-Proustian seven-volumes-and-counting or to a single modest sentence ("She blew out the ten candles on her cake, and when the smoke cleared, there were sixteen"). It may even happen that the interval ten-to-sixteen doesn't get mentioned in Irma's life story at all: One characteristic of the myths of wandering heroes, for example, from all cultures and centuries, is that typically little or nothing is said of the interval between the hero's miraculous birth and narrow escape from infant death to the time of his setting out in manhood upon his heroical career.

What prompts this excursion into the crevices and crannies of the coastline measurement problem is that, as aforementioned, I've just wound up *a* story of my own, quite non-heroical life — the first two acts of that life, anyhow, from about age zero to about age forty — and, not surprisingly, I'm impressed (and pleased) by how much I left out, for various reasons; likewise, by how many other ways that particular floating opera might have been scored. As it happens, I chose to sing it under the aspect of *vocation*: the "calling" that any artist who persists in any art must feel more or less strongly. Given that particular theme, the story's turning points are a, b, and c, et cetera, rather than x, y, and z, as they might have been if the theme were something else: a political or intellectual or spiritual or sexual case history, say.

The truth is, even the particular theme of Vocation might have been sung in any number of other keys and tempos than the ones that seemed to me best to suit my purposes — but let that go. My modest point is that a story of your life might be told as a series of career moves, or love affairs, or intellectual friendships, or houses lived in, or ideologies subscribed to (even magazines subscribed to), or physical afflictions suffered, or what have you, and that every one of those series might be recounted from very different perspectives, to very different effect.*

All this by way of saying that having just rehearsed the first four decades of my life under the aspect of Vocation, I find myself more than usually appreciative of other aspects under which those

---

*The late Raymond Queneau's little book *Exercises in Style* (1947) exploits this inherent plasticity of the storyteller's material: Queneau retells the same banal anecdote 99 times, in 99 several modes, and it yields 99 quite distinct effects — in effect, 99 different stories.

same decades might have been sung, not excluding the aspect of libraries — and so we arrive at our proper subject.

Salman Rushdie once told me that when he was a child in Bombay, his father enthralled him with bedtime stories about characters named Aladdin, Ali Baba, and so forth — stories that Rushdie learned only later, to his disappointment, had been lifted from *The 1001 Nights*: He'd thought his dad was inventing those wonderful stories for his son. My first "library," if I may stretch the term a bit, was a single book, also of bedtime stories: a no doubt quite unremarkable Depression-era collection called *365 Bedtime Stories*, given to my twin sister and me at some Christmastime early in Franklin Roosevelt's first presidential term. Unlike Rushdie with his tales from Scheherazade, neither my sister nor I can recall a single item from *365 Bedtime Stories*. What we both recall well and warmly, some sixty years later, is being duly bedtime-storied by our mother from that book for nearly a year as we lay in our (twin) beds in Cambridge, Maryland: It is our earliest memory of narrative. I say "nearly a year" because although the book rationed its contents by calendar date, we kiddie sultans sometimes demanded of our matronly Scheherazade more than one narrative hit per night to toddle us off. The original vizier's daughter, geared for the long haul, typically stretched her stories over several nightly installments (by my count, in Richard Burton's famous edition of *The 1001 Nights* Scheherazade tells only 267 complete stories, despite Burton's own claim that there are "upwards of 400"; the longest of them, with its tales within tales within tales, takes Scheherazade exactly 100 nights to tell*). The items in *365 Bedtime Stories*, on the contrary, were often so abbreviated that we could coax our mother to read ahead of the book's calendar.

Needless to say, this narrative pacing was neither the only nor the most important difference between our situation in 1930ish Tidewaterland and King Shahryar's in medieval Islam. Setting

---

*For further Scheherazadean statistics, see my analysis "Don't Count on It: A Note on the Number of *The 1001 Nights*," in *The Friday Book*.

aside the utter forgettability of our bedtime fare compared to what Scheherazade was serving up — she had, after all, prepped for her job in her father's very considerable library, and by Night One she had the whole rich corpus of traditional narrative literature under her belt — there are also the cardinal differences that in our house nobody's life was on the line (despite our blood-chilling bedtime prayer, "If I die before I wake"), and that in the innocent nature of our situation, there was no erotic voltage on the connection be-tween teller and told, such as obtained between Scheherazade and the king. I have made much of this sex-and-death aspect of narra-tivity here and there in my writings; enough here to say that what was true literally for Scheherazade is true figuratively for all story-tellers: Our professional life is always on the line, and properly so. We're only as good as our next story, and this relation between teller and audience, while perhaps terrifying, is also at least poten-tially fertilizing. Among the reasons for there being 1001 nights rather than more or fewer is that it takes just about that much time to conceive, gestate, and deliver the three children for whose sake Scheherazade begs for her life on Night 1001. Three sons, they are (this being a patriarchal venue): "one walking, one crawling, one suckling. . . ."

The king then orders Scheherazade's tales set down by the scribes and published in thirty volumes for posterity: a small li-brary in itself. The fate of our *365 Bedtime Stories* was less dignified. Soon outgrown by us and consigned to the attic, it had a raffish second life in my early teens, when, under the evil influence of certain pals in the neighborhood, I looked for a place to conceal the verboten cigarettes that we sometimes sneaked and smoked. What more innocuous hiding place than a kiddie bedtime book? And so with a single-edge Gillette razor blade that I normally de-ployed for cutting model-airplane parts from sheet balsa, I excised and discarded the inch-thick text, leaving only the hard-covered margins, and I stashed our contraband Camels inside like a genie in a lamp. It's not as if I were trashing Ali Baba and Aladdin, I tell myself, still with a pang of guilt. I was reminded of this loaded vol-ume a quarter-century later, when I finished a book called *Lost in the Funhouse: Fiction for Print, Tape, Live Voice* and wondered briefly with my editor whether we shouldn't include an audio cassette with the printed book (cassette tapes were a hot new item in 1968) and, if we did, how the combination might best be packaged. In the event, I vetoed the cassette idea as too gimmicky — but I sure knew how we'd have packaged the thing if I had felt otherwise.

In the museum of the Vatican library, if I'm not mistaken, there is an elegantly bound little breviary that once belonged to some seventeenth-century prince or politically involved cleric — anyhow, to someone in need of other than merely divine protection, for the sacred text has been excised even more ingeniously than was the text of *365 et ceteras* and replaced not with contraband cigarettes but with a deadly little pistol (still a hot new item in the seventeenth century) mounted to fire through a hole in the gilt-edged leaves of the prayer book when triggered with a tug of the silken bookmark by the wily friar (let's say) accosted in mid-devotion. In the end, too, was the Word.*

My fascination with books put to symbolic purposes other than mere reading persists: the old Sears catalogues that farm families patiently dog-eared page by page into buoy-shaped doorstops, or tore off page by page for privy-paper — a direct, if complex, statement about American consumerism. Or that wonderful book-shaped entity constructed by some pop artist back in the Sixties, big as a small house, with entrances and exits, stairways, various rooms, even a flush toilet, as I remember. Who hasn't had the experience of a novel, for example, so capacious and absorbing that as readers we virtually inhabit it?

Once upon a time, my wife and I needed to know the weight of a roast that we were about to roast, and in the absence of a proper kitchen scale, the only thing available to weigh it on was an antique balance scale with just two poundsworth of assorted counterweights. So I used those counterweights to weigh the American hardcover first editions of my novels (which happened to be at hand) in the order of their publication, noting the heft of each in turn and setting it aside to use as a supplemental counterweight:

*And one remembers that other notorious cut-out scripture in Flannery O'Connor's "Good Country People": no cigarettes or pistol inside, but a flask of whiskey, a pack of naughty playing cards, and a package of condoms.

The Floating Opera, 16 oz.; *The End of the Road*, a svelte 13 oz.; then *The Sot-Weed Factor*, 2 lb. 8 oz.; *Giles Goat-Boy*, 2 lb. 6 oz. (my first heavy period), et cetera. By then putting selected items of my bibliography in one pan of the scale and our roast in its other pan, and switching a couple of the bona fide counterweights back and forth for fine-tuning, I was able to weigh precisely the meat on our table with the books that had helped put it there. Most gratifying.

Browsing back to the subject of unofficial libraries: The second of importance in my life, a few years after *365 Bedtime Stories*, involved a quantum jump from that single, ill-fated quarto volume to twenty folio volumes plus index: a children's encyclopedia called *The Book of Knowledge*, silver-tooled blue bindings in a dedicated bookcase that came with the package* — a pricey package, I imagine, that the Grolier Society's sales reps must have had an uphill job of selling to financially strapped New Deal–era moms. Ours, bless her, took the bait, despite truculent resistance from us young beneficiaries, whom I remember sitting in a sulk on the living-room staircase because the sales pitch, to which we had been corralled to listen, was keeping us from play. Who wants an encyclopedia? I believe I grumbled at one point — to which the sales rep smoothly replied, Maybe you *know* already why the sky is blue?

Well, he had me there, and my sister likewise. The sale was made, the self-contained mini-library presently delivered (with its gothic-lettered custom presentation page tipped into Volume 1) and the special bookcase proudly installed just inside our living-room door. My disgruntlement must have passed, for I believe that over the next several years I read every page of every volume of *The Book of Knowledge* — though not in the willfully, perversely systematic order with which, in my undergraduate years, I plowed through Dr. Eliot's entire Five-Foot Shelf of *The Harvard Classics*, one after the other, left to right, while ostensibly working as a night-shift timekeeper in the Chevrolet factory out in East Balti-

---

*Much ado about this set in *Once Upon a Time: A Floating Opera*.

more. *The Book of Knowledge* invited browsing; it leavened its encyclopedic-informational burden with stories retold from classical mythology and a recurring feature called "Things to Make and Things to Do," which had a formidable turn-of-the-century labor-intensivity about it:* To make a little bathtub-toy steamboat, for example, we kiddies were directed to procure from a tinsmith sheet metal and tin-snips, from a hardware store solder and flux and a soldering iron, from a pharmacist a certain quantity of naphtha (something to do with propulsion). Talk about deferred gratification! No young Tom Edison, I was generally content just to *read* such ambitious recipes for their own sake and to confine my building to the generous limits of my Gilbert Erector Sets — labor-intensive enough themselves with their endless little nuts and bolts in that pre-plastic, pre-snap-together era.

Annie Dillard fondly memoirizes similar encyclopedic browsings from twenty years later than my own American childhood — as she remembers other adventures in more official libraries. I was not blessed with Dillard's fine and precocious sensibility (nor was my family blessed with anything like the privileges that she was born into), but I certainly shared, anyhow came to share, something of her thirst for the entire (lowercase) book of knowledge. Once having nibbled the addictive fruit of that tree, one craves the whole pomegranate, the whole crop, plus leaves, limbs, bark, heartwood, roots. "You Must Know Everything," declares the haunting title of one of Isaac Babel's stories — haunting perhaps especially to us novelists. In later life I've met enough bona fide polymaths to know that I'm far from being one; my curiosity, however, remains moderately encyclopedic, even if my capacity and memory fall short. What we failed encyclopedists are left with is the eclecticism of the autodidact, which for many purposes will suffice — particularly in the case of novelists, who in this respect are the opposite of icebergs. Eight-ninths of what a novelist knows about any subject that comes up in her/his novel is likely to be right there on the surface, worked up for the occasion.

---

*Adverted to in the Friday-piece "A Few Words About Minimalism," herein.

Au revoir now, *Book of Knowledge*: I still remember, from your pages, why the sky is blue — and what fraction of an iceberg is below the surface. I also know that the children's encyclopedia that I bought for my own youngsters in the 1950s — the Little Golden Book set, I believe it was, colorfully illustrated but thin on substance — couldn't fetch tea for the Grolier Society's 1930s product.

One goes on to elementary and junior high and high school, and no doubt those institutions were equipped with libraries even on the poor old lower Eastern Shore of Maryland in World War Twotime; but I have little memory of those libraries beyond Jack London's *White Fang*, the complete works of that intrepid and mischievous adventurer Richard Halliburton, and Paul de Kruif's *Microbe Hunters*. Same goes for the Dorchester County Public Library, in my hometown: Like many more kids back then than nowadays, I suppose, my sister and I were busy readers who duly ran through that library's shelves of Hardy Boys, Tom Swift, and Tarzan for young Jack, the Bobbsey Twins and Nancy Drew for young Jill — all a benign blur, as is indeed my entire school education between kindergarten and college (we had the privilege of an excellent private kindergarten, in a time and place where there were no public ones, and I lucked into Johns Hopkins). Nothing in between "took," in the school-and-library way, whether because they weren't what they ought to have been or because I wasn't what I ought to have been.

The really important library for me in the last throes of my adolescence was another unofficial one. Paperback "pocket books" had been invented by then (we're in Harry Truman's first term now), and my father sold them in his soda-fountain/lunchroom, along with magazines, comic books, and piano sheet music. His children were allowed to bring any number of pocket books home to read, as long as we didn't bend them out of shape for selling, and — perhaps exactly because those stacks of paperbacks "from the store" *were* unofficial in their librarihood — I found them an inexhaustible and ever-changing smorgasbord, much more to my taste than the hardbound and call-numbered offerings of the bona fide libraries available to me, such as they were. Although neither of my parents had been educated beyond public high school, they both enjoyed book-reading, as did nearly everybody in those pre-TV days: the end of the golden age of mass literacy. My father preferred serious nonfiction on the order of Winston Churchill's memoirs (though he also enjoyed a paperback series called *The Ribald Reader*, of which more presently); my mother doted on westerns and romances. They neither guided their children's reading on the one hand nor censored it on the other; any pocket book for sale in Whitey's Candyland was ours to read, and it is from my binges in this line — especially through the long, subtropical, un-air-conditioned tidewater summers — that I trace the first stirrings of my vocation.

Was there any nonfiction in the store's inventory? I don't remember any (Dad's Winston Churchill and company were hardcover gift items). *Novels* is what there mainly was up there: Mother's westerns and romances, neither of which I had a taste for, and tons and tons of Raymond Chandler, Agatha Christie, Ellery Queen — I think I read them all, and from that total immersion I must have osmosed unconsciously some sense of narrative architecture, pacing, and suspense (there wasn't much else there to osmose; certainly not depth of theme, emotional complexity, or richness of characterization and language). Even more to my taste, when I discovered them, were the neo-gothic supernaturalists, as I guess we might call them: writers like Abe Merritt, John Collier, Lord Dunsany, and H. P. Lovecraft, whom I found in the Avon Fantasy Reader series — a refreshing change of literary aesthetics and metaphysics (though I wasn't thinking in those terms at the time) from the hard-boiled realism of James M. Cain and company, which I also enjoyed.

And then one day, as we storytellers like to say, round about high-school graduation time, amid this indiscriminating voracity, this pop-fiction feeding frenzy, I accidentally bit into something altogether different — indeed, *two* things altogether different, both from Abe Merritt/Agatha Christie and from each other. One was *Manhattan Transfer*, by John Dos Passos; the other was William Faulkner's *Sanctuary*. What were they doing in the stacks of Whitey's Candyland? Lord knows; it was some regional distributor who stacked those stacks, not my busy father. But I read them right through, the Dos Passos and the Faulkner, and however much my memory might be reorchestrating the experience, I know that I recognized at the time that here was something quite other not only than my mysteries and supernaturals but than *White Fang* and *Ivanhoe*, too (Walter Scott didn't take for me). Here was — I understood later but did not then — a different kind of realism: non-generic, non-commercial; *real* realism, complete with italicized "cinematic" chapter-headnotes in the Dos Passos and corncob dildos in the Faulkner. Here was a different kind of plotting (*two* different kinds of plotting), a different deployment of language (in the Faulkner especially; Dos Passos was no great stylist). Here was, in a word, capital-L Literature, but of a very different, more alluring and intriguing sort (for me, at least) than the items in our high-school English syllabus. Heavy stuff, maybe, this was, but hot stuff, too, both in matter and in manner. Here as well, by the way — so I sensed but couldn't have said — was High Modernism. And I liked it; I liked even the passages or aspects of it that I didn't understand, the way you can strongly enjoy certain music that you know has a lot more going on in it than you can follow; the way you can relish other kinds of experience that you'd be at a loss to explain. So this is Modern lit, huh? I liked it plenty.

I liked it so much, in fact, that I searched for and found some more Faulkner up there in Whitey's Candyland, and I liked *it*, too — *The Wild Palms*, and *Pylon*, and *Soldier's Pay* — and so I looked farther for items in that line, whatever that line was, and found none. But my eager browsing after the non-generic led me to at least one other discovery, which will lead us to this browsing's end.

I was, be it remembered, a healthy male adolescent, ipso facto horny; also omnivorous — the old *Book of Knowledge* effect. That *Ribald Reader* series aforementioned had not escaped my eye, with its mildly titillating cover drawings of harem girls, bosomy milkmaids in fetching décolletages, et cetera. Their presence on my unabashed father's lap — the books, I mean — gave me the green light, for Dad was a conservative and eminently respectable fellow, though no prude. Anyhow, I had Faulkner's Popeye and Temple Drake and corncob phallus under my belt by then, so to speak. Therefore I reveled in the *Ribald Readers* — pretty tame stuff, actually, on the level of their soft-porn content, as these items were for sale in a Norman-Rockwellish small-town soda fountain, after all, in Harry Truman's postwar America. On the level of literary quality, however, what I was in fact being introduced to was not only my future muse Scheherazade (several of whose racier tales were included, but by no means the raciest of them, as I would later discover), but also certain of her farther-Eastern forebears and contemporaries (from the *Panchatantra* and other Sanskrit sources), along with a smattering of naughty classical Romans (excerpts from Petronius, Apuleius, Juvenal), plus the rich tradition of medieval European *fabliaux* and the great horny Renaissance writers, mainly but not exclusively Italian, who recycled the oriental tale-cycles and the medieval folk-fabliaux into more or less high literature in the thirteenth to sixteenth centuries: Straparola, Basile, Boccaccio, Aretino, Poggio Bracciolini; also Geoffrey Chaucer and Marguerite d'Angoulême and François Rabelais. What a bounty — and while I was devouring it under the uncritical aspect of Horny Teenager, I was in fact scarfing down quite high-protein (and quite addictive) stuff.

It turns out, therefore, that although I matriculated at Johns Hopkins so academically unprepared that I barely survived my first two undergraduate years at that rigorous university, I was not so altogether innocent of literature as I believed myself to be. When my Gilman Library book filing led me into the haunts of the *Decameron/Pentameron/Heptameron* crowd, and the *Kitab Alf Laylah Wah Laylah*, or Book of the Thousand Nights and a Night, and the *Panchatantra* and the *Vetalapanchavimsati*, or Twenty-five Tales Told by a Vampire, and the *Kathā Sarit Sāgara*, or Ocean of Story, it was as much reunion as discovery, a provisional induction into that riotous society as much as an introduction to it.

No: not yet an induction, for I was only beginning a long and strenuous apprenticeship, discovering vocation in the most hesitant, tentative, trial-and-error way. I had all the other great Moderns to discover and learn from, including even the rest and best of Faulkner; likewise the great ancients, not every one of whom had been risqué enough for inclusion in the *Ribald Reader* series. But two important elements — significant preliminary doses of them, anyhow — were in place, thanks to those several unofficial libraries that preceded and prepared me for the vast and rich and serious official ones that were now mine to browse in. By the time I made my way out of the tide marshes and across the Chesapeake to Baltimore, I was in love already with the ancient tale-cyclers, especially the bawdy ones, and likewise with the startling, challenging, more or less high-tech High Modernists. Through years of apprenticeship, I imitated first the one and then the other: bogus Faulkner, bogus Boccaccio, bogus Joyce, bogus Rabelais. In my rearview mirror I can see that what I needed to do in order to get into gear down my own professional road (in addition to running up sufficient *non*literary mileage on my experiential odometer) was to jigger these two powerful influences into a particular sort of synergy — a synergy that I now grandly declare to be Postmodernism, though we didn't have that term yet, in that sense, at that time.

But that is another story, involving yet other unofficial libraries: a generation's literary movement, if you like, from Bennett Cerf's old Modern Library (which included both the ancients and the Modernists, though not Somadeva or Pietro Aretino or the *Gesta Romanorum* or *The Tale of Genji*, for example*) to the Postmodernist library of Donald Barthelme, Samuel Beckett, Jorge Luis Borges, Italo Calvino, Robert Coover, John Hawkes, Gabriel García Márquez, Elsa Morante, Vladimir Nabokov, Grace Paley, Thomas Pynchon, Salman Rushdie — a splendid library indeed, in which one can be proud to see one's own efforts occasionally included.

---

*Genji — as noted in the Friday-piece "It's a Long Story" — was later added to the series as a Modern Library Giant.

Four Forewords

. . . *to five works of fiction: my first five, which, in the latter 1980s,
their original publisher saw fit to reissue in a uniform trade paperback edition.* The prospect pleased me: More of my books than not
have led short first lives in hardcover and then resurfaced to commence their more extended second lives in mass-market or trade
reprint editions. The condition of reissue, in this instance, was an
authorial foreword to each volume in the series. As I am, for better
or worse, the sort of wayfarer who keeps a mindful eye on his backtrail not only through a story in progress but from book to book as
well — "deciding where to go by determining where I am by reviewing where I've been," says somebody somewhere in those books — I addressed that work of retrospection with some curiosity, along with a
skipperly interest in dead-reckoning my position. To paraphrase
E. M. Forster, how could I tell what I think about what I've said until I saw what I said about it?*

*In the process of so saying, seeing, and re-seeing (I see now), I
worked out the House Myth, so to speak, of those novels' genesis and
my own: an account whose several themes have been here and there
re-sounded elsewhere in this collection. Narcissism? I call it narrative navigation.*

*NY: Anchor Press/Doubleday, 1988. In point of fact, the first was published
originally by Appleton-Century-Crofts and republished by Doubleday in a revised hardcover edition in 1967.

The Floating Opera and
The End of the Road*

⌒— MY BOOKS TEND to come in pairs, as did their author; I am half of a set of opposite-sex twins.

Our parents didn't plan it that way. Nor did the progenitor of
my first two published novels, *The Floating Opera* (1956) and *The
End of the Road* (1958). Insofar as I had any literary plan at all in
the early 1950s, it was simply to write a publishable novel if I
could and perhaps in the process learn who I was, at least in the
medium of fiction.

As is the case with most apprentices in the arts, I had been attempting unsuccessfully for years, by trial and error, to find out
what if anything my muse, like King Kong or Dr. Frankenstein's
monster, was trying to say to me. Such basic messages, so apparently obvious after the fact, can be far from clear to the fledgling
writer. What is his essential subject matter? What will be his
"characteristic" handle on it? Having discovered or decided (as I
had by age nineteen or twenty) that your vocation is for writing instead of, say, music, and further that it is for fiction rather than poetry or drama or journalism, you may face still a number of questions the answers to which are by no means self-evident: Are you
essentially a novelist or a short-story writer? Is your muse the lady
with the grin or the one with the grimace? Are you a realist or a
fantast? Ought you to make your art for its own sake or engage it
in the service of the revolution or some other cause? Are you
more interested in the thing said than in its saying (the Windex
approach to language) or vice versa (the Stained Glass approach)?

*Issued as a single volume, not inappropriately, in the Anchor Press edition.
Footnotes added for this reprise.

Is less really more? Shall you sing white whales or scarlet letters or green extraterrestrials or the black urban underclass or WASPs in the pink or none of the above, and shall you do so out of your private experience or avoid autobiographical fiction as one avoids flashers and confessional drunks?

Good lyric poets frequently hit their stride early. Fiction writers, however — novelists in particular — often don't find their answers to these questions until age thirty or thereabouts; frequently later.

In my case, it happened at age twenty-four. I was living and teaching in central Pennsylvania then, inadequately supporting a wife and three small children on an entry-level academic salary and not quite facing the fact that after five years of industrious literary apprenticeship, things weren't panning out, musewise.* I had published a couple of stories in ephemeral literary magazines, but my first two book-length efforts — an ersatz-Faulkner novel and a projected Boccaccian cycle of one hundred Chesapeake tide-marsh tales — had justly failed to find a publisher. Their author was neither a Faulkner nor a Boccaccio. Once before, after high school, I had discovered (at the Juilliard School of Music) that I had not a certain talent that I'd hoped I had. But I had been single then, a callow kid with the smorgasbord of college waiting for him down the road; changing career plans was no big deal. The situation this time was more consequential, and the pressure was on: The family could not make ends meet, and with neither substantial publication nor the Ph.D. I had no academic future. Moreover, while I'd previously thought I wanted to be a musician, I *knew* I wanted to be a writer. Indeed, in some gut way and despite ample evidence to the contrary, I knew I "was" one — that was perhaps the only thing I knew about myself for sure — as clearly as I knew that nothing I had written thus far was "for real." *Vocation* implies both a summons and an able response; I had the call, but not yet the calling.

---

*More on this, if anyone craves more, in *Once Upon a Time: A Floating Opera*, as well as in sundry of the foregoing Friday-pieces. To plot a fix, your careful navigator takes multiple bearings.

My problem, I believe in retrospect, was how to integrate on home grounds — the tidewater Maryland area where I had grown up, and where my imagination was still rooted like marsh grass — the two large sources of literary inspiration exemplified in those abortive early projects: the great Modernists like Joyce and Faulkner on whom I had cut my apprentice teeth, and the old taletellers like "Scheherazade" and Boccaccio whom I had devoured extracurricularly. But the clock was running. It appeared that I would be obliged to resign my Penn State instructorship, borrow money from god knows where, and return to Johns Hopkins to complete if I could the doctorate in literary aesthetics that I had abandoned earlier to try my luck with the muse. Before I made that disagreeable decision, however, I had a season (the spring of 1955) to attempt one "final" literary project.

High and dry in the Pennsylvania uplands, I used to pore nostalgically over albums of Marylandia by the Baltimore photographer A. Aubrey Bodine. In one of them I found shots of Captain James Adams's Original Floating Theater, a tug-towed showboat that I remembered having seen as a boy at the municipal wharf in my hometown (Edna Ferber spent a season aboard while writing her novel *Showboat*, the basis of Jerome Kern's musical; but Captain Adams's homely, sturdy Chesapeake vessel was a far cry from Mississippi Riverboat Gothic). Its portentous name suggested allegory; I made notes toward a fiction in the form of . . . well, a philosophical blackface minstrel show. I had picked up from the postwar *Zeitgeist* some sense of the French Existentialist writers and had absorbed from my own experience a few routine disenchantments. I imagined myself something of a nihilist — but by temperament a smiling nihilist, not the grim-faced kind. I would write some sort of nihilist minstrel show.

It turned into a novel, *The Floating Opera*, because I found the minstrel-show conceit too artificial to sustain and because, while dreaming up a tidewater story of which the showboat-show might serve as climax, I discovered by happy accident the turn-of-the-century Brazilian novelist Joaquim Machado de Assis (*Epitaph of a Small Winner, Philosopher or Dog, Dom Casmurro,* etc.). Machado — himself much under the influence of Laurence Sterne's *Tristram Shandy* — taught me something I had not quite learned from Joyce's *Ulysses* and would not likely have learned from Sterne directly, had I happened to have read him: how to combine formal sportiveness with genuine sentiment as well as a fair degree of realism. Sterne is pre-Romantic; Joyce is late- or post-Romantic; Machado is playful, wistful, pessimistic, intellectually exuberant, both romantic and Romantic. He was also, like myself, a provincial, although his novels are set in the sophisticated ambiance of late-nineteenth-century Rio de Janeiro, as was his adult career. Machado's tone and manner, as much as his narrative technics, showed me how I might get my disparate gods together on a tidewater showboat.

Whatever its shortcomings, the novel came together more surely and quickly than anything I had written before. I drafted it in the spring of '55, spent the summer revising it on location in Maryland, turned twenty-five, and in the fall drafted even more swiftly a companion piece, *The End of the Road*. The problem of economic survival did not go away: It took nearly a year for the *Opera* to find its first publisher, who brought it out only on condition that it conclude on a less "nihilist" note (see my preface to the 1967 Doubleday revised edition, which restores the original, apocalyptically shrug-shouldered ending*). But I knew I was finally and truly on track. The family skimped and did without for another semester while I finished and revised *The End of the Road*, began *The Sot-Weed Factor*, and put off the abandonment of my writerly ambitions. Early in 1956, just when that abandonment could be postponed no longer — I had actually reapplied and been readmitted to that doctoral program in Baltimore — my agent telephoned to say he had a contract at last for *The Floating Opera*. Not so much elated as unspeakably relieved, I canceled the move and went back to my writing desk for keeps.

No doubt some of the discouragement of those raw years, masquerading as general philosophic principle, comes through in *The Floating Opera* and even more in *The End of the Road* (whose

---

*The operative passage from that preface: "One [publisher] finally agreed to launch the *Opera*, but on condition that the builder make certain major changes in its construction, notably about the stern. I did, the novel was published, critics criticized the ending in particular, and I learned a boatwright little lesson."

bleak title was another acquiescence to New York: My working title had been *What to Do Until the Doctor Comes*; my then editor, the late Edward Aswell of Doubleday, feared the novel would be mistaken for a treatise on first aid). The *Opera* I regarded as a nihilist comedy, *Road* as a nihilist catastrophe: the same melody reorchestrated in a grimmer key and sung by a leaner voice. Their situations have in common that they are narrated by the Other Man in a more or less acknowledged adulterous triangle complicated by an ambiguous pregnancy. The personnel of the two triangles — their ages, social positions, attitudes, and moral voltages — are dissimilar, but the narrators share a radical alienation that fascinated me at the time. "A man may smile and smile and be a villain," Shakespeare reminds us. Todd Andrews, of the *Opera*, embodies my conviction that one may smile and smile and not only take his own life but blow up the whole show — or, failing in the attempt, shrug his shoulders and come to a conclusion beyond Albert Camus' (in, e.g., *The Rebel* and "The Myth of Sisyphus"): namely, that one may go on living because there is no more justification for suicide than for going on living. Jacob Horner, of *The End of the Road*, embodies my conviction that one may reach such a degree of self-estrangement as to feel no coherent antecedent for the first-person singular pronoun. Horner cobbles up a "self" to deal with the crisis of the plot — arranging an illegal abortion for his pregnant lover lest she commit calm suicide — but his efforts lead to a mortal fiasco, and Horner abdicates personality altogether. If the reader regards either of these egregious conditions (as embodied by the narrators) as merely psychopathological, then the novels will make no moral-dramatic sense.

By the time *The Floating Opera* was launched, in 1956, its builder had turned away from (what were by my standards) realism and minimalism to the high-energy extravagancies of *The Sot-Weed Factor* and *its* sort-of-twin, *Giles Goat-Boy*. Although the *Opera* had the good fortune, especially for a first novel, to be nominated for that year's National Book Award in fiction, its hardcover run was brief; it has lived its gratifyingly long half-life mainly in paperback editions. Ditto *The End of the Road*, although it was made into what ought to have been an excellent movie: Stacy Keach as

Jacob Horner, James Earl Jones as the Doctor, Harris Yulin as Joe Morgan, and Dorothy Tristan as Rennie Morgan. Those first-rate ingredients failed to make a first-rate cake; the film was X-rated by the Production Code Administration for scenes nowhere to be found in the novel (man rapes chicken, etc.) and Z-rated by the muses. "The principal difference between the novel and the film," remarked the critic John Simon, "is that the novel concludes with a harrowing abortion, whereas the film is an abortion from start to finish." Fairly said, alas.

So: (1) an unsuccessful mass-murder/suicide attempt by a middle-aged small-town bachelor lawyer with prostate trouble and a hair-trigger heart condition; and (2) an unsuccessful abortion, fatal to the mother, made necessary by a failed condom in an era of unreformed abortion laws and arranged by the adulterous antihero, a walking ontological vacuum: These are the plot-armatures of my first pair of opposite-twin novels. That *The Floating Opera* and *The End of the Road* are again in reprint thirty years later* suggests to their author that there may be more to them than their "nihilist" materials; that the how of their telling is at least as important as the stories told.

Truth to tell, I knew it all along.

— *Langford Creek, Maryland, 1987*

---

*And now (1994) nearly forty years later, muse be praised. "That one's books (at least not all of them) not die before their author — that is success enough," I have said somewhere, and in fact believe.

The Sot-Weed Factor

IT SOUNDS LIKE an element in a situation, most likely deleterious, shady, or potentially threatening: the China Syndrome, the French Connection, the Sot-Weed Factor. And indeed, "sot-weed" (Colonial American slang for tobacco, as later Americans would refer to marijuana as "pot" or "grass") was thus called for the narcotic and addictive properties that made it so enormously popular in the Old World when it was introduced from the New; that made tobacco not only the chief money-crop of the middle-Atlantic colonies but, for a time, money itself: the very medium of exchange. It was a weed with which both Europe and white America — and the economy and agriculture of Colonial Maryland and Virginia — quickly became besotted. Robert Burton writes of it in his *Anatomy of Melancholy* (1621):

> Tobacco, divine, rare, superexcellent tobacco, which goes far beyond all . . . panaceas, potable gold, and philosopher's stones, a sovereign remedy to all diseases. A good vomit, I confess, a virtuous herb, if it be well qualified, opportunely taken, and medicinally used; but as it is commonly abused by most men, which take it as tinkers do ale, 'tis a plague, a mischief, a violent purger of goods, lands, health; hellish, devilish, and damned tobacco, the ruin and overthrow of body and soul.

And three hundred years later, an American undergraduate named Graham Lee Hemminger writes in the Pennsylvania State University *Froth* of 1915:

> *Tobacco is a dirty weed, I like it.*
> *It satisfies no normal need. I like it.*

It makes you thin, it makes you lean,
It takes the hair right off your bean.
It's the worst darn stuff I've ever seen.
I like it.

But in the English of the American Colonial period, a "factor" was a trading agent (still the term's first definition in my desk dictionary, though I've never heard it used that way). Thus the place called Moose Factory, Ontario, for example, is not an establishment for the manufacture or processing of moose, but the site of a former fur-trading post up there in moose country; and the sotweed factor in seventeenth- and eighteenth-century Maryland was the man who exchanged consignments of English manufactured goods for hogsheads of tobacco from the tidewater plantations.

One such fellow is the luckless hero of what is generally held to be the very first American satire: a fierce and funny narrative poem whose title page (in the most available edition) reads *The Sot-Weed Factor: Or, A Voyage to MARYLAND. A SATYR. In which is describ'd, The Laws, Government, Courts and Constitutions of the Country; and also the Buildings, Feasts, Frolicks, Entertainments and Drunken Humours of the Inhabitants of that Part of* America. *In Burlesque Verse. By* Eben. Cook, *Gent.* LONDON: *Printed and Sold by* B. Bragg, *at the* Raven *in* Pater-Noster Row. *1708. (Price* 6d.*).* Its narrator is a young man down on his luck:

> *Condemn'd by Fate, to wayward Curse,*
> *Of Friends unkind, and empty Purse, . . . [I]*
> *Was forc'd my native Soil to fly,*
> *And the old World must bid Good-b'ye.*

He arrives in the fabled New World to try his hand at tobacco factoring; but instead of the cultivated Eden commonly depicted in Colonial American press-agentry — a land of noble savages, honest tradesmen, civilized planters and their chaste womenfolk on elegant plantations — he finds tidewater Maryland to be a barbarous, pestilential place. The Indians stink of bear grease; the colonials are drunken, brawling, illiterate sharpsters whose hospitality is not to be trusted; their women are sluttish, their courts corrupt. Among other misadventures, the novice sot-weed factor is robbed of his clothes, treed by dogs, bitten by mosquitoes, nearly carried off by the "seasoning" fever so often fatal to new arrivals, and ultimately cheated out of his goods. A ruined man, he takes ship homeward from ". . . that Shore where no good Sense is found,/But Conversation's lost, and Manners drown'd." The poem closes with his malediction:

> *May Wrath Divine . . . lay these Regions wast*
> *Where no Man's faithful, nor a woman chast!*

About the author of this entertainment, scholars of early American literature have pieced together a fair amount of information over the past two decades: J. A. Leo LeMay's *Men of Letters in Colonial Maryland*, for example (1972), and Edward H. Cohen's 1974 study *Ebenezer Cooke: The Sot-Weed Canon*. In 1956, however, when I set about to write a novel based on his satirical poem, not much more was known about "Eben. Cook" than that he usually spelled his surname with an *e* (despite the title page quoted above).

That name appears on certain Maryland real-estate transactions and other legal documents and petitions in the last decades of the seventeenth century and the early decades of the eighteenth, as well as on "The Sot-Weed Factor" and a handful of other poems: four occasional elegies (at the foot of which he tantalizingly appends to his name the title "Laureate of Maryland"); a not-so-funny satire on Bacon's Rebellion in Virginia; a late and rather heavy sequel to "Sot-Weed" called "Sot-Weed Redivivus" (1730), wherein the "old *Poet*" laments the destruction of Maryland's forests and depletion of its arable land by ill-regulated tobacco farming; and a revised and less biting edition of "The Sot-Weed Factor" itself. He seems to have been born in England and to have practiced law in Maryland, where his father, Andrew Cooke, owned property; he seems to have had a sister, Anna, to whom that property was jointly bequeathed (they later sold it). After the 1731 revision of "Sot-Weed," his name is found no more in the archives of the period. There is no record of his death or burial.

Cooke Point — a long, narrow, much-eroded strip of woods and farmland where the broad Choptank River meets the even broader Chesapeake Bay — was so named by Andrew Cooke, who in the 1660s established there a thousand-acre tidewater estate and manor house. The point lies a dozen or so miles downriver from the town of Cambridge, on Maryland's Eastern Shore, where I was born and raised; I knew the name (minus its terminal *e*, dropped by later mapmakers) and the geography long before I knew anything of its history. Toward the end of my literary apprentice days, I conceived the ambitious, Boccaccio-like project of writing one hundred tales about my marshy home county at all periods of its recorded history; in the course of my researches, I came across Ebenezer Cooke's "Sot-Weed Factor" poem and drafted a few tales based on the premise that its misfortunate narrator was the poet himself, whom I imagined arriving in the colony with the innocence, though perhaps not the programmatic optimism, of Voltaire's Candide.

The larger tale-project proved beyond my capacity; I abandoned it halfway through but saved the manuscript and attendant historical homework for possible future use. Almost immediately thereafter, in 1954, I found a more congenial narrative voice, and, with an ease and speed that astonish me now, I wrote what were to be my first two published novels: *The Floating Opera* and *The End of the Road*. Their materials are local but not historical; they are short and relatively realistic novels, in the mode of what would soon after come to be called "black humor." Indeed, I cheerfully thought of them at the time as not only pessimistic but nihilistic, and with the energetic optimism of an ambitious twenty-five-year-old, once they were done I saw them as the first two-thirds of an imaginable nihilist trilogy, to consist, in order, of a nihilist comedy; a nihilist . . . well, hardly tragedy, let's say catastrophe; and a nihilist . . . what?

Extravaganza, perhaps. I went back to those shelved Ebenezer Cooke tales, and — re-viewing their anti-hero from the "nihilist" perspective of *The Floating Opera* and *The End of the Road* — I projected an extravagant novel indeed: one that would reorchestrate a number of twentieth-century melodies in eighteenth-century style. The melodies were familiar American ones, not all of them modern: the tragic view of innocence, the comic view of experience, the New World (not new to its natives) versus the Old (still new to me, back then), the problematics of personal and national identity. The style would echo that of the big eighteenth-century comic novelists, especially Henry Fielding: a style and attack very different from those of my first two books. The objective was to conclude my "trilogy" with something like a narrative explosion, if I could manage one: a story at least as complicated, and if possible as energetically entertaining, as Fielding's *Tom Jones*; a novel fat enough so that its publishers could print its title comfortably *across* the book's spine rather than down it. Those earlier novels had taken me half a year each to write; I reckoned this one might take as long as two years.

It took four, of immersion in *The Archives of Maryland* and other documents and studies of American Colonial history as well as in the great inventors of the English novel and, of course, in the sentences, paragraphs, and pages of the work in progress — my conception of which rather changed as I drove the poor sot-weed factor through the obstacle course of my plot. For one thing, I came to understand that *innocence*, not nihilism, was my real theme, and had been all along, although I'd been too innocent myself to realize that fact. More particularly, I came better to appreciate what I have called the "tragic view" of innocence: that it is, or can become, dangerous, even culpable; that where it is prolonged or artificially sustained, it becomes arrested development, potentially disastrous to the innocent himself and to bystanders innocent or otherwise; that what is to be valued, in nations as well as individuals, is not innocence but wise experience.

Moreover, out of all that homework and sentence making there emerged another, unintended theme. My Ebenezer Cooke is not merely a naive (and programmatically virginal) tobacco factor misadventuring in the New World; he is also — whatever his foolishnesses, misdirections, and innocent pretensions — a *writer*, sure in his calling though not in his gift. While regaining his lost estate by sacrificing his ever-more-technical innocence, he is also learning the hard way some facts of literary life, finding a real voice under all his rhetorical posturing and attitudinizing, discovering his true subject matter and most congenial form — in short, becoming the writer that he had innocently presumed himself to be.

So was I.

Perhaps for that reason, *The Sot-Weed Factor*, whatever its imperfections, remains the novel that gives me the most satisfaction to remember having conceived, planned, and written. It was first published by Doubleday in 1960, a few months after my thirtieth birthday, in an edition that has since become something of a collector's item, certainly in part because the jacket was drawn by the artist Edward Gorey. Despite the formidable problems of translating a mid-twentieth-century novel that echoes late-seventeenth-century English (an English that in the documents of Colonial America frequently sounds Elizabethan), it has been rendered with apparent success into German, Italian, Polish, and Japanese.* In 1967 Doubleday reissued it in a slightly slimmed-down edition, which I prefer: about sixty pages shorter than the original. No plot-protein was removed, only some excess verbal calories. It is this *Sot-Weed* (no warning from the Surgeon General necessary) that I'm pleased to see here in a new edition. . . .

— *Langford Creek, Maryland, 1987*

---

*And, more recently, Spanish. The German and Polish titles retain the sense of a tobacco *trader*; the Italian and Spanish mistranslate him into a planter (*Il coltivatore del Maryland*; *El plantador de tabaco*). The Japanese I cannot vouch for.

Giles Goat-Boy

AS WE LOOK back at the period now, the American 1960s may be thought of as having begun on November 22, 1963, with the assassination of President John F. Kennedy, and as having ended on Yom Kippur 1973, with Egypt's attack on Israel and the consequent Arab oil embargo.* By this definition, *Giles Goat-Boy* — written between 1960 and 1965, and first published in 1966 — has one foot in the Fifties and one in the Sixties, as its hero has one foot in the library of "the University" and one (at least) in the campus goat-barns.

At the end of "the Fifties," the Cold War was chilly indeed: Both the U.S. and the U.S.S.R. by then had operational hydrogen bombs, intercontinental ballistic missiles, and nuclear submarines. The successful Sputnik launch of 1957 had triggered both the "space race" and an epidemic of academic gigantism in the United States: a massive effort to "catch up," fueled by an inpouring of federal money that would fertilize the groves of Academe right through the Sixties. And the Cuban missile crisis of 1962 — another reasonable benchmark for the change of decades — had brought home to many, as the atmospheric testing of thermonuclear weapons had not, the specter of apocalypse. On other fronts, the nation was already considerably involved in Vietnam, the black civil rights movement was in full swing, commercial jet airline service had recently been established, and tape recorders and stereo music systems had been added to television for our domestic entertainment. The personal computer was still well into the

---

*These negotiable decade-calendrics are adverted to in the Friday-piece "Postmodernism Revisited" and are of the architectural essence of *Once Upon a Time: A Floating Opera.*

future, but large mainframe computers were "in place," especially on the booming university campuses, and electronic data processing had unequivocally impinged upon the public consciousness. Hippies had not quite invented themselves yet, but Beatniks were well-known, with their countercultural aura of Zen Buddhism and narcotics. In American fiction, the phenomenon called Black Humor was not only established but had pretty much run its course.

Numerous of these elements echo through *Giles Goat-Boy*, transmogrified into the simple — I would even say the deliberately, programmatically "sophomoric" — terms of the allegory, which is not an allegory at all in the Dante or Kafka sense, but merely a manner of speaking. There too reverberate some of the author's literary-professional preoccupations at the time — less sophomoric, I hope — as well as a few personal-historical circumstances.

To speak first of the former: By 1960 I had completed what I regarded as a loose trilogy of novels — *The Floating Opera*, *The End of the Road*, and *The Sot-Weed Factor* — and I felt, particularly in the course of writing that extravagant third item, that I had put something behind me and moved into new narrative country. Just what that movement was, I couldn't quite have said; today it might be described as the passage made by a number of American writers from the Black Humor of the Fifties to the Fabulism of the Sixties.* For four years, writing *Sot-Weed*, I had been more or less immersed in the sometimes fantastical documents of U.S. colonial history: in the origins of "America," including the origins of our literature. This immersion, together with the suggestion by some literary critics that that novel was a reorchestration of the ancient myth of the Wandering Hero, led me to reexamine that myth closely: the origins not of a particular culture but of culture itself; not of a particular literature, but of the very notion of narrative adventure, especially adventure of a transcendental, life-changing and culture-changing sort.

*But it has also been described as the movement from late Modernism into Postmodernism. Professor Heide Ziegler, for example, of the University of Stuttgart, who regards Gertrude Stein as "the mother of Postmodernism," has seen fit to call *The Sot-Weed Factor* "the first American Postmodernist novel."

Deep stuff. I was living at the time in a rural village in central Pennsylvania and teaching at a huge state university that got huger every semester. My own alma mater had been small, intense, and fairly elite, at least academically; I was charmed and impressed by the great scale, the Jacksonian democracy, and the multifarious-ness of American land-grant universities, not a bad microcosm of the land itself. In an English department of nearly one hundred members, I taught my classes not far from an experimental nuclear reactor, a water tunnel for testing the hull forms of missile sub-marines, laboratories for ice-cream research and mushroom devel-opment, a lavishly produced football program with halftime shows on the Hollywood scale, a barn-size computer with elabo-rate cooling systems (if I remember correctly, the machine was never shut down, even when "off-line") — and the literal and splendid barns of the animal husbandry departments, surrounded by vast experimental farms and barnyards where, among other livestock, radioactive turkeys prowled, as did I and my then-small children.

No goats. I would supply that defect from my imagination.

I had crossed a border much remarked by poets, the age of thirty, and was approaching another much remarked in heroic myth, the age not so much of midlife crisis as of maturational crux: thirty-four, -five, or -six, depending on whether you have in mind Jesus's crucifixion, say, or Dante's impasse in the Dark Wood (halfway through the biblical threescore and ten), or Carl Jung's actuarial individuation point. In *Giles* I make that age $33\frac{1}{3}$: the long-playing moment* when the mythic hero — who is all of us, writ large — is summoned to his mysterious destiny. He must leave his (usually adoptive) home and parents, the familiar daylight world of conscious reality and sundry ego-tokens; he must pass through the twilit territory of dreamish forms and porous cate-gories; aided by guides, helpers, intuitions, tricks, and secrets, he must deal with initiatory riddles and ordeals, with irreal (but not unreal) monstrosities of the subconscious; he must attain at last

---

*Readers in the age of compact disks may need reminding that $33\frac{1}{3}$ rpm was the rotational speed of "long-playing" disk recordings in the decades here evoked. CD players, by contrast, operate at an initial speed of about 600 rpm and decel-erate as the disk proceeds.

the Princess, the Elixir: unmediated, noumenal knowledge in that dark, unconscious, nameless center, the bottom of things.

This has ever been, literally or figuratively, a spiritual/psychological adventure as well as a physical one. Historically, each has represented the other: The mystic's progress toward unitive transcendence is reported in images of literal journeying and hazarding, the wandering hero's quest in images of descent or ascent to, and communion with, the gods. Moreover (as the great pragmatist William James makes poignantly clear in his chapter on mysticism in *The Varieties of Religious Experience*), it is an adventure with a quasi-tragic sequel. Having attained Davy Jones's locker, or the hand of the ogre's beautiful daughter, or the vision of the Rose or of Rome, the hero must now return to the everyday working world and do real work in it. Fortified by an illumination essentially ineffable, he must translate that illumination into action — into laws and cities, religions, poems, novels — knowing or discovering that such translation will inevitably compromise, betray the vision. (In some wise languages, the verbs for "translate" and "betray" are the same; *Giles Goat-Boy* has been betrayed into several tongues.) Here is where mysticism, traditionally associated with "the wisdom of the East," crosses paths with the classically Occidental tragic view; where the wandering hero Oedipus fatefully reencounters somebody older than himself.

But Oedipus's crossroads, we recall, was a place where *three* roads meet, not two; and indeed, this talk of encounters between Tragicism and Mysticism* has fetched us a long way from my line of work, the comic novel. Beside the tragic view and the mystic view of human experience has always run another, in Western Civ at least: the comic view. "Gaiety transfiguring all that dread," as Yeats writes of Hamlet and Lear in "Lapis Lazuli." And not only in the Western tradition: Yeats's great poem ends with the image of two Chinese sages on a mountain top:

> *On all the tragic scene they stare.*
> *One asks for mournful melodies.*

*See "Mystery and Tragedy: The Twin Motions of Ritual Heroism," in *The Friday Book*.

Accomplished fingers begin to play.
Their eyes mid many wrinkles, their eyes,
Their ancient, glittering eyes, are gay.

I had another reason, too — other than the fact that my muse is the one with a smile on her face — for approaching the mystic and the tragic by way of the comic: It has to do with what the Italian semiotician/novelist Umberto Eco calls "ironic double coding" (a hallmark of the postmodern condition, in Eco's opinion). In an age of hyperself-consciousness and lost innocence, straightforward mysticism (or tragicism or mythicism) is as likely to off-put the knowledgeable reader of fiction as — to borrow Eco's example — the naive declaration "I love you madly" is likely to off-put a sophisticated lover. The knowledgeable and sophisticated, however, may still need to make and receive declarations of love, as people still need the tragic and the mystic perspectives — without, as Eco puts it, succumbing to false innocence or to disregard for "the already-said." Comedy — especially comic irony, a certain sort of satire, and what might be called impassioned, compassionate parody — can sometimes come to the rescue. "As they say in hack romantic novels," Eco's lover might say in effect to his beloved: "I love you madly."* Late in the historical day, a declaration of love has still been made and, perhaps, received.

Mystery, tragedy, comedy: The place where those three roads met for me was *Giles Goat-Boy*: the adventures of a young man sired by a giant computer upon a hapless but compliant librarian and raised in the experimental goat-barns of a universal university, divided ideologically into East and West Campuses. Assigned a riddling series of tasks upon his matriculation, he must come to terms with both his goathood and his humanhood (not to mention his machinehood) and, in the very bowels of the University, transcend not only the categories of East and West but all the other categories as well;† transcend language itself — and then return to

---

*The full quotation from Eco may be found in the Friday-piece "Postmodernism Revisited."
†The passage wherein Giles achieves this transcension, I am flattered to report, was declared by a visiting Korean scholar at Johns Hopkins to be the best account he knew of in English of the Mahayana Buddhist view of mystical enlightenment.

the daylight campus, drive out the false Grand Tutor (whom he understands to be an aspect of himself), and do his best to eff the ineffable.

I wrote the novel between my thirtieth and thirty-fifth birthdays. Begun in State College, Pennsylvania, continued in goat-rich southern Spain, and completed in Buffalo, New York, it represents, needless to say, a passage for its author as well as for its caprine hero. It was my own (still ongoing) attempt to do what Giles the goat-boy and every one of us must: understand on the deepest level what's what with ourselves and our life in the world, and endeavor — tragically, comically, however — to *do* something with that understanding.

— Langford Creek, Maryland, 1987

Lost in the Funhouse

SHORT FICTION IS not my long suit.* Writers tend by temperament to be either sprinters or marathoners, and I learned early that the long haul is my stride. The form of the modern short story — as defined and developed by Poe, Maupassant, and Chekhov and handed on to the twentieth century — I found in my apprentice years to be parsimonious, constraining, constipative. Much as I admired its great practitioners, I preferred more narrative elbow room.

The pre-modern *tale* is another matter: especially the tale-cycle, as told by the likes of Scheherazade and Boccaccio. I virtually began my narrative career with one of those, but set it aside for the even more hospitable space of the novel and the more hospitable project-rhythms of the novelist. Your congenital short-story writer faces the blank-faced muse once every few weeks (in the case of early Chekhov, every few days). Your congenital novelist prefers to dream up a world once every few years; to plant and people it and dwell therein for maybe a whole presidential term — or the time it takes a new college freshman to complete the baccalaureate — before reconfronting the interterrestrial void.

But after a dozen years of writing and publishing the novels reprinted in this series — *The Floating Opera, The End of the Road, The Sot-Weed Factor, Giles Goat-Boy*† — in the mid-1960s I found myself hankering to reattempt the short form, for assorted reasons:

• For one thing, Less really is More, other things equal. Even quite expansive novels, if carefully written, have their own econ-

---

*A deficiency remarked and expanded upon in the Friday-piece "It's a Short Story," which essentially recapitulates the argument of this foreword.
†The series currently includes as well *The Last Voyage of Somebody the Sailor*.

omy and rigor; but *Sot-Weed* and *Giles* are long novels indeed, and writing them increased my respect for the mode that comes least naturally to me. The clown comes to want to play Hamlet, and vice versa; the long-distance runner itches to sprint. Just as there are musical ideas that won't do for a symphony but are just right for a song, there are narrative ideas suitable only for a short story: quick takes, epiphanies that even a novella would attenuate, not to mention a novel. Over the years, I had accumulated a few such narrative ideas in my notebooks.

• Moreover, I teach stories as well as telling them, and like most writing coaches I find the short story most useful for seminar purposes. You can hold a short story in your hand, like a lyric poem; see it whole; examine the function of individual sentences, even individual words, as you can't readily do with *Bleak House* or *War and Peace*. (This pedagogical convenience, together with the proliferation of creative-writing programs in the USA, must be largely responsible for the happy resurgence of the American short story — at a time when, paradoxically, the popular audience has never been smaller.) But those model stories that I was teaching came from classroom anthologies in which (novels being hard to excerpt coherently, and excerpts being formally less useful than complete works) my own fiction was seldom included. I consoled myself, maybe flattered myself, with the consideration that such eminent non-short-story-writing contemporaries as Ralph Ellison and William Styron were likewise seldom included — but I wanted to be in those anthologies. Not all of a writer's motives are pure.

• It was about this time that I came across the writings of the great Argentine Jorge Luis Borges, whose temper was so wedded to the short forms that, like Chekhov, he never wrote a novel, and whose unorthodox brilliance transformed the short story for me. Writers learn from their experience of other writers as well as from their experience of life in the world; it was the happy marriage of form and content in Borges's *ficciones* — the way he regularly turned his narrative means into part of his message* — that suggested how I might try something similar, in my way and with my materials.

*More on this in the Friday-piece "Borges and I: a mini-memoir."

The result was *Lost in the Funhouse* (I was in fact, at age thirteen or so, once briefly mislaid in a boardwalk funhouse, in Asbury Park, New Jersey; end of autobiographical reference). Incorrigibly the novelist, I decided at the outset to write not simply some short stories but a *book* of short stories: a sequence or series rather than a mere assortment. Although the several stories would more or less stand alone (and therefore be anthologizable), the series would be strung together on a few echoed and developed themes and would circle back upon itself: not to close a simple circuit like that of Joyce's *Finnegans Wake*, emblematic of Viconian eternal return, but to make a circuit with a twist to it, like a Möbius strip, emblematic of — well, read the book.

The series was written and assembled between 1966 and 1968. The High Sixties, like the Roaring Twenties, was a time of more than usual ferment in American social, political, and artistic life. Our unpopular war in Vietnam, political assassinations, race riots, the hippie counterculture, pop art, mass poetry readings, street theater, vigorous avant-gardism in all the arts, together with dire predictions not only of the death of the novel but of the moribundity of the print medium in the electronic global village — those flavored the air we breathed then, along with occasional tear gas and other contaminants. One may sniff traces of that air in the *Funhouse* ("Fictions for Print, Tape, Live Voice"). I myself found it more invigorating than disturbing. May the reader find these stories likewise.

— Langford Creek, Maryland, 1987

$4\frac{1}{2}$ Lectures
The Stuttgart Seminars on Postmodernism, Chaos Theory, and the Romantic Arabesque

Through the peak of the Atlantic hurricane season — early August to mid-October — the Barths are reluctant to venture far from home. Our Langford Creek establishment sits vulnerably in the Chesapeake Bay floodplain, just a few feet above mean high water, exposed to a very long fetch (and lovely view) off the Chester River — no land in sight at all in one southerly direction — and we maintain a veritable flotilla of small craft at our dock: a cruising sailboat and its tender for extended sailing, an old outboard runabout for water-skiing and guest-entertaining, a Sunfish sailboard for daysails, a venerable canoe for calm-weather exercise. As of this writing, the Chesapeake has not suffered a direct hit since Hurricanes Connie and Diane, four days apart in August 1955. Toward summer's end, however, we wait like tenpins at the end of Mother Nature's bowling alley, knowing she's going to roll half a dozen or more big ones over from Africa and up from the Caribbean, and hoping they'll all be gutter balls. We shake our heads in awe and anxious sympathy as an Andrew devastates south Florida or a Hugo lays the Carolinas waste. While pursuing our businesses and pleasures (categories fortunately much overlapping in our house), we track each tropical depression's path and stand by to take what protective measures we can should our stand-by escalate to an official Watch, that Watch to a Warning. Come corn-harvest time, when the geese arrive from Canada and the leaves begin to turn, we uncross our fingers for another ten months.

For this reason, among others, I was reluctant to join my American writer-friends Raymond Federman and William H. Gass, my

*cordial acquaintances the critic Ihab Hassan and the British novel-
ist Malcolm Bradbury, and my German critic-friend Heide Ziegler
in the inaugural Stuttgart Seminar in Intercultural Studies,
scheduled for the middle two weeks of August 1991, under Professor
Ziegler's energetic direction and the provocative title "The End of
Postmodernism: New Directions." It looked to be a fortnight of
fairly intensive seminaring, with (given the meteorological circumstances) no time for Europe-touring fore and aft. Except for the odd
Friday-piece, aesthetic theorizing is not my cup of tea, whereas to
those others — professional intellectuals all — it comes as naturally
as breathing air. Moreover, a new fiction project was under way in
my shop, and I was loath to set it aside even for the space of that seminar, not to mention the weeks required to work up my presentations.
Finally, I had no proper subject: On the matter of literary Postmodernism, I had long since said my amateur say;* I had no particular
interest in re-revisiting that subject.*

*On the other hand, I warmly disagreed that that problematical
aesthetic had shot its bolt (Ziegler's title was designed to invite such
disagreement); as one of the few "Postmodernist" writers who un-
complainingly accept that designation, I wanted like Mark Twain
to make the case that reports of my demise were being greatly exag-
gerated. And those were friends and comrades-in-arms, with whom
the prospect of a German reunion was appealing. Germany itself
was newly reunited since our last visit there, a dozen years before,
and we were curious to have a look at the updated Deutschland,
side-of-the-eye as our glimpse would have to be. The seminar fellows
were to be a couple dozen bright young assistant-professorial men
and women mainly from the newly "free" Eastern European countries, including Romania, Bulgaria, even Albania — much more
cut off from Western intellectual fashions of the previous four
decades than had been their counterparts in Hungary, Czechoslovakia, and Poland, for example. It would be interesting to make their
acquaintance.*

*Finally, having declared that I had no subject, I recognized that
on some back burner of my mind there had been gently stewing for*

*In the Friday-pieces "The Literature of Exhaustion" (1968) and "The Literature
of Replenishment" (1979), collected in *The Friday Book*; also in "Postmodernism Revisited," in the present collection.

months certain tantalizing resonations between and among contemporary chaos theory (about which I had a layman's curiosity), the Romantic concept of the arabesque (I had just published a postmodern arabesque novel, The Last Voyage of Somebody the Sailor), and the aesthetics of Postmodernism as I understand or misunderstand that term. The prospect of formally addressing those nebulous interconnections was daunting. All the same . . .

Our fingers duly crossed, we went, and found our colleagues duly collegial, our glimpse of reunited Germany duly impressive, and the Stuttgart Seminarians a lively and knowledgeable crew — the more so considering the hard regimes under which most of them had managed their university training. Chaos theory (aka chaotics, chaology, nonlinear dynamics, or simply complexity theory, although there is nothing simple about it) was fairly new to them. The Postmodernist writers under discussion in the several seminar groups were known to them principally as names and reputations; they were thirsty for actual texts (the Stuttgart photocopy machines ran day and night, surely an excusable bending of copyright regulations). On the subject of the Romantic arabesque, however, and of German Romanticism in general, a number of my "students" were, as I had hoped and expected, more knowledgeable than I. Whatever the state of health of that aesthetic phenomenon labeled Postmodernism ("made in America, studied in Europe," Malcolm Bradbury quipped), it enjoyed a vigorous workout along the banks of the Neckar that August fortnight.

I remain persuaded that among the three subjects here considered there are interconnections worth exploring — and that that exploration wants a less amateur theorist than myself.* With relief we returned to Maryland, and I to making fiction rather than theorizing thereupon — and sure enough, after the long transatlantic flight, as we drove bone-weary from Dulles International across the Chesapeake Bay Bridge toward the Eastern Shore and home, we were met by flashing emergency signs along the highway: AVOID SHORE

---

*G. R. Thompson's 1989 monograph on Edgar Poe's Narrative of Arthur Gordon Pym ("Romantic Arabesque, Contemporary Theory, and Postmodernism: The Example of Poe's Narrative"), published in ESQ: A Journal of the American Renaissance 35, nos. 3–4, is an excellent beginning, much leaned upon in these lectures.

POINTS: HURRICANE WARNING. *Instead of piling straightway into bed and leaving suitcases to be unpacked next day, we were obliged to spend much of that jet-lagged night battening hatches for Hurricane Bob, already off the Carolina capes and roaring up the coast. In the event, it only grazed tidewater Maryland — deflected from its course, I like to imagine, by some Butterfly Effect of my airing these speculations in the Schlosshotel Monrepos, outside Stuttgart.*

I re-air them here in their original lecture form and tone, much edited but hitherto unpublished (though percolated in samizdat photocopy through Romania and environs), for what they may be worth: a working professional novelist's amateur reflections upon a subject that would better be left to professional intellectuals if it were not too unimportant *— and, to some of us Monday-through-Thursday field hands, too interesting — to be left to them, like war to the generals. The whole voluminous Sturm und Drang of Postmodernist theory and counter-theory is a teapot-tempest, in my view — and, as aforedeclared, not this storyteller's cup of tea at that. Notwithstanding my Tragic View of Categories aforestated,* however, I believe it to be as human an enterprise to classify and label our experiences of life and art (and earnestly to debate our classifying labels) as it is to render those experiences into, for example, narrative fiction.*

*In "Postmodernism Revisited."

1. PM/CT/RA:
An Underview

AS A WORKING novelist, I am in the habit of giving my first attention to my fiction in progress, including the reverberations in it of what I've written before, the retrospective illumination of old themes by new variations and reorchestrations, and the possible foreshadowing of future projects. This priority may be reprehensible — morally, politically, intellectually — but it is an established habit.

My second attention, I suppose, goes to my present experience of life in the world, including the reverberations in it of my past life-experience, the retrospective illumination of that past experience from the present, and occasional prospective illumination of what's down the road. This experience of life in the world includes also what experience I've had of art in general and of literature in particular — an experience neither massive nor systematic in my case, but reasonably wide and decidedly eclectic.

A third level of attention goes to the world around me apart from my life in it, insofar as those can be separated. Such matters as literary history, literary-aesthetic theory, and high-tech literary criticism go into this third category, along with science, economics, philosophy, political history and ideology, social justice, physical sports, cool jazz, and a great many other things. They engage my interest more or less from time to time, but for better or worse they rank lower on my agenda of concerns and my categories of expertise than those earlier-mentioned matters.

As I have acknowledged, perhaps my priorities — even my literary priorities — should be otherwise. If I happened to be South African, African American, or European Jewish, for example, they would no doubt be otherwise whether I wanted them to be or not.

But as a white Anglo-Saxon (lapsed) Protestant of just the right age and location to have missed all the wars of our century, I have had the remarkable privilege of being largely left alone by history and politics, and I have largely returned them that courtesy.

Regarding literary theory in particular, in which these Stuttgart seminars on "The End of Postmodernism" ineluctably embroil us: It is true that I have been a university professor for all of my adult life, generally in departments of literature — but my professorships have been mainly of a peculiar American sort: as a coach of apprentice fiction writers, not as a scholar/teacher of literary texts, theory, and criticism. Great literature is so agreeable to read and think about and discuss that I often envy my scholar-friends whose professional life consists of doing just that. But my own consists of adding to the pile of texts for them to examine, and of helping younger writers to pile that pile even higher, perhaps burying my efforts under theirs. I find time to give no more than a side-glance even to what the critics say about *my* work, not to mention what they say about literature in general.

That being the case, one might reasonably ask what I'm doing here. Why have I left my pleasant tidewater-Maryland writing room and crossed the Atlantic to audit (indeed, to protest, even to deny) "The End of Postmodernism" and to address the fancy topic of "Postmodernism, Chaos Theory, and the Romantic Arabesque" — matters on which I am no expert at all? It is a reasonable question, to which I am not at all sure that I can offer an acceptable reply. But because I *am* here, of my own volition, having chosen the topic myself, and because I dislike sailing under false colors, I propose to address the question, if not answer it.

Let me say a few things that doubtless go without saying.* Speaking again as a working novelist, I agree with Aristotle that the subject of literature is our human experience of life, its happiness and its misery. But I recognize that our human experience of life importantly includes our experience of language and ideas, and I recognize further that for educated people (whom, as a working novelist,

---

*And that, nevertheless, have been said more than once already in these Friday-pieces: e.g., in "It Goes Without Saying."

I find to be no less interesting than uneducated people), the experience of language and ideas includes some experience of texts: literary, historiographical, philosophical, scientific, sometimes even critical and aesthetic-theoretical.

In my house it is an article of faith (perhaps an occupational bias) that of all the various categories of texts, the one best suited to the rendering of the invisible universe of sensibility — the registration of sensation, the *experiencing* of experience — is fiction in general and the novel in particular. It is a further article of faith *chez moi* that that invisible universe is indeed worth rendering into language. For that reason, it doesn't surprise me to find reflected in the work of novelists new developments or changes of coloration in their culture's general aesthetic sensibility. It wouldn't surprise me even to discover, conversely, that novels may occasionally affect as well as reflect literary-aesthetic theory. In my shop, that sort of reciprocal influence is called "coaxial esemplasy" — a term I like better than "feedback loop," for example, because the adjective "coaxial" evokes the high-tech-electronic here and now, while the noun "esemplasy" is a coinage of the German Romantics, circulated through Samuel Taylor Coleridge across the Atlantic and up the Chesapeake Bay to me. I hope to recirculate that coinage, the *coaxially esemplastic*, from time to time in the days ahead — thus returning it to the country of its origin, with my thanks.

It further goes without saying (and therefore I shall say it) that both the art of the novel and literary-aesthetic theory can be impinged upon by events and strong ideas from outside the realms of literature in particular and aesthetics in general: events and strong ideas from such realms as history, politics, and the social, physical, and biological sciences — even from mathematics. The career of the term "Postmodernism" is one obvious example: My Stuttgart colleague Ihab Hassan* tells us that it is first to be found in a work of literature: an anthology of Hispanic poetry compiled in 1934 by Federico de Onís, who employs the term to distinguish the writings of such Hispanic Americans as the Nicaraguan Reubén Darío and the Argentine Leopoldo Lugones, for example, from Spanish

---

*Whose landmark study *The Dismemberment of Orpheus: Toward a Postmodern Literature* (NY: Oxford U. Press, 1971) made the term and the concept common currency in American literary-critical discourse.

modernismo, a phenomenon that has little to do with the Modernism of Thomas Mann, Franz Kafka, James Joyce, T. S. Eliot, and Ezra Pound. (Spanish *modernisto* poets, I'm told, were much preoccupied with images of swans, and the *postmodernistos* spoke of their movement as "wringing the neck of the swan" — perhaps an echo of Paul Verlaine's advice in "*Art Poétique*": "Take eloquence and wring its neck." Not much connection here with the way we use the term today.) At about the same time, and no doubt coincidentally, Arnold Toynbee is reported to have used the term "postmodern" somewhere in his immense work *A Study of History*, without reference to aesthetics. Neither of these instances was of general aesthetic consequence; as the American critic N. Katherine Hayles remarks (about chaos theory), "Although ideas may be conceived at any time, they are converted into a tradition only when they can be synthesized into the prevailing paradigm."* In the case of European and North American Postmodernism, that conversion and synthesis take place in the 1960s, when the term resurfaces in architecture and the graphic and plastic arts and is returned to literary aesthetics by Professor Hassan & Co. Thereafter, as everybody knows, it spreads to the electronic media and to the culture at large and becomes so popular that by now no two culture-watchers agree on what it refers to. You may read the Barth line on this subject in my essay "Postmodernism Revisited," and we shall visit it further in the second lecture of this series, a fairly extended lay sermon on the subject.

That same process of "conversion into a tradition and synthesis into the prevailing paradigm" characterizes the history of chaos theory, or "chaology," as a rigorous and systematic enterprise. Chaos has been around for a long time, as those of you who hail from the Balkan Republics may have noticed. Chaos theory, however, I understand, originates in the work of the American meteorologist Edward Lorenz in the early 1960s — work inspired by earlier, less systematic observations of turbulence and nonlinear dynamics in other areas, at least as far back as Leonardo's careful drawings of swirling water. Lorenz's seminal paper goes virtually unnoticed for a decade thereafter, whereupon it is picked up by

*Hayles, *Chaos Bound: Orderly Disorder in Contemporary Literature and Science* (Ithaca NY: Cornell U. Press, 1990). More presently from this source.

mathematicians such as Benoit Mandelbrot and by thinkers in other sciences, both physical and biological, to illuminate nonlinear phenomena previously resistant to quantification. Inevitably it comes to infect literary theory as well (at least it seems to promise such benign infection), and it may even have promise for the practice of literature itself, as part of a working aesthetic for writers, as well as for the illumination of existing works whose authors were quite innocent of chaology — if not of "turbulence" and "chaos" in their experience of life. Like Claude Lévi-Strauss's structuralism and René Thom's catastrophe theory, chaos theory is an idea too rich, a metaphor too powerful, not to spread "rhizomatically" out of its original bounds into other fields, like crabgrass on a suburban American lawn. It is worth noting that this spreading itself can be illuminated by a term from chaos theory: "mode locking," or "entrainment" — the tendency of one regular cycle to synchronize with another where their ratios are close to a whole number. "Mode locking," I have read, is what accounts for the moon's always turning the same face to the earth, and for the tendency of pendulum clocks on the same wall of a watchmaker's shop to synchronize their pendula:* an example, by the way, of "coaxial esemplasy." Another way to put it (I'm using Professor Hayles's jargon here) is that chaos theory is one of those "heuristic fictions" so rich in "surplus meaning" that even a working novelist might conceivably find some use for it in his or her shop.

As for the third leg of our tripos, the arabesque: Its root meaning, of course, is simply "Arab-like." In its oldest sense the term refers to a three-thousand-year-old Arabo-Oriental tradition of figuration. In the late eighteenth and early nineteenth centuries it gets appropriated from art history (especially from discussions of "Persian" carpet design, of which more later) into the literary aesthetics of German Romanticism — particularly by Friedrich von Schlegel, who applied the term *Arabeske* to framing narratives of a certain character and incorporated it into his theorizing about the genre of the novel (*der Roman*). In both usages, the arabesque strikes me as a jim-dandy meeting ground, or the uncanny prefiguration of a meeting ground, for these several ideas. I used to tell

---

*Not to mention the current tendency of apprentice writers in American fiction-writing workshops to turn into clones of the late Raymond Carver.

my undergraduate students, as a sort of shorthand or mnemonic, that Enlightenment plus Industrialism engendered Romanticism, and that Romanticism plus revolution — political, technological, scientific — engendered Modernism, and that Modernism plus cataclysm (and skepticism) engendered Postmodernism. Speaking as a confessed Postmodernist, I report to you that I have always felt more affinity with my Modernist parents (Joyce, Kafka, Mann, and Faulkner, for example) and with my premodernist great-grandparents and great-great-grandparents (Sterne, Diderot, Cervantes, Rabelais, Boccaccio, Scheherazade) than with my Romantic grandparents. For that reason, it was illuminating to me to be reminded rather recently that the German inventors of Romantic literary aesthetics were navigating by the same eighteenth-century stars (and seventeenth-to-thirteenth-century stars) that *I* was navigating by, as a working novelist, well before we revived the term *Postmodernism*. It appears that I owe a considerable debt to Karl Wilhelm Friedrich von Schlegel that I was altogether unaware of, and it is to acknowledge and explore that debt (if not necessarily to repay it) that I have come to Stuttgart.

For the *discovery* of my debt to Schlegel, I am further indebted to a contemporary American scholar, G. R. Thompson of Purdue University, in Indiana. Professor Thompson's specialty happens to be the writings of my fellow Baltimorean Edgar Allan Poe: I met him (Thompson, not Poe) a few years ago on Nantucket Island, off the coast of Massachusetts, at a conference on Edgar Poe's only novel, *The Narrative of Arthur Gordon Pym of Nantucket*,* which Thompson not only classifies but attempts to vindicate as an example of the Arabesque. He was kind enough to send me subsequently his excellent new monograph called "Romantic Arabesque, Contemporary Theory, and Postmodernism: The Example of Poe's *Narrative*,"† in which he does me the honor of quoting from my essays a couple of times. In return, I shall frequently be quoting him in this series, for although Professor Thompson does not persuade me that Poe's *Pym* is a good novel (indeed, his monograph acknowledges, in a footnote, that Poe's *Pym* is as much a failure as a "novel" as is Schlegel's

*See my headnote to the Friday-piece " 'Still Farther South.' "
†Full bibliographical citation in the introduction to these lectures.

Lucinde), he most certainly persuades me that Poe was an ingenious writer who quite understood Schlegel's notion of *die Arabeske*. It is Thompson's extended discussion of Schlegel and Postmodernism that revealed to me my unwitting debt, aforementioned, to my German Romantic grandparents.

I have spoken of "the uncanny prefiguration," in Schlegel, of a meeting ground for chaos theory, Postmodernism, and the arabesque. A few quick quotations (most of them not from Professor Thompson) should suggest the possibility. James Gleick, in his recent popular history of chaos theory called *Chaos: Making a New Science*,* defines the Chaos of chaologists as "an orderly disorder generated by simple processes"; he quotes the American physicist Joseph Ford as saying that "[biological] Evolution is chaos with feedback." This sentiment echoes that of the British pathologist Ivy McKenzie on the subject of Parkinson's disease: Oliver Sacks, in his book *Awakenings*,† quotes McKenzie as writing in 1927 that "The pathological physiology of Parkinsonism is the study of an organised chaos." And *that* echoes our man Friedrich Schlegel's beautiful definition of arabesque romance (in *Literary Notebooks 1797–1801*, #1356) as "a structured, artful chaos" ("*ein gebildetes künstliches Chaos*"). Pausing for just a moment on each of Schlegel's adjectives, we see that *gebildetes* differentiates Chaos from mere anarchy and entropy on the one hand and from Cosmos on the other (it also differentiates what Felix Guattari and Gilles Deleuze call the "arborescent" from the "rhizomatic," of which more eventually, and the arabesque from the grotesque, of which more quite soon), while *künstliches* differentiates the structured chaoses of art from those of nature and of mathematics. *Künstliches* implies an artist behind the structure, an artful controller of the controlled indeterminacy.

We have, I believe, brought chaos theory and the Romantic arabesque to our hypothetical meeting ground; two more quotations should serve to invite Postmodernism to the picnic. In my essay "Postmodernism Revisited," I cite the American art critic Tom

*NY: Viking, 1987.
†NY: HarperPerennial, 1990.

McEvilly's characterization of (lowercase) postmodernism as the swing of the pendulum of western civilization from the romantic-mystical pole (of which twentieth-century Modernism is certainly an instance) to the rational-skeptical pole; thus McEvilly can speak of an Egyptian postmodernism of the Middle Kingdom and a Roman postmodernism of the Silver Age. This characterization of McEvilly's corresponds nicely to N. Katherine Hayles's view of postmodern science as a skeptical moving away from the grand global syntheses characteristic of many disciplines in the late-nineteenth/early-twentieth centuries — a moving away of which nonlinear dynamics is one instance. Hayles thus speaks of chaology as an essentially postmodern science. And listen to Benoit Mandelbrot (whose fractal geometry is one of the best-known and most appealing manifestations of chaos theory) on the subject of Modernist versus pre- and Postmodernist architecture: "Bauhaus architecture," Mandelbrot declares, "manifests a Euclidean sensibility, [whereas] art that satisfies lacks *scale*; it contains important elements at all scales, all sizes." In this instance, Mandelbrot happens to be contrasting Mies van der Rohe's Seagram building in New York City with l'Opéra in Paris, but the contrast would serve as well for much Postmodernist architecture, to which the element of "nonfunctional" decoration has been restored at various scales. Mandelbrot's view of l'Opéra also echoes the art historian Sayed Hosayn Nasr (as quoted by Professor Thompson) on Islamic architecture, in which "solid surfaces are dissolved, as it were, by filling the whole surface with smaller and smaller decorative units and motifs, [to suggest] the temporary character of all earthly structures and the impermanence of human existence." I'm not at all sure that "the impermanence of human existence" is what Philip Johnson and the other Postmod architects have in mind, but the first part of Nasr's description certainly suggests Mandelbrot's self-similar fractals and the High Baroque. It also echoes what our man Schlegel remarks about the writings of Cervantes and Shakespeare (the remark appears in Thompson's monograph): Schlegel admires their "artfully ordered confusion, charming symmetry of contradictions, the wonderfully perennial alternation of enthusiasm and irony ... *even in the smallest parts of the whole. . . .*" [my italics].

I conclude my overture to this series with another theme from Friedrich von Schlegel; in this case, his very useful distinction between the grotesque and the arabesque, as that distinction is elaborated by Professor Thompson. Speaking of Edgar Poe's 1840 framed-tale collection called *Tales of the Grotesque and Arabesque*, and of the assumption by Poe critics that "grotesque" refers to the comic stories and "arabesque" to the serious ones, Thompson argues that for the German Romantics by whom Poe was influenced, "each term has a double meaning, and each definition shares some properties of the other." The two modes share a tendency to juxtapose disparate, even contradictory elements: humor and horror, illusion and reality, the realistic and the fantastic, the sublime and the vulgar. The term "grotesque," Thompson reminds us, in both its comic and its sinister sense, comes from the Italian *grottesco*, indicating the "grotto" paintings discovered on the walls of ancient Rome below the modern street level. These grotto paintings (which inspired the literal sculptured grotto-grotesques of a later period) showed human heads growing out of tangled vines and other fusions of plant and animal, organic and inorganic. "The implication of entanglement," Thompson writes, "of looping and twisting lines, is especially strong in grotesque design; radically different elements entangle and accommodate one another."

> In this effect, it shares connotations with "arabesque." . . . But the basic denotation suggests an important difference between grotesque and arabesque: namely, the difference between hopeless entanglement and orderly symmetry, [between] total indeterminacy and controlled or contained indeterminacy.

In short, both are nonlinear, but in the language of Deleuze and Guattari, the grotesque is "rhizomatic," while the arabesque is "arborescent." In the language of Friedrich von Schlegel, the grotesque would be "chaotic" in the traditional sense of that adjective, whereas the arabesque is *"ein gebildetes künstliches Chaos."*

To wind up this overture: The aesthetic of literary Postmodernism (as I understand the term and the aesthetic, and as at least some of us *apply* that aesthetic at our tidewater writing tables) appears to me to have been remarkably anticipated by the Romantic arabesque, especially by Friedrich von Schlegel's notion of *die Arabeske*. And so far from being exhausted, that aesthetic seems to me to be potentially revalidated — refreshened, reinforced, replenished — by contemporary chaos theory. Indeed, I have come to think of my own working aesthetic, when I think about it consciously at all, as "romantic formalism," or "chaotic-arabesque Postmodernism." How's that for a potential manifesto?

As for our menu: Tomorrow's entrée will be "Postmodernism Visited": a professional novelist's amateur review (with a little help from his friends) of the history of the term and the history of the spirit; of Postmodernist art and postmodern culture, or the postmodern condition. Thereafter, we shall look more closely at the nature of the arabesque, particularly at anticipations of Postmodernism in German Romanticism. That will be our opportunity to review the older senses of "arabesque": "Persian" carpets, for example, and "Orientalism" in general in Western art and culture, both as an aesthetic phenomenon in itself and as a spin-off from the silk-and-spice trade and from European colonialism. There too we can zoom in on the preoccupation of the German Romantics, Schlegel especially, with *der Roman* in general and *die Arabeske* in particular as models of Romantic values, and on Schlegel's own major experiment with the literary arabesque. The pedagogical muse willing, we shall then focus on chaos theory as an example of postmodern science and as a possible literary model resonant with echoes of both Postmodernism and the arabesque. After that, let's glance at some literary progenitors, both of the Schlegelian arabesque* and of "chaotic" Postmodernism, as well as at contemporary literary theory and the theories of arabesque romance and of chaology. My position will be that inasmuch as literary Postmodernism is a descendant of the Romantic arabesque, they share the same ancestors — including, but not limited to, *The Arabian Nights* and its own ancestors, such as Somadeva's eleventh-century Sanskrit *Kathā Sarit Sāgara*, called in English *The Ocean of Story*, also Boccaccio's *Decameron* and *its* ancestors,

---

*Schlegel himself declares the arabesque to be "the oldest and most original form of human imagination."

such as the Italian *Novellini*; also Chaucer's *Canterbury Tales*, Rabelais's *Gargantua and Pantagruel*, Cervantes's *Don Quixote*, Shakespeare's plays, Laurence Sterne's *Tristram Shandy*, Denis Diderot's *Jacques le fataliste*, and (along with Schlegel the amateur novelist) such later arabesquers or proto-Postmodernists as Edgar Poe and a particular favorite of mine, the late-nineteenth-century Brazilian novelist Joaquim Machado de Assis — plus anybódy else we can think of who deserves a place in our genealogy. And perhaps we should conclude our seminars with something like "Chaos Theory, Postmodernism, and the Arabesque — So What?"

That last question — So what? — returns me to those priorities that I spoke of at the outset. In my fiction-writing seminars at Johns Hopkins, I try to impress upon apprentice writers the difference between the readerly responses "So what?" and "Ah, so!" as a dramaturgical litmus test. "So what?" means that you have our attention, but you haven't yet paid your narrative-dramatic bills. "Ah, so!" indicates that your dramaturgical bookkeeping is in good order. In the present case, I for one will be not much more than academically interested in the mere demonstration that there are affinities between and among chaos theory, the aesthetics of literary Postmodernism, and the Romantic arabesque. I would like to know further what those affinities *portend*; what use, for example, if any, a working novelist might make of them, and why sentient citizens who happen not to be novelists should give a damn.

On with the story?

2. Postmodernism Visited: A Professional Novelist's Amateur Review

LET'S SIDLE UP to the grand topic of Postmodernism by way of two nit-picking questions: whether the term should be hyphenated and whether it should be capitalized. The latter question doesn't come up *auf Deutsch*, but it does in English, for example,* with certain consequences.

In a recent issue of the *New York Times Book Review* (June 23, 1991), Professor Bernard Williams, a philosopher at Oxford and Berkeley, reminds his readers that the adjective "postmodern" has come to have at least two quite different primary meanings: In the arts, says Professor Williams, especially in architecture and music, "a post-modern style represents a rejection of the formal austerities of the modern movement† in favor, roughly, of eclecticism, historical reference and greater jollity."

In other connections, however, and above all in relation to politics, post-modernism hopes to overcome *modernity*, which is a phenomenon, and a spirit, identified with such things as the Enlightenment and the ambitions of 19th-century political theory. Since modernity set in not later than the 18th century, and [since] modernism, flourishing in the first half of this century, rejected many of [modernity's] most typical products, such as naturalism and romanticism, [the] conflation of the two conceptions produces an epical degree of historical confusion.

---

*The 1991 Stuttgart Seminars were conducted in English.
†For reasons presently to be set forth, I wish he would say "Modernist" instead of "modern."

That strikes me as well said indeed — except that if Modernism rejects Romanticism, I would say that it does so in the way that some children reject their parents, while still carrying their genes. There is much more Romanticism in the Modernist program, it seems to me, than there is in Postmodernism. Anyhow, inasmuch as Postmodernist artists ineluctably live in a climate of cultural postmodernity, I'm not optimistic about keeping the distinction clear. It's hard enough to come to an understanding in the matter of whether the terms should be capitalized or lowercased, and whether the prefix "post" ought to be hyphenated from or run into what follows it. There is no way of knowing what Professor Williams's preferences are in these weighty matters, inasmuch as he is writing for the *New York Times*, which (as I know from sore experience) insists on its own house style — in this instance, lowercase initial letters for such terms as "Modernism," "Postmodernism," and "Romanticism," and hyphenation for the term "Postmodern."* Looking around the critical landscape, I see that whoever wrote the copy for the brochure of our Stuttgart Seminars — "The End of Postmodernism: New Directions" — also prefers the lowercase initial (except in titles), but drops the hyphen. Likewise the notable French theorist Jean-François Lyotard, in his 1979 book *La Condition postmoderne* — but of course, the French language is as averse to uppercase letters as the German language is fond of them; French book titles are all lowercase after the first noun. Likewise too Professors G. R. Thompson and N. Katherine Hayles, on whom I shall be relying heavily in these lectures: lowercase, no hyphen. I have not yet personally consulted the pope of the church of Postmodernism, our colleague Professor Hassan, as to his preference; his bibliographical credits in our seminar brochure follow the style of that brochure: no hyphen, uppercase in the titles but lowercase in the text.† That seems to be the rough consensus in languages other than German, although British English inclines, *New York Times*like, to the hy-

---

*Also the omission of commas before conjunctions in serial items ("eclecticism, historical reference and greater jollity") and the digitalization of century-names (18th, 19th), both practices frowned upon by the present author's house style and by his publishers' as well.

†Likewise Hassan's seminal *Dismemberment of Orpheus*, aforecited.

phen (I don't know how it goes in Japanese, although I can attest from firsthand, on-site experience that the Japanese are keenly interested in whatever it is that we *gaijin* mean by the term "Postmodern").

As for myself: You will be excited to hear that I shrug my shoulders at the question of hyphenation, but am inclined to prefer the uppercase initial, and not merely out of respect for the German side of my ancestry. There is a difference, and not only in quality, between the lowercase-romantic novels of Barbara Cartland and the uppercase-Romantic novels of Goethe and Schlegel, between the lowercase-romantic aspects of candlelight and wine and the uppercase-Romantic aspects of a hike through the Bavarian Alps. Just as I find the adjective "Modernist" more precise than "Modern" when speaking of the dominant aesthetic movement of the first half of the twentieth century in Europe, the United States, and elsewhere, and the adjective "Postmodernist" more precise than "Postmodern" when speaking of an aesthetic movement that follows Modernism in one spirit or another, so also I find it useful to employ the uppercase when referring to contemporary aesthetic Postmodernism, because doing so leaves us a lowercase postmodernism to describe analogous phenomena in other times and places: Tom McEvilly's Middle Kingdom Egyptian postmodernism and Silver Age Roman postmodernism;* perhaps Friedrich von Schlegel's uppercase-Romantic lowercase postmodernism of the late-eighteenth/early-nineteenth centuries.

You get the idea: It is the difference between Burgundy from the Burgundy region of France and burgundy from the Napa Valley of California (in this instance, not necessarily a difference in quality). Thus I shall try to use the adjective "Postmodernist" when speaking of contemporary aesthetics, and the adjective "Postmodern" when speaking of other aspects of our contemporary culture, on the grounds that we need every possible aid to clarification when we're snorkeling such muddy waters. And I shall use the uppercase noun "Postmodernism" when speaking of the latter-twentieth-century aesthetic phenomenon, and to hell with the rest, for the

---

*Cited in "Postmodernism Revisited."

inarguable reason that postmodernism as a condition, like post-industrialism, looks queer to me in the upper case.

In this matter of usage I seem to have the eminent Octavio Paz on my side (at least in the English translation of his recent volume of essays called *Convergences: Essays on Art and Literature**) — though inasmuch as Paz has published (in the Mexican literary journal *La Jornada Semanal*) an attack on my essay "The Literature of Replenishment" wherein he denominates me *un bobo* for writing that essay, I imagine that he wouldn't enjoy being on my team any more than I enjoy being on his. In any case, we are in sweet agreement only on the question of uppercase initial letters, for Paz reserves the term "Modernist" exclusively for Hispanic *Modernismo* — he prefers such terms as "Avant-Gardism" or "Expressionism," or the more particular terms "Dadaism" and "Surrealism" and so forth, to describe what was going on in the rest of Europe and in North America — and by "Postmodernist" he means Hispanic *Postmodernismo*, of which more presently. (Among Spanish-language copyeditors, by the way, there seems to be at least as much inconsistency in the typesetting of these terms as there is in other languages.)

Here is Paz on Hispanic *Postmodernismo*, in an essay called "A Literature of Convergences," undated, from the aforementioned collection. After asserting that the literatures of both North and South America are marked by alternating impulses, even periods, of "Cosmopolitanism" ("the sallying forth of ourselves and our reality") and "Americanism" ("the return to what we are and to our origin"), Paz writes:

> An example of the first was the initial phase of Hispano-American Modernism, between 1890 and 1905, characterized in poetry by the influence of European Symbolism and in prose by that of Naturalism. This phase was followed around 1915 by so-called Post-modernism, which represented a return to our hemisphere and to colloquial speech.

*San Diego: Harcourt Brace Jovanovich, 1987.

It is quite clear that Paz in Mexico City is not talking about what we're talking about here in Stuttgart.*

In other instances, his usage is less clear. For example, in (interestingly enough) a 1970 essay called "The Tradition of the Haiku," speaking of a 1918 volume by the Mexican poet José Juan Tablada, Paz writes,

> The . . . book was still Modernist; its relative novelty lay in the appearance of those ironic and colloquial elements which historians of our literature have seen as the hallmarks of a movement that, with notorious inexactitude, they label Postmodernism. This movement is a textbook invention: Postmodernism is simply the criticism that, within Modernism and not venturing beyond its aesthetic horizon, certain Modernist poets level against Modernism. It is the line of descent, via [the aforementioned poets] Darío and Lugones, of the anti-Symbolist Symbolist Laforgue.

The context does not make it altogether clear whether, in this case, Paz is extending the term to include non-Hispanic Postmodernism (his phrase "the line of descent" suggests that possibility). Given the date of the essay — 1970, when Ihab Hassan was just bringing the term "postmodern" to our gringo attention — I suspect that Paz added this remark by way of an update when he was putting together the collection *Convergences*. But perhaps not; he is a knowledgeable and sophisticated hombre. Despite the dismissive tone of his remark, I think it does in fact describe one kind of literary Postmodernism: an essentially Modernist criticism of Modernism; one that (rather like my own) not only declines to throw out the baby with the bathwater, but maintains a high regard for that bathwater as well. I daresay that something of that sort is what William Gass has in mind when he describes such writers as Samuel Beckett and Italo Calvino (and himself and me and Donald Barthelme and Robert Coover and John Hawkes) as late-Modernists, and reserves the term "Postmodernist" for the

---

*I should add that he does not, at least in this essay, go on to describe any subsequent phase of Hispano-American Modernism after that "initial" phase of 1890–1905.

likes of Raymond Carver, Frederick Barthelme, and Ann Beattie: the "Diet Pepsi minimalists."

One more quotation in this vein from Señor Paz before we bid him *hasta la vista*: this one from an excellent 1970 essay called "Blank Thought." The essay deals with Tantric art (Paz was once the Mexican ambassador to India), but its opening paragraph sounds to me like a call for a kind of Postmodernism more substantial than the "mere textbook phenomenon" that he earlier dismissed:

"We are living at the end of linear time," he writes, "the time of succession: history, progress, modernity" (note the appropriate lower case):

> In art the most virulent form of the crisis of modernity has been the criticism of the object; begun by Dada, it is now ending in the destruction (or self-destruction) of the "artistic thing," painting or sculpture, in celebration of the act, the ceremony, the happening [remember that Paz is writing in 1970], the gesture. The crisis of the object is little more than a (negative) manifestation of the end of time; what is undergoing crisis is not art but time, our idea of time. The idea of "modern art" is a consequence of the idea of a "history of art"; both were inventions of modernity and both are dying with it. . . . Is another art dawning? In certain parts of the world, particularly in the United States, we are witnessing different attempts to resurrect Fiesta (the "happening," for example).* . . . I recognize [in these attempts] the old Romantic dream, taken up and transmitted to today's younger generation by the Surrealists: that of erasing the boundaries between life and poetry. An art embodying images that satisfy our world's needs for collective rites. At the same time, how can we not imagine another art satisfying a no less imperative need: solitary meditation and contemplation? This art would not be a relapse into the idolatry of the "art object" of the last two hundred years, nor would it be an art of the destruction of the object; rather, it would regard the painting, sculpture, or poem as a point of departure. Heading where? Toward presence, toward absence, and beyond. Not the restoration of the object of art but the instau-

---

*A charming idea: The Fiesta as a prototype of the Happening!

ration of the poem or the painting as an inaugural sign opening up
a new path.

"My reflections on Tantric art," Paz concludes, "are situated
within the framework of such concerns." And very astute reflections they are. But Paz's call, or wish, for "another art" besides de-
funct Romanticism/Modernism on the one hand and the destruction of the art object or erasure of "the boundaries between life
and poetry" on the other hand sounds to me very much like a call
for Postmodernism — though not for the Hispanic *Postmodernismo* at which he has already sniffed, and not for *my* kind of
gringo Postmodernism, which has no grand quarrel with the art
object, at least in its manifestation as the Postmodernist novel.*

I conclude my consideration of Paz the Potential Postmodernist
with two reflections and a more recent quotation. The first reflection is that, as a novelist, I am uneasy with the notion of the
art object regarded *mainly* as a point of departure "toward presence, toward absence, and beyond" (whatever that language
means) rather than as a wonderful thing in itself, while at the same
time I protest that artistic *Meisterstücken*, even less-than-*Meisterstücken*, have always also been points of departure for "solitary
meditation and contemplation," to a degree depending, I suppose,
on the particular *Meisterstück*, the particular reader, viewer, or auditor, and the particular circumstances of their encounter. The second reflection is that I do not see how this "other art" that he
imagines "dawning," even if it has prefigurations in Tantric art,
for example, can be regarded otherwise than as something new in
the ongoing history of Western art — a prospect that does not
bother *me* in the least, but that seems to contradict Paz's original
thesis concerning the end of time, succession, history, and all that.
I'll return to this "end of" business presently, with respect to "The
End of Postmodernism." But I cannot resist a final quotation from
Mr. Paz — this from his speech accepting the 1990 Nobel Prize for
literature — to demonstrate how seriously (though eloquently) he
equivocates his terminology while attempting to clarify it (the

---

*In general, Paz has little to say about novels, even the exemplary Postmodernist
novels of his fellow Mexico Cityman Gabriel García Márquez.

speech is reprinted by Harvest/HBJ in the volume *In Search of the Present*):

> What is modernity? It is, first of all, an ambiguous term: there are as many types of modernity as there are societies. Each society has its own. The word's meaning is as uncertain and arbitrary as the name of the period that precedes it, the Middle Ages. If we are modern when compared to medieval times, are we perhaps the Middle Ages of a future modernity? Is a name that changes with time a real name? Modernity is a word in search of its meaning. Is it an idea, a mirage or a moment of history? Are we the children of modernity or are we its creators? Nobody knows for sure. . . . Since 1850 [modernity] has been our goddess and our demoness. In recent years there has been an attempt to exorcise her, and there has been much talk of "postmodernism." But what is postmodernism if not an even more modern modernity?

In my judgment, Mr. Paz is simply playing in a not very interesting way with that conflation of meanings that Bernard Williams remarked upon earlier. "Modern" and "postmodern" are ambiguous adjectives; "Modernist" and "Postmodernist," while certainly arguable, are much less ambiguous (especially with uppercase initials and outside their particular Hispanic literary-historical reference); the nouns "modernity" and "postmodernity" (especially with lowercase initials) unfortunately include both sets of adjectives. We must endeavor steadfastly to keep our terminology clear, but we need not throw up our hands. It may be valid, though it is not especially clever, to say that a Postmodernist writer like Italo Calvino and a Postmodernist architect like Philip Johnson are "more modern Modernists"; but it is not valid to say that they are more Modernist Modernists than, for example, Wallace Stevens and Ludwig Mies van der Rohe. No: They are better described by the term "Postmodernist"— a term that does, after all, have meaning.

Let's turn now briefly to the subject of postmodernity, or the postmodern condition, before coming back to Postmodernist art in general and PM fiction in particular. In preparation for these

Stuttgart seminars, I duly took a look at some major studies of Postmodernism that have appeared or come to prominence since the last time I did such homework (i.e., since 1979, when I wrote the essay "The Literature of Replenishment" in preparation for my visit to the Tübingen meeting of the *Deutsche Gesellschaft für Amerikastudien*) — in particular, at reflections on the subject by the British architect Charles Jencks, the Italian semiotician/novelist Umberto Eco, the French philosopher-critics Jean-François Lyotard and Jean Baudrillard, their German counterpart Jürgen Habermas, and the American critical theorist N. Katherine Hayles. Some of these — the ones that I believe I understand, like Jencks and Eco — I have quoted already in my essay "Postmodernism Revisited." Eco's parable of the postmodern condition I find particularly "in synch" with my own position on the subject, in part no doubt because his example involves the problem of *getting something said*, which obviously speaks to my condition, but also because he avoids extended abstractions. I cannot say the same for Lyotard and Habermas, whom I do not understand very well at all, although I don't doubt that each knows not only what he himself is talking about but equally what the other is talking about. Reading them, alas, I find myself back in the eminent philologist Leo Spitzer's doctoral seminar at Johns Hopkins in the 1950s, when I realized that the classmates on my right and my left were going to be among the scholar-critics of their generation, and that I was going to have to make it as a fictionist, if at all. In the face of extended theoretical argument, unless it is laced with splendid concrete examples and dynamite one-liners, my eyes glaze over; my attention wanders to the nominalist world outside the classroom windows; I am obliged to push my head back and down with my hand to the next line of text, like the carriage of an old manual typewriter, until presently I close the book and go take a swim, or pick up a novel. There, back in my student days, went Hegel (but not Nietzsche or Schopenhauer); there in later years went Lacan and Derrida and other seminal figures, to my loss; and there, alas, went much of Lyotard and Baudrillard and more of Habermas this past spring. I apologize.

On the other hand, I don't want to cast myself as the Huckleberry Finn of Johns Hopkins University. Do I understand, for example, Lyotard's preliminary definition of postmodernism (the postmodern condition, I presume he means, not Postmodernist art) as "incredulity toward metanarratives"— by which he means, e.g., the "legitimating narrative" of science as the search for objective truth? I believe that I do understand that proposition; I would even second it if he substituted the word "skepticism" for "incredulity" — but M. Lyotard has the Gallic taste for hyperbole that used to give me trouble with Roland Barthes.* I quite agree with Lyotard that the postmodern condition involves (not *is*) skepticism (not necessarily *incredulity*) toward "metanarratives." So far, so good. And I like his remark (in the essay "Answering the Question: What Is Postmodernism?") that "eclecticism is the degree zero of contemporary general culture: one listens to reggae, watches a western, eats McDonald's food for lunch and local cuisine for dinner, wears Paris perfume in Tokyo and 'retro' clothes in Hong Kong. . . ." That pervasive eclecticism is an aspect of what N. Katherine Hayles calls "the denaturing of context" and what G. W. S. Trow (speaking of contemporary Americans) describes as living one's life "within the context of no context." I like also Lyotard's observation that "the essay (Montaigne) is postmodern, while the fragment ([Schlegel's] *The Athenaeum*) is modern" — an observation that echoes McEvilly's characterization of postmodernism as rational-skeptical as opposed to mystical-romantic — although I would have preferred Lyotard to say that Montaigne is postmodern*ist*, like the Middle Kingdom scribe Khakheperresenb, while the fragment is modern*ist*.

I like even better, because I understand it better, Fredric Jameson's observation (in his introduction to the American edition of Lyotard's book) that "Postmodern architecture . . . comes before us as a peculiar analogue to neoclassicism, a play of ('historicist') allusion and quotation that has renounced the older high mod-

---

*Barthes's proposition in *Writing Degree Zero*, for example, that "the whole of literature, from Flaubert to the present day, becomes the problematics of language." If only he had been content to say that "the problematics of language" — indeed, the problematics of every aspect of the medium of literature, not language alone — becomes one of several prominent field-identification marks of our literature after "Flaubert." But that kind of reasonable modification, I suppose, de-zings such zingers.

ernist rigor and that itself seems to recapitulate a whole range of Western aesthetic strategies. . . ." Jameson goes on to cite architectural instances of

> a mannerist postmodernism (Michael Graves), a baroque postmodernism (the Japanese), a rococo postmodernism (Charles Moore), a neoclassical postmodernism (the French, particularly Christian de Portzamparc), and probably even a "high modernist" postmodernism in which modernism is itself the object of the postmodernist pastiche. This is a rich and creative [architectural] movement, of the greatest aesthetic play and delight, that can perhaps be most rapidly characterized as a whole by two important features: first, the falling away of the protopolitical vocation and the terrorist stance of the older modernism and, second, the eclipse of all the affect (depth, anxiety, terror, the emotions of the monumental) that marked high modernism and its replacement by what Coleridge would have called fancy or Schiller aesthetic play, a commitment to surface and to the *superficial* in all the senses of the word.

Despite the inappropriate lowercase initial letters, that seems to me well said, perhaps even transferable to Postmodernist fiction, although I suspect that these aesthetic movements seem clearer to us fiction writers when the illustrations are from architecture or painting. In any case, I begin to hear Roland-Barthesian hyperbolical paradox and Octavio-Pazian equivocation in such passages as this (from the same essay by Lyotard, to which we now return):

> What, then, is the postmodern? . . . It is undoubtedly a part of the modern. All that has been received, if only yesterday . . . must be suspected. . . . A work can become modern only if it is first postmodern. Postmodernism thus understood is not modernism at its end but in the nascent state, and this state is constant.

I believe that I understand what Lyotard is saying here, but I disapprove of his saying it because he is unnecessarily muddying the waters that had seemed so clear when he and Jameson were talking architecture. He is stretching the terminology like Paz until it becomes all but meaningless.

And then we come to those passages of theoretical abstraction that make my eyes glaze over with incomprehension: passages like this one, that have the sonority of sense but that defy my comprehension:

> The postmodern would be that which, in the modern, puts forward the unpresentable in presentation itself; that which denies itself the solace of good forms, the consensus of a taste which would make it possible to share collectively the nostalgia for the unattainable; that which searches for new presentations, not in order to enjoy them but in order to impart a stronger sense of the unpresentable. A postmodern artist or writer is in the position of a philosopher: the text he writes, the work he produces are not in principle governed by preestablished rules, and they cannot be judged according to a determining judgment, by applying familiar categories to the text or to the work. Those rules and categories are what the work of art itself is looking for. The artist and the writer, then, are working without rules in order to formulate the rules of what *will have been done*. Hence the fact that work and text have the characters of an *event*; hence also, they always come too late for their author, or, what amounts to the same thing, their being put into work, their realization (*mise en oeuvre*) always begin too soon. *Post modern* would have to be understood according to the paradox of the future (*post*) anterior (*modo*).

To the extent that I comprehend this paradoxical passage, it sounds to me like a banality, as much a manifesto of the Romantics and the Modernists as of the Postmodernists. Every "innovative" work of art is a leap into the unknown, an exploration of aesthetic possibilities, a quest; Friedrich von Schlegel understood that as well as Fredric Jameson and Jean-François Lyotard do. But I'm not at all sure that I *do* comprehend the passage just quoted, and in any case it does not seem to me to go very far toward distinguishing between the spirit of García Márquez's *Cien años de soledad* and the spirit of James Joyce's *Finnegans Wake*: the homely practical task that I addressed in my essay "The Literature of Replenishment."

Finally (with respect to Lyotard), there are aspects of the contemporary situation of artists and writers in late-capitalist societies of which Lyotard disapproves, but which Umberto Eco and I,
for example, do not find to be self-evident disvalues: "Artistic and
literary research [in postmodern society]," Lyotard writes (I believe he means "research" here in the sense of artistic experimenta-
tion), "is doubly threatened":

> . . . once by the "cultural policy" and once by the art and book
> market. What is advised, sometimes through one channel, some-
> times through the other, is to offer works which, first, are relative to
> subjects which exist in the eyes of the public they address, and sec-
> ond, works so made ("well made") that the public will recognize
> what they are about, will understand what is signified, will be able
> to give or refuse its approval knowingly, and if possible, even to de-
> rive from such work a certain amount of comfort.

To this I would reply, Why on earth not, if the thing can be
done with proper artistic responsibility? The situation Lyotard describes is that of Umberto Eco's postmodern lovers (aforecited in
"Postmodernism Revisited") trying to give voice to their love —
passionately but uninnocently, in full awareness of and responsibility to "the already said." It exemplifies the difference between a
magnificent Postmodernist writer like García Márquez and a
merely interesting one like, say, Georges Perec.

One could go on comparing and contrasting the prominent theorists of Postmodernism, I suppose, until the phenomenon really
does come to an end: Jürgen Habermas ("Modernity versus Postmodernity"), Andreas Huyssen ("Mapping the Postmodern"),
Craig Owens ("The Allegorical Impulse: Toward a Theory of Postmodernism"), Hal Foster ("Postmodernism, a Preface"), and of
course Ihab Hassan, a charter member of the club. I myself have
not yet read every one of these theorists; I begin to suspect that I
never shall. But before I restate my own position on Postmodernist
aesthetics, I want briefly to consider one more theorist — the
earlier-cited N. Katherine Hayles of the University of Iowa —

because I will be depending on her assistance when the time comes to relate chaos theory to Postmodernism.

In her most recent book, *Chaos Bound*, while acknowledging Lyotard's definition of cultural postmodernism as "an incredulity toward metanarratives," Hayles constructs her own narrative of the evolution of postmodernism and then speculates intelligently on the aesthetics of high-tech Postmodernist literary narration. Her definition of cultural postmodernism is somewhat different from Lyotard's; its root, she declares, is "the realization that what has always been thought of as the essential, unvarying components of human experience are not natural facts of life but social constructions." These essential life-components — whose "denaturing" in our century has, in her view, led to cultural postmodernism — include language, context, time, and "the human" itself, for in Hayles's opinion "The postmodern anticipates and implies the posthuman" (she is, remember, speaking of postmodern culture, not necessarily Postmodernist art). She proceeds to examine in some detail the denaturing of these erstwhile natural facts into social constructions. Radically summarized, her argument goes like this:

First, as to language: Its denaturing consists of its coming to be seen "not as a mimetic representation of the world of objects but as a sign system generating significance internally through a series of relational differences. . . . Denatured language," says Hayles, "is language regarded as ground painted under our feet while we hang suspended in a void. We cannot dispense with the illusion of ground, because we need a place from which to speak. But [that illusion] is bracketed by our knowledge that it is only a painting, not natural ground." This vertiginous state of affairs, Hayles maintains, is the historical consequence of two main currents of thought: in mathematics, physics, and philosophy, the undermining of Whitehead and Russell's *Principia Mathematica* by Gödel's theorem, of Einstein's special theory of relativity by quantum mechanics, and of logical positivism by such philosophers of science as Kuhn, Hanson, and Feyerabend, "who argued convincingly that observational statements are always theory-laden." And in linguistics, the Saussurean view that "language is inherently self-referential and ungrounded . . . an interactive field in which the meaning of any one element depends upon the interactions present in the field as a whole." The resultant denaturing of language, in Hayles's narrative, constitutes the first wave of cultural postmodernism, a wave cresting in the period between the two world wars — although, to be sure, we can hear clear anticipations of it at least as early as Flaubert.*

The second wave, says Hayles — the denaturing of context — crested after the denaturing of language and is, in her view, an effect of the postwar explosion of interest in information theory and technology. "Initially," she writes, "messages were separated from contexts because such a move was necessary to make information quantifiable. Once this assumption was used to formulate a theory of information, information technology developed very rapidly. And once this technology was in place, the disjunction between message and context which began as a theoretical premise became a cultural condition." Hayles proceeds to illustrate this blurring of the distinction between text and context with persuasive examples — from advanced weapons systems, from biogenetics (test-tube babies), from MTV, from satellite image-enhancement, and even from literature (citing, e.g., Borges's stories "Pierre Menard, Author of the *Quixote*" and "Tlön, Uqbar, Orbis Tertius").

She then turns her attention to the denaturing of time, declaring that the "cutting loose of time from sequence, and consequently from human identity, constitutes the third wave of postmodernism. Time still exists in cultural postmodernism, but it no longer functions as a continuum along which human action can be plotted." She cites Heidegger and Derrida and then asks the question "How did we come to believe that the future, like the past, has already happened?" Her engaging answer is that "The rhythm of our century [had come to seem] predictable. World War I at the second decade; World War II at the fourth decade; World War III at the sixth decade, during which the world as we know it comes to an end. But somehow it did not happen when it was supposed to. By the ninth decade, we cannot help suspecting that maybe it happened after all and we failed to notice. Consequently time splits into a false future in which we all live and a true future that

---

*E.g., in *Madame Bovary*: "Language is a cracked kettle that we beat on for bears to dance, when all the while we wished to move the stars."

by virtue of being true does not have us in it." She illustrates this interesting state of affairs as manifested in Nabokov's *Ada*, Walker Percy's *Love Among the Ruins*, and a number of movies, and then applies it to Postmodernist aesthetics, citing for example the critic Michel Serres's view that the temporal aesthetic of nineteenth-century realism gives way in our century to "a spatial aesthetic focusing on deformations, local turbulence, and continuous but nondifferentiable curves" — a hint of chaos theory already, and reminiscent of William Gass's recent lectures on "spatial form" in literature. And Hayles concludes her discussion of the denaturing of time by pointing out that it makes paradoxical the writing of a *history* of postmodernism. The various theorists whose names we keep mentioning are all "concerned to locate postmodernism in a sequence that began with modernism."

> They vary in their estimations of how successful, and even what, modernism was; they disagree about whether it is continued or refuted by postmodernism. Whatever their stance, however, they concur that postmodernism *has a history*, and thus that it has roots in such intellectual issues as the self-referentiality of symbol systems, the Kantian sublime, the cultural logic of late capitalism, and so forth.

The case is very different, she declares, for those who *live* postmodernism rather than theorize about its history:

> For them, the denaturing of time means that they have no history. To live postmodernism is to live as schizophrenics are said to do, in a world of disconnected present moments that jostle one another but never form a continuous (much less logical) progression. The prior experiences of older people [such as all those theorists] act as anchors that keep them from fully entering the postmodern stream of spliced contexts and discontinuous time. Young people, lacking these anchors and immersed in TV, are in a better position to know from direct experience what it is to have no sense of history, to live in a world of simulacra, to see [even] the human form as provisional. The case could be made that the people in this country [the USA] who know the most about how postmodernism *feels* (as dis-

tinct from how to envision or analyze it) are all under the age of sixteen.

I want to return to this distinction presently: not between the young and the old, but between those who theorize about postmodernism and those who live it (some of that latter group, I know for a fact, are older than sixteen, and not all of them lack a sense of history or live like schizophrenics). But there remains to be considered the prospective fourth wave of Professor Hayles's narrative of cultural postmodernism: the denaturing of the human, by which she means something considerably more ominous than the famous "dehumanization of art" that the Spanish philosopher José Ortega y Gasset was applauding back in the 1940s. I'll surf down this fourth wave quickly, first because it happily has yet to break fully upon us, and second because Hayles's discussion of it has mainly to do with such things as cyborgs and the new "cyberpunk" fiction of William Gibson and his confreres, which I resist as I resist most science fiction, as being artistically thin, as a rule, however occasionally ingenious. But Hayles is surely correct when she writes that "the denaturing process arouses intense ambivalence, especially as it spreads to envelop the human."

> Language, context, and time are essential components of human experience ... [whereas] the human is a construction logically prior to all three, for it defines the grounds of experience itself.* If denaturing the human can sweep away more of the detritus of the past than any of the other postmodern deconstructions, it can also remove taboos and safeguards that are stays, however fragile, against the destruction of the human race. What will happen to the movement for human rights when the human is regarded as a construction like any other? Such concerns illustrate why, at the heart of virtually all postmodernisms, one finds a divided impulse.

That said, Hayles concludes her study by applying Lyotard's postmodern "incredulity toward metanarratives" to her own narrative of denaturing and to narrative itself, asking rhetorically,

---

*Which, we might recall here, is the Aristotelian "subject of literature."

What are the essential components of narrative construction, if not
language, context, time, and the human? The denaturing of experience, in other words, constitutes a cultural metanarrative; and its
peculiar property is to imply incredulity not just toward other
metanarratives but toward narrative as a form of representation. It
thus implies its own deconstruction.

That seems to me to be reasonably said, particularly if we follow my advice and substitute "skepticism" for "incredulity."
What sort of narrative fiction, for example, might one write out
of a fundamental postmodern skepticism toward narrative itself?
"In a fully denatured narrative," Hayles argues, "one would
expect the language to be self-referential; the context to be self-
consciously created, perhaps by the splicing together of disparate
contexts; the narrative progression to be advanced through the
evolution of underlying structures rather than through chronological time; and the characters to be constructed so as to expose their
nature as constructions." As a working Postmodernist literary
aesthetic, that certainly sounds close to the mark, although it
leaves out a few things that I regard as essential. It also sounds a
lot like Rabelais, Sterne, Diderot, and company, and Hayles (unlike Lyotard) wisely acknowledges that Postmodernist texts have
no monopoly on these literary strategies. "What could be more
self-referential than the end of *A Midsummer Night's Dream*," she
asks, "or more effective at representing the denatured human than
Frankenstein?" What makes a text postmodern (and, I would add,
what makes it Postmodernist as well) is not the above-mentioned
literary strategies in isolation, but rather "their connection
through complex feedback loops with postmodernism as a cultural dominant. Other times have had glimpses of what it would
mean to live in a denatured world. But never before have such
strong feedback loops among culture, theory, and technology
brought it so close to being a reality."

To this I say Brava, Professor Hayles — even before we examine (somewhere down the road) how she fits chaos theory into her
postmodern Weltanschauung and how the Romantic arabesque
can be said to bear upon both.

*   *   *

I now return briefly to the overall subject of these Stuttgart seminars, "the end of postmodernism," and to my own position on these matters as a working writer.

As to the former: Whether or not Hayles's apocalyptical "denaturing of the human" comes to pass — and I for one profoundly hope and almost believe that it will not — there is no reason to doubt that the experience of being human will continue to be *refigured* by changes in technology, as it has been being refigured dramatically ever since the industrial revolution, and that this refiguration will be reflected in — even anticipated by — whatever passes for art in the next century (to look no farther). Even the "denaturing of time" will not prevent our artistic successors from doing things rather differently from the way we've done them, and therefore what we call Postmodernist literature, for example, will by no means prove to be the last word. On the subject of the future of literature as a medium of art and entertainment I'll have my say another time* — but I do not doubt that by the year 2030, let's say, when I turn one hundred, we won't be calling what we do Postmodernist. The ending of this century and of the millenium has already prompted so many "endgames" — the end of history, the end of nature, the end of Western linear time that we heard Octavio Paz speak of earlier — that 2000 seems an appropriate target date for winding up Postmodernism as a cultural and aesthetic dominant, just as 1950 or thereabouts was a historically tidy date for bidding auf Wiedersehen to High Modernism.

What's more, for writers "like myself" and of my approximate age, whose product has been classified over the decades as existentialist, black humorist, fabulist, and now Postmodernist, it wouldn't surprise me if that last term turns out to be the one we're stuck with in the history books, if there continue to be such things as history and history books. I here report that that prospect is quite okay by me. I have never resisted the term "Postmodernist"; indeed, QED, I have, if not quite embraced it, at least accepted it and attempted to understand how it applies to what I've done and what I'm doing in my daily practice. I have never written anything because it was the Postmodernist thing to write; I've written what

---

*See this collection's concluding Friday-piece: "Inconclusion: The Novel in the Next Century."

I've written because I have seen fit to do so, whereafter others (myself more or less included) have seen fit to classify the product as Postmodernist. In many respects, I think, that adjective describes my output better than those earlier classifications did, and so if it turns out that I am too far along in my curriculum vitae to get to be called a post-Postmodernist or whatever in my old age, I am quite prepared to shrug my shoulders and get on with the story.

Because (to conclude) while I know that there is a feedback loop between my thinking about postmodern culture and Postmodernist aesthetics and my practice of writing fiction — a "coaxial esemplasy," each shaping the other — I continue to affirm the primacy of the work. Following Professor Hayles's Postmodernist literary aesthetic might well make a work Postmodernist, but it won't ipso facto make it wonderful, and for me, as you have heard,* the important thing is that it be wonderful. Can it be wonderful (Donald Barthelme once asked†) even if it drags along after it "the burnt-out boxcars of a dead aesthetic"? Maybe so, maybe not. But I am convinced that blockbustingly wonderful novels, for instance, can influence literary fashion at least as much as literary fashion influences more routine specimens of the genre. I would contend that James Joyce affected literary Modernism at least as much as Modernism affected Joyce, and that the Postmodernist novel has been influenced more by the example of Gabriel García Márquez than he has been influenced by Postmodernist literary theory. Rousseau and Goethe don't owe nearly as much to Romanticism as Romanticism owes to them. The individual terrific writer, the individual terrific work, is the main thing. The labels are neither meaningless nor unnecessary; but by whatever name we label it, on with the story.

*E.g., in "Postmodernism Revisited."
†In his 1985 *Georgia Review* essay, "Not-Knowing."

3. The Arabesque

NOW THAT WE have successfully clarified for all time the concepts of postmodern culture and Postmodernist art, let's do the same for the idea of the arabesque — first in its original sense, then as it enters Western literary thinking by way of the German Romantics (especially Friedrich von Schlegel), and finally as it bears upon at least one variety of Postmodernist fiction.

In its oldest sense, as G. R. Thompson reminds us,* the term refers to an Arabo-Oriental tradition of figuration that predates Islam (Professor Michael Craig Hillmann, a leading American authority on this subject, estimates the tradition to be three thousand years old). The root meaning of the term is a style of design and ornament most commonly associated with, but not confined to, the "East"; but as Professor Thompson points out, "What 'the East' means in this context is not simple." As everybody knows who has had dealings with a rug dealer, carpets are often called "Persian" and "Arabesque" even if the design inspirations originate outside the borders of Iran, as far away as China and India — and it's worth establishing at once that the Persians themselves have not been innocent of this sort of "Orientalizing": The mise-en-scène of the Persian frame story of *The Arabian Nights* is neither Persia nor Arabia, but "the Islands of India and China." In the Islamic world, says Professor Thompson,

> ... the concept of later arabesque design applies as well to wall decorations on mosques, the design of mosques themselves, the

*In the monograph aforecited. All subsequent quotations from Thompson in these lectures are likewise from that monograph.

aspect (especially the skyline) of Islamic cities as viewed through
Western eyes, a style of illuminations and other graphic design in
Eastern and Western books and manuscripts from the Middle Ages
and the Renaissance through the 19th century, medieval and Re-
naissance oil paintings, and charcoal and pen-and-ink drawings.
"Arabesque" as geometric design also applies to ballet. . . .

But the basic pattern symbolism that we call arabesque evidently originates with ancient weaving, and it might be worthwhile to listen to Professor Hillmann's review of this subject*
while bearing in mind the literary parallels that intrigued Friedrich
von Schlegel and company at the turn of the eighteenth/nineteenth
centuries.

The fundamental subject matter of "Persian" carpets, Hillmann
tells us, from the most naturalistic to the most geometric, is generally floral. The Islamic prohibition against reproducing natural
forms in graphic art did not originate, but served to reinforce, a
long-established "Arabic" development of "highly intricate patterns of geometric designs (floral or otherwise) involving struc-
turally repeated, symmetrically developed lines, loops, concentric
and interpenetrating curvilinear, triangular, rectilinear, and quincunxial structures."

> An often repeated version of the latter pattern is the interlineated
> *quincunx*, a figure with five points of reference, four outer points
> forming a square or parallelogram, the fifth point in the center [e.g.,
> the "five" card in any suit of a deck of cards, or the face of a die]. In
> these designs, often an outer rectilinear frame will be doubled or
> trebled, and grotesque† curvilinear patterns will decorate or in-
> habit, symmetrically, the four interior corners and envelop the vi-
> sual middlepoint.

The Ur-pattern of such carpets includes a main border or
frame, secondary borders that may interpenetrate the main border,
and a framed field with four corner elements and a central medallion (commonly with pendants top and bottom that to my eyes

*In his book *Persian Carpets* (Austin: U. Texas Press, 1984).
†The adjective as used here has nothing to do with Thompson's earlier-quoted
distinction between "grotesque" and "arabesque."

look a lot like Mandelbrot fractals: Compare Figures 1 and 2, below) in a quincunxial arrangement — the field itself often filled with proliferated ornamentation that interpenetrates both the borders and the medallion and corner elements:

Fig. 1: The "Ur-pattern" of Arabesque" carpet design:
in this instance, the Kerman pattern
(from Hillmann, reprinted in Thompson, op. cit.)

These formal properties are strongly suggestive of arabesque narrative as we'll hear it defined presently by Schlegel, and in at least some Romantic instances (Schlegel's *Lucinde*, Poe's *Pym*) they inform the architecture of the text on both the macroscale and the microscale.

"The act of weaving itself," says Hillmann (as quoted by Thompson, as quoted by me — another kind of double framing), may be "viewed as potentially symbolic," part of the "arabesque" sense of "the rhythm of life" in harmony with "cosmic rhythm. . . . The creative repetition that physically characterizes carpet-weaving . . . parallels such internal rhythms as inhalation-exhalation and biorhythm as well as exterior diurnal, tidal, seasonal, solar, and sidereal rhythms." He adds: "Mirroring an imperfect world, deliberate flaws are woven into Persian carpets to ward off the evil eye." My wife and I have amused ourselves by searching for such flaws

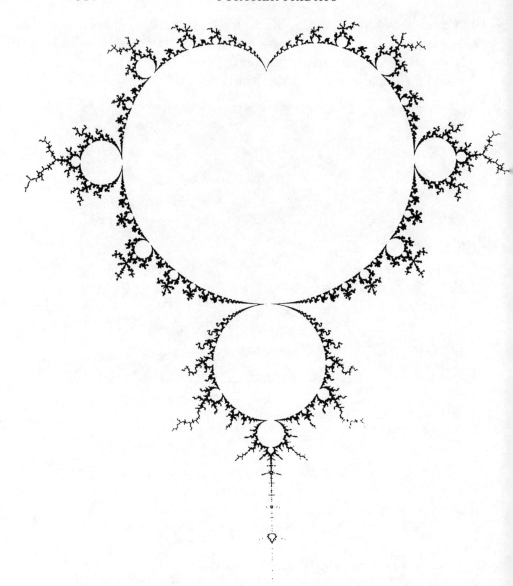

Fig. 2: A computer-generated Mandelbrot "fractal" (reprinted in Gleick, op. cit.)

in our own Oriental rugs — Tabrizes, Karajas, Bokharas — and we've found a number of them; but whether they were put there deliberately to ward off the evil eye I would not presume to say. The Navajo Indians in America traditionally did the same thing in their carpets and pottery (we remember also the Olympians' grudge against Arachne in Greek mythology), and certain unwittingly arabesque novelists such as myself have followed their example. Todd Andrews, the narrator of my first novel (*The Floating Opera*, 1956), is as ignorant of the Romantic arabesque as was I when I invented him, but he speaks of the Navajo tradition of programmed imperfection apropos of certain lacunae in his own narrative.

Hillmann goes on to say that "In some cases, the subject matter [of 'Persian' carpets] is itself the pattern," and Thompson properly adds that "sometimes, or perhaps always ultimately, the pattern is the subject matter — an effect apparently not lost on Schlegel in his formulation of literary arabesque." And just as the symbolism of the process of weaving is part of the meaning of the carpet, so in Romantic literary arabesque (and in a fair amount of Modernist and Postmodernist fiction) the process of writing or narrating becomes a significant feature of the content, as is the case with such precursors as *The 1001 Nights*, *Don Quixote*, and *Tristram Shandy*.

Here is more on the elements of arabesque carpet design, from the same sources. Writes Thompson:

> Within the double or infinite implicature of the *quincunx* exists the archetypal arabesque leaf, symbol of the garden, earthly symbol of paradise — or of a *glimpse* of paradise through the *gateway* to paradise. The basic symbol is repeated within repeated patterns within repeated borders to suggest infinity [another echo of Mandelbrot's fractal geometry]. [The] question of the function and symbolism of borders in such designs gets to the heart of East/West differences in perception; in addition, such "ambiguous" framing suggests a central concept of Friedrich Schlegel's arabesque. Put simply, the question is, Are borders limiting or limitless?

And Hillmann cites a tradition in Turkish carpet design, dating back at least to the thirteenth century, of regarding the border not as circumscribing a finite field but as framing a detail of "the infinite": When the border cuts through single motifs of the central field, he declares, it implies that the field is to be imagined as endless. Fractal geometry, needless to say, affords much more dazzling instances of interplay between finite and infinite: With such a figure as the Koch snowflake, e.g., it is literally the case that a finite area is surrounded by an infinitely long border:

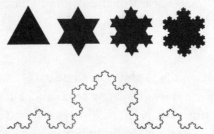

Fig. 3: "Snowflake" generated through the first several of a potentially infinite series of algorithmic iterations called the Koch curve, after the Swedish mathematician who first described it in 1904 (reprinted in Gleick, op. cit.)

Contrariwise, another fractal figure called the Sierpiński carpet has a finite border enclosing an infinity of squares, while its three-dimensional counterpart, the Menger sponge, has an infinite surface area enclosing zero volume:

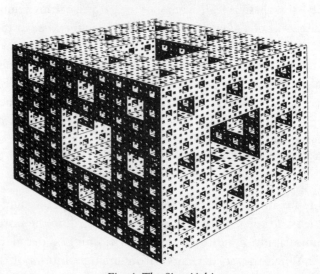

Fig. 4: The Sierpiński
carpet and the Menger
sponge (Gleick, op. cit.)

One wonders what literary use Schlegel might have made of such high-tech figures.

Thompson winds up his discussion of arabesque figuration by remarking that the basic Arabic patterns of architectural decoration and carpets reflect both "traditional Islamic aversion to the representation of animal forms and human figures" and also "the denaturalization of nature" (a phrase reminiscent of N. Katherine Hayles) —

> that is, the attempt to represent the supernatural by abstracting natural forms into geometrical designs that reveal the mind of God. Into this rarefied void the observer also dissolves. Self disappears into the great Void. . . .

The secular literary analogue to this dissolution, I suppose, is the commingling of the authorial writing self into the written self, and — in Schlegel and in others — the commingling of both writing and written selves and the text. I am reminded of Octavio Paz's observation that Tantric art on the one hand and Surrealist art and "happenings" on the other are analogs to "the old Romantic dream of erasing the boundaries between life and poetry" — or better, between life and art.

A second "Arab" source of the arabesque, Thompson reminds us, is the collections of tales and poems introduced to the West at the end of the seventeenth century from Arabic-speaking countries of the Middle East, notably the *Rubáiyát* of Omar Khayyám and *Kitab Alf Laylah Wah Laylah*, the Book of a Thousand Nights and a Night (whose frame-story dates from thirteenth-century Persia, while the stories framed date from the eighth to the sixteenth centuries and come from all over "the East"). Antoine Galland's multivolume French translation appeared between 1704 and 1712, was immensely popular, and generated a flood of "orientalism" through the rest of the eighteenth century and into the nineteenth: a craze for fiction and poetry with "Eastern" locales, such as Byron's *Turkish Tales* and Thomas Moore's *Alciphron* and *Lalla Rookh*, down to Kipling's *Gunga Din*. For the German Romantics, however, and for Western literary *theory* as opposed to popular literary fashion, the significant European appropriation from Arabo-Oriental literature and art history is not subject matter but design: "arabesque" in the sense of elaborately and/or subtly *framed* design. On this matter, I shall quote Professor Thompson at some length:

> The framing of frames [as in "Persian" carpets and Scheherazade's tales within tales within tales] suggests pure design; and the arabesque became the norm of a "pure" standard of beauty for Immanuel Kant: "abstract design," structures and patterns with no "inherent meaning." . . . By analogy to a sense of elaborately symmetrical yet open-ended design, "arabesque" as a European literary term came to indicate deliberate inconsistencies in the handling of narrative frames and . . . intricate ironic interrelationships among many tales within a frame or a series of nested frames.
>
> In the German romantic period in particular, Schlegel, Novalis, and others appropriated the term "arabesque" to indicate an intricate geometric or abstract narrative design into which incongruity in detail and antithesis in character and structure are consciously insinuated. In the arabesque, the relationship between a framing narrative and one or more story strands severely strains or calls into question overt narrative illusion, which may be further undermined through involuted narrative conventions, complex digressions, disruptions or incongruities, and the blurring of levels of narrative reality. The writer of arabesque calls attention to the narrativity of the text, the fiction of its mimesis, the artifice of its conventions, and then frequently turns all these conventions on their heads, beginning at the end or in the middle, or failing to end the narrative in the expected way. . . . Taking as his supreme examples the novels of Sterne, Diderot's *Jacques le fataliste*, and (with reservations) the novels of "Jean Paul" [Johann Paul Friedrich Richter], Schlegel uses the term "arabesque" to denote a *form* characterized by involutions, complex and seemingly aimless digression, and wandering back and forth between temporal and spatial settings [N. Katherine Hayles's "denaturing of context"] as well as between levels of narrative reality.

Before proceeding with the Schlegelian arabesque, I want to put in a kind word here for the Western tradition of "Orientalism," a

tradition whose ramifications have been most authoritatively doc-
umented by Edward W. Said of Columbia University.* More or
less originating as a spin-off from the spice and silk trade, enhanced by such almost legendary adventurers as Marco Polo in the
thirteenth century and Christopher Columbus in the late fifteenth,
and potentiated from the sixteenth through the twentieth centuries
by European colonialism, the ongoing fascination of Western
artists and their audiences with the exotic "East" is an impressive
and ambivalent phenomenon indeed, whose artistic provenance
Said traces as far back as the oldest extant Athenian play, Aeschylus's
The Persians. Said's real subject, and the focus of his own ambivalence, is Orientalism as an academic discipline all too often allied,
consciously or unconsciously, with the power structures of European colonialism. However much he deplores that colonialism,
and whatever his reservations about the patronizing or politically debatable aspects of academic Orientalism, he has no real
quarrel with the artistic product of this tradition: Ingres's and
Matisse's odalisques, Verdi's *Aida*, Puccini's *Madama Butterfly*,
Rimsky-Korsakov's *Scheherazade* — the list is endless, and Said
does not much concern himself with it, particularly in the nonliter-
ary arts. He acknowledges, moreover, that Orientalism is but one
manifestation of a more general sympathetic curiosity on the part
of the arts of one time and place concerning the arts of another:†
Think of all the polonaises, schottisches, danses russes, and the
like in Western music; think of Shakespeare's "Italy of the heart"
and of the Renaissance and post-Renaissance fascination with
"the glory that was Greece and the grandeur that was Rome."
Note too the European "Americanism" analogous to Orientalism
and Hellenism: Rousseau's noble savage, Karl May's cowboy-and-
Indian novels, Puccini's *Girl of the Golden West*, and the later Italian "spaghetti western" movies. I have noted already one example
of Middle Eastern "Orientalism" — the frame-story of the *Kitab
Alf Laylah Wah Laylah* — and I'm sure there are many others.
I note as well the interesting though less pervasive countertra-
dition of "Occidentalism," from Japanese "Impressionism" (and

---

*In *Orientalism* (NY: Putnam, 1978).
†"There is nothing especially controversial or reprehensible," he grants *(Orientalism*, p. 60), "about such domestications of the exotic; they take place between
all cultures, certainly, and between all men."

curious renderings of us *gaijin*) to the current Japanese fashion for "American" T-shirt inscriptions (frequently quite mysterious to us Americans) and for more or less English automobile names, often unpronounceable by many Japanese themselves (Langley, Corolla — spelled out in Roman-alphabetical characters rather than Japanese, even on cars made in Japan for domestic sale). In short, such Western Orientalisms as the Romantic arabesque may have their patronizing or otherwise questionable aspects, but they may also be manifestations of innocent curiosity, sympathy, and admiration.

Back to Friedrich von Schlegel: He was notably preoccupied (toward the very end of the eighteenth century) with "Romantic irony" in general and with the genre of the *Roman* and the sub-genre of the *Arabeske* in particular as models of Romantic values. Whole books have been written about Schlegel's thinking on each of these several items; here is my quick amateur impression of their relevance to our topic:

The "Romantic irony" of life experience, for Schlegel, I understand to be centered in the perception that "truth" changes "from experience to experience and that wisdom depends on a recognition of the fickleness of truth."* In literature, therefore, Romantic irony characteristically (and not surprisingly) involves one or another sort of *quest*: instinctive, unconscious, intellectual, philosophical, mystical — including the author's search for himself and for the realization of his work in progress. The processes of living and writing become interwoven; there is a "coaxial esemplasy" between the writing self and the written self, as in Escher's famous drawing of a hand with a pen drawing the hand with a pen that draws and is drawn by it. "Irony," Schlegel remarks, "is a permanent *parabasis*" (an ongoing aside, of the chorus to the audience or the poet to the reader). Elsewhere (*Ideas*, #69) he declares, "Irony is the clear consciousness of eternal agility, of an infinitely teeming chaos."

In its literary manifestation, Romantic irony informs both the *Roman* as Schlegel conceives it and *die Arabeske*. My impression

---

*I'm quoting the *Columbia Encyclopedia*.

is that for Schlegel, the *Roman* comprises far more than Randall Jarrell's famous definition of the novel: "a prose fiction of a certain length that has something wrong with it." The Schlegelian *Roman* is a genre that comprises all other genres; an anti-generic genre made coherent by *Witz* (of which *die Arabeske* is an expression). The *Roman*, says Schlegel (in his "Brief über den Roman"; section three of the *Gespräch über die Poesie*) "*ist ein romantisches Buch*." One is to understand this proposition not as a tautology, but as a paradox comprehensible by *Witz* — that aspect of Romantic irony that Schlegel returns to again and again in his writings. *Witz*, I gather, is considerably more than cleverness; it is the faculty of imagination that perceives similarities and makes connections even among disparate and hidden things. It is what controls the "controlled indeterminacy" of the arabesque: the "eternal agility" that presides over, or at least deals with, "infinitely teeming chaos."

Both Romantic irony and the arabesque, Thompson observes, are centered on the "playful treatment of artistic form; . . . the discussion of the work or form or medium along with the actual object of portrayal; [and, indeed, in extreme instances, the portraying of the] form or the medium *instead* of the object." The arabesque *Roman*, as has been mentioned already, characteristically involves the rupture of illusion by references in the text to its author, to the process of writing, and so forth; the transgression of the boundary between the reality of reader and author and the reality of the characters and world of the text; the privileging of the "*interplay* between and among norms, forms, voices, themes, and languages. . . ." Authorial self-reference in the Schlegelian arabesque is particularly problematical because the author behind the text also *is* the text, as the Logos is *with* God and *is* God. "God speaks Himself into existence, the world is the ultimate fiction; the self is never single and unified; single selfness is no more than a (sometimes) useful fiction, an *Als Ob*" (Thompson).

All of these so-familiar notions, the very stock-in-trade of late-twentieth-century "metafiction," are involved in Schlegel's concept of the arabesque *Roman*. Thompson concludes: "To generate 'dialogue' between the 'two romanticisms' — the light and the dark, the positive and the negative, and the redoubled binary within each of positive and negative — is in part the function of the arabesque as a form."

Before we have a look at Schlegel's *practice* of the literary arabesque, including his fascination with its aspects of constrained or harmonious chaos, it may be well to recall Thompson's useful distinction between "arabesque" and "grotesque," at least as literary modes: Both characteristically involve coexisting elements of the sinister, the fearful, the awesome, the sublime, the beautiful, the ugly, the positive, the negative, the serious, the humorous, the ironic, the indeterminate. But the indeterminacy of the arabesque is framed, constrained, ordered, and relative. There may be "wild" cards in the deck of the arabesque, but there are rules to the game. I think of Dioneo's special privilege in Boccaccio's *Decameron*: He takes his narrative turn with the rest, but need not speak to the topic of the day. Dioneo is Boccaccio's programmed relief from the constraints of his own narrative program.

On now to chaos. I understand from Professor Thompson that the term implies for Friedrich von Schlegel not disorder but a unity pre-existing the cosmos, which is to say, the world and its dichotomies. That is not yet quite the *"gebildetes künstliches Chaos"* of the Schlegelian arabesque on the one hand, nor on the other the undifferentiated pre-cosmos of Hesiod's *Theogony* — and in fact, in his 1799 novel *Lucinde*, at least (Schlegel's only novel, as *Pym* was Edgar Poe's only novel), I find the author's deployment of the term not altogether consistent. Sometimes Schlegel uses it in the traditional, "Hesiodic" sense of mere anarchical disorder; at other times he uses it in the sense of an impressive and perhaps fecund though not orderly disorder, the breeding-ground of cosmic order; and occasionally he uses it in the "arabesque" sense of an orderly disorder that is an end in itself, not the vestibule to something else.* On page 76 of the U.S. edition of *Lucinde*, for example,† the narrator, Julius, remarks to

---

*Among contemporary chaos theorists, too, as shall be seen, the term is deployed in more than one sense.
†Minneapolis: U. Minnesota Press, 1971.

Lucinde, "Society is a chaos that only wit can organize and bring into harmony." In passages like this, it isn't clear whether Schlegel is contrasting chaos with anti-chaos or anarchical chaos with a harmonized chaos. Similarly, speaking of the power of the written word, Julius declares: "It is the letter with which the irresistible will of that great magician, Fantasy, touches the sublime chaos of all-encompassing nature . . . and calls the infinite word to light, the word that is an image and a mirror of the divine spirit, and that mortals call the universe." (p. 58)

Here the chaos is sublime, all-encompassing, and natural, though not yet either *gebildetes* or *künstliches*, and the universe that the infinite word calls to light seems pretty clearly to be the traditional cosmos, not a structured chaos.*

"I could go on like this," says Schlegel's Julius, and indeed he does, declaring for example on page 106 that "Through the magic of joy, the great chaos of conflicting forms dissolves into a harmonious sea of forgetfulness." Again, it's not clear whether that harmonious sea is a *gebildetes Chaos* or an anti-chaos, and both terms of the proposition are ambivalent: The chaos of conflicting forms is called "great," and the harmony that the magic of joy works upon it is not a *re*solution, but a *dis*solution. To Lucinde again (Lucinde the woman, in this instance, not *Lucinde* the work in progress), Julius writes: "You too, my dear friend, should cast off all remnants of false shame, just as I've often torn off your hateful clothes and strewn them all over in a lovely chaos" (52). No structure there, that I can see; just libido.

Elsewhere in the novel, however, Schlegel/Julius comes closer to the "arabesque" sense of our term. Of another of his lovers, Juliane, Julius observes (63) that she has "as much poetry in her as she does love, as much enthusiasm as wit; but each quality is too isolated in her and so she will sometimes react with feminine terror to the daring chaos of this work" — a chaos in which, we

---

*Likewise in #71 of the *Ideas*: "Confusion is chaotic only when it can give rise to a new world." Here, indeed, Schlegel seems to imply *three* states of affairs: mere "confusion," which resembles the traditional notion of chaos; "chaotic confusion," which is pregnant with the possibility of order; and "a new world," which sounds to me more like cosmos than like *gebildetes Chaos*.

presume, those four disparate qualities are harmoniously conjoined. Even more to our point, Julius declares early in the novel: "I want to attempt to shape raw chance and mold it to the purpose. No purpose, however, is more purposeful for myself and for this work, . . . for its own structure, than to destroy at the outset all that part we call 'order,' remove it, and claim explicitly . . . the right to a charming confusion" (45).

Note that his target is not order itself, but what we commonly *call* order. Later in the same passage, Julius affirms that the work in progress "should and must achieve . . . the re-creation and integration of the most beautiful chaos of sublime harmonies and fascinating pleasures." There, I would say, is a mini-manifesto of the Romantic arabesque.

Inasmuch as it is in *Lucinde* that Schlegel makes his most sustained attempt to practice his preachments about the arabesque, G. R. Thompson's excellent summary-analysis of the novel is worth quoting almost in full:

> . . . *Lucinde* (1799) [is] a "static" narrative about how the artistic mind conceptualizes itself as it writes the "romantic" book about composite characters who are all part of the author's love object. This once famous "novel" about "free love" is neither a novel in the conventional sense nor about free love as conventionally understood. It symmetrically yet elliptically exfoliates its essay-narratives, attempting to create an arabesque of abstract design exemplifying the structure of the *Mittelpunkt*.
>
> Like Melville's *The Confidence-Man*, Schlegel's *Lucinde* tells no chronologically ordered linear "story"; and it represents mental reflections rather than actions outside the mind (that is, what were traditionally called "events"). In the middle chapter (chap. 7) is a "confessional" *Bildungsroman* that traces the development of the character Julius up to the point where the novel "begins" six chapters earlier. On either side of the central bildungsroman are six chapters, each in a different literary form, each a permutation on the theme of love. Julius is the fictive author of the book, who in an early chapter announces that a progressively unfolding chronological narration is unsuitable for his purposes; he will instead give the reader a chain of connection not necessarily visibly complete, but

rather fragments of a whole to be pieced together in the mind of the reader.

In the first half, Julius describes a series of sexual or love encounters with six different women, all of whom constitute the figure or persona of Lucinde, who is also the book *Lucinde* created by the author-character Julius, whose love is Lucinde, the composite person and the composite text *Lucinde*. This complex doubling is prefigured by a portrait of Wilhelmina in chapter 3, who, Julius says, is "the novel itself." In chapter 4, called an "allegory," Julius gives a humorous account of how the novel *Lucinde* came to be written. *Witz* shows to the writer four figures at a crossroads, representing the four novels he could "now" (at this very point) write by going off in one direction or another in his narrative.

And so Schlegel's *Roman* spins out, creating a quincunxial arabesque of abstract symmetrical design around a *Mittelpunkt* from multi-leveled, multi-toned, multiply framed "narratives" and "narrative-essays" that mutually reflect, refract, and re-reflect one upon the other. The narrative movement is like being lost in a funhouse, knowing that you are in a labyrinth, journeying "ever inward," participating in, yet "soaring" above all Chaos — seeing self-replications as in an "endless succession of mirrors."*

Clearly, whatever its weaknesses as a novel and however "chaotic" we may find Julius's frequent allusions to chaos, Schlegel's "arabesque romance" is more than just the "charming confusion" that Julius claims a right to or the incidentally "lovely chaos" of Lucinde's discarded clothes when the narrator strips her. It is decidedly a *"gebildetes künstliches Chaos"* — and a fascinating work of literature (as is Poe's failed novel *Pym*), though scarcely to be compared with such of its models as *Tristram Shandy* and *Jacques le fataliste*, or such of its late-nineteenth-century successors as Machado de Assis's *Braz Cubas* or *Dom Casmurro*. In his *Critical Fragments* (#89) Schlegel asks rhetorically, "Isn't it unnecessary to write more than one novel, unless the artist has become a new man?" I would reply that if the novelist is

---

*Those concluding images (all except the funhouse) are Schlegel's own, from his *Athenäumsfragment* #116 — the text that Jean-François Lyotard called "modernist" in contrast to the "postmodernist" Montaigne. Chaos everywhere.

Herr Schlegel, the answer to that question is probably yes. Even given the Romantic presuppositions of the question (e.g., that the purpose of a novel is to express the full sensibility of its author), I would regard it as impertinent — except that Schlegel himself prudently undermines his own question in the next sentence of the same fragment: "It is obvious that frequently all the novels of a particular author belong together and in a sense make up only one novel." If *that's* what he means, then I have no objection.

Thus concludes my amateur review of the arabesque tradition in general and, in particular, Friedrich von Schlegel's application of it to literary theory and practice. Lyotard classifies the *Athenaeum Fragments* as (proto)modernist, and in form they certainly are, although they're even more quintessentially Romantic: a deliberate less-than-wholeness, like the torsos of Romantic sculpture and the "broken" columns of Romantic landscape architecture — an example of medium-as-message that reminds me of Donald Barthelme's famous one-liner (in his story "See the Moon?"), "The fragment is the only literary form I trust." But the *substance* of Schlegel's remarks on *der Roman* and *die Arabeske*, while also first and foremost quintessentially Romantic, seems to me to have more affinity with Postmodernist than with Modernist fiction — at least as I use the term "Postmodernist." There is a popular misconception of the Romantics as rebelling against all formal constraints in favor of untrammeled freedom (as in their fondness for "wild" gardens around those "broken" columns), and indeed we have heard Schlegel's Julius explicitly rejecting "all that . . . we call 'order'"in his *Lucinde* project. But it is clear that in fact he and his creator as well have a veritable passion for form — in Wallace Stevens's famous phrasing,* a "rage for order"— and that what they're rejecting is only certain *conventions* of order and form. I prefer to think of Schlegel as a "romantic formalist" — a term that I apply to myself as well — and I will venture to say that the principal difference between Romantic romantic formalism and Postmodernist romantic formalism is that the latter, more than the for-

*In the poem "The Idea of Order at Key West."

mer, inclines to the ironic (though impassioned) reorchestration of older conventions — including the classical and the neoclassical — rather than to their rejection in favor of "new" forms.

It remains for us now to add contemporary chaos theory to this goulash of Postmodernism and the Romantic arabesque — and then to see whether the admixture provokes a "So what?" or an "Ah, so!"

4. Chaos Theory: Postmod Science, Literary Model

WE HAVE HEARD Friedrich von Schlegel's Julius (and Schlegel himself) ruminating in his Romantic-fragmentary way — and not always consistently — about a sort of chaos different from mere anarchy and entropy: a *gebildetes Chaos* that, in the mode of the literary arabesque, may become a *künstliches Chaos* as well. And in my introductory remarks to these lectures I quoted no less an authority than Benoit B. Mandelbrot of IBM, the formulator of the Mandelbrot set and the father of fractal geometry, disapproving of the "Euclidean" monoscale of Bauhaus Modernism in contrast to the more satisfying "scalelessness," or multiscalarity, of the Paris Opera. The text of my present sermon is an observation by the Belgian/French mathematical physicist David Ruelle, as quoted by James Gleick in his popular account of chaos theory.* Speaking of the aesthetic appeal of what the chaologists call "Strange Attractors" — those phenomena in mathematical "phase-space" that give rise to such characteristic patterns of nonlinear dynamics as those in Figures 5 and 6 (below) — Ruelle says: "These systems of curves, these clouds of points suggest sometimes fireworks or galaxies, sometimes strange and disquieting vegetal proliferations. A realm lies there of forms to explore, and harmonies to discover."

My proposal is that the Romantic arabesque is one prefiguration of this realm, and that at least some Postmodernist writers and critics may find in chaology a ground metaphor (the postmodern term would be "paradigm," I suppose) as suggestive for them as "Persian" carpet design and "Eastern" frame-tale collections

---

Chaos: Making a New Science, aforecited.

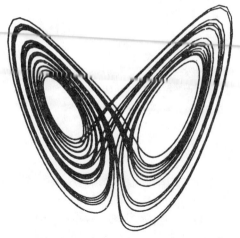

Fig. 5: The Lorenz attractor (Herbert Hethcote)

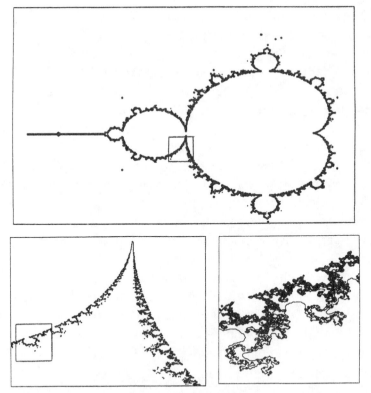

Fig. 6: A Mandelbrot set with progressively greater magnifications of boxed areas to show self-similarity reiterating toward infinity (Nural Akchurin)

were for Schlegel and his comrades. I'll attempt to illustrate each point I make about chaos theory with some literary analogue.

Nonlinearity and *constrained indeterminacy* strike me as the two most obvious links between and among the four terms that we're considering: arabesque design, the Romantic arabesque *Roman* (and its predecessors and successors), the Postmodernist novel, and chaos theory — although, as we shall see, "nonlinearity" can be an equivocal term in this context. To make a proper arabesque quincunx we need a fifth item; the one that I shall nominate is the very recent theory (it dates from 1987, much more recent than chaos theory in general) of the physicists Per Bak, Kurt Wiesenfeld, and Chao Tang called "self-organized criticality," or "weak chaos." I'm not sure which of these five elements deserves the honor of being the *Mittelpunkt* of our quincunx, the medallion of our arabesque carpet.

Now: I am a faithful reader both of *Scientific American* and of *Sciences*, the periodical of the New York Academy of Science; moreover, one of my grown children is a publishing neuroscientist and another is a designer of computer software. But I myself am a mere curious tourist in the lands of science and mathematics — even more so than in the land of literary theory. I visit science in the same spirit in which Coleridge attended the chemistry lectures of Sir Humphry Davy, "to renew my stock of metaphors." (In Coleridge and Schlegel's time, I gather, the connection between science and literature was more coaxial than it is today; while Coleridge was renewing his stock of metaphors and Keats was writing poems in his anatomy classes, Sir Humphry Davy was composing sonnets of his own.) Because the subject of chaology *is* highly technical, and because James Gleick's book does such a fine job both of making it understandable and of narrating its history, I propose to make the quickest possible review of those aspects of chaos theory that seem most pertinent to our concerns and then to get on with the consideration of what their pertinence is.* The aspects that I have in mind include the general nature of chaotic sys-

---

*Neither of my scientific/mathematical sons, by the way, uses the term "chaos theory" except when talking to civilians like me or — as N. Katherine Hayles says about workers in this discipline — when they're applying for research grants. Among themselves, they prefer the less glamorous term "nonlinear dynamics," or simply "complexity theory."

tems, the postmodernity of chaos theory, and the conflicting or at least contrary emphases of the two main branches of chaos theory (what some people call the "order-out-of-chaos" branch and the "strange-attractor" branch); also the principle of self-similarity and that particular modification of chaos theory called "self-organized criticality."

As to the general nature of chaotic systems, or "complex" or "composite" systems, as they're sometimes called: Everybody agrees that they are *disordered* in the sense that, unlike linear systems, they are unpredictable, but ordered in the sense that they possess recursive symmetries that almost, but not quite, replicate themselves over time. In short, they are deterministic despite their unpredictability. N. Katherine Hayles (in *Chaos Bound*) lists five characteristics that such systems share:

First, they are *nonlinear*, in the sense that the magnitudes of causes and effects in such systems may be startlingly disproportionate. This is one aspect of the famous Butterfly Effect in meteorology and elsewhere: Edward Lorenz's half-serious supposition that the flutter of a butterfly's wings in the rain forests of Brazil might trigger tornadoes in Texas. It has also been called the Horseshoe-Nail Effect, after the proverbial loss of a kingdom for want of one horseshoe nail. One can readily cite otherwise conventional novels whose plots illustrate this nonlinear correlation of cause and effect: e.g., from contemporary American fiction, Thomas Rogers's *The Pursuit of Happiness* (1968) and Kurt Vonnegut's *Deadeye Dick* (1985), in both of which comparatively unremarkable "initial conditions" — an automobile accident, the idle firing of a bullet into the air — escalate to disproportionately large consequences, that disproportion being, indeed, the point of the story. In a recent *Scientific American* article cited by Hayles, it was estimated that if an effect as small as the gravitational pull of one electron at the edge of the galaxy is neglected in a predictive computer model, the trajectories of colliding billiard balls become unpredictable *within one minute.*

Second, the forms of chaotic systems are *complex* in a way that makes their measurement, for example, contingent on scale, as in fractal geometry. My memory is that Bertrand Russell, half a century ago, first remarked that the length of a coastline depends on the scale of its measurement — whether one measures around every little creek and cove, every rock, every grain of sand, every atom of every grain of sand. More recently that famous example has become associated with the Mandelbrot set, and I have learned that Russell must have been quoting his countryman Lewis Richardson, who wrote about the coastline problem in the 1920s.* Another way to put it is that nonlinear dynamics posits a qualitative difference, not merely a quantitative difference, between linear and complex systems. All narrative, I would venture, is "complex" in this respect; I have often pointed out to apprentice writers that the amount of narrative distance between any point A and point B — even if the two points are as apparently close as the character's picking up of a telephone and her saying hello — can be anything from zero to infinity, depending on the degree of "atomization" of the action, the interposition of digressions, the deployment of literary "freeze frame" effects, and so forth. Sterne's *Tristram Shandy* and Diderot's *Jacques le fataliste* illustrate this principle, as does such a contemporary specimen as Robert Pinget's *L'Inquisitoire* (1971).

Third (and following from the foregoing), in the study of "chaotic" systems the focus is shifted from individual units of the system to *recursive symmetries between scale levels*. Instead of trying to follow individual molecules in a turbulent flow, for example (as one might in a laminar flow), the nonlinear dynamicist models the flow as swirls within swirls within swirls, replicated (but never quite duplicated) over numerous scale levels, appreciative of the fact that even microscopic fluctuations at the coupling-points between scale levels can rapidly have macroscopic effects and send the chaotic system off in a new direction (a manifestation of the Butterfly Effect). I think of those several stories of Scheherazade's — stories within stories within stories, in some cases — in which she or one of her lower-scale "inside" narrators tells King Shahryar of innocent people under threat of imminent death, like herself, who postpone or are excused from their fate by beguiling their would-

---

*As acknowledged in the earlier Friday-piece "Ad Lib Libraries and the Coastline Measurement Problem."

be killer with stories. If the king happened to recognize and be displeased by the parallel, Scheherazade's own life story would take a radically different turn.

This delicate interrelationship among scale levels leads to a fourth characteristic of chaotic systems, abbreviated in English to "SDIC": their *sensitive dependence on initial conditions* — the first zillionth of a second of the big bang, for example, which affects the shape of the ensuing universe. It is like imagining that Scheherazade's sexual and narrative success on Night One of her 1001 affects not only her continuance (as it obviously does) but also the content and arrangement of her entire subsequent narrative and gynecological/obstetrical program (as it does not, except occasionally*). One sees, in any case, that "SDIC" applies rather strongly to the way some writers write — especially poets and short-story writers, whose first-articulated line really can have a strong determining effect on what follows. The narrator of Donald Barthelme's story "The Dolt"† concludes, "Endings are elusive, middles are nowhere to be found, but worst of all is to begin, to begin, to begin."

Finally (in Hayles's catalog of field-identification marks), complex systems share *feedback mechanisms* in which output loops back into the system as input. With this process, every writer is familiar; it is epitomized by E. M. Forster's famous obiter dictum "How can I tell what I think until I see what I say?" Thus, for example, I agree to come to the Stuttgart Seminars, and I choose the topic "Postmodernism, Chaos Theory, and the Arabesque" because I suspect that they bear upon one another meaningfully, but I am by no means sure what their interrelations are and what I think about them. So I make a few notes and I read a few books, and then I make further notes on what I read in those books, meanwhile going forward with a sort of novel-in-progress‡ about a man slightly older than myself, lost in the labyrinthine salt marshes of my native Maryland in the autumn of 1992 and unable to find his way out except by taking some long way around

---

*See "Don't Count on It: A Note on the Number of *The 1001 Nights*," in *The Friday Book*.
†Collected in *Sixty Stories* (NY: Putnam, 1981).
‡*Once Upon a Time: A Floating Opera* (1994).

through time and space. The Stuttgart prospect affects my thinking about this narrative, and vice versa, in a way that goes well beyond feedback loops to what I have called coaxial esemplasy; I understand that I am writing (and living) some sort of "chaotic arabesque" while preparing more material on that subject for Stuttgart than I had originally intended to do. A line from the poet Theodore Roethke becomes a refrain in my house: "I learn by going where I have to go" (from Roethke's villanelle "The Waking"). I come to understand intimately the double meaning of that line: "I learn where it is that I have to go by going there," and "By going where I have to go [e.g., to Stuttgart], I learn" — learn what it is that I'm going there for, and, to that extent, learn who the *I* is who's going there. Another way to put it (and to novelize it, as I attempted to do in *The Last Voyage of Somebody the Sailor* [1991]) is that the voyager is changed by the voyage, but the voyage is also changed by the voyager: dynamic feedback loops. Coaxial esemplasy.

Having pointed out these five characteristics that all "chaotic" systems share, Professor Hayles distinguishes between two branches of chaology; it appears that like Schlegel's Julius in his shifting moods, the workers in these two branches understand the word "chaos" in different senses. One branch of the field sees chaos as the precursor and partner of order rather than as its opposite and adversary, and focuses on the spontaneous emergence of self-organization from a chaos that in itself at least approaches pure randomness. In the language of the field, this branch of chaology concerns itself with the "dissipative structures that arise in systems far from equilibrium, where entropy production is high" (Hayles). The Belgian Ilya Prigogine, whose work in irreversible thermodynamics won him the 1977 Nobel Prize in physics, exemplifies for Hayles this approach to chaology; Prigogine's book on the subject is aptly titled *Order out of Chaos*. The other branch of the field — the "strange attractor" branch — concerns itself with finding the hidden order *within* chaotic systems. Quoting Hayles: "Whereas truly random systems show no discernible pattern when they are mapped into phase space, chaotic systems contract to a confined region and trace complex patterns within it." The world evidently contains a wide range of such systems, "from lynx fur returns to outbreaks of measles epidemics, from the rise and fall of the Nile to eye movements in schizophrenics." The study of such systems focuses on the "orderly descent into chaos [Hayles could just as well say "the descent into an orderly chaos"] rather than on the organized structures that emerge from chaos."

In Hayles's opinion, "the order-out-of-chaos branch has more philosophy than results, the strange-attractor branch more results than philosophy." I happen to believe that both varieties of chaology are of potential literary interest. The order-out-of-chaos approach, for instance, obviously applies to the way that poems and novels and Stuttgart Seminars and all sorts of other things come into existence. But it is the strange-attractor branch of chaology that strikes me as having more affinity with Postmodernism and the arabesque. When Hayles says, for example, "Almost but not quite repeating themselves, chaotic systems generate patterns of extreme complexity, in which areas of symmetry are intermixed with asymmetry down through all scales of magnification," she is describing the systems studied by Edward Lorenz, Michael Feigenbaum, and Benoit Mandelbrot — but her description also brings to mind arabesque carpet design, Friedrich von Schlegel's praise of self-similarity in Shakespeare, perhaps such a novel as Thomas Pynchon's *Gravity's Rainbow*, perhaps even my own most recent "arabesque," aforementioned.

One final observation from Hayles's *Chaos Bound*, having more to do with chaology's relation to postmodern culture than its relation to Postmodernist literature. Hayles's overall "narrative of postmodernism," as she herself calls it, is this:

> In the early years of this century, efforts were made in a variety of areas to construct unified field theories that would eliminate ambiguity and self-reference. These efforts failed; but the failures brought to light certain intrinsic limits to representation. Having swung as far as it could in the direction of closure, the pendulum began to swing the other way as people became interested in exploring the implications of ungrounded representation. At the same time that global networks of communications, finances, energy sources, weapons research, and so forth made human lives on the

planet more interdependent than they had ever been before, theoretical postmodernisms put forth urgent claims for fragmentation,
discontinuities, and local differences. Cultural postmodernism
arises from loops that build up between these seemingly divergent
trends.

She finds this divergence in chaos theory as well:

The science of chaos shares with other postmodernisms a deeply in-
grained ambivalence toward totalizing structures. On the one hand,
it celebrates the disorder that earlier scientists ignored or disdained,
seeing turbulent flow not as an obstacle to scientific progress but as
a great swirling river of information that rescues the world from
sterile repetition. On the other hand, it also shows that when one
focuses on the underlying recursive symmetries, the deep structures
underlying chaos can be revealed and analytical solutions can
sometimes be achieved. It is thus like other postmodernisms in that
it both resists and contributes to globalizing structures.

But she distinguishes chaology from certain other postmodernisms, such as deconstructionist literary theory, by pointing out
that chaos theorists "do not perceive themselves as creating chaos,
either through their discourse or through their representations.
They believe that they merely recognize what was always there but
not much noticed before. In other postmodernisms, it is not so
clear that chaos inheres in the system rather than [in] the theorist."
   I like the sound of that, but inasmuch as I know little about de-
constructionism, I cannot vouch for the validity of Hayles's observation.* I want to close my exposition (or self-exposure) by mildly
taking issue with something Hayles said a moment ago, and then
by turning to the fifth term of our quincunx, not mentioned by
Hayles or Gleick: "self-organized criticality," or "weak chaos."
   My quibble is with Hayles's characterization of theoretical
postmodernisms as "put[ing] forth urgent claims for fragmentation, discontinuities, and local differences." That may be quite

---

* "... since texts were not generally perceived to be chaotic before [the advent of]
deconstruction," she adds reasonably, "the burden of proof is on [the deconstruc-
tionist] to show that it is not she who creates the chaos she reveals." Amen.

true of postmod culture in general, but here as elsewhere the application to Postmodernist literature is more problematical. One might say of such Modernist monuments as James Joyce's *Ulysses* and *Finnegans Wake* that they are indeed efforts at a novelistic "global synthesis" akin to those in modern science as opposed to postmodern science. But the "fragmentation" and "discontinuity" that Hayles sees as the characteristic claims of "theoretical postmodernisms" seem to me to be field-identification marks more of Modernist than of Postmodernist art and literature, at least as I tried to formulate the distinction in my 1979 essay "The Literature of Replenishment" (and we remember Lyotard's characterization of Schlegel's *Athenaeum Fragments* as modernist). It was the Modernists, I declared in that Tübingen essay, "carrying the torch of Romanticism," who "taught us that linearity, rationality, consciousness, cause and effect, naive illusionism, transparent language, innocent anecdote, and middle-class moral conventions are not the whole story," and it is the Postmodernists (in my view) who remind us that "the contraries of these things [including fragmentation and discontinuity] are not the whole story either." I believed that in Tübingen in 1979; I continue to believe it here in Stuttgart in 1991.

My disagreement with Hayles on this matter must be one of those "local differences" that she finds characteristic of theoretical postmodernisms. At first glance it might seem to point to a larger discrepancy between chaos theory and Postmodernist art: namely, that chaotic systems are by definition nonlinear, whereas (in my view, and evidently in Jean-François Lyotard's as well) "nonlinearity" is at least as characteristic of Modernist as of Postmodernist narrative, for example, if not more so. But perhaps all we have here are two different senses of "nonlinearity": In chaology, it has to do with the disproportional relation of causes and effects; in fiction it has to do more with narrative straightforwardness. Ilya Prigogine's irreversible thermodynamics is nonlinear in the first sense but not in the second; the whole point of the "arrow of time" is that its movement is one-way. A better literary analogy is turbulent flow: As in *The 1001 Nights* and *The Ocean of Story* and *Tristram Shandy*, the local motion may be in any direction, even retrograde, but the net global narrative motion is forward, though far from *straight*forward. I believe that to be one reason why *Tristram Shandy* and *Jacques le fataliste* are more engaging than Schlegel's genuinely "static" novel *Lucinde*.

Now to the last of the cards that I want to put on our table in this ramble: *self-organized criticality*, as distinct from the self-organizing *systems* that Ilya Prigogine's branch of chaology concerns itself with as they arise spontaneously from "chaotic" randomness. What some later investigators have found (the Danish-born Per Bak and his colleagues, whom I mentioned earlier) is that large interactive systems may not only organize themselves into being but "organize themselves into a critical state in which a minor event starts a chain reaction that can lead to a catastrophe." I'm quoting an article on the subject by Per Bak and Kan Chen, from the January 1991 *Scientific American*, in which the authors go on to define the theory of self-organized criticality more specifically: ". . . many composite systems [among them, seismic faults, economic markets, ecosystems, snowfields on a mountainside] naturally evolve to a critical state in which a minor event starts a chain reaction that can affect any number of elements in the system." What is different here from René Thom's earlier catastrophe theory, for example, and from the general emphasis in chaology on the nonlinear relation of causes and effects, is this:

> Although composite systems produce more minor events than catastrophes, chain reactions of all sizes are an integral part of [their] dynamics. . . . [T]he mechanism that leads to minor events is the same one that leads to major events. Furthermore, composite systems never reach equilibrium but instead evolve from one metastable state to the next.

I hear echoes of Hegel and Marx in that description. "Self-organized criticality," the authors go on to maintain, "is a holistic theory":

> . . . the global features, such as the relative number of large and small events, do not depend on the microscopic mechanisms. Consequently, global features of the system cannot be understood by

analyzing the parts separately. To our knowledge, self-organized criticality is the only model or mathematical description that has led to a holistic theory for dynamic systems.

I cannot vouch for that proposition, although I believe that I understand it. From the scientific point of view, the important thing is the rigorous experiments and mathematical formulations generated by this theory of "weak chaos" — which differs from "full chaos" in that "Fully chaotic systems [such as the weather] are characterized by a time scale beyond which it is impossible to make predictions," whereas "weakly chaotic systems lack such a time scale and so allow long-term predictions. . . ."

The uncertainty [of weak systems] increases according to a power law rather than an exponential law. [Such] systems evolve on the border of chaos. [Their] behavior, called weak chaos, is a result [not only of their self-organization, but] of their self-organized criticality.

What interests me here as an amateur chaos-watcher is that the theory of self-organized criticality appears to bridge, or at least to narrow, the gap remarked by Hayles between the two branches of chaology: Per Bak's examples come as often from the order-out-of-chaos branch as from the strange-attractor or fractal-geometry branch of chaos theory. What interests me here as a professional novelist and an amateur thinker about narrative fiction is the possibilities that I sense in "self-organized criticality" and "weak chaos" as paradigms, if not for human life in general, then at least for the way many people live, and for certain aspects of narrative construction — as I shall now attempt to illustrate.

Way back in the early 1970s, when such forerunners of chaos theory as "systems theory" and "catastrophe theory" were just beginning to impinge on the sensibility of amateurs like myself, I formulated a half-serious definition of Aristotelian dramaturgy in the language of systems analysis (partly for the purpose of alarming my American writer-friend John Hawkes). *Plot*, I declared, can be rigorously described as "the incremental perturbation of an unstable homeostatic system and its catastrophic restoration to a complexified equilibrium." The "unstable homeostatic system" of this definition corresponds to what I call the dramatic "ground situation" in classical dramaturgy: a potentially volatile state of affairs antedating the present action of the story. Its "incremental perturbation" is of course the conventional dramatic conflict and its complication in the story's present action. The "catastrophic restoration" — catastrophic in René Thom's sense, not necessarily in the Greek-tragic sense — is the plot's climax, the *peripateia*; and the "complexification" of the resultant equilibrium is simply an affirmation of the Aristotelian principle that the action of drama must be consequential; that, in the language of classical physics, the plot must not only expend effort, but accomplish work.

To harmonize this systems-theory definition of dramaturgy with Per Bak's paradigm of weak chaos would seem to require only three adjustments, which, while not difficult to articulate, imply a Weltanschauung significantly different from that of classical dramaturgy. First, the "incremental perturbation" of the dramaturgical "ground situation" toward catastrophe would need to be seen as *self-organizing*, an aspect of the system itself rather than something imposed upon it from outside. The incremental escalation of such a plot would not be the result of "dramatic" exterior causes, but merely Hamlet's "thousand natural shocks that flesh is heir to": the little snowflakes that build to an avalanche; the injustices that accumulate until one more apparent trifle triggers the revolution. Second (as in proverbial wisdom), the straw that breaks the camel's back ought to be no different from the straws that preceded it; just one more small quantitative change that happens to effect a very consequential qualitative change. And third, the ensuing "complexified equilibrium" needs to be seen not as a stable state but as a "metastable" one, inclined like its predecessor to organize itself toward criticality. Nor should this serial evolution from instability to instability be regarded as a naively "progressive" dialectic, I suppose, but rather in the sense of the historian of science Thomas Kuhn's model of the structure of scientific revolutions (itself an excellent example of self-organizing criticality).

Our human experience of life certainly abounds with this sort of "weak chaos." As a literary paradigm, it strikes me as readily applicable not only on the macroscale, as a worldview, but on other scales as well; a way of thinking about such practical matters as dramaturgy, form, characterization, narrative viewpoint — the whole works.

I want to close this sermon by addressing the very basic question of why a writer should be interested in applying such paradigms as chaos theory and self-organized criticality on the local as well as the global scale; on the level of incidental action, perhaps even on the level of syntax, as well as on the levels of overall plot construction and worldview. It seems to me that we have at least two reasons for doing so. First, to apply such paradigms across the range of scales is to follow the admirable principle that art critics call "significant form" and that I take beyond form and call "the principle of metaphoric means," a principle older than chaos theory and Postmodernism (one finds it in the Modernists and the Romantics, and much farther back as well). By this principle I mean the writer's investiture of as many aspects of the text as possible with emblematic significance, until not just the "form" but the plot, the narrative viewpoint and process, the tone, the choreography, in some cases even the text itself, the fact of the artifact — all become signs of its sense (the way Dante's *terza rima* reflects, on the microscale, the macroscale of his three-part *Commedia*, itself a reflection of his tripartite eschatology). The second reason for doing so is that one does not write a truly contemporary novel, for example, merely by writing about contemporary matters (as my distinguished countryman John Updike does so eloquently — and premodernistically — in his "Rabbit" novels), any more than one writes an arabesque merely by writing eloquently about Arabs. One writes a contemporary novel by writing it in a contemporary way.

Do I believe that following this advice will make anyone a better writer? Not for a moment. Do I believe, on the other hand, that (other things being approximately equal) a novel that artfully deploys and embodies the principle of metaphoric means is aesthetically stronger and richer than one that does not? As a confessed "romantic formalist," I most certainly do believe that. And so much the better if the metaphor involved is as strong as the paradigms of chaological chaos and self-organized criticality — although in the final analysis it is a writer's literary genius, not his or her technical up-to-dateness, that matters. Much of Shakespeare's natural history, like Dante's eschatology, is as obsolete today as chaos theory may be fifty years from now; their writings are not.

$4\frac{1}{2}$. PM/CT/RA: "So what?" or "Ah, so!"?

TWO BRIEF CLOSING points — after making which ". . . I shall fall silent," as the valet Arsene says in Samuel Beckett's *Watt*, "and you will hear my voice no more, only the silence of which the universe is made" — a silence to which perhaps a case has been presented for adding complexity and self-organized criticality. The first point has to do with Friedrich von Schlegel's assertion, cited earlier, that ". . . the arabesque is the oldest and most original form of human imagination." The second concerns obvious differences between the Romantic arabesque and the Postmodernist or "chaotic" arabesque. After considering these two matters, let's address the bottom-line question: "So what?" or "Ah, so!"?

I'm not sure how seriously we can take Schlegel's assertion. "Originality" is a matter of opinion, I suppose, more than of empirical verification, but to the extent that "original" means "novel" or "innovative" rather than "aboriginal," that which is "most original" cannot very well also be "oldest," since it has to be an innovation from something older than itself, some preexisting state of affairs. On the other hand, to the extent that "original" means "aboriginal" rather than "innovative," "original" and "oldest" mean the same thing. Perhaps something is being lost in English translation (I haven't checked the "original"). More likely, I suspect, Schlegel's remark is a casual obiter dictum, the real sense of which is that the arabesque goes back a long way before Schlegel himself took an interest in it. With *that* proposition there can be no quarrel.

If we assume that Schlegel is talking in this instance about literature and not about carpet design, then his conception of the arabesque does indeed have a long provenance, though I don't see how it can intelligibly be called the oldest form of human literary imagination: Various creation-myths, epics like Gilgamesh, and papyri like "Khakheperresenb's complaint" have nothing of an arabesque character about them, and they certainly antedate what Schlegel has in mind: namely, the juxtaposition of the fantastic and the earthily realistic, the vulgar and the sublime, the terrifying and the comic, etc., within a more or less dynamic and interactive narrative frame, the overall narrative exfoliating in a "nonlinear" (i.e., non-straightforward) way, with digressions, reiterations, "self-similarities" across scale levels, tales within tales, perhaps authorial asides and other proto-metafictive touches, perhaps also with lacunae or other "deliberate" imperfections and disorders in the narrative program: in short, "*ein gebildetes künstliches Chaos.*"

If we take these to be the chief field-identification marks of the literary arabesque, and if we do not insist that every one of them must apply to a particular candidate for admission into our club, then the genealogy of the Romantic arabesque certainly includes, from the "East," Scheherazade and her numerous predecessors.* The "Western" side of the genealogy would include *Il novellini* (the anonymous thirteenth-century *Cento novelle antiche*), Boccaccio's *Decameron* and its many spin-offs, such as Giovanni Basile's *Pentameron* and Marguerite of Angoulême's *Heptameron*, also Chaucer's *Canterbury Tales*, Rabelais's *Gargantua and Pantagruel*, Shakespeare's plays (which Schlegel seems to have regarded, charmingly, as one large *Roman*, just as he and I regard *The 1001 Nights* as a *Roman*), and then of course *Don Quixote*, *Tristram Shandy*, *Jacques le fataliste*, and the rest.

---

*E.g., the Sanskrit *Panchatantra* and *Vetalapanchavimsati* (Twenty-five Tales Told by a Vampire) and *Kathā Sarit Sāgara* (The Ocean of Story), which happens to include both the entire *Panchatantra* and *Vetalapanchavimsati* as cycles within the main cycle, and which Salman Rushdie uses as a ground metaphor in his 1990 novel *Haroun and the Sea of Stories*. For more on the extraordinary framing story of *Kathā Sarit Sāgara*, see the Friday-pieces "It's a Long Story," herein, and "The Ocean of Story," in *The Friday Book*.

I nominate Plato's *Symposium* and Ovid's *Metamorphoses* for associate membership in this confraternity. Once upon a time I did an informal survey of more than a hundred specimens of frame-tale literature, in the course of which I discovered that a rigorous examination of the *Symposium* reveals an extraordinarily subtle and complex nest of frames — seven levels deep at one point, in a genre that very rarely reaches five degrees of narrative embeddedness — and that Ovid sometimes goes at least four levels deep (a story within a story within a story within a story), which is as far as Scheherazade ever goes.* And both the *Metamorphoses* and the *Symposium* — especially the *Symposium* — display those abrupt shifts of tone and changes of pace that we associate with the arabesque: sententious Agathon, witty Aristophanes, Alcibiades drunk and disruptive, Socrates himself in all his gadfly serenity, and then Socrates ventriloquizing the even more serene Diotima. I'm sure there are other Western candidates for membership in the club.

When these Eastern and Western traditions come together in the European seventeenth and eighteenth centuries, they generate not only "the novel as we know it" (as in Cervantes's successful fusion of fantastical chivalric romance and "earthy" realism), but also the Western arabesque, ready for theoretical elaboration by the German Romantics and for Postmodernist reorchestration by the likes of us.

That brings me to my second point: the difference, if any, between the Romantic arabesque, as manifested in Schlegel's *Lucinde* and Poe's *Narrative of Arthur Gordon Pym of Nantucket*, for example, and the Postmodernist or "chaotic" arabesque (Chaotical? Chaotistic?), as manifested in whatever examples we choose to choose: perhaps Pynchon's *Gravity's Rainbow*, or Kundera's *The Unbearable Lightness of Being*, or Calvino's *If on a Winter's Night a Traveler*, or — to go back just a bit — Nabokov's *Pale Fire*. They have in common the "arabesque" juxtaposition of fantasy and realism, humor and horror, illusionism and counterillusionism, presided over by a high degree of authorial *Witz*. The Calvino and

*For more of this, see "Tales Within Tales Within Tales," in *The Friday Book*.

the Nabokov, at least, deploy narrative frames no less ingenious than Poe's and Schlegel's — more so, in my opinion. In both sets of examples, the narration is anything but straightforward: The chronological ending of Kundera's *Lightness* occurs well before the final chapter; the terminal V2 rocket in Pynchon's *Rainbow* remains narratively suspended in its trajectory; the chronology of *Pym*, like the ontological status of the text, is vertiginous.* I have not read critical analyses of the contemporary works above-cited, but my professional intuition is that they are every bit as "romantically formalistic" as is the Schlegelian arabesque.

In what meaningful ways, then, do they differ from it — other than in the circumstance that neither *Lucinde* nor *Pym* happens to be as rich and artful a work of fiction as any one of those contemporary specimens? No doubt their differences come down to the differences between the "cultural dominant" of German Romanticism and the cultural dominant of Postmodernism, at once linked and separated by the intervening cultural dominant of Modernism. The Romantics enthusiastically and optimistically rejected neoclassical forms; the Postmodernists are just as likely to embrace such forms, although the embrace is seldom unskeptical or unironic, however impassioned it may be underneath its coolness. The Romantics, arabesque and otherwise, aspired to make a new literature of individual sensibility; the Modernists seem to have imagined that their art could change the world (we remember Joyce's Stephen Dedalus setting about to "forge in the smithy of [his] soul the uncreated conscience of [his] race"). The Postmodernist program is more modest and skeptical; Nabokov declared that his objective was simply "aesthetic bliss," and while Pynchon's and Rushdie's and Kundera's novels certainly have a vigorous political dimension,† I doubt that their authors aspired to any considerable political effect. (In Rushdie's case, there has *been* a considerable and lamentable political effect, but it wasn't in the author's program.)

That said, I find really quite impressive the affinities of spirit between, say, Schlegel and Calvino, however finer Calvino's talent

*See the Friday-piece "'Still Farther South,'" herein.
†As also does Elsa Morante's wonderful *History: A Novel* (1974), which, though not "arabesque," surely deserves full membership in the Postmod canon.

and however cooler his literary *Witz*. I'm tempted to say that a principal difference between them comes from the happy circumstance that Schlegel's aesthetics, I'm told, influenced Russian Formalism, which influenced European Modernism, which influenced such late-Modernist/Postmodernist groups as Raymond Queneau's "Oulipo,"* which influenced and was influenced by the genius of Italo Calvino — with the result that whereas Schlegel's arabesque is a Romantic reconfiguration of Scheherazade, Sterne, Diderot, and company, Calvino's arabesque might be said to comprise a reorchestration of all those plus Schlegel and Klebnikov and Vladimir Propp and company as well: an arabesque on the tradition of the arabesque.

Enfin, let's bear in mind that, as aforementioned, a work does not become Modernist simply by addressing the phenomenon of modernity, or Postmodernist by chatting about the postmod condition. The same goes for the arabesque and the chaological: Edward Said's treatise on Orientalism is not an arabesque, whereas Poe's *Narrative of Arthur Gordon Pym* arguably is, although it never refers to anything "Arabian." And James Gleick's account of chaos theory is not in any sense chaotic; it is straightforwardly linear. On the other hand, there certainly are novels that talk about what they're doing while they're doing it, as do some prestidigitators, and sometimes for the same reason — to distract their audience from noticing their sleight of hand. That sort of metafictivity is part of the Postmodernist syndrome, from Cervantes and Fielding through Sterne and Diderot and Schlegel down to Beckett, Barthelme, Brautigan, and the rest of us "usual suspects."

Postmodernism, chaos theory, and the Romantic arabesque: If there are demonstrable affinities between and among them, so what? I regard that question as answered, in the general way, before it's asked: It goes without saying — Doesn't it? — that the essentially human characteristic of general intellectual curiosity interests itself in the demonstration of previously unremarked

---

*An acronym for *Ouvroir de la Littérature Potentielle*, the Workshop for Potential Literature, whose informal membership included Calvino, Georges Perec, and the American Harry Mathews.

interconnections among apparently disparate phenomena, as part of our ongoing project of making sense of the world. Somewhat different, and more rigorous, is the novelist's *So what?*, which I believe I have addressed by the way already in these lectures but will readdress by way of auf Wiedersehen to the Stuttgart Seminars:

In the *Nicomachean Ethics*, Aristotle argues in effect that while on the one hand a coherent ethical theory (such as his) will not in itself make anyone more virtuous, and while on the other hand there are "naturally virtuous" people, innocent of ethical theory, who seem to have the gift of acting rightly without deliberation (*proairesis*), it is in his view more fully human — and therefore, by Aristotelian standards, more excellent, more "virtuous" — to choose the right action *deliberately*, out of a coherent ethical theory. Aristotelian by temperament, I reaffirm that while first-rate aesthetic theorists are by no means ipso facto first-rate artists, and that most good artists are at best amateurs in the realm of aesthetic theory, the best artists have a keenly intelligent feel, however intuitive, for just the sort of demonstrable interconnections that I've been fumbling with in these lectures,* and for the relevance of those interconnections not only to their own artistic practice but to the circumstance of being humanly alive and vigorously sentient in a particular historical time and place.

Ah, so?

---

*See, e.g., Leonard Shlain's book-length elaboration of this point in *Art and Physics: Parallel Visions in Space, Time, and Light* (NY: Quill/Morrow, 1991).

Inconclusion
The Novel in the Next Century

Back to less theoretical, if still hypothetical, ground.

When Harvard College was established in 1636 as the first American institution of higher education, the Università degli Studi di Macerata, in the Adriatic Marches of Italy, was already 346 years old, approximately Harvard's present age. In 1990, in celebration of its 700th anniversary, the university hosted an ongoing international symposium on "The Novel in the Next Century." What follows is adapted from my remarks to that symposium, subsequently published in the literary journal Conjunctions *19, 1992.*

WITH THE SUBJECT of the novel in the next century I have both a certain sympathy and a certain problem. The sympathy is understandable enough: I am a practicing novelist, not as old as the University of Macerata or the genre of the novel but, like them, not as young as I used to be. A new novel of mine — my ninth — is scheduled for publication in 1991;* with luck I will commit yet another novel before our cataclysmic century expires,† and it is not altogether out of the question that I might perpetrate yet another after that in the early years of the century to come, before *my* expiration date arrives. Even if fate should decree otherwise (as it has done, alas, for Italo Calvino and Raymond Carver and Donald Barthelme and other of my distinguished contemporaries), I maintain a benevolent interest in the future of the art form that I have devoted my professional life to; likewise, for that matter, in the institution of universities, in which

*The Last Voyage of Somebody the Sailor (1991).
†I have duly so done: *Once Upon a Time: A Floating Opera* (1994).

I have agreeably spent that professional life. I have rather more confidence in the persistence of the university as an institution in the century to come than in the persistence of the novel as a medium of art and entertainment in that century — but I'll save my prophesying for later in these remarks.

As for the problem: I have been preceded in the Macerata symposium by a number of distinguished scholars, critics, and novelists, from various countries — including, from the United States, my comrades Robert Coover, Stanley Elkin, William Gass, and Ishmael Reed — "the usual suspects," I'm tempted to say.* Gifted and knowledgeable writers and thinkers every one, and although I wasn't present to hear their contributions to the symposium, I am acquainted enough with them and their writings and opinions to know that they are hard acts to follow. What can I imaginably say on the subject of the novel in the next century, I wonder, that one or all of them and/or their counterparts from other countries will not have said already, and better?

As soon as I put that discouraging question to myself in those discouraging terms, I am immediately encouraged — encouraged by its resemblance to the question that every thoughtful practitioner of the art of literature doubtless asks him/herself at least occasionally, and that some of us ask ourselves relentlessly from project to project. The phenomenon of the novel is many centuries old (just how many depends on your definition); the medium of written literature goes back very much farther yet — at least four millennia, to an Egyptian papyrus of the Middle Kingdom complaining eloquently that language may already have been exhausted† — and the institution of storytelling goes back immeasurably farther than the invention of writing. Furthermore, what applies on the macroscale of history applies also on the microscale of a writer's own career, if that writer is lucky enough to have survived this century's plenteous catastrophes and to have published,

---

*And have already so said, in the Friday-piece immediately preceding this and elsewhere — but the roster of usual suspects keeps changing.
†"Khakheperresenb's Complaint," aforecited in "Can It Be Taught?" and wherever else I have a chance to echo that exemplary utterance, first brought to my attention in Walter Jackson Bate's excellent study *The Burden of the Past and the English Poet* (Cambridge MA: Belknap/Harvard U. Press, 1970).

as I have, some five thousand pages of fiction. What's left to say, for me as a working novelist and for the novel as a working category of art and entertainment?

With that question I feel exactly as much at home as I do at my writing table and in my own skin, and so here we go — *in bocca al lupo*, I believe the Italian phrase is: into the wolf's mouth. Familiar territory.

The text of my sermon is also Italian, from the eminent fifteenth-century Roman humanist and storyteller Gian Francesco Poggio Bracciolini. Poggio's *Facetiae* of 1450 is a collection of mainly ribald anecdotes, from which Rabelais and Marguerite d'Angoulême and many another writer borrowed; it has been called the world's first best-seller* as well as the archetype of the modern joke. Tale LXXV of the *Facetiae* tells of a simple fellow in the town of Camerino who desires to travel and see the world. A clever acquaintance of his, one Ridolfo (who figures in a number of Poggio's tales), suggests that he begin by going no farther than Macerata, not a very long distance away. When the fellow returns, Ridolfo says to him, "Now you have seen the entire world. What else is there on earth besides hills, valleys, mountains, fields both cultivated and uncultivated, woods, and forests? All these things you have now encountered, in the area between here and there."

Ridolfo of Camerino himself, we may presume, was as cosmopolitan as was Poggio Bracciolini. Only the very well-traveled are entitled to make such ironic disparagements of traveling, just as only the very well-read are entitled to say, with Gustave Flaubert, that "it is enough to have read five or six books well." Reading Poggio's anecdote as a parable, we might say that one position to take about novels in the next century is that we scarcely need any more of them, when there are already in the existing corpus — "in the area between here and there" — more admirable specimens than the most voracious reader is likely to get through in a lifetime. If anyone takes that position, may it be in the ironic spirit of Ridolfo of Camerino and not in the unironic spirit of those Muslim fundamentalists† who would maintain that even

---

*Poggio scored early on the invention of movable type and before the establishment of copyright laws.
†Already mentioned, in this connection, in the Friday-piece "Browsing."

Flaubert's reading list is too long; that only *one* book is necessary, the Koran, inasmuch as all the others either agree with it, in which case they are redundancies, or disagree with it, in which case they are heresies.

As for myself, when I consider the Story Thus Far of the novelistic "area between here and there," it occurs to me to imagine the 1990 Macerata symposium as only the latest in a series of such symposia on the subject; symposia held once every century since the founding of that ancient university. Before risking prophesy myself, I'll speculate on what might have been said about the novel in the next century in 1890, in 1790, in 1690, right back to the hypothetical original gathering in 1290.

Let's begin at the beginning:

The symposiasts of 1290, gathered at the brand-new University of Macerata, would not have found our topic intelligible — not that *that* ever deterred a real symposiast from holding forth. From the corpus of late-classical literature there survived a few extended prose-fictional narratives, more or less realistic, satirical, and fragmentary, such as Petronius's first-century *Satyricon* and Apuleius's second-century *Golden Ass*. There was the more recent vogue in Europe of highly fanciful chivalric romance. And over in Japan there was one extraordinary, undeniable specimen of the novel, already two hundred years old: Murasaki Shikibu's *Genji Monagati*, or *The Tale of Genji*. But our panelists would not have heard of Baroness Murasaki, whether or not they had heard of Japan, and the noun "novel" (as we use it nowadays in English, Spanish, and Portuguese) wasn't yet available to them — nor for that matter was the noun "century," in the historical sense of a hundred-year period called, for example, the thirteenth century. The most we can reasonably imagine is that they might have heard of *Il Novellino* — the *Cento novelle antiche*, or *100 Old Tales* — just then being collected anonymously in northern Italy: the collection of earthy, often satirical anecdotes that historians say gave us (us Europeans) both the literary prototype of the novel and the name we call it by in the languages mentioned above.* But "novelty,"

---

*But not in Italian, French, and German, which prefer variants of the term "romance."

even "a hundred antique novelties," as I like to translate the *Cento novelle antiche*, wouldn't have had the appeal in 1290 that it has had since the Romantic period. Even if our thirteenth-century symposiasts had heard of *Il Novellino*, it is unlikely that they would have predicted how influential that work and that form would become in the "century" ahead — most particularly with Giovanni Boccaccio, soon to be born, the future author of the *Decameron*, and Giovanni Sercambi, the future author of the *Novelle* — and how even more influential it would be in the two centuries after that, with the likes of our man Poggio Bracciolini and Matteo Bandello and Giovanni Straparola and Gianbattista Basile and their ribald counterparts outside Italy. Inasmuch as cultural change of any sort was not a prominent feature of medieval times (despite the "novel" institution of universities and the fetal stirrings of the Italian Renaissance), I imagine that our panelists of 1290 would have agreed (1) that chivalric romance would continue to be the major category of narrative fiction indefinitely, in prose, in verse, and in mixtures of the two; (2) that prose fiction was not a serious category of art in any case, so that even if the *novellino* were to outgrow its diminutive suffix, it would still be of diminutive artistic stature; and (3) that even poetry is but the handmaiden of philosophy, itself but the profane sibling of theology, and that only the classical poets (Virgil in particular) merit consideration in university curricula and symposia.

The equally unlikely Macerata symposia of 1390, 1490, and 1590 would have agreed. The fantastical romances of King Arthur, Roland/Orlando, Amadis of Gaul, and company remained enormously popular but not a matter of curriculum. Boccaccio's *Decameron* was imitated everywhere as the model of racy, more or less minimalist realism, but the author himself in his serious old age had repudiated it for its licentiousness. The Renaissance had full-flowered; the noun "novel" had entered the English and Iberian vocabulary (the *Oxford English Dictionary* attests it in English to 1566), but it was applied indiscriminately to short satirical tales and chivalric romances alike. So what lay ahead for the seventeenth century? Not even Cervantes, who was on the very verge of inventing "the novel as we know it," could have predicted to the symposium of 1590 that he was about to do so. In 1590, Cervantes was forty-three years old, a destitute war veteran, occasional poet, failed playwright, and perpetrator of the first half of a pseudo-classical pastoral romance (*Primera Parte de la Galatea*) of which he would never write Part Two: an increasingly desperate scrambler already excommunicated by the church for certain irregularities, about to be sent to jail not once but two or three times for nonpayment of debts, and, very possibly during one of these imprisonments, about to begin writing *Don Quixote* — "just the sort of thing that might be begotten in a jail," the author himself remarks in his famous prologue to Part One. In short, a middle-aged hombre on the cusp of changing literature forever after with his winning combination of satiric realism and *quasi*-fantastic adventure — but one may doubt whether he himself realized the size of what he had achieved even after he achieved it, much less before. The first written notice of *Don Quixote* is by the author's eminent compatriot and fellow dramatist Lope de Vega (with whom Cervantes had had a falling out): Having read Part One in manuscript, Lope wrote to a friend in 1604, "no poet is as bad as Cervantes, nor so foolish as to praise *Don Quixote*." So much for professional critical foresight.

As everybody knows, *Quixote* was immediately as popular as the chivalric romances that it satirized; by 1690 it was making its influence felt much as had the *Decameron* in the several centuries before. I find it not impossible to imagine that some canny prognosticator at that year's Macerata symposium might have foreseen — might perhaps have forewarned — that this novel form of readerly entertainment could well achieve some prominence in the next century.* And indeed, "the novel as we know it" was in fact so explosively successful through the 1700s that one of its great English inventors, Samuel Richardson, by 1758 was already predicting its demise. "There was a time," Richardson writes to Lady Barbara Montague that year, "when every bookseller wanted something of that kind. But Millar [Richardson's own publisher] tells me that the fashion has passed."

*I say "readerly" instead of "literary" entertainment because the word "literature," in the sense of a canonical body of verbal art, doesn't enter our vocabulary for another hundred-plus years. Our symposiasts do, however, now have the word "century" in the sense we mean — first attested in English in 1638 — as European historical consciousness was raised in the seventeenth century.

There we have the first reference that I know of to that Modernist theme, "the death of the novel," in the same generation that established the novel as the dominant form of literary entertainment for that rapidly growing class, the reading public. One feels a touch of déjà vu: that Egyptian scribe at the very dawn of written literature, fretting that he may have arrived on the scene too late. . . . But note how disingenuous Richardson's letter is: Lady Barbara has been pressing the successful novelist for help in getting one of her friends' novels published, and middle-class Richardson is trying to say no without offending a lady of the gentry, while at the same time shifting responsibility from himself to his publisher. I have been in comparable positions from time to time, and I sympathize; it is a situation right out of an epistolary novel by Samuel Richardson.

Disingenuous or not, Richardson's pronouncement that the fad had passed was ignored by readers and writers alike. By the time of our hypothetical 1790 Macerata symposium, the future of the *epistolary* novel in the century to come might well have been questioned, so overworked was that particular mode thanks to Richardson's example, but no one would likely have doubted a robust future for the novel itself as literacy spread to the masses in the nineteenth century. By 1790 even one or two upstart Americans had written novels; to our Macerata symposiasts, that would surely have signaled that *anybody* could now get away with it, and they would have been virtually correct. Indeed, some farsighted participant might have begun to worry about the audience for poetry in the century to come; another might perhaps have noted premonitions of a gothic revival. Would any of them, I wonder, have quite foreseen the remarkable flowering of Romanticism, the famous "inward turn" of narrative and the general rebellion against established forms in all the arts that would distinguish the European nineteenth century? It's not impossible: Jean-Jacques Rousseau was history by 1790, and the French Revolution was news. Goethe had published *The Sorrows of Young Werther*, and the other German writers and philosophers whom we now call the heralds of the Romantic movement — Kant, Herder, Schiller, E. T. A. Hoffmann — had done or were doing their main work. But the phenomenon was still mainly Teutonic and suspect, oper-

ating under such aliases as "Gothicism" and "Sturm und Drang."
My guess is that most of the 1790 symposiasts would have concurred with Goethe's own later pronouncement: "Classicism is
health; Romanticism is disease" — without suspecting how
healthy the virus itself was, how contagious it was about to become, and how persistent it remains to this day.

We come to 1890, with a wistful sigh. To the Macerati of 1890,
the empire of prose fiction in general and of the novel in particular
in the century to come would surely have seemed as secure, for
better or worse, as the British raj and the other European colonial
empires. In 1890 we are at the climax of the period of general
bourgeois literacy and the regnancy of the novel. Hugh Kenner
reports* that even ordinary English agricultural journals of the
time — the *Dairyman's Fortnightly* and so forth — regularly published fiction, as did all the innumerable newspapers. On every
level of sophistication, supply could scarcely keep pace with demand, and it is important to remember that in the realm of fiction
those levels of readership were happily still less demarcated than
they were soon to become; less demarcated by far than were the
levels of social class among readers themselves. The great novels of
the nineteenth century were not invariably best-sellers, but by and
large they were widely read, if still not commonly accepted as
proper subjects for university study. And *writing* novels was almost as fashionable as reading them: A surprising number of
Bonapartes, for example, perpetrated novels among their other di-
versions (the Emperor himself did not), and we remember
Nathaniel Hawthorne's complaint about "hordes of damn'd scribbling women." What a lovely time, novelistically speaking: It is
the period from which dates the still-persisting notion that somewhere in each of us there lurks a *novel* waiting to be written. I'll
return to this notion presently.

No doubt there were in 1890 premonitory signs of trouble
ahead, but who was sharp-eyed enough to see them for what they
were? The seeds of Modernism, for example, were already sown
and germinating — Roland Barthes dates "the fall of literature"
from the 1850s (i.e., from Flaubert), noting as a symptom of its

*In *A Sinking Island: The Modern English Writers* (NY: Knopf, 1987).

fall from innocent unself-consciousness that the term "literature" itself had just come into use. But such news traveled more slowly back then than it does nowadays, and the fateful division of the genre we're concerned with into art novels and pop novels had scarcely begun: that Modernist division much remarked by Leslie Fiedler and others, which some of us who are called Postmodernists aspire to see bridged, although Fiedler tells us that we have yet to bridge it.

Such portents were there to be read, but I daresay that no one at the Macerata symposium of 1890 could have foreseen the turn of events far more consequential for the future of the novel in the next century than was the Modernist polarization of novelists into, shall we say, James Joyces on the one hand and James Micheners on the other. I mean the great usurpation of the kingdom of narrative by the visual, especially the electronic, media: the invention and development first of movies and then of television and videocassette recording; along with these, in America particularly though by no means exclusively, the ubiquitous soundtrack of rock music and the combination of these ingredients in MTV— from all which has followed the famous "new barbarianism" of the "electronic global village": the very substantial decline (some would call it calamitous) in *reading* as a source of information and entertainment, and the attendant, quite measurable decline in verbal skills among both students and their teachers and thence among the general population. Again, it is not a peculiarly American phenomenon, although my impression is that the situation is more acute in my native land than in the other developed democracies. Public school education in Japan and Germany, for example, is no doubt superior in most respects to ours, but my academic friends in those countries shake their heads just as we do at their students' addiction to television and their general aliteracy — and I noted for myself on a recent visit to Japan that among Tokyo high-school boys and young men on commuter trains, pornographic comic books and photonovels appeared to be at least as popular as print (the girls and young women seemed to prefer talking to one another).

*   *   *

We have arrived at our 1990 symposium; it is time to prophesy, and the general lines of my prediction are themselves predictable enough from my characterization of the present state of readerly affairs as it bears upon the art of and the audience for that grand old literary institution, the novel. First I'll describe, and then I'll offer some judgments upon, what I read of its future in the tea leaves of the present.

To begin with, I certainly see no grounds for imagining that the trend away from reading in general will reverse itself. On the contrary. As things stand now in the much diminished realm of prose fiction, if we leave out of account assigned reading by students and professional reading by teachers, writers, editors, reviewers, critics, and booksellers, my personal impression is that in America, at least, novels are still read for pleasure these days principally on resort beaches, cruise ships, and wide-body airliners. I have myself also received encouragement from readers in such outlying areas as Alaska's North Slope, in the extended care facilities of hospitals, in the rear areas of various U.S. military operations, and in jail. Let me say at once that I am most gratified by these observations and reports, regardless of the literary merit of the novelists being read, for I believe that *haute cuisine* is likely to be better where the *cuisine ordinaire* is widely relished, and that the chances of turning out great opera singers or chess players (as well as opera and chess fans) are improved where lots of ordinary folk go around singing Puccini or playing chess in the public parks.

Two reasons for the persistence of these last bastions of extended pleasure-reading are obvious: At our present level of technology, it remains inconvenient to bring the electronic visual media to the beach, for example, and/or people in such circumstances as those just remarked have more time on their hands than even high-tech entertainment can entirely fill. I note, however, that the novel readers in those situations are most often the middle-aged and older, and not only because it is they who can more often afford to be on resort beaches, cruise ships, and other extended care facilities. Their younger counterparts — what the *New York Times* recently* called "the lost book generation"— are more likely to be "wired," and I cannot decide whether it's more dis-

*In its Education Supplement, January 6, 1991.

tressing to see them hooked on the headphones and the Tom Clancy novel simultaneously or the Sony Walkman *tout court* (headphones and Chekhov would certainly be dismaying).

In the century to come, no doubt, the technological impediments to VCRs in the beach bag or attaché case will be overcome; or it may be that those surviving habitats of the endangered species of novel-readers will themselves disappear, supplanted by teleportation, say, and the seductions of computer networking and interactive electronic "virtual worlds." Of this prospect, too, more presently, as of the question whether *any* amount of leisure time is too large for such very-high-tech allurements. Before we leave the category of diminishing habitats, however, two others should be noted, of similar dubiety but perhaps different fragility. First, in Central and Eastern Europe, as in the Soviet Union, one imagines that for a while yet the habit will persist of looking to novelists and even poets for political-moral news unavailable via state-controlled media.* But this habit can be expected to weaken as and if political conditions in those countries continue to liberalize. Philip Roth's memorable distinction between "us" and "them" will less and less apply: that in America anything goes and nothing matters, whereas behind the old Iron Curtain nothing went and therefore everything mattered — even novels, even poems. Good-bye to all that, I suppose and am obliged to hope, by 2090. Second, and somewhat analogously, it has been speculated that the future of the novel may lie in the "developing countries" — where, I presume, the electronic competition is less developed also, and where novelists might incline to address the kinds of social and political issues addressed by many of their great nineteenth-century predecessors. Leaving aside the possible condescension of this speculation, I think it quite likely that the social-economic "Third World" will still be with us a century hence;† but to the question whether there lies the future of the novel, I would respond only that there lies a considerable slice of its past as well.

---

*A writer-friend returning not long ago from the then Soviet Union remarked to me that when a Russian says the word "literature," he still tends to put his hand on his chest, as if about to sing an aria.
†The Harvard historian Paul Kennedy worries (in his best-selling worrywork *Preparing for the Twenty-first Century*) that it might well not only be with us, but overwhelm us.

Now I'll swap my tea leaves for a crystal ball and offer the scenario for the novel in the next century that I see least dimly reflected in its pollution-enhanced mists. Not so long ago I used to see two scenarios in there, the darker of which involved thermonuclear apocalypse: The condition of the novel in the next century, after all, presupposes that there will *be* a next century. Indeed, one aspect of the movement from Modernism to Postmodernism, as I have remarked elsewhere,* is that many who used to worry about "the death of the novel" (a characteristically Modernist anxiety) have been more likely in the last three decades to worry instead about the death of the reader, and/or of the planet. The nuclear swords have by no means yet been beaten into plowshares, but it looks now as though we may turn our concern to the plowshares themselves, so to speak: to the attrition of the biosphere. That too can be regarded as apocalyptic, but it's an apocalypse in slower motion, with more hope of there being a symposium in 2090.

I am left therefore with only one scenario, though it comes in two flavors, the pessimistic and the guardedly optimistic. The scenario itself, as I see it, is this: The once-vast dominion of the novel, together with the even vaster dominion of printed literature of all sorts as a medium of entertainment and edification, continues in the next century the inexorable shrinkage that we have witnessed in ours. Nonprofessional readership keeps on declining, except for reference and special-communication purposes via video display terminals, fax machines, and whatever technology follows them. In the more pessimistic version of the scenario, reading and writing skills in the general population of technologically developed countries atrophy even further from lack of exercise, perhaps "bottoming out" at levels somewhat lower than those of today's public high-school seniors in the USA (average 1990 verbal SAT scores of 424, down from 476 in 1951, on a test that spots you 200 points virtually for spelling your name right) — or perhaps *not* bottoming out, but regressing even farther toward an oral culture deafened by high-decibel pop music more circumambient than the loudspeakered propaganda in George Orwell's *1984*. The reading of extended, even of brief, fictional narratives becomes

*E.g., in the Friday-piece "Postmodernism Revisited."

ever more a special, more or less elite taste, akin to chess or equestrian dressage; akin most of all to a taste for poetry, old and new, in the generations since the ascendancy of the novel did to the audience for poetry what the ascendancy of the electronic media has done to the audience for prose fiction (and for books in general). Already in 1990, most of us "serious" novelists must plan our economic lives the way most poets have always had to do; we practice what the critic Earl Rovit has described as "a full-time profession that is, paradoxically, a part-time occupation," and we do not expect to be able to live even modestly on our royalty income alone. By the second half of the twenty-first century, it may be that even the Stephen Kings and the James Micheners, the Danielle Steeles and Judith Krantzes and whoevers, will be obliged to do likewise; "desktop publishing" and small print runs from small presses will be to the twenty-first century what poetry-by-subscription was to the eighteenth and nineteenth. In this version of the scenario, a really quite widely read new novel, even of what nowadays we regard as the purely commercial sort, becomes as unusual a phenomenon as today's occasional "literary bestseller" by Gabriel García Márquez, Umberto Eco, John Updike, William Styron.* A certain number of aficionados, hard-core literati, will continue to concern themselves with new fiction, just as today such "early Christians" (as Thomas Mann was already calling them in 1903) remain *au courant* with contemporary poetry. But the mass of the bourgeoisie, including the "college educated," will be as ignorant of and indifferent to the medium of prose fiction as are their present-day counterparts with respect to the medium of verse.

That's the pessimistic forecast: It all but precludes the likelihood of there being a symposium in 2090 on the novel in the twenty-second century, though it optimistically allows that the University of Macerata, for example, will still exist on its eight hundredth anniversary. Before we turn to the alternative prognosis, perhaps we should consider exactly why what I've just described is bad news, except for novelists and their publishers. Why

---

*How such exceptions are to be marketed, in the presumable absence of large trade fiction publishers and institutions of distribution and sale, is beyond my competence to imagine.

should we (we the people) care whether one particular medium of entertainment, even of art, is supplanted by another? Narrative literature, after all, did reasonably well before the invention of movable type, not to mention before the rise of the novel: There was the oral tradition for the unlettered and manuscript reading for the very small literate population; in my scenario, the former is replaced by the electronic visual media, the latter by small presses and desktop publishing. If reading any great literature for pleasure in the electronic global village becomes as rare as reading Homer in Greek today; if the audience for the William Faulkner or the García Márquez of the next century is as small and special as today's audience for Seamus Heaney or James Merrill, what will we have lost? In my opinion, our losses will be two at least; I classify them as civil and aesthetic.

As for our civil loss: The ascendancy of the novel is historically associated with the ascendancy of the middle class and the spread of general literacy, and those in turn, in the West at least, with the development of the institutions of liberal democracy and the civil state. In this area I am far from expert, and it may be that I'm mistaking correlations for causations. But it seems to me to have been democratically healthier back when every major American city, for example, had three or four competing newspapers instead of one without competition (my own father, a small-town storekeeper without a high-school diploma, used to read four newspapers daily, from three different cities, plus the entire *New York Times* on Sundays), and when citizens read those newspapers, each at his own pace, his own depth of understanding, and his own agenda of concerns, rather than passively receiving the show-biz presentations of television newscasters at *their* pace, according to *their* agenda. In the same way, it seems to me to be better mental exercise, civically healthier exercise, to be *reading* for pleasure — great fiction, junk fiction, nonfiction, anything — than to sit hypnotized by that "satanic glass screen," as the writer Mark Helprin calls it. No doubt I am being both biased and superstitious, but because of that historical connection I think of the novel (and, by extension, of general literacy) as a canary in the coal mines of democratic civil society. I have read, and I believe it, that people are more manipulable by the visual media than by print (I know that *I* am).

Television may inspire a certain cynicism among its devotees, but it doesn't do much for critical thinking; the "couch potato" makes sarcastic comments about the programming as he grazes remotely from channel to channel, but he doesn't turn the set off. Reading even a spy thriller or a "bodice ripper" is much more of an *activity* than "channel surfing" is. If this particular canary really does go belly-up, I'm old-fashioned enough to fear for the general civic air.

The other loss is aesthetic. In the scenario as given, an elite remnant of the literate will be spared this loss (I don't imagine that libraries will disappear, for example), but I'm democratic enough to regret that the larger community won't be spared it. A work of prose fiction — even a slick commercial novel or a slick commercial short story (back in the days when there was still a market for those) — is a considerably more individual, idiosyncratic affair than is a movie or a television drama. I write a novel with invaluable editorial assistance from my wife, from my official editor, and from my meticulous copyeditor and fact checker; that novel is published with the further assistance of designers, graphic artists, printers and binders, publicists, salespeople, bookstore managers and clerks, and others. Nevertheless, the book is much more "mine" than any film or television play can ever be its "author's": My book's effect on whatever readers it may find does not depend on the exigencies of casting, directing, production budgets, and technical staff. Far fewer contingencies stand between me and my readers than stand between any dramatist and his audience. Compared to fiction and poetry, all theater and cinema and television — even *"auteur"* cinema and television — is committee art: "team sports," Truman Capote called them. I have no quarrel with the collaborative arts; I am a failed musician myself, and know the joys of submerging one's individuality in the ensemble. But surely we'll be poorer for it if the collaborative arts come to be all there is. I am persuaded that it is this low-capital individual-voiceness that accounts for the runaway popularity of creative-writing courses in American colleges and universities — a paradox indeed in a culture not much given to reading.

Another reason for their popularity brings us to another kind of aesthetic loss that we'll suffer if my pessimistic scenario comes to pass. The graphic and the plastic arts, after all, may be said to be just as "individual," as a rule, as writing is; but whereas comparatively few of us ordinary taxpayers go about our daily business imagining that inside our unprepossessing exteriors there lurks a great painting or sculpture waiting to be born, *not* a few folk imagine that they have a story to tell, even a novel, if they could only get it down on paper. Sometimes, astonishingly, they actually do — and the reason for the novel's singular hospitality to amateurs over the centuries, no doubt, is that while only a small number of people draw and carve and paint en route to work or at their office desks or amid their housework, nearly all of us use our language all day long: talking and listening, telling how it is, hearing how it was.

Now, it goes without saying that every medium of art has its particular assets and limitations.* The great limitation of written narrative, for example, as opposed to stage, film, and television drama, is that it deals directly with none of the physical senses. There are no literal sights, sounds, smells, tastes, and feels in a novel, only their names. This technically *anesthetic* aspect of writing no doubt accounts for the comparative ease with which we can be moved to physical tears, laughter, and excitement by even rather mediocre drama, and only comparatively rarely by even first-rate writing. But this great limitation is offset — more than offset, in my opinion — by the fact that the written word can address directly, like no other medium, the invisible universe inside the head and under the skin: the universe not of direct sensation but of sensibility; the *experiencing* of human experience.

This incalculable asset is what is lost when people no longer read novels and stories and poems. The oral narrative tradition supplied it to some extent once upon a time, but at the sacrifice of audience control, so to speak — and here is my point: Not only is the *writing* of fiction a more individually controlled enterprise than the production of visual drama; the reading of it, too, is more individually controlled than the spectating of drama. Granted, the various buttons on our VCRs restore some measure of control to the individual auditor;† but what we're rather awkwardly and in-

---

*More on this goes-without-saying item in "The Limits of Imagination," earlier in this collection.
†A measure to be greatly increased by the predicted imminent arrival of highly interactive media combining television with computers.

frequently controlling in that quite limited way is non-narrative: It lacks the mediating, selecting, registering, interpreting, rendering sensibility of the *narrator*, as well as the irreplaceable virtues of the written word. Visual media and even oral narrative are meals fed to us regardless of our individual appetites and digestive capacities; the printed word we savor at our own pace.

So highly do I esteem these two virtues of prose fiction — all power to the individual (relatively speaking) in both production and consumption, and direct access to the invisible universe of sensibility — that I am impelled to imagine a less pessimistic version of my scenario for the novel in the next century. Even in this happy version, the novel goes the way of the elephant and the rhinoceros — how can it not, given the forces competing against it? But its extinction is by no means complete; the special parks and preserves in which it carries on its much-diminished life turn out to be rather less remote, precarious, and minuscule than our cultural ecologists had feared. Indeed, like the tropical rain forests and the African game reserves, the novel becomes something of a cause, even something of a craze: Save the Whales! Hortatory T-shirts and bumper stickers promote the cause; literary Greenpeace activists stage silent read-ins and book giveaways at video rental outlets, and although their tactics alienate a few moderates, the agreeable mental exercise of reading (reading fiction in particular) catches on in the overdeveloped countries like the physical exercise of aerobics and off-road biking.* Excessive televiewing comes to be regarded, and not only by the elite, as on a par with excessive alcohol consumption and single-crop agriculture. Billboards and signs on city buses extol the hygienic pleasures of reading (in my city already, every municipal bus-stop bench proclaims, perhaps quixotically, READING ZONE — BALTIMORE: THE CITY THAT READS). Reading rooms spring up in our teleportation terminals, furnished nostalgically with period chipboard bookshelves from the twentieth century; special no-viewing, no-listening seats are available on whatever passes for public vehicles. Even the irresistible virtual

---

*In a recent tour of some first-rate American bookstores, I was told that their volume of business has been increasing lately by as much as 20 percent annually. May it be so.

worlds of interactive whole-body computer simulation come to include virtual armchairs in which one can virtually read virtual novels, non-interactive except in the wonderful way that readers and writers have traditionally interacted.

In these benign though diminished and somewhat artificial preserves, I like to imagine, the old art of the novel (and the much older art of written literature in general) not only survives the twenty-first century but adapts, modestly flourishes, and contrives even to evolve. To change the metaphor: I note that Italy, Spain, France, and Great Britain, for example, though no longer the imperial centers that they once were, remain still distinctive, important, more or less prosperous places. I hope the same for Russia and the United States as their former empires dissolve in the century to come, and I wish no less in that century for the noble genre of the novel, both as entertainment and as art.

End-Note

REVIEWING THESE FRIDAY-PIECES, I note with mild dismay but only small apology the frequency with which the books therein referred to are my own. This is because, whatever their merits and shortcomings, those are of all books in the world the ones I've lived with most intimately; also because their production has been and remains, for better or worse, so central to my life-concerns that almost whatever else I think about from hour to hour, day to day, year to year and decade to decade, I think about at least partly with respect to that production — par for most artists' course, I suppose. Finally, as aforeproposed in *this* book,* it is by reviewing where he's been that the navigator dead-reckons where he is in order to set course for the next waypoint of his voyage — perhaps even to discover his destination — and those books are where, all these Mondays through Fridays, I've mainly been.

On with the voyage.

*In the Friday-piece "Once Upon a Time: Storytelling Explained."

Index